Diary of
Skeleton Steve
The Noob Years

An Unofficial Minecraft Series

FULL SEASON ONE!

Books 1-6

Skeleton Steve

<u>www.SkeletonSteve.com</u>

D1367455

Copyright

"Diary of Skeleton Steve the Noob Years – Season ONE Box Set"

"Diary of Skeleton Steve the Noob Years – Season 1 Episode 1 (Book 1)"

"Diary of Skeleton Steve the Noob Years – Season 1 Episode 2 (Book 2)"

"Diary of Skeleton Steve the Noob Years – Season 1 Episode 3 (Book 3)"

"Diary of Skeleton Steve the Noob Years – Season 1 Episode 4 (Book 4)"

"Diary of Skeleton Steve the Noob Years – Season 1 Episode 5 (Book 5)"

"Diary of Skeleton Steve the Noob Years – Season 1 Episode 6 (Book 6)"

www.SkeletonSteve.com

To join Skeleton Steve's free mailing list, for updates about new Minecraft Fanfiction titles:

www.SkeletonSteve.com

Table of Contents

Contents

Book Introduction by Skeleton Steve

Love MINECRAFT? **__Over 86,000 words__ of kid-friendly fun!**

This high-quality fan fiction fantasy diary book is for kids, teens, and nerdy grown-ups who love to read epic stories about their favorite game!

All Six Episodes from "The Noob Years" First Season in ONE!!

Thank you to <u>all</u> of you who are buying and reading my books and helping me grow as a writer. I put many hours into writing and preparing this for you. I *love* Minecraft, and writing about it is almost as much fun as playing it. It's because of *you*, reader, that I'm able to keep writing these books for you and others to enjoy.

This book is dedicated to *you*. Enjoy!!

After you read this book, please take a minute to leave a simple review. I really appreciate the feedback from my readers, and love to read your reactions to my stories, good or bad. If you ever want to see your name/handle featured in one of my stories, leave a review and *tell me about it* in there! And if you ever want to ask me any questions, or tell me your idea for a cool Minecraft story, you can email me at steve@skeletonsteve.com.

Are you on my **Amazing Reader List**? Find out at the end of the book!

February the 14th, 2017

For those of you who love my Noob Years Series, and like a good deal, enjoy this Full Season ONE Box Set! If you'd like to see me continue the adventures of Skeleton Steve, Elias the Enderman ninja, Slinger the Spider, and their other friends, please let me know in the review comments!

- Skeleton Steve

P.S. - Have you joined the Skeleton Steve Club and my Mailing List?? *Check online to learn how!*

You found one of my diaries!!

This a Bundle of Tales about ... well ... *me!!*. Fresh out of the end of the 'Enderman Ninja' series, Elias the Enderman ninja and I went on to many adventures, back when I was just a *noob* skeleton! You'll see appearances from Zebulon the Zombie Knight, new friends like Slinger the Spider, and others as the episodes go on! You are holding the *FULL SEASON ONE* Bundle of my diary entries as a young adventurer on Diamodia!

Be warned—this is an *epic book!* You're going to *care* about these characters. You'll be scared for them, feel good for them, and feel bad for them! It's my hope that you'll be *sucked up* into the story, and the adventure and danger will be so intense, you'll forget we started this journey with a *video game!*

So with that, dear reader, I present to you the tale of **Skeleton Steve the Noob Years**, Full Season ONE...

S1E1 – "My First Journal"

S1E2 – "Trying to Remember"

S1E3 – "The Mountain of Wisdom"

S1E4 – "The Mysterious Tower"

S1E5 – "Into the Nether"

S1E6 – "Invasion in the Rain" *Season Finale!*

Season 1, Episode 1:
My First Journal

The very first diary of Skeleton Steve himself!!

Welcome to a new adventure. Follow along the 'The Noob Years' of Skeleton Steve, Minecraft writer and adventurer, back when he first started his travels on Diamodia! Fresh out of the "Enderman Ninja" series, Skeleton Steve and Elias the Enderman Ninja are traveling east to explore a distant village on the Enderman's map. The village's library is a great place to find an empty journal for Skeleton Steve's first diary, right??

But when the village turns out to be a zombie village, what manner of trouble will the two adventurers run into? And when a mysterious baby zombie offers to give Skeleton Steve the library's last empty book in exchange for finding his missing tome about his "Knight's Code", will Elias and the memory-challenged skeleton be up to the task?

S1E1
1 – Beginnings

Where to begin?

Right now I'm sitting on the roof of the watchtower in *Zombietown*, writing in this nice, new journal!

How did I even learn how to write? How do I understand these words? What unknown memories in my undead brain guide my bony fingers to move the quill and ink over these pages?

My name is Skeleton Steve.

Or, at least, that's the name they *gave* me.

I don't know who I am.

I guess a good place to start with would be back when Elias and I were on the road heading to Zombietown. I didn't know it was called 'Zombietown' back then—we gave this place that name later. We just sort of ... started calling it Zombietown. But at the time, it was a Tuesday morning, the square sun was high in the sky, and the forest was bright and beautiful around us.

"So where are we going, again?" I asked.

The tall, black-skinned Enderman walked along beside me, moving in graceful, easy strides. The tails of his blue ninja headband fluttered in the breeze, and the sun glinted on the white symbol over in its center, the symbol of his *ninja order*.

He looked down at me with an unreadable face. His purple eyes glowed.

"*To the east*," Elias said, his voice inside my head, "*there's a village on the map*."

It was still very strange to me—communicating with this Enderman via telepathy—speaking inside our heads. The ninja never made a sound otherwise. Never a word, never a *grunt*. The only times he spoke to me was with my *thoughts*, like I was thinking those words myself, in my own voice.

But it *wasn't* my voice. It was his.

"Oh," I responded. "Oh yeah..."

Elias stopped and cocked his head, blocking out the sun for a moment. "*Are you okay? How's your memory?*"

"What a funny question," I replied out loud. The Enderman spoke inside my head, but *I'd* speak out loud. If anyone else was ever watching our conversations, it would look like Elias was staring at me, and I was talking to myself! "*How's your memory?*" I repeated. "If my memory was acting funny, would I have *any* idea?"

We moved on.

"*Valid point, Skeleton Steve,*" he said.

I looked down at my skeletal hands as we walked. Flexed my fingers—watched them open and close.

Who am I? I thought. Who *was* I?

My slender, bony feet crunched through the dirt and grass, and my pack flopped against my hip-bones as I walked. We'd been traveling all morning, following Elias's direction.

Sometimes, the Enderman ninja would stop, and pull his *compass* out of thin air (he called it his *dimensional pocket*), look at the instrument for a moment, glance up at the sun, look up ahead, then, we'd move on...

I realized that this must be very slow for the powerful creature—walking with me like this. I've seen him jump around like magic, *zipping* around using his ... teleportation power. Elias could really cover a lot of ground in a hurry like that!

But ... he wanted to be with me.

To walk with me.

And I appreciated him for it.

Was Elias my friend? I don't know—I didn't even know who I was. Or who I *used* to be. The Enderman claimed that he wanted me to travel with him. He said he wanted to help me get my memories back.

I *guess* he was my friend...

"So what's gonna happen when we find this village?" I asked. "Won't the villagers freak out and not want anything to do with us?"

"*That seems likely,*" Elias replied.

"So ... what's the point??"

"*One reason to go there is to find you a journal, remember?*"

"Well," I said, "wouldn't it make more sense to just go back to the village where you're *already* a hero, and get one there?"

The Enderman looked at me for a moment. I couldn't tell what he was thinking or feeling—not like with the Minecraftians. Those creatures were pretty easy to read. Elias's face however, was just ... *blank*. Black and smooth and blank. With glowing purple eyes that mostly just looked ... gentle and uninterested.

What was going on behind those passive purple eyes? An Enderman *sigh?*

"*I have picked up many Ender seeds in the area of the last village already*," Elias responded. "*It is good to explore, to cover new ground.*"

"Your *Seed Stride?*" I asked. "That's why?"

"*That is one of many reasons, Skeleton King,*" he said. I winced at the name. "*There is also a compelling reason to seek out new villages, and new areas—to become more familiar with this map.*"

The Skeleton King.

Who was the man—the skeleton—that existed *before* the Skeleton King??

My memories from being the monster were almost gone now—just hazy shadows in the back of my mind. At times, when I stayed quiet for too long, I started looking *through* this bright, sunlit world, and caught flashes of an army of skeletal archers; brief glimpses of clashing with this Enderman ninja in mortal battle; quick memories of ... *red*...

The Enderman put a slender, black hand on my shoulder.

"*I apologize, Skeleton Steve,*" he said. "*I did not mean to use that name...*"

Had I stopped?

Did I stop walking and go into some sort of weird flashback again??

We started moving again.

"It's okay, Elias," I said. "I'm ... sorry too." I shook my skull. "How far do you think the village is?"

"*Well,*" the Enderman said, "*From the last time I looked at the map, judging by the time of day, and the plains to the south...*" He pointed to our right and, through the trees, I could see a bright, open area of green grass peppered with yellow and red flowers. "*I surmise that we will be walking for today, and tomorrow, then should reach the unknown village.*"

"Not bad," I said. "You know what?" I looked up at him and smiled.

"*No, I do not,*" he responded blankly.

I smirked. Elias was a weird guy. He *definitely* didn't understand that expression. But, how did I??

At every turn, thinking about the mechanics of this ... amnesia ... seriously boggled my mind. How did I know some things and not others? How did I know how to speak? Or how to use expressions like, *you know what?*

"Err ... know what? I kind of *like* this traveling like this," I said.

"*That is good, Skeleton Steve,*" Elias responded. "*This world of Diamodia is immense. It is good to see much of it—to learn much of this place. I have come to understand, from my Seed Stride and my first mission for my order, that there is much self-improvement and growth to be had in journey and adventure...*"

"Journey and adventure, huh?" I asked. "Yeah, I like that."

"*Take this creeper for example,*" Elias said, waving a hand off to our left.

Creeper??

I looked, and didn't see anything. Green. Trees.

And suddenly, a freaking *creeper* stepped out from the woods! Right next to us! Its skin was green like the leaves, and crackly, with four stubby, green legs, and a frowny face with deep, sad eyes like black holes in a dense bush...

"Whoa!" I exclaimed. "Where'd *you* come from?"

"Ssss," the creeper replied. Its voice was dry and scratchy. "I walk through the treesss, ssskeleton!" It approached us and stopped.

"What could you learn from this creature?" Elias went on, in my mind. I had no idea if *only I* heard his mind voice, or if the creeper was hearing it too. *"This creeper may just be another mob, but he has a name, and has been here longer than you have. All of these beings of Diamodia have their own stories—their own lives."*

The creeper stared at us blankly.

"Uh ... *hi there*, creeper!" I said, turning to it. It didn't respond. "What's your name?"

"Cho'thosss," the creeper responded. "Why'sss a *ssskeleton* want to know?"

"Just curious, I guess," I said.

Elias stood by like a silent sentinel, watching our interaction.

This felt weird. What was the Enderman trying to do? Make me have a conversation with the creeper?

The creeper suddenly looked up at Elias, and watched his face for a while.

"Yesss, Ender," the creeper said. "There'sss a cassstle to the wessst. What'sss with hisss eyesss? They glow *red!*" It glanced at me with its sad, deep eyes, then turned back to Elias.

They looked at each other's faces for a while longer. Elias must have been talking to the creeper with his *mind voice*, and I wasn't a part of the conversation...

"Not that I know of," Cho'thos responded, its voice like leaves and gravel. "I have not gone much farther eassst..."

20

The Enderman ninja gave the creeper a small nod.

"Good travelsss," the creeper said to both of us, then walked around us, continuing to the south.

"Uh ... nice to *meet* you, Cho'thos!" I said after him. I looked at Elias. "What was *that* about? Asking him about the village?"

"*Yes*," my companion replied. "*He's familiar with this area, and the Minecraftians' castle, but hasn't been much further east than we are now.*"

"Yeah, I got some of that," I said, and we walked on for a while.

When the sun went down and the world became dark, Elias insisted that we stop for the night. Neither of us needed to sleep, but the Enderman preferred to stop at night to meditate and recharge his *Chi*—whatever *that* was.

We both sat in a small clearing between tall oak trees, and I watched the Enderman as he sat straight, crossed his legs, and put a slender hand on each knee. Appearing very serene, Elias closed his eyes, and stayed like that for the rest of the night. Only the blue tails of his ninja headband moved, drifting up and down in the night breeze.

I sat in the dark, watching and listening to the strange world around me, wondering if those zombies and spiders I heard and saw in the distance ever had a taste for *bones*...

S1E1
2 – On the Road

When the square moon set, and the sun brightened the day again, we continued our journey.

Elias stopped every once and a while to do his weird Enderman stuff.

His *Seed Stride*.

Sometimes, gliding along like the long and limber creature from another world he was, Elias would stop, close his eyes, then head off of our path a bit, holding his hands out in front of him. With those powerful and lean arms, he'd dig his fingers into the dirt, and pull up a block or two. Occasionally, he'd have to dig and set aside *block after block* until he found the dirt block he was looking for...

They all looked the same to me.

But Elias sure acted *funny* about those blocks, treating *some* of them like they were nothing interesting at all (*they weren't interesting of course—just dirt*), and others like they were full of *diamonds* or something! His eyes would flare, and he'd look over those 'special' dirt blocks like they were the coolest things he'd ever seen. And then, he'd slip them away into nothing—into his *dimensional pocket*.

"What do you see in those?" I asked, eventually.

The Enderman was regarding one of those 'special' blocks. He held it up for me to see, treating it with gentle care.

"*Behold,*" Elias said. "*What do you see?*"

Dirt.

It was a block of dirt.

"Just looks like dirt," I said.

"*Inside this dirt,*" he replied, "*is an 'Ender Seed'—something sacred to my people.*"

"Like, some kind of ... *egg?*" I asked.

24

"*Not exactly,*" Elias said. "*Each of us Ender has an Ender Pearl inside, which is an amplifier for our Chi, and allows us to channel much of our power into the techniques you have seen me use— my ability to warp, my mind voice, and other, more subtle things.*"

"And they come from *dirt?*"

"*This world, Diamodia, has three connected planes. Do you know of them?*"

"What are *planes?*"

"*The End, which is my home, the Nether, and this world—the Overworld. All are planes, like worlds within a world.*"

"What's that have to do with the dirt??"

"*All planes are connected, and are vital to each other. We Ender, who live in The End, rely on the Overworld to produce the Ender Seeds, which grow naturally in the soil of the world. When my people go on our Seed Strides, we collect the seeds to bring back to the dragon's island, where they will grow into new pearls for Ender younglings.*"

Dragon??

"Um ... dragon island? Is there a dragon??"

"*The Ender Dragon*," Elias replied. "*The ancient beast bound to my people's civilization that grows the pearls.*"

"Can I *see* the dragon?" I asked.

"*Perhaps, one day, I will lead you to The End. But, for an Overworld-dweller like yourself, that would be a very involved adventure. You cannot reach The End as easily as I can.*"

"Can't you just *teleport* us there?"

Elias seemed to smile. "*I can return there at will*," he said. "*But I cannot take you with me.*"

As we walked, I listened to spiders hissing and climbing around in the trees around us. Looking up, I watched their multiple, glowing red eyes regard us from the shadows.

"Um ... Elias?" I asked.

"*I sense that you are distressed about the mobs around us,*" he said in my mind. "*You do not need to fear.*"

"Do you think I could at least … have a weapon?? A bow or something? I mean—I know the Minecraftians didn't want me to have one, but they're long behind us now, you know?"

The memory echoed in my head:

"*Do you think I could have a bow?*" I asked. "*Just in case … uh … I dunno … we run into trouble??*"

"*No way,*" Xenocide99 said.

"*Not a chance,*" said WolfBroJake. "*You might be a wimpy skeleton now, but yesterday you were the Skeleton King!*"

My first memories of transforming into a normal skeleton after being … that *monster* … were kind of hazy, but I could still remember the Minecraftians and Elias standing around me, as I waited in my cage for them to decide on my fate…

I was truly grateful that this Enderman spoke up and didn't allow the Minecraftians to *execute* me. They sure had every right to...

"*Why do you feel the need to have a weapon?*" Elias asked.

"What if those spiders attack?"

Elias shook his head, and looked up into the trees. He stared at the individual arachnids handing out in the upper branches as we walked on. After a while, he looked down at me again, then pointed at one of them. The spider's glowing red eyes glared down at me.

"*That spider's name is Sidney. He's up there because he likes to spend the day in the sunshine at the top of the trees. He feels happy and warm.*" Elias pointed to another. "*That one's name is Sophia. Sidney's her best friend, so she hangs out with him a lot, and is hoping they're going to go explore a certain cave nearby after lunch.*"

"Okay ... what about that one?" I asked, pointing at a third.

"What *about* me?!" the spider called down from above with a hissing voice.

"*That's Seth,*" Elias said. "*He just wanted to see what the other two were doing up there.*"

I felt a bit silly.

"Oh, *nothing* ... Seth. Have a nice day!"

"You too, bones!" Seth replied.

"Hey, you guys!" the spider named Sophia cried out in a spidery voice. "Watch out for the Minecraftians! There are a *bunch* of them living nearby!"

She must have meant the Minecraftians in the castle *behind* us.

"Thanks!" I said, and we walked on.

"*You don't have much to fear from other mobs here, Skeleton Steve,*" Elias said. "*Don't forget—you are one of them, yourself!*"

"Still," I said. "I'd like to have a weapon. If something bad happens, what am I gonna do? You have your awesome ninja skills, but I'm just … I'm just a bunch of bones."

"*Soon,*" the Enderman replied. "*Be patient, Skeleton Steve. You are still recovering from being … the other. We must make sure that … your state of mind is safe.*"

We walked in silence for a while.

"What was I, Elias?" I asked. "What was the Skeleton King? Who am I now? Was I *always* the Skeleton King before?"

Elias shook his head. "*I do not believe you were always the Skeleton King, Skeleton Steve,*" he said. "*From what I could tell, you were … distorted … by a magical artifact—an evil magical item that is no longer on this plane. I feel rather certain that you were something else, or someone else, before the artifact made you into the Skeleton King.*"

"Can you show me?" I asked.

"*Show you what?*"

"With your *mind power*. Can you make me see myself, as the Skeleton King, from your own memories, maybe?"

"That is an odd request, Skeleton Steve," Elias responded. *"Why would you want to remember being the Skeleton King? That's not who you are now..."*

"Maybe it'll help me remember who I was—you know—before!"

"Are you sure?" the Enderman said. *"I could send you ... images, short memories, I suppose. But will it really help you? It will likely cause you pain."*

"Please," I said. "I *want* to see."

Elias stopped, and we stood in tall grass.

The monster stood in the room directing his skeleton minions as they carried more of the heavy metal blocks over from a corner of the room. In the shadows, spared from the red light, I caught a glint of steel.

Were the blocks made of solid iron?

My eyes darted back to the Skeleton King.

The abomination stood twice as tall as the skeletons around him—taller than me. And he was thick and wide, with heavy ribs and dense limbs. The Skeleton King's bones were overall more massive than normal skeleton bones, and he had a broad lower jaw that made him appear even more menacing. As I expected, his eyes held the same fierce, red pinpricks of glowing light as the other skeletons. The monster's shoulders were armored, and he held a huge, black bow in one chunky bone hand.

No ... not in his hand. On his hand!

The Skeleton King was armed with a great, black bow that was bolted sideways onto a bracer of some kind that was attached to his right arm.

"Move it!" he yelled, his voice like thunder. "Get those blocks in there!"

The skeletal minions struggled with the heavy blocks to finish their work on the pyramid.

I shook my head.

That was weird. I was suddenly aware of the tall grass around me again. Elias stood before me, regarding me with a passive, smooth face and glowing purple eyes. I looked up at the blue sky above me and felt the sunshine on my face.

"Are you alright?" Elias asked. *"Did you see?"*

"I..." Pausing, I tried to collect my thoughts. "*That* was weird. I was suddenly ... in a castle? The Minecraftians' castle??"

"Did that ... stir any memories?" Elias asked. *"Did the monster feel like you?"*

Nothing.

"No, not really. I was just seeing the Skeleton King from *your eyes*. It didn't *feel* like me. Can you do it again, maybe a ... *stronger* memory??"

Elias pressed his hands together. He seemed resistant to the idea, although I couldn't read his strange, Enderman face for the life of me...

"Very well," he said, and my mind was swooped away into a ... flying kick!

Flying through the air, I visualized my kick hitting the Skeleton King in the center of his chest. Then, just as my foot was about to connect, I was shocked when the Skeleton King's massive ribcage split apart up the center and opened up like a sideways chest—like a great clam-shell trap—and my body crumpled inside of it!

The ribcage trap slammed shut on me, crushing me inside the abomination's body.

Pain...

I cried out, and roared in agony!

The Skeleton King's chest was large enough that such an attack would have totally swallowed up a Minecraftian. But I, as an Enderman, was too big to be completely enclosed, so I was tangled up in a deathtrap of bones, crushed, stuck...

Then, the ribcage opened up and spat me back out onto the ground.

I landed in the dirt, feeling broken.

Trying to get to my feet, I barely noticed the Skeleton King raise his bow to me again.

Zip.

I teleported just a few feet away as he fired, the black arrow hitting the ground where I was.

When I appeared, I collapsed onto the ground again.

Clunk clunk clunk clunk clunk clunk clunk. The skeleton army around us beat their bones in a constant rhythm song of hand-to-hand combat...

I was exhausted and broken.

The Skeleton King turned, and raised his bow again.

Fired.

The black arrow pierced my chest and almost pinned me to the ground! The pain was unbelievable...

"Give me the beacon!" the Skeleton King roared.

I could barely see.

Clunk clunk clunk clunk clunk clunk clunk.

Looking up at him, I tried to get to my feet, then fell again.

"Give me the beacon or DIE!!" the *abomination bellowed.*

I heard the voice repeating in my head...

Die...

Die...

Die...

When I came to, Elias was trying to help me stand from the ground. I was sprawled out in the grass, holding my chest. The huge, black arrow that pinned me to the ground was...

Wait.

There *was* no black arrow...

That was from a memory that wasn't mine.

And that's all it was.

The Skeleton King was a terrible monster, but he wasn't me at all!

Seeing the abomination wiping the floor with Elias, from the ninja's point of view, was *horrifying*, but it didn't remind me of anything. Seeing that massive, menacing creature was no different than … if he was standing in front of me as … something else…

It was all very confusing, but it didn't help at all.

"Oh … that's … oh my—" I stammered as the Enderman helped me to my feet.

"*Are you okay, Skeleton Steve?*" he asked, his *mind voice* serious and concerned.

"Elias … I'm … *are you??* That was terrible! How did you … I'm *so sorry!*"

"*I am okay now,*" Elias replied. "*I will always have the scars from my battles with your other form, but the Skeleton King was also a great mentor to me, in its way, and helped me grow as a ninja.*"

"I'm sorry, Elias," I said. "The … weapons … never mind. I'm sure I'll be fine. I've got *you*, after all. Just … whenever you think I'm ready? A bow or something?"

Not much later, just as the sun was setting in the western sky behind us, we saw the distant lights of torches across a darkening plateau.

The village…

"*Skeleton Steve*," Elias said. "*We will rest here, and approach in the morning, after I have recharged my Chi…*"

"Okay, Elias," I said, my thoughts still on the terrible memories from the Enderman's mind.

So, my memories of being the Skeleton King probably won't help me. I had to remember who I was *before* I became the monster! But, since the moment I became a normal skeleton again, I couldn't remember *anything* from before!

Who was I before?? Just a random skeleton?

Hopefully starting a journal would help me to remember…

38

S1E1
3 – Zombietown

We approached the village in the morning with caution.

After all, the villagers wouldn't know us from any other random skeletons and Endermen out there. They wouldn't know that Elias was a *hero*, an ally to Balder's village—Balder was the blacksmith who gave the ninja his map. They wouldn't realize that he was a friend of the Minecraftians—the *hero Enderman ninja* who saved the village from ... well ... from *me*...

Elias figured that we should scout out the village real quiet-like. There was also the possibility that some *other* Minecraftians lived here, and they probably wouldn't be friendly.

"*I'm not sensing any villager energy*," the Enderman said in my mind. "*Nothing Minecraftian, either.*"

"So what's out there? What's going on?" I asked.

"*Let's find out*," my companion replied.

The closer we came to the village, the stranger it seemed. Even though it *looked* like a normal village, there was something … *off* about it.

There were no crops. The farming fields were empty—rows of bare dirt with troughs full of water in between.

And there were no villagers.

No bustling, energetic, always-moving-around villager creatures. No constant opening and closing of doors.

Instead, the people we saw standing in the streets … were zombies!

"A zombie village?" I asked.

"*No living villagers*," Elias replied. "*All mobs. All undead.*"

I had a much better look when we stepped into the streets. There weren't many zombies out and about, because most of them were inside the houses. It was broad daylight, after all. Any of the undead that were out in the street were sticking to the shadows, standing under the eaves of the homes, hiding under overhangs from the deadly sunlight that would otherwise set them on fire!

Other than the fact that the farms were dead and there were no villagers running around, this place looked a lot like a normal village!

Except ... also ... all of the *doors* were broken down.

Mostly.

There was one place in town where a hole was blown out in the cobblestone street and the walls of the surrounding homes—likely from a past creeper explosion.

But this was a zombie town, alright.

"Zombietown," I said.

Elias nodded.

"Let's find the library," he said.

As we walked through the streets, I saw green-skinned zombies standing in the open doorways, staying out of the sunlight. Looking through the windows of the houses, I saw more of them inside, like a strange reflection of a normal village.

It truly was a *Zombietown*. They lived here.

"Hello ... uh ... skeleton ... Ender ..." a random zombie said as we passed by. His voice was thick and dull.

Elias stopped, nodding to the creature, so I stopped too.

"Hi there, eh ... zombie?" I said. "What's your name?"

"Zed," he replied.

"Good to meet ya, Zed. I'm Skeleton Steve, and this is Elias," I said, pointing to my companion.

"Welcome to the village," Zed said. "How do you walk around in the sun without burning up?"

How did I? I thought.

My hands went to the metal helmet on my head. I thought I remembered the Minecraftians saying something about that...

"*Don't take that off*," Elias said into my mind suddenly.

I pulled my hands away.

"I don't know," I replied to Zed. "Because I'm a *skeleton* I guess?"

"Can't be that," the zombie said. "Skeletons burn up, too." He blinked.

"What's the deal, Elias? Now *I'm* curious," I said, looking up to the Enderman.

"*It's your helmet, Skeleton Steve*," Elias said. "*The Minecraftians gave you that helmet after the battle so that you could travel with us in the daylight protected from the sun. But don't ever take it off during the day, or you'll be set on fire!*"

I smirked. "Well, gee, *that's* good to know..."

"Who are you talking to?" Zed asked, scratching his face slowly.

Was Elias just talking to *me* again with his *mind voice?* He didn't include the zombie? I must have looked like I was just talking to myself...

"Oh, sorry," I said, looking back to the zombie. "It's the *helmet*. Wearing a helmet protects you from the sun."

"Really??" Zed asked. "Uh ... can I have it?"

"Ha ... no ... I'm sorry, I need it!" I said, and laughed.

"Oh..." the zombie said, looking down.

"Hey, maybe I can find you one sometime, eh?" I replied. "So, Zed, could you tell us the way to the *library?*"

"What's a ... library?" His mouth gaped.

"A place with books," I said. "*Lots* of books."

Zed scrunched up his green face, and I could see the wheels turning ... slowly ... behind those dull, black eyes. He pointed down the street, the same way we were already walking.

"Zebulon's house," he said. "It has some books. Turn right at the next street, and you'll see it. Big house."

"Thanks," I said. Elias nodded to the zombie, and we continued down the street.

We walked, turned, walked some more, watching the many zombies of the undead village peer at us from inside their houses. Passing by several more small homes of cobblestone and wood, most with broken doors and many shattered glass windows, we eventually came across a somewhat *larger* house, with a raised floor, and a sloped roof. The door on this house was bashed open, as well, like the others.

"*This looks like the place*," Elias said. "*I sense a single zombie inside*..."

Taking slow steps up the cobblestone stairs, I headed inside.

"Hello?" I said as I entered. "We come in peace!"

The inside of the building was fairly open, with two plain, wooden tables, benches, and another strange wooden table that looked like a Minecraftian tool—a cube of wood, bedecked with hand tools and drawings. Along the walls were rows and rows of bookshelves ... mostly *empty*. Sitting at one of the tables, with a large, red book in front of him, was a small, green zombie—the size of a *child*, really—dressed in the normal zombie blues, looking over the cover of the book with glittering black eyes.

The little zombie looked up, startled by my intrusion, and *jumped* to his feet!

"*Back*, interloper!" it cried out in a very large, but also tiny, zombie voice. "This is *my* house! What is the meaning of this??"

I put my bony hands up in front of me. That little zombie was so full of energy and so fast! For a moment, I was afraid that it was going to jump at me and start wailing on me with its tiny fists!

"Whoa! Sorry there, buddy—"

"Buddy?! Who are you calling *buddy*, bones? You cannot just come waltzing into my house with your ... your..." The little zombie looked up behind me.

Elias pushed through the too-short doorway, standing to his full height once he was inside. His head almost touched the ceiling.

"*Greetings, zombie,*" Elias said into my mind. He must have been talking to the little zombie, too. "*You must be Zebulon.*"

The small zombie calmed himself down, crossing his arms over his little chest, looking up at the Enderman standing behind me.

"I *am*, Enderman! *Zebulon the zombie!* Are you speaking *inside* my head?"

His little voice projected like the voice of a creature *much* bigger than he really was.

Elias nodded, then went on. "*We have come to this village seeking the library. Is this the only library in town?*"

Zebulon looked at both of us, then looked at the empty bookshelves. Only a small handful of books remained, along with many scraps of paper.

"Tis *indeed*, Ender," the zombie replied. "It *was*, anyway. Many of the books have been *pilfered* over time by those dastardly Minecraftians, they have!" His voice was calming down. "I must *apologize* for my outburst when you came in. My good travelers, it has been a ... *rough day*."

"It's alright, Zebulon." I said. "What's wrong?"

The little zombie scrutinized me again with bright, glittering black eyes. He was different than the others, for sure. While the other zombies we've seen—Zed and the other 'citizens' of Zombietown—were slow and sloppy, with dull eyes, dirty, untucked clothes, and gaping mouths, Zebulon was *bursting* with energy, and seemed really on top of things! His eyes were sharp, his clothes clean and neat, and his movements sure and confident. What an *interesting* little fellow...

"Good travelers, you two know *my* name, but I have not had the pleasure of learning *yours*!"

I stepped further into the room. "Well, Zebulon, my name is Skeleton Steve, and *this* is Elias."

"Very good, sirs!" Zebulon replied. "*Skeleton Steve* and *Elias*, what can humble Zebulon do for you two this fine day?? Why do you seek this *library?*"

"*We seek a book,*" Elias said. "*An empty book, so that my friend, Skeleton Steve here, can start a journal.*"

"Ahhhh..." Zebulon replied. "A good practice, to be sure! Someone ... in *one* of these books ... said that *Journal writing is a voyage to the interior!*"

"That's what we're hoping for!" I said.

"What an *odd* thing to say, Skeleton Steve!" Zebulon replied. "Why are you seeking *voyage to your interior?*"

"Well," I said, "I don't really know who I *am...*"

"We're thinking, good Zebulon," Elias said, *"that if Skeleton Steve starts writing a journal, it may help him remember who he once was. Stir up some memories..."*

Zebulon put a hand to his chin and thought for a moment. "Tis a *good quest*, Skeleton Steve! The only problem is, as you can see, this library is nearly out of books! And the last empty book available..." he pointed to the red leather-bound book on the table, "I need for *myself* after I lost my *own* journal earlier today!"

So *that* was the rough day...

I looked down.

Oh well. There must be another village within a few days walk from here. Once we had a minute to look at the map again, we'd—

"Zebulon," Elias said suddenly in our heads, *"Is that book still empty? Is there any way we could convince you to give it to Skeleton Steve? Finding his memory is not only important to him; it's important to all of—"*

The little zombie interrupted him.

"I'm afraid not, Enderman sir! *Believe* me—I see *many* zombies with memory problems, all the time around here! A lot of the undead are always trying to figure out who they used to be—your friend's not an exception. But now that *my* journal is gone, I need *another* so that I can continue my … wait a minute!"

Zebulon stopped and thought. He looked Elias up and down, looked at me, then looked back at the red book…

"What is it?" I asked.

"As an *Enderman* … you may be able to reach it!" he exclaimed, smiling suddenly. "*You* can get my old journal!"

"*An exchange?*" Elias asked.

"*Yes*, good sirs!! Yes! An exchange!" Zebulon exclaimed, grinning from ear to ear. "I thought it was lost, but it's not! Not when *you* can get it!" He settled down, and his face became *all* business. "If you bring me back *my* journal, which I lost earlier today, I will give you the *last* empty book. Do we have a deal??"

Elias and I looked at each other.

"Where is it?" I asked.

"Okay," Zebulon said, taking a breath. "So last night, I was in my favorite place up the river from town. There's a waterfall, and a *fantastic* ravine—a deep cave—it's a nice place I like to go, to *read and write*. To think..." He moved back, and pulled himself up to sit on the table as he talked. "I was there, reading my book under a tree, when I was suddenly attacked by a *crazy spider!* In the fight, the foul beast pushed me to the edge of the ravine, and as I fought for my life, I dropped my precious book over the edge!"

"So your book is at the bottom of a ravine, and you have no way to get to it," Elias said.

"That's right!" Zebulon said, "But *you*, an Enderman! You can just teleport down there, get it, and teleport back up again!"

"That stands to reason," the Enderman responded. *"Tell us more about the book."*

"Well," Zebulon said, "it's bound in leather, like that one," he pointed to the red book behind

52

him, "but it's just brown. And on the *front* of it, I painted the words, *The Knight's Code*, along with a picture of a sword!"

"Knight's Code, huh?" I asked. "Sounds distinctive. Of course, it's probably the *only* book at the bottom of the ravine..."

Elias turned to me. "*Do you want to do this to acquire this empty journal, Skeleton Steve?*" he asked, staring at me with his glowing, purple eyes.

"Sure," I said. "Sounds easy enough..."

"You should go right away!" Zebulon said, "While the day is still new! If the spider is still there, well ... spiders *tend* to be more *easy-going* during the daytime."

"*How do we find this place?*" Elias asked.

"Go to the east side of town. If you look to the south from there, you'll see a river running past the village through the plains. If you follow the river up toward the mountains for an hour or so, through the forest, you'll get to a place where the trees *open up*, and you'll see a waterfall joining up with it. There's a big ravine in the trees there, but the opening is narrow and hard to see. Watch your step! If you fall in, tis a *long way down*..."

"What about the spider?" I asked.

Elias looked at me. "*Don't worry about the spider*," he said.

"Well, the beast has gone crazy!" Zebulon replied. "I could not reason with it. It refused to speak like a *civilized* mob! *Take care* if it is still there..."

With that, we left the library, headed for the eastern edge of town.

S1E1
4 – The Spider and the Book

"See?" I said. "Crazy spiders! Now, can I have a bow? A sword? Something?!"

Leaving Zombietown behind us, we were crossing a large, grassy field, making our way to the deep blue river in the distance, which stretched out, weaving and winding its way through the plains. I couldn't tell which way was 'upriver' yet, but it looked like we'd be following the river to the left, since it wound its way in that direction *up* into rising forested hills. I could even see mountains farther away. To the right, it seemed that the river continued into flat lands as far as I could see.

"*I am sure there is a reasonable explanation for this,*" Elias said. "*Mobs don't just 'go crazy' like Zebulon claimed.*"

"Yeah, I guess we'll see, right? At least I don't have *skin*, like zombies, for when the spider tries to bite me..."

"*No need to fear, Skeleton Steve,*" my companion responded. "*If the spider is … aggressive, I'll take care of it.*"

"Hey, man," I replied, "Don't confuse 'fear' with feeling the need to have something I can *defend* myself with, okay? I'm not *scared*. I just want something better than my *fists* to fight off monsters with!"

Elias stopped and looked at me. His blue ninja headband tails fluttered in the wind.

"*It is interesting, my friend, that you refer to other mobs as monsters, or feel the need to protect yourself from them. You are, after all, one of them. You are a mob. You're undead! Yet, you act like you're not. Why is that?*"

Now that *was* an interesting thought, and it gave me pause.

It's true, come to think of it, that I've been thinking about this journey from the point of view of an adventurer surrounded by monsters!

But I'm *one* of the monsters. *Aren't I?* These creatures are my allies.

Why don't I *feel* that way?

We continued, turning left at the river, and followed it up into the hills. The trees were thick and dark.

Dark oak.

And, compared to the time it took to walk from the Minecraftians' castle to Zombietown, traveling an hour upriver was *nothing*.

Before long, we found a place where the trees opened up, and I saw a bright and blue waterfall flowing from above a high hill, down to a small pool, which fed a creek that connected to the river. In the middle of the beautiful grass clearing was a single large dark oak tree.

I could imagine Zebulon sitting under that tree, the waterfall splashing softly on his right, reading his book while the warm sunlight bathed the river in front and the grassy field around him...

Well, it was nighttime when he was here. But it sure was pretty in the sun.

Yep. It was definitely a nice reading spot.

"This must be the place," I said. Elias didn't respond.

I listened for the hissing sounds of a spider, but heard nothing but the wind and the moving water.

As we approached the large tree, I looked all around for a menacing set of glowing red eyes; searched the shadows of the woods, peered up into the treetops...

Nothing.

"*Take care looking for the ravine,*" Elias said. "*If I slip, I can save myself, but if you slip into the ravine as Zebulon described it...*"

"Yeah, yeah," I said. "I know. I don't *bounce*. I'll check over here..."

Moving around to the back of the huge oak, I made my way to the tree-line, keeping a careful eye out for a crazy, murderous spider. Once I was in the shadow of the forest, I started watching each step to make sure I didn't wander over an edge, or into a hole, and plummet to my doom, deep in the ravine!

Zip.

I heard Elias teleporting around.

Zip. Zip.

His way of searching for something was probably *much* more efficient than mine. I laughed.

"*Over here,*" Elias said in my mind. But without hearing an actual voice with my ears, I had no idea where he was speaking from...

Looking around, I saw the faint remains of one of his 'warp paths', and followed the dim, trickling motes of purple light, drifting down to the forest floor, until I saw my pal. A short distance away from me, I could see his eyes glowing in the shadows of the trees.

"There you are," I said, and made my way to him, being careful of my steps.

As I approached Elias, I saw the opening in the ground. It was narrow indeed—only a few blocks wide—and the rift stretched along the forest ground ... I don't know how far!

Inside, was *darkness*...

The Enderman ninja was momentarily preoccupied by a dirt block that must have contained an *Ender Seed*. Elias held the block lovingly, and closed his eyes, as if he was trying to feel the energy of the seed with one of his palms, gliding over the dirt surface. He slipped the block into his dimensional pocket and turned to me.

"*Here it is. Be careful*," he said.

"Do you see anything? See the book?"

I approached the edge, taking two quick looks behind me. I couldn't avoid imagining the crazy spider sneaking up behind us and trying to push us into the ravine!

Looking down, I saw that the rift extended *far* into the darkness, and that the very bottom was somewhat lit up by a river of lava, burning bright and orange down below. Around the lava was a long, stone ravine floor with glittering pools of water here and there. The forest floor—where we were standing now—must have been a pretty large *overhang*, because the ravine was a lot wider under the surface than the rift we were looking through was.

All along the sheer walls of the ravine were various natural ledges and cliffs. An explorer down there could walk along the ledges for a while if they were careful, but would always hit dead ends and have to either cut through the rock to *extend* the ledge, or climb to somewhere else.

Some ledges were closer than others.

And on *one* of the ledges, maybe twenty feet below the surface, there was something sitting on the stone floor; some kind of small, dusty, leather...

"The book!!" I exclaimed. "There it is!"

"*Well done, Skeleton Steve,*" Elias said. "*I can see it now, too.*"

"How are we going to get to it? Can you teleport over there?"

"*I can,*" Elias said, "*though the shape of the opening here compared to where the cliff is there does make it a little more difficult. It will be harder to warp back out...*"

I wasn't about to try to understand the mechanics and angles of how Endermen teleport.

"So what are we gonna to do?"

"*I can warp in, and if I have a hard time warping out, I'll need to build up a bridge of dirt toward enough of a line of sight to allow me out again. Of course, that would take me some time. Alternatively, we can build a bridge of dirt down to the cliff, from here to begin with, and go down together.*"

My imagination suddenly played a scene in my head of Elias stuck down in there, on the cliff with the book, taking the time to build his way back up to here with dirt … while I waited up here all alone, unable to defend myself…

"I prefer the *second* option." I said. "Let's go together."

"*Very well,*" Elias said, then began looking around. He immediately pulled up the dirt block at the edge of the ravine, further opening the rift and getting us closer to the ravine's inner wall. The ninja set the dirt block aside.

I watched for the spider as the Enderman continued digging up dirt blocks, one at a time, making a pile to use for the bridge, working his way through the forest floor to the ravine wall.

"Do you ... ah ... *sense* the spider?"

Faced away from me with a dirt block in his hands, Elias stopped for a moment, then resumed his work.

"*No,*" he said. After a while of moving blocks, Elias spoke up again. "*Alright. We've got a way in.*"

I walked over, past the dirt pile, and looked inside. There was the wall—stone and dirt. From here, the Enderman would be able to make a dirt path down to the ledge holding the book. We'd be in and out of there in no time!

And Elias did exactly that. Once the hole was big enough, he started placing those dirt blocks from the forest floor along the wall in a way that I could get down to the ledge without trouble—building something like a *staircase* of dirt...

So talented, I thought.

Eventually, we followed those dirt-block stairs down into the ravine, down several steps until we reached the ledge with the book...

And Elias stopped in his tracks.

"There's..." he said in my mind, the word fading while he focused on something else. *"Something ... red..."*

"Red?" I asked, still on the dirt block behind him. "What are you *talking* about?"

The Enderman turned, and looked back at me. His purple eyes flared.

"Skeleton Steve, get the book, and stay on your toes. There's something wrong down here. Something..."

"Wait, uh, what are *you* gonna do??"

Zip.

With that, Elias disintegrated into purple motes of light right in front of me, and I saw his warp path bolt toward another ledge across the ravine! He reappeared there, looking around frantically. Purple light-dust flickered and drifted down into the rift.

Zip.

He teleported again to another ledge farther along.

What's going on?!

I hustled down the dirt blocks, down to the stone ledge, and made my way carefully to the book. If I was too careless now, I might fall over the edge. I could *see* it, at the far end of the ledge ahead, brown, covered in dust form the fall, words scrawled on it in black paint. A little black sword on the cover…

"Got it," I said to myself, closing the distance, and I reached down to grab the book.

The moment I picked it up, I heard a loud *hissss*…

Clutching the book to my ribcage, I pressed my back to the stone wall as a *large spider* scrabbled up from the edge right in front of me. Its multiple eyes glared at me, burning red, and its fangs trembled...

"Uh ... *hi* there ... uh ... spider," I stammered. "Are you ... um ... the crazy one??"

Hisssssss!!!

I tried to step back, but I was already up against the wall. It might be possible to turn back to the dirt stairs and make a run for it, but the spider would surely catch me when I turned away...

"Elias!!" I cried. "It's *here!!*"

As I looked into the crazy spider's eyes, I saw something *deeper* inside there. Strange, fiercely burning points of red light *blazed* inside the spider's normal red eyes. Something was ... different. Something ... *red*...

"Elias!! Help!"

I'd have to run.

As soon as I bent my knees to try and take off from where I was standing, the spider flexed its own eight, furry black legs, and I watched its fangs open as it *leapt* toward me...

Zip.

In a sudden flurry of motion, all I could see the next moment was black and purple. Little purple motes of light exploded all around me, and Elias was suddenly standing right next to me, in a low, martial arts pose, and with lightning speed, he launched a *powerful kick* at the spider as it attacked, connecting with the middle of its body with a surprising *squish!*

The mob screeched in pain, stopped in its midair leap, and flew away from us, launched by Elias's kick, out into the open space of the deep ravine.

Then, something weird happened that *neither* of us expected...

The wounded spider, in mid-flight, seemed to ... shake and ... *glitch!*

Suddenly, there were *two* spiders, but in the same position of pain, legs pulled in, both falling in the same way ... down ... down ...

Splat!!

"What?!" I cried. "What the—what just happened??"

"*Are you okay?*" Elias asked, his mind voice perfectly calm.

I felt the book, still held tight against my chest. Looking back to the dirt stairs, I glanced over the cliff's edge at the dead spiders again, then up to my friend's glowing, purple eyes.

"Yeah, I'm … it didn't get me. What *was* that?! It turned into two spiders??"

"*Yes, strange,*" Elias replied. "*There's a very bad energy in this place. I will have to study the area. Oddly enough, I feel that the energy here is related to the energy of the Skeleton King and the artifact. This is bad news for Diamodia. I will have to consult my master back on The End for his advice on how to proceed.*"

"What would the … um … *Skeleton King energy* be doing way over here?"

"*I don't know, Skeleton Steve. But we've got to find out. And in the meantime, we've got to make sure that no mobs venture into this ravine.*"

"And that none get *out*, right?"

"*Correct*," the Enderman said. "*Whatever is happening here, we wouldn't want it to spread anymore...*"

After climbing back out of the ravine (and destroying the dirt steps), I watched helplessly as the Enderman ninja spent the better part of the afternoon moving dirt blocks around to *completely* seal the rift. Every once and a while, he found a dirt block containing an Ender Seed, and stashed it away in his 'dimensional pocket', then went on.

By the time evening was near, the work was done, and Elias had crafted a small landmark from dirt to remind us of where to dig down and access the ledge again in the future.

With the book in my pack, we head back to Zombietown...

Psssssst!!
Liking the story? Don't forget to join my Mailing List! I'll send you *free books* and stuff! (www.SkeletonSteve.com)

S1E1
5 – The Knight

I looked at the cover of Zebulon's book while we walked.

Zombietown was just off in the distance as we hiked away from the river, across the huge, grassy plain, and as the sun went down, I could see, even from here, that the town was really coming alive!

The undead come out at night.

Zebulon's "The Knight's Code" was a *thick* book, and I was very curious about all of the information and musings within. The little black words and cartoony sword beckoned to me...

"*Open the book,*" I heard in my mind. "*Open the book.*"

Eh, I thought, and returned the tome to my pack. As much as I wanted to read Zebulon's book, it was also a *journal*, at least in part—a personal diary. And I just didn't feel right about looking at someone's diary without their permission.

But that *did* give me some ideas.

I thought about Elias's diary. And that beautiful, empty red book back at Zebulon's place, which I'd start filling up myself. I thought about Sidney the Spider who likes to be warm in the sun at the top of the trees during the day. And Cho'thos the creeper, who's very sneaky! And even Zed the Zombie, who really wants a helmet so he can prowl around in the sunlight.

Maybe it'd be fun to ... I dunno ... make friends and document their *own* stories? To start amassing journals from mobs *all over* Diamodia?

Perhaps Zebulon would let me read *his* diary one day...

As we approached the village, I was surprised at *how many* zombies there were! It looked like there were *way more* than I saw in the shadows and inside the houses during the day. Where'd they all come from??

The undead mobs all roamed about, chatting with each other, talking about various mundane things that happened through the day. I heard more than a few of them mention a mysterious Enderman and a skeleton with red, glowing eyes...

We stepped into the library.

"Zebulon?" I said, moving through the doorway. "We're coming in! Don't be mad!"

I saw the little zombie sitting at the table with a different book. Looking up at the shelves, I saw the bold, red journal, what was to become my new diary, sitting all alone among scraps of paper. Zebulon looked up at us and smiled.

"Ah haaa!" he exclaimed. "You *return!* Hello, Skeleton Steve! Hello, Elias! Did you find my book?"

I pulled the tome from my pack as Elias squeezed through the doorway behind me.

"*Greetings, Zebulon,*" the Enderman said into our heads. "*We have the book, and also came across the 'crazy' spider.*"

"You do!" he exclaimed, smiling. "You did??" His smile turned to a frown. "Are you *okay?*"

"Yeah, we're fine," I said, approaching the small zombie. I put his book on the table in front of him, and he snatched it up with a grin, pulling it to his chest.

"Thank you both!" he said, standing, and moving quickly over to the red book on the shelf. "Fine job!"

"*Zebulon,*" Elias said. "*You say that the spider attacked you on the surface? Where did this happen?*"

The little zombie pulled the red book from the shelf and approached us. "Well," he said, "I was sitting under my tree, and it attacked me while I was reading."

"*Did it bite you?*" the Enderman asked.

Zebulon shook his head, then, handed the red book to me. "No," he said. "I wrestled it back a few times, and we circled each other while I tried to *talk* to it. I had to dodge out of the way of its *jump attacks* a couple of times—that's how we

74

ended up so close to the ravine's edge, and I dropped the book!"

The *red book* in my bony hands just … felt right. I loved it. As far as I knew, I'd never owned a book before. And now *this* was mine—this book I'm writing in at this very moment, these words you're reading right now. I was so proud…

"*How did you get away?*" Elias asked.

"After I dropped the book, I ran into the trees and lost the foul beast there," Zebulon said. "I may not *look* like it, but I'm *very fast*, you know!"

"*Have you seen any more of these spiders, or other crazy, unresponsive … aggressive mobs?*"

"Thanks for the book," I said.

Zebulon smiled at me, then turned back to Elias with a serious face. "Good Ender, *why* all the questions??"

Elias folded his hands together. "*There was something wrong with the spider—something dangerous to us all. I intend to investigate this disturbance and help if I can, but know that I have sealed the ravine. You, and the other zombies here, should stay away from that area for now."*

Zebulon sighed, then replied with his big voice. "I was *afraid* you were going to say that! *Very well*. I suppose I'll just have to find another reading area."

"Zebulon," I said, looking at his book on the table, "what's this *Knight's Code* of yours?"

He looked back to his brown book and smiled.

"Ah, Skeleton Steve, *that* is a question that will indeed lead you onto a *noble* path!"

Walking over to the table, Zebulon closed the book he was reading before we returned, and stretched to put it back on the shelf. I didn't catch a good glimpse of its cover, but I was able to make out the words:

King Arthur and his...

"What's this *noble path* of yours?"

Elias watched silently.

"Ah, my friends, *fellow warriors*. I live in this world of *books and knowledge*." Zebulon gestured to the shelves, then frowned. "Well, at least what is *here*. I am always looking for more! And these books have shown me distant lands, and other ways of life. Glimpses into worlds very different than our own!"

"*Where do these books come from?*" Elias asked.

Zebulon paused. "I honestly do not know, Elias!" He smiled. "But they were here when I found this village, and they have *changed* my life! For, you see, we are *more* than just mere zombies. More than a skeleton and an Enderman. We can be anything we want to be!"

I laughed. "What do you mean? A zombie can't be a ... an *Enderman*, for example..."

"No, of course not, Skeleton Steve!" he replied. "We are what we are in our bodies, and what those bodies can do, after all. But our *minds*, and who we are ... only *you* can tell yourself who you are. You, Skeleton Steve, can be a skeleton archer, wandering around in the dark looking for Minecraftians to shoot at—"

"If I had a *bow*..."

"Yes, if you had a bow—*what?!* You can be a typical skeleton and do what everyone expects you to do, or, you can go your *own* way, and choose your own course! You have chosen to travel! You have chosen to perform an act of bravery in order to earn *that book!* What else will you choose? Will you, in time, become a hero? Will you do good deeds for your fellow mobs?"

"What have *you* chosen, zombie?" I asked.

Zebulon smiled.

"I think of myself, good Skeleton Steve, as a *knight* in training."

"*What is a knight?*" Elias asked.

"A champion of good!" Zebulon exclaimed. "A warrior of the light, and defender of mobkind. A follower of the *Knight's Code!*"

"So what's the *Knight's Code?*" I asked.

Zebulon puffed out his little chest, then thought for a moment, as if trying to assemble something he memorized...

"On my honor," he began, "I dedicate my heart to *valor*. I will fight injustice and avenge the wronged. I will have courage in sword and deed. I dedicate my blade to the innocent. I will be strong ... and defend ... the weak. I will ... undo ... the wicked ... and..." The little zombie scrunched up his green face in concentration. "Undo the wicked and ... have faith in goodness!! And I ... and..."

Elias and I exchanged glances.

Zebulon gave up, and laughed, a long hearty laugh.

"Ah well, good sirs," he exclaimed, chuckling. "I am a knight *in training* after all. Still working on it!"

"That's really cool," I said. "I guess the world can really use more good like that, right?"

"*It is, indeed, a good collection of ideals*," Elias said.

Zebulon beamed. "Thank you, Skeleton Steve and Elias. And thanks again for returning my book! Now, if you don't mind, I'll get back to my studies. Feel free to visit me *any time!*"

S1E1
6 – Minecraftians

As I sat on the roof of the Zombietown watchtower, the square moon slowly passing by overhead, I began to write these words. My skeletal fingers were clumsy at first with the quill and ink, but eventually I got the hang of it.

Elias sat next to me, his blue headband silvery in the cool moonlight. My Enderman friend sat lightly with his legs crossed, and his hands on his knees, calm and serene. Soon, he would start meditating, I supposed. His eyes were almost closed.

"That was some interesting stuff Zebulon said."

The ninja opened his eyes, their purple glow bright in the dark night.

"*Indeed,*" Elias said. "*It is interesting how he has evolved into that mentality on his own, using books.*"

"And he's just a good person, really."

"Most mobs are."

"I *have* been noticing that," I replied, "except for that crazy spider!"

We were silent for a moment. I wrote some more words on the page.

"The spider is … disturbing," Elias said. *"There's something dark and dangerous going on here on Diamodia. And I fear we're all threatened by it. You, me, your world and mine. Even the Nether."*

"What did you sense in the ravine that made you go teleporting off like that?"

"The red," Elias replied. He stared up at the moon.

"The artifact?" I asked.

"Maybe," the Enderman said. *"Or maybe the artifact was just a piece of something bigger. Maybe there's a portal to that … other universe … down there somewhere."*

"Did I...?"

I didn't quite know where I was going with that. My thoughts were going crazy with images of the Skeleton King, and wondering about where I came from. Who am I? Who was I before??

What was *my* relation to all of this??

"*Don't worry about it,*" Elias said. "*I'm going to take another look down there tomorrow, and go back to The End to consult with my master. We'll find out more soon. In the meantime, we've got to figure out how to help you recover your memories!*"

I sighed, and looked back down at the journal.

"Well," I said, "hopefully *this* will help."

"*I suspect that if you continue documenting your days and your thoughts,*" Elias said, "*it may help your mind become more organized, and you may start to remember more about who you were before you were corrupted by the artifact.*"

"Then I will. I'll keep writing. Let's hope this works."

"*It's a good idea*," the Enderman said, closing his eyes again.

"Elias?" I asked.

His eyes popped open.

"*Yes, Skeleton Steve?*"

"What about you and me? What's the plan next? How long will you be with me?"

"*I was intending to stay with you, to help you with your memories, for the duration of my Seed Stride,*" he replied. "*After that, I must return home to go through my promotion trials, and I will be sent on missions for my order from then on...*"

"How long is your *Seed Stride?*"

"*Until I feel it is complete.*"

"And what about you going back to tell your master about the ravine? Will that change things?"

"*Perhaps,*" he said. "*There's no way to know about that tonight. You should get back to writing...*"

"Alright," I said.

Looking down, I penned more words in my journal under the light of the moon.

Until I heard the rustle of leaves near the tree-line down below.

I heard the constant moaning and footsteps of the many zombies down in the streets, their dull voices chatting with each other in the darkness of Zombietown at night, but *this* was something different.

Scanning the forest ahead of me down below, I looked for the source of the noise.

... And saw a pair of *Minecraftians* running around in the dark.

None of the zombies down below seemed to notice them, at least not yet.

The creatures ran around in a random pattern just inside the trees, as if they were torn between running toward the town, and just intently investigating every tree, every bush. They were strange—not like the three Minecraftians I had met before; not like Elias's friends.

One Minecraftian was dressed in leather armor, and carried a wooden sword. His face was plain and featureless, his eyes without emotion. The other was dressed in orange and blue rags, with wild black hair that seemed to grow in all directions, and bare, muscular arms. At the moment, the orange guy wasn't holding a weapon. One of them threw something at the other, who picked it up.

Chomp chomp chomp chomp chomp….

The Minecraftian in leather ate something, then burped loudly.

Then, I heard them speak. While I was able to understand the other Minecraftians, Elias's friends, before, I could not comprehend *any* of these guys' words!

Elias opened his eyes, and looked down at them.

"What are they saying?" I whispered.

"*It doesn't make much sense,*" Elias responded. "*One of them said something like, 'you need hearing aids', and the other said 'thank you, dumb guy, thank you'—babble, mostly.*"

"I wonder what they want…"

The Minecraftians didn't seem all that interested in coming into Zombietown—not right now anyway, but they hovered around the tree-line for a few more seconds.

Then they looked up at me.

And I looked back down at them.

And they fled into the darkness…

Season 1, Episode 2:
Trying to Remember

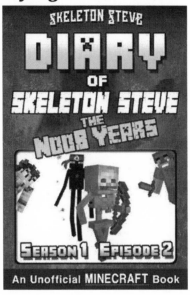

Trying to remember ... and Skeleton Steve gets a bow!

After discovering a dangerous disturbance in the energy of the world, Elias must return to his master in The End to report the situation. But first, Skeleton Steve and the Enderman explore Zombietown to see what his amnesiac mind remembers about Minecraft life!

Before leaving the Overworld, Elias finally gives Skeleton Steve a bow, and it's a good thing, too! Those strange Minecraftians outside town look like they're going to assault the village! Will Skeleton Steve and Zebulon the little zombie knight be able to defend Zombietown without the help of the powerful Enderman ninja?

S1E2
1 – Burning Zed

As the square sun rose in the eastern sky, the zombie citizens of Zombietown fled for the darkness and the safety of their abandoned villager homes. Daylight was deadly to the undead.

I felt the sunshine warm up my bones.

With my *helmet*, given to me by Elias's Minecraftian friends (who live a few days' travel to the west), I didn't have to worry about sunlight if I wanted to roam around during the day.

"*The sun rises*," Elias said to me with his mind voice, inside my head.

I closed my diary and put the red leather-bound book back into my pack.

"So what's the deal for today?" I asked, standing.

My bones *clunked*.

We were on top of the village's watchtower, which was quickly becoming our local *hangout*, since it was *likely* that all of the ruined houses of Zombietown were already claimed.

You know … by *zombies*.

Elias, my Enderman companion, remained seated in his meditation posture—back straight, legs crossed under him, one hand on each knee. The blue headband of his ninja order was bold against the smooth, black skin of his forehead, and the white 'novice' symbol glimmered in the morning light. The tails of the headband floated up and down gently in the breeze coming from the southeast.

He opened his eyes, and the purple light inside them flared.

"*I have two things in mind for us to do today,*" the Enderman said. "*First, we should explore this village. With the problems present inside the ravine with the red energy, we may be here a while. It may also do well to see if there is an unoccupied dwelling that we can use for a … 'base', as the Minecraftians would say…*"

"That's cool," I replied. "Good idea. This watchtower roof is a little cramped anyway, and what are—"

I was interrupted by the sound of raging flames and zombie cries of pain. Several undead down below started moaning and lamenting.

"I'm on fire!" a zombie cried. "Oh, I'm on fire!"

"He's on fire!" another said.

I looked over the edge.

"Now *I'm* on fire!" yet another said.

Just outside the nearest house, there was a zombie enveloped in billowing flames, wandering around on the cobblestone street blinded by the fire all around him. I could hardly see the guy inside the blaze—only his green hands protruded, as he flailed around, grasping blindly at the world in front of him!

"Get inside!" I shouted down from above. "Get out of the *sun*, you oaf!"

Elias was still sitting, watching me, not paying attention to the fiasco down below.

I saw a second zombie wander by on fire as well.

"Can you help him?" I asked my companion.

"*This happens every morning, Skeleton Steve,*" the Enderman responded. "*Zombies ... and skeletons ... come and go. They appear from the wilderness in great numbers during the night, and those that don't seek shelter burn up in the daylight. I've seen countless undead perish in the mornings.*"

"What?!" I said, crossing my bony arms. "That's nuts! You don't at least *try* to help them?"

Elias looked up at me as I stood, stretched over the wooden railing, watching the zombies wander around on fire below.

"*The undead are many. I have tried to save them in the past, yes, but for every zombie I convince to stay out of the sun, several more burn up without much thought. And even then, I've seen the ones who are safe for the moment, unless they're trapped somehow, forget about the dangers of the daylight, and wander out to burn up again!"*

The sound of the flames died down, and looking back to the street, I saw just a pile of ash and charred zombie flesh.

"Forget??"

"Yes," Elias said with his mind voice, standing. His long Enderman body towered over me in the sunlight. *"Most zombies have problems with their minds, and forget things very quickly. They live in the moment, every moment, and don't last long. You ... are unique, Skeleton Steve. Zebulon is unique too, it seems. Both of you have retained sharp minds in your undead states. But, even still, you don't know who you are, and our main quest, during my Seed Stride, is to try to recover your memories. You, my friend, have problems with your own mind as well..."*

"Yeah, I guess so," I replied.

Foom!

I heard another gout of flame from down below.

"I'm on fire! I'm on fire!!" a zombie shouted.

"Zed's on fire! It's Zed!" another cried.

I scoffed.

"Oh, come *on!!*" I shouted, dropped down to the ladder, and scrambling to get out to the street. "Really?!"

Running through the open doorway, stepping over the remnants of the shattered wooden door, I saw *another* zombie on fire, wandering around the cobblestone street. Flames sputtered and sparked and licked at his body and clothes—I couldn't even see his face.

"Zed?!" I asked. "Is that you??"

"I'm on fire!" Zed said. "I'm on fire!" I recognized his voice.

Crud.

I figured I *had* to help the guy—I was just talking to him yesterday about maybe finding him a helmet so he didn't burn up in the sun anymore!

"Get back inside!" I cried, approaching to try to steer him back to the house across the street.

The flames were hot, and I suddenly realized that if I touched the zombie, I might catch on fire as well!

Looking around on the ground, I saw a stick lying in the grass next to the watchtower. I snatched it up, and ran back to Zed.

"I'm on fire!" he repeated, half-heartedly.

Oh, gee, look at that, the tone of his zombie voice seemed to say. *I'm on fire. How interesting. I happen to be on fire...*

I stabbed at him with the stick, directing him back to the house where he was presumably hiding before be wandered out into the street.

It worked.

Pushing against his chest with the stick, which started to smolder whenever I prodded into the pillar of flames that Zed had become, convinced the zombie to walk in the direction I was pushing him.

After a few seconds of directing Zed, he stepped blindly back into the house, and the flames died down. The zombie I met yesterday was now charred and crispy, but still alive ... er ... *undead alive*. His dull, black eyes stared at me in surprise from a sooty, blackened face.

"Uh, *thanks*, Skeleton Steve!" he said in a slow voice, his green skin still sizzling.

I smirked.

"Sure thing, Zed," I said. "Just ... ah ... stay inside, *okay?*"

"Okay." He smiled, his cooked face crackling.

Zip.

I heard Elias use his teleporting power, and saw him materialize standing right next to me, down on the street. Little purple motes of light drifted down to the ground around him.

"*Shall we look around?*" he asked in my head.

"Sure, let's go," I replied.

S1E2
2 – Exploring Zombietown

We approached *another* cobblestone house.

The door was bashed in, the wooden pieces mostly gone by now, but the walls and cobblestone stairs were still in good repair. I stepped up to the doorway and looked in.

Inside the house, the main room was rather small, and was sparsely furnished with a table and chair, and nothing else.

Did villagers even *sleep?*

Maybe there was a bed in here once, but perhaps, after whatever battle or calamity happened that resulted in the living leaving and the undead moving in, it was taken or destroyed.

Two zombies stood inside, and a third sat in the oak chair.

I looked at them, and they stared back at me dully.

"Howdy," I said.

"Hello," they all said, then continued to stare. One of them let out a long, low moan.

"See ya!" I said, giving a wave, and ducking back out of the doorway.

"Bye!" one of them said.

I looked at Elias, who stood waiting in the street.

"So how many Minecraftians *are* there on this world?" I asked.

The Enderman ninja shook his head. "*I don't know, Skeleton Steve,*" he said. "*I have not wandered Diamodia much longer than you have by now—at least in your current state of mind. So far, while on my Seed Stride, I have only seen the three back at the castle—LuckyMist, WolfBroJake, and Xenocide99—and the two we saw in the forest last night.*"

"What was *with* those guys last night?" I said, laughing. "Should we be worried?"

We continued walking, and I approached a similar small house. Looking inside, through the busted door, I saw a similar scene: a small, modest dwelling housing a handful of zombies.

One of the zombies looked like it might have been a *villager* before. A long, green nose hung over its mouth, its lips pressed together, and it almost *glared* at me with dull, dark eyes under a thick, black furrowed brow.

"*I'm not sure yet,*" Elias responded. "*I did not sense hostile energy from the two. Only … wild impulses. A strange energy. Not like the dangerous energy in the ravine—more like … the unchecked and blazing energy of … younglings.*"

"Kids?!"

"*Perhaps. I do not know how to tell the age of Minecraftians. While one of them wore armor, and they looked similar in build to my friends back at the castle, it was like they had the minds of children, yes.*"

"I also didn't understand them," I said. "Which is weird, because I understood your Minecraftian buddies just fine..."

"*Perhaps they spoke in a different Minecraftian language? A language you have not heard? Fortunately, the mind voice allows me to communicate with all manner of creatures, since I am bypassing the inconvenience of the verbal word.*"

"How many different Minecraftian languages could there be?" I asked.

We approached another home. This one had an intact door!

I reached out without hesitation, and opened the door, letting myself in.

Elias stopped.

"*It is indeed curious that you understand Minecraftians in the first place, Skeleton Steve.*" He approached the doorway and looked inside. "*My friend, do you realize that you just opened a Minecraftian door??*"

I paused, and looked down at my bony hand.

"Uh ... is that a big deal?"

The home was another small one—maybe slightly larger than the last two—and it was *empty*. I looked back to the open door.

"*Mobs do not open doors*," Elias said.

Interesting.

"I did," I said.

"*Yes,*" Elias responded. "*Curious. I am capable of opening doors as well, but the Minecraftian technology was alien to me, and I spent a significant amount of time trying to figure out how to do so. And if it wasn't for my involvement with LuckyMist at the time, and the other Minecraftians, I probably would have never bothered to learn.*"

"So ... whoever I was ... I was able to *open doors*, I guess."

Elias nodded silently.

"Incidentally," I said, gesturing to the interior of the house, "I think we've found a *place!*"

The Enderman *zipped* through the open doorway into the house. Little, purple motes of light sprinkled down around us.

Inside the house, Elias had enough headroom for his height, and the floor was clear of any rubble or debris. Only a single window was broken. We would have enough space here to deem this house as our *Zombietown Adventure Base of Operations!*

I laughed, thinking about it.

"*I sense that you are comfortable with this place,*" Elias said into my head.

"Yeah, it'll do," I said.

"*Indeed. It will do.*" My tall, slender companion turned back to the open doorway. "*And now, I must go. I need to take another look inside the ravine.*"

"Well, I'll come with you!" I replied, moving to follow him.

The Enderman ninja turned, and his purple eyes glowed in the darkness of the bare house.

"*Wait here, Skeleton Steve,*" he said. "*The evil energy surrounding the artifact, your other self, and the spider is extremely dangerous.*"

He didn't want me to come along??

But ... I could *help* him! Somehow. If I had a weapon, I could watch his back! Two sets of eyes are better than *one* and all that...

"Can't you use my help?" I asked.

My voice must have betrayed a little bit of hurt, or, perhaps, Elias just sensed it in me. He had a power to read the minds of other mobs that I didn't quite understand.

The Enderman put his long, black hand on my shoulder.

"*Skeleton Steve,*" he said. "*If it was anything else, I would surely take you with me. But I've got to move quickly, and warp from ledge to ledge in a way that you cannot follow me. And most importantly, I need to be sure that the infected mobs can't make their way up to the surface.*"

"Like, you think it can *spread??*"

"*Perhaps. We don't know. But, I can say that the red energy in the spider was the same as the red energy in the Skeleton King, and in his artifact.*" He was speaking about the Skeleton King as if it was another person—not me. "*And this ravine is quite a distance from where I first met the monster and his army...*"

I smirked.

"Well, I guess I'll ... explore the town some more..."

Elias nodded.

"*Good idea,*" he said. "*Explore the town. Stay in the village. Perhaps see if you can find any other Minecraftian technology that you can manipulate—see if anything helps you remember.*"

"When will you be back?" I asked.

The Enderman looked outside to the sky and squinted his purple eyes against the brightness.

"Maybe in a couple of hours? I need to explore the ravine's interior, see if there are any more infected mobs, and seal it up again when I leave."

Just a couple of hours?

Oh yeah, I thought. Elias can move like the wind when he's not slowed down by a *walking* mob like me. He'll just teleport from 'warp to warp' as he calls it, all the way there and back again...

"Okay," I said. "I'll stick around." I smirked.

There must be more to see around here.

With that, Elias nodded, and with a *zip*, he was gone...

Purple flecks of light drifted down around me, disappearing when it hit the wood floor. I looked at the home's interior. Bare, cobblestone walls. Two windows, one broken. Wooden rafters in the ceiling.

What did it mean to have a place? A home of my own? What would I do, as a *mob*, in a house like this?

I didn't need a bed; didn't need to eat!

Maybe I could just use this place as a 'base' in Zombietown, like a storage space—perhaps to hold all of the stuff Elias and I will find on our adventures?

It could hold anything I didn't want to carry around in my *pack*, anyway...

I pulled the leather satchel open and looked inside.

There was my red diary. A quill and ink.

That was it.

This felt like the beginning of a *new life* of adventure!

I sighed. If only I could remember my *old* life...

Eventually, I took to walking around the village on my own, closing the door to my new place behind me so that zombies wouldn't wander into the house and claim it for themselves.

Most of the homes were the same small shacks with a doorway and a single window or two, usually bare inside, but occasionally furnished with a table or chairs, or both. All of the doors were bashed to bits. I figured that this must have been a *normal* village a long time ago, until the zombies took over and killed, ate, or drove away all of the living villagers.

And, for whatever reason, the zombies *stayed*.

Even though Zombietown was only the second village I'd ever seen, as far as I could *remember* anyway, for some reason I thought that a town inhabited by zombies was just ... *not normal*. Like, if a typical village was overrun by the undead one night, the mobs would probably just *move on* or burn up in the morning, leaving the place a *ghost town*.

But not Zombietown.

There was one other larger home, like the one Elias and I had claimed, but its door was broken down just like all of the other houses here, and a handful of zombies waited inside for nightfall.

Another interesting find in Zombietown was a building that Elias would later tell me was *the blacksmith*. The living quarters were as small as the other tiny shacks, and there was a large, cobblestone addition to this place, with a huge porch and roof, *open* to the outdoors. On this porch, around the corner from the doorway to the inside, was a stone container of burning lava, sputtering and spitting little chunks of molten rock onto the cobblestone floor, as well as several stone and metal containers—some sort of Minecraftian tools, I presumed.

Inside the living quarters was a wooden container—a *chest*, that creaked open with ease when I tested it.

Hmm, I thought. *So I was familiar with chests, too...*

Inside the wooden container were several pieces of Minecraftian food (nothing that appealed to me), three bricks—ingots—of polished, grey metal, and a handful of small, baby *trees*...

I picked up the food and inspected each piece, held in my bony fingers.

Firm, red balls. Sweet smell. Three of them.

Apples, I thought.

"These are ... apples," I said to no one.

There were five large chunks of brown, squishy food. The smell was ... distinct.

Bread.

I tore a loaf of bread in half and smelled the white insides.

Minecraftian food. *How did I know what this was?*

The metal ... hard and cold and grey ... was ... *iron*.

These are 'ingots' of iron, I thought, holding one of the heavy metal bricks in front of me.

What are they for?

I turned an ingot over and over in my bony hand, contemplating its shape and edges.

All in all, there were three apples, five pieces of bread, three iron ingots, and five oak saplings.

I put them all into my pack.

True, I had no intention of eating the apples or the bread. I didn't even know if I could *try* to. But they might come in useful later…

Closing the chest, I looked it over.

Open … *creak*.

Close … *creak*.

I tried to move it, but it seemed either too heavy, or, it was bolted to the wall or the floor. Maybe if I had the right kind of tool, I could break it down somehow…

114

Or maybe I'd just wait for Elias to move it *for* me.

That would be a cool thing to have in our little Zombietown home...

Over the rest of the time I waited for Elias to return, I explored the remainder of the town—not going into *all* of the buildings, but at least looking for anything else Minecraftian that I could try to play with.

But there wasn't much else of note.

In the middle of town was some kind of *well*, a source of water for the villagers that lived here before. But now, the blue water sat still inside, untouched and unused.

I also looked over the farm plots until I determined that they were all the same. The raised rectangular pads of dirt with water-filled trenches were surrounded by timber logs, and probably grew *plenty* of Minecraftian crops once upon a time, but were now just barren dirt.

Elias finally returned before the evening, gone a bit more than a couple of hours. When I saw him appear near me out of a warp, I was shocked to see the ninja *injured*—I could barely make it out! On his deep, black skin, I barely saw a couple of wounds that were even *darker* black with his Enderman blood...

"Elias!" I cried. "What happened?!"

I ran to my companion, my bones clunking.

"*Do not worry, Skeleton Steve*," he said, purple motes of light settling around him. "*I will heal when I return to The End. It's not bad*."

"I guess you ran into more ... eh ... *infected* mobs?"

The ninja nodded. "*I did, yes*," he said into my mind. "*Down near the floor of the ravine, I encountered a group of mobs ... with red eyes, like yours, who were ... aggressive*."

"What's with the red eyes? And why does everyone keep *pointing out* my eyes??"

"*Have you seen your reflection?*" Elias asked.

It occurred to me suddenly that I had no idea what my face looked like!

Ever since I transformed into my ... current self, I had never thought of seeking out a mirror or some other way to *see* myself. Oddly enough, it just never struck me as something to do. We've seen skeletons here and there in the village, and on the road, and I guess I assumed that I looked like *them*.

But the Minecraftians had mentioned my eyes. And so had Zebulon. Had Zed? I couldn't remember...

Where could I find a *reflection* ...?

"Uh, *this* way!" I said, leading Elias from the farm plot where he found me back to the middle of town. The Enderman followed.

When I reached the village's well, I climbed the steps and stared into the blue waters. But this time, instead of just taking a second to notice that the water was still and unused, I focused on my shadowy reflection until I could see...

My skull was a lot like the other skeletons I'd seen, just as I figured.

Maybe I was a little more … *smirky*.

But the big difference between myself and all of the other mobs we'd come across on Diamodia … were my *eyes!*

Skeletons had empty, dark, hollow eye sockets—nothing there. Just the empty holes of an undead skull.

But inside each of *my* dark eye sockets, right in the middle like a ghostly pupil, was a bright pinprick of blazing red light!

The red…

My skeleton jaw gaped as I looked at my reflection…

No *wonder* everyone mentioned my eyes! They really stood out! And as I stared at my red, glowing eyes and the rest of my bony face, those little pinpricks of light darted around like a ghostly parody of real eyes—like *living* eyes.

"Wow!" I exclaimed.

"*Indeed,*" Elias replied, standing behind me. "*You are unique, Skeleton Steve. It is important for us to figure out who you are—what you are...*"

"My eyes, they're like ... the infected?"

"*When you were the Skeleton King, your eyes burned the same, as did the eyes of every single skeleton archer in your army. And the eyes of the creatures in the ravine ... are the same as well.*"

"So I'm ... like them??" I asked, watching my eyes in the water transform with concern.

"*I'm not sure,*" Elias replied. "*I believe that you are somehow connected to the red energy, but once the corruption of the artifact was broken, and you became who you are today, you're somehow different. You may be a special case. And it is important for the safety of this world that we figure it out...*"

I turned away from the burning red eyes, and looked at my friend.

He watched me with his glowing, *purple* eyes, and I couldn't read that alien Enderman face. What was he thinking? What did he feel when he saw me—especially after just fighting some bad mobs that were somehow *related* to me? How could he even treat me so nicely after I tried to kill him and his friends when I was the Skeleton King??

He put a hand on my bony shoulder.

Elias *cared* about me.

Or, I thought, *he was keeping me close, because I might be the key to removing the red energy from his world*...

No, I thought. He didn't find out about the ravine until *after* we were traveling together.

"I found out some more interesting stuff," I said, looking up at him.

"Did anything help you remember?"

"Sort of," I replied. "I found some stuff in a chest—a wooden container—and could remember the *names* of the stuff..."

"Show me," Elias said.

So I took him to the blacksmith's and showed him the chest. The Enderman had clearly seen chests before, but was more interested in how I immediately knew how to open and close it, as well as how I remembered the names of the items within. I showed him the apples, the bread, iron ingots, and saplings.

"*Come with me,*" he said. "*I'd like you to try something else...*"

The ninja led me to Zebulon's library. After we went inside and chatted with the zombie knight-in-training for a while, Elias led me to the *crafting table* I noticed the first time we found this place.

"What is it?" I asked. "Looks *Minecraftian*, but I don't remember it."

"*It's called a 'crafting table'. This block of wood and its small tools makes up a vital piece of technology for Minecraftians. With this, they can create tools, weapons, armor, and other things—a very important item.*"

"How does it work?"

"*You tell me,*" Elias responded. "*I have seen the Minecraftians out west build shields, armor,*" *swords, doors, and many more things with this. Experiment with it—see if it reminds you of anything..."*

I approached the wooden desk. Small Minecraftian hand-tools hung from its sides, and the top was decorated with lines of paint—perhaps some sort of *measuring grid*...

Laying my bony hands on its wooden surface, and tried to think. Running a fingertip along the lines, I tried to let the memories come back to me. I tinkered around with the small tools hanging on the sides, then, returned them to their places.

Nothing.

"Did *you* make anything with this?" I asked Elias.

"*No,*" he replied. "*I just watched as the Minecraftians used it. Or, one like it. And they built these out of wood from the trees whenever they needed to build more tools.*"

"I don't remember anything," I said. "Sorry."

After leaving Zebulon's, we spent the rest of the evening and part of the night wandering around town looking for anything else to help spark my memory. When the sun went down, the zombies and other mobs all came out into the streets again, and eventually, we retired to our new home so that Elias could do his meditations.

S1E2
3 – The Bow

In the morning, I climbed up the ladder of the watchtower again after making sure all of the zombies were safe and out of the streets.

Elias thought it was silly, but I didn't want to run around again rescuing any lame-brains from burning up in the sun today. Zed, the first zombie I talked to when we *found* this village, was still blackened from his little *roast* the morning before!

Sitting up in the sunlight on the roof of the village's watchtower, I worked a little in my journal, and enjoyed the sun warming up my bones.

Until I saw those weird Minecraftians again!

"Elias!" I called.

Peering down from the tower railing, I watched the tree line of the forest nearby, and saw the same two weird Minecraftians, jumping and flitting about in the trees, randomly swinging their swords and arms at anything nearby.

The one dressed in orange and blue had an angry face and spiky black hair that stuck out in all directions. His eyes were dark and focused, but I couldn't read his face—it was always in a *scowl*, and never changed. His orange and blue shirt had no sleeves, revealing his muscular arms, and he wore no shoes, bounding around in the forest with bare feet, punching the trees as he excitedly spoke to his friend in a language I didn't understand.

The other was dressed the same as he was the other night I saw him—brown leather armor covered his entire body and the top of his head, his face bland and unreadable with strange, blue eyes. The *leather guy* bounced and jumped and sprinted around, swinging a wooden sword in front of him. Sometimes he hit the trees, doing little damage, something he swung at nothing at all.

They chatted and shouted at each other constantly in their strange language.

The orange man and the leather guy...

Zip.

126

In a subtle shower of purple light dust, my Enderman pal appeared on the watchtower roof next to me.

He regarded the Minecraftians for a moment, squinting his purple eyes against the bright morning.

"That's like meta spooky man," Elias said. *"Am I 29? Do I sound 29? What are you freaking fruitcases talking about?"*

"Uh ... what?!" I asked.

He looked down at me.

"That's what they are saying. In their own language. Gibberish," Elias said.

"Oh," I said, looking back out at them. "Are they dangerous?"

The Enderman crossed his long arms over his chest.

"I'm not sure," he said. *"We should follow them and see where they live."*

"Good idea."

"*But not now,*" Elias went on. "*I must return to the End to discuss the ravine with my master. The red energy issue is the most important thing right now.*"

I looked up at him. "But what if they *attack?*"

Elias thought to himself for a moment, then reached into his dimensional pocket.

"*I believe you may be ready for this, Skeleton Steve,*" he said, producing a brand new *wooden bow*. I grinned. "*This was crafted by LuckyMist. She gave it to me to give to you at the right time. It seems that the right time is now...*"

"Oh, awesome!" I exclaimed. "*Thanks*, Elias!" I straightened my face and got rid of the smile. "I won't let you down, you know. I'm not the Skeleton King ... not anymore!"

"*I know,*" he said, reaching back into his dimensional pocket. His long, black hand emerged again and again with several clutches of arrows. I put them into my pack.

Holding the bow felt right. The string was tight, and the wood was smooth. The grip seemed like it was made for my hand...

"This might be a odd question," Elias said, *"since you're a skeleton, and, all skeleton archers are great with bows ... but ... since you've been acting like you're* not *a normal skeleton, remembering all of those Minecraftian details and all ... do you know how to use it?"*

I laughed.

"Of course I—"

But I stopped.

Come to think of it, I didn't have any memories of ever holding a bow before. Even those weird memories of me beating up Elias as the Skeleton King, from the ninja's point of view, had me shooting a weird, sideways *arm-mounted* bow. Not like this bow in my hand now...

"I guess ... I'm not sure," I said.

We left the watchtower and walked to the field on the opposite side of the village from where the Minecraftians were playing in the woods. After hiking a short distance away from town, Elias stopped me, then made several stacks of dirt in a few positions, two blocks high.

"Targets?" I asked.

"*Yes*," he replied. "*Take some shots and see what you remember...*"

"Okay," I said, holding the bow in my left bony hand, pulling the first arrow from my pack with my right. Then, I stood, looking at the bow in one hand, and the arrow in the other.

Nope.

Nothing.

Zilcho.

I was *not* an expert marksman. Not by a long shot.

It was like starting over...

"Um..." I said, trying to position the arrow onto the bow above my grip. I tried putting the arrow on the inside of the bow, then moved it to the outside...

"You don't remember..." Elias said.

I smirked, then forced a laugh.

"Ah ... yeah. Right. A skeleton who can't use a bow, right?? I mean ... I'm sure it can't be *that hard*..."

Sure, I was starting over. But I was smart. I'd figure this out. Obviously, the arrow rested on the bow above the grip, and the part behind the feathers fit into the bowstring...

I raised the bow with the arrow in place, and started to pull the arrow back against the string. When the bow was raised to the right height, I found that I could look down the length of the arrow, using my right eye, to aim at the dirt block...

Pulling the arrow back until I couldn't pull any farther, I held still, then slowly released the string. The bow launched the arrow through the air with a *whistle*, the string *slapped* my bony forearm of the hand that held the grip, and I watched my first arrow sail through the air…

It sank into the grassy ground next to the dirt block!

"Okay…" I said.

"*It's okay*," Elias said. "*I have given you so many arrows that you won't need any more for a long time. You'll just have to practice.*"

I scoffed. "Yeah," I said. "I guess."

"*I must go*," the Enderman said. "*I'm not sure how long I'll be away, but I'll try to hurry back after I learn what my master wants me to do about the ravine.*"

"Um … what about the Minecraftians?"

"*Well, now you have a bow*," Elias said. "*I expect that the two of them won't attack an entire village full of zombies with just one wooden sword. But they are very strange and chaotic, so … there is no way to be sure. Do not venture out of the village except to practice here. And practice! Now, you can*" *defend yourself. You just have to learn your weapon again..."*

I turned to my friend, and shook his hand.

"Good luck, Elias," I said. "Come back soon!"

"I will try," he said. *"Goodbye for now, Skeleton Steve."*

"Good—"

Zip.

Elias disappeared in a puff of purple light dust. The motes of ender stuff drifted down to the grass, and my friend was gone.

I stared at where he was standing for a while, hoping that he'd come back *very soon*, then focused my attention back on the dirt block targets again. Reaching into my pack, I pulled out another arrow.

S1E2
4 – The Calm

I spent the rest of the day practicing with my bow in the field.

Shooting a bow wasn't very difficult, I supposed.

After a hundred arrows or so, I was finding that I could hit a dirt block pretty regularly. Eventually, I also tried shooting at different *distances*, walking closer or stepping farther back, to figure out the *arc* of the arrow from various ranges. After several shots, I felt that I had at least a *basic idea* of how to adjust my aim for targets that were closer or farther.

And I'm not an idiot, of course.

I realize that someone can't be a master of the bow and arrow after a few hours of practice!

I'm sure that there were *many* other things to practice and learn. Heck—all of the shots I took were from a standing position. Standing *still*. I bet

I'd totally flub my shot if I tried *moving* at the same time as shooting, or if I had to crouch or *hide behind a wall* at the same time or something...

And even though I could hit a block-sized target, I realized that such a large target wasn't exactly a *bullseye*. Could I hit a block-sized bad guy right between the eyes? Probably not. But I could probably hit him ... somewhere.

If he was standing still.

And I was standing still.

I scoffed and walked back to the village when the sun went down.

Yeah, there was still a lot to learn, obviously.

But it was a *start*. That was enough for the day.

As I walked through the streets of Zombietown, I greeted the various zombies that emerged from the houses in the growing darkness.

Among the throngs of undead, I saw a familiar zombie wave at me.

It was Zed. His face was a little more normal. He was gradually healing from being cooked extra-crispy in the sun yesterday morning, looking a little more *green* than black now...

"Hi there, Zed!" I said, approaching.

"Oh hi, Skeleton Steve!" he replied, his voice thick and dull. His skin wasn't crackling anymore. He pointed at my weapon. "Hey, you have a *bow* now! Cool!"

"Yeah," I said, my bones clunking as I lifted it. "Elias gave it to me."

"Good thing," he said. "You can use it when the *Minecraftians* attack soon!"

What?!

"Ummm ... *come again*??" I asked.

"When the Minecraftians attack, I said! You can use the bow to *fight* them!" The zombie smiled at me, his dark eyes glazed over and glittering a little in the light of the torch on a street post nearby.

"What do you mean, *when the Minecraftians attack?*"

"Oh—the Minecraftians outside of town!" he said slowly. "It's about time for them to attack again. They come and kill some of us every few days or so..."

"What?!" I asked. "Why?"

"Eh," Zed shrugged. "Dunno..."

"So what happens?"

Zed scrunched up his brow and frowned at me. "What do you *mean?* They run in, attack us, then run away! Last time one of them got killed— the orange guy. It was cool. But he killed *seven* of us first! Those guys are *scary!*"

I frowned at Zed, and looked at the bow in my bony hand.

"Umm, well," I said, "you tell me if you see them, okay? And stay out of the sun!"

Zed grinned. "Okay, Skeleton Steve! See ya later!" Then, he turned and walked away to strike up a conversation with a handful of zombies nearby.

I had to talk to *Zebulon*. He'd know more about this apparent regular attack...

Walking briskly through the streets, my bones clanked and clunked, and I eventually found my way to the library. I stepped inside.

"Zebulon?" I called.

Looking around, I saw the benches and table, the shelves full of paper scraps and just a handful of books, the crafting table, but *no* Zebulon...

"Ah, man, where is he?" I said to myself, then stepped outside again.

Passing by several zombies in the streets, I made my way to the watchtower, then climbed up the ladder to the roof.

The night was clear and calm.

I looked up at the moon.

Several loud zombie moans drew my eyes back down.

What's the racket? I thought.

And I couldn't tell why they were making so much noise all of a sudden.

The zombies were interesting, but they weren't very much like me. They were, largely, somewhere *in between* clear-thinking, intelligent creatures—like Elias's Minecraftian friends—and mindless undead.

Most of them, anyway.

And this town was pretty-much *all* zombies.

Zombietown...

These last few days (and nights) of living here, I've seen other mobs passing through; skeletons, and spiders, and even a creeper ... but that's just it—they were *passing through*. Even now, I could hear the *clunk* of bones somewhere in the streets below me, as a random skeleton joined the village of zombies for the night, probably wandering in from the wilderness.

Sometime soon, I'd have to chatting with other skeleton archers, too. Were they more like me? Did they act and talk and *think* like me?

I looked at my bow and laughed.

I wasn't much of an archer myself, I thought.

Zebulon was different. He was unique. There was something *special* about that little zombie—he wasn't like the others.

Without Elias here with me, I suddenly felt very alone...

Then, something caught my eye.

Looking over, several rooftops away, I saw the shadow of a little zombie sitting on the roof of one of the larger buildings.

It was the zombie knight-in-training. Little *Zebulon*.

I watched him for a moment, and saw small guy kick back on the cobblestone roof, put his little zombie hands behind his head, and watch the moon...

"Zebulon!" I called from several roofs over.

He must have been on top of his library...

The little zombie sat up and looked over at me. He waved.

"Greetings, good Skeleton Steve!" he called back with a hearty voice.

I waved.

"What are ya doin?" I asked.

Zebulon looked back up at the moon, raised a finger and opened his mouth to speak, then shook his head.

"Just a moment, my friend!" he shouted. "I'll be right there!"

I waited as the zombie knight-in-training turned and disappeared over the other side of the cobblestone ridgeline. Among the moans and slow chatting of the zombies down below, I could just barely make out the rapid *pitter patter* of his little feet moving quickly, as he dodged between all of his larger undead brethren on the way to the watchtower. Then, I heard him climbing the ladder,

142

and stepped back as he popped out of the hole in the roof.

"Hey there," I said, and smiled.

"Hello, citizen!" he exclaimed, beaming brightly, then sat down next to me. "Tis a good night for star-gazing, is it not?"

"Yeah, I guess," I replied. "What are *you* up to?"

Zebulon smiled and sighed.

"On *some* nights, Skeleton Steve, especially when the moon is full, like tonight," he pointed to the large, bright square moon with a small, green finger, "I like to spend time outside, on the roof, thinking, *meditating* ... I watch the moon and think about the *direction of my life*."

Full moon, huh? I guess I recognized that it was full, but what whether the moon was full or *anything else* didn't really ring any bells in my mind...

"Well that seems like a good idea, I suppose," I replied.

"Truly, it is!" Zebulon replied. "Most mobs don't take the time to sit and think. Tis a good idea for gathering your mind—figuring out *who you are*. If you always *go, go, go* all the time, and never take the time to stop and *think*, tis like going through life without a map!"

I nodded, and we sat in silence for a while, listening to the zombie moans and watching the moon move across the sky.

Suddenly, Zebulon clapped me on the back. My bones *clunked*.

"I see you now have a *bow*, Skeleton Steve!" he exclaimed in his big, little voice.

"Yeah, I do," I replied, pulling it off of my shoulder and looking it over again. "Elias gave it to me earlier."

"Good for you!" Zebulon said. "And where *is* the good Enderman warrior now?"

"Oh," I said. "Elias had to go home for a short while. He said he'd be back soon."

"I see," the little zombie said. "Have you found a place to stay? Or are you still resting up *here?*"

"I did. There was an empty house with a door."

"Ah ... the *last* remaining home with a door! Did you *bash down* the door?"

"No," I replied. "Didn't have to. I can *open doors*, I guess."

The little zombie's black eyes grew wide. "Really?!" he said. "Now *that* is fascinating, Skeleton Steve! Never before have I met an undead mob who could open doors!"

"Yeah, I don't know how I did. It didn't *occur* to me that it was strange—I just reached down and *opened it*."

"So *that* must be the reason why Elias had you try to use that strange device in my library earlier, yes? Trying to see what *other* odd behavior may be hiding inside you, eh?"

"I guess," I said. "But I didn't remember anything."

Opening my pack, I reached in, and pulled out one of the iron ingots. The brick of polished metal gleamed like silver in the moonlight. Zebulon stared at my pack in wonder.

"What on Diamodia is *that?!*" he asked.

"Oh," I replied, looking at the chunk of metal, "this is an *iron ingot*. That's the *other* thing. I looked inside the blacksmith chest, and could remember the names of all of the—"

"No, not *that*," Zebulon said, "although that is interesting as well. But, I mean to say, what is that *pack?* The *leather satchel* strapped to your bones??"

I looked down at it.

I've always had it, and never thought anything of it. The strap ran up over my ribs and shoulder, and I kept the small, leather pack cinched close to me so it didn't move around when I ran.

"Eh ... it's just my *pack*. I've always had it. It's where I keep my stuff."

"Skeleton Steve," Zebulon said, looking up at me. "Other skeletons, other undead mobs, do not wear such a thing. Where did you get it??"

"Well, I don't remember. I've had it since the beginning of ... well ... as far back as I *can* remember."

"My good warrior friend," Zebulon said. "Have you considered the possibility that *you* are *not* a mere skeleton?"

Of course I had.

But I didn't know what to make of it yet—I needed more clues. Needed to *learn* more. See more.

"Kinda," I said.

"Your path is bound to be an interesting one, good sir," Zebulon said. "I can see you have *quite an adventure* ahead of you!"

"Yeah, thanks," I said. "I'm starting to see that, myself."

S1E2

5 – Minecraftian Hooligans

Zebulon hung out with me on the watchtower roof until sunrise, and just before the sun spread its light out across the valley, we were both startled by weird, excited voices behind the tree-line...

"What is that?!" I asked.

"Another day for *battle*, it seems!" Zebulon exclaimed. "*Behold!*"

I could hear the sounds of the zombies in the streets hustling to get indoors as the sun started peeking out over the eastern horizon, casting deadly sunlight into the village. It was like a strange parody of when living villagers all run around suddenly just before nightfall, slamming the doors of their little houses and locking themselves inside before the dangers of the *night* come...

Here in Zombietown, there were only the dangers of the *day*...

And here was *one* of them, apparently.

At the edge of town, across the field and past the crops, hiding just inside the trees, were the two weird Minecraftians.

Kids, I remembered.

The orange man and the leather warrior chaotically bounced around inside the trees, babbling to each other loudly in that language I couldn't understand.

"Are they going to attack?" I asked, pulling out my bow. Reaching into my pack, I grabbed a handful of arrows.

"Tis likely!" Zebulon shouted. "It has been several days since their last attack. The hooligans are *back for more!*"

"What are we going to do??" I asked. "The zombies can't fight them in the sunlight!"

"Why, that is how the Minecraftians *fight*, good Skeleton Steve!" Zebulon replied. "They will come, and draw the zombies into the sun. Those two—the man in orange and the warrior in leather armor—they are not very *strong* Minecraftians, but they are *unpredictable*, and are definitely *smarter* than zombies! When the citizens perish in the flames, the Minecraftians will loot whatever they can. Those vandals will pilfer our village until they are driven back, then, will return in several days again!"

"Then let's get 'em!" I exclaimed.

"I am *with you*, brave Skeleton Steve! I am among the *few* zombies here who will *not* burn in the sun, and will *fight* by your side!"

"How's that?" I asked, turning away from the two wild Minecraftians and looking down at the little zombie. "Why don't you burn?"

Zebulon shrugged, then ran to the edge of the tower. He looked down into the streets.

"Zombie brothers!!" the little knight-in-training shouted over the edge. "The Minecraftians come! Get into your homes! Get out of the streets—the day is coming! The day is coming!!"

A cacophony of moans erupted down below, and I could hear the undead shuffling around with heavy footsteps.

And with a speed like lightning, the two Minecraftians sprinted into the village, running around in random patterns, and stopping just shy of the cobblestone streets. They yelled at each other in their own language, and looked around with blank, unreadable faces, swinging their fists and wooden sword (wielded by the leather guy) constantly as they darted around.

I moved to the edge of the watchtower and nocked an arrow. Raised my bow.

The closest Minecraftian was the orange man.

But he was so fast!! The strange creature with his orange and blue sleeveless shirt and ... martial arts pants?? (*How did I know that?*) ... darted this way and that, looking at his friend, looking at the zombies. He looked up at me as I released an arrow. The creature's *eyes*, white with black pupils, glared at me unchanging—his face so *alien* to me...

My arrow whistled through the air down at the orange man, but the chaotic Minecraftian dodged to the side with ease, and my missile just hit the dirt…

"*Good try*, Skeleton Steve!" Zebulon declared.

I nocked another.

"No!" I yelled, seeing a handful of zombies moan and venture out into the street, heading toward the Minecraftian harassers. "Get back inside!!"

Foom!

Three zombies burst into flames, wandering out into the field, their arms held out in front of themselves, making a bee-line to the orange man.

I lost track of the leather guy.

This is nuts! I thought.

If only Elias was here!!

I fired again at the orange man, and missed. He was just so *fast*, and never stopped moving! He

153

even jumped around constantly, as if he thought that if he paused—even for a second—he'd die.

Well, I thought. *He was right!*

I'd shoot him dead if only he'd ... stand ... still!

I fired again.

The arrow whistled at the orange man, and he must have zigged when he should have zagged—I heard a low grunt of pain as my arrow hit him in the back!

Yes!!

I nocked another arrow.

Three burning zombies reached the Minecraftian, just outside of town, and he danced around out of their reach, darting in to *punch* one of them every few seconds. The orange man never stopped *babbling* his excited gibberish.

One zombie fell to the ground, burned up into ash.

"Get back inside, you fools!!" Zebulon shouted down from next to me.

More zombies caught on fire.

I watched, aiming, focused, and *waited* as the orange man darted around with the remaining two zombies. Waited for just the right time...

The Minecraftian lunged in to punch one zombie, then sidestepped the other, was still for a moment—

I fired ... and *hit!!*

My arrow sank into the Minecraftian's chest, and surprised, he looked down at his wound, looked up at me, and stumbled as he tried to dodge out of the way of a flaming zombie.

The zombie *bashed* the orange man in the back, and he fell to the ground, his orange and blue martial arts suit catching fire!

Then, he promptly *disappeared* in a puff of smoke, dropping several items onto the ground around him!

"I did it!!" I cried. "We did it! He's dead!"

"Alas, poor zombies!" Zebulon replied, as the other two burning zombies, including the one that landed the killing blow on the orange man, likewise disappeared, burned up to ashes. Only charred zombie meat remained...

"Where's the other one??" I asked.

"There!" Zebulon cried, pointing to an area at the edge of the village nearby. Just out of my line of fire from the watchtower, around a few houses, I saw a similar scene. The leather-armored guy was attacking a handful of burning zombies, dancing around just out of their reach, and stabbing at them with his wooden sword here and there. "We must fight that hooligan on the ground!" Zebulon said. "Let's go!!"

Turning to the hole in the floor, we took turns sliding down the wooden ladder, then ran out into the brilliant, sunlit field. Taking a few steps into the grass away from the village, I had a clear shooting lane again.

The leather guy hadn't seen us, and had no idea I was about to have him in my sights...

"I can hit him from here," I said.

"I will *flank* him!" Zebulon replied, then, he turned and pitter-pattered back into the cobblestone streets of the village, around a corner, and was gone!

Flank? I thought.

Taking careful aim, I used the same strategy that let me beat the orange man. I waited until the Minecraftian was in a position where he had to change direction, or dodge a zombie's attack— anything that would force him to stand still for *just a second!*

When the leather guy took the time to swing his wooden sword at a zombie, while also dodging a *second* zombie who came up behind him, I had my chance!

Taking careful aim, doing my best to be perfectly still, I released the bowstring from my bony fingers, and my arrow whistled through the air, striking the Minecraftian in the leg!

Distracted by my attack, the leather guy took another hit from one of the burning zombies, and stabbed the undead mob straight through the chest with his wooden sword. He sidestepped the other zombie, and got some distance from the group.

My arrow was still stuck in his leather armor, and zipping around with him as he ran and jumped through the air trying to evade the fiery zombies.

He looked at me with passive blue eyes and a blank face.

For a moment I thought he'd abandon the zombies and *charge* at me!

I nocked another arrow and aimed again...

When I fired, my arrow flew straight at him, but the Minecraftian *jumped*, and my shot passed under him, landing somewhere in the grass.

But just then, as the burning zombies were closing in again, I saw a small flash of green and blue, and then little *Zebulon* was *on him*, punching the leather guy again and again, *pounding* on him with his little fists!!

The Minecraftian turned away from me to deal with the new threat, raising his sword into the air...

I nocked another arrow, aimed, and fired!

The missile flew through the air quickly, and struck the Minecraftian in the back!

Dropping the wooden sword, the leather guy grunted in pain, then fell to the ground...

"Yes!!" I shouted. "We did it!"

Zebulon backed away from the dying Minecraftian, his face beaming, then, turned to yell at the burning zombies. The leather man disappeared in a puff of smoke, all of his leather armor falling in a heap to the grass!

"Get back inside! Get back in—" he started, then faced me again, eyes widening. "Skeleton Steve, *behind you!!*"

I spun, nocking another arrow onto my bowstring, and saw a *third* Minecraftian charging at me without a sound! This creature was dressed in a light blue shirt, dark blue shorts, and had some kind of white *hood* with ... *bunny ears?* ... on his head. His face was strange, but similarly unreadable. A small bit of yellow hair stuck out from under his hood, green straps over his shoulders hinted at a green *backpack* on his back, and his wooden sword was held high...

Aiming as quickly as I could, I released the shot.

My arrow struck him in the chest, knocking him backwards a little and stopping his charge!

The Minecraftian recovered, lifted his sword again, and charged again...

Crud.

"Oh man!" I yelled, scrambling to nock another arrow as quickly as possible.

My bony fingers did their work quickly, and I pulled back on the bowstring again.

Don't miss, I thought. *Don't miss or he'll kill you*.

Just before the Minecraftian reached me, I fired again, hitting him square in the middle of his chest.

He staggered, and I reloaded again.

"Oh man, oh man, oh man!!" I stammered, and fired *again* just before the *bunny ears guy* recovered and made it to me with that sword...

Hitting him in the chest once more did it...

The Minecraftian fell back, dropped his sword, and disappeared in a puff of smoke when he hit the ground.

I heard the *pitter patter* of rapid, small feet coming up behind me.

"*Good shooting*, Skeleton Steve!" Zebulon exclaimed.

I pulled another arrow, nocked it, and scanned around.

Were there any others?

Any more??

But, other than the moans and pain sounds of the burning zombies, it seemed that things were quiet again...

"You were going to *flank* him!" I said, then, laughed. "So *that's* what that means!"

Zebulon laughed, and clapped me on the back.

"You were nearly *flanked* yourself!" he said, letting out a long, hearty laugh.

I relaxed, releasing a tense breath I didn't realize I was holding.

Turning to look at little Zebulon, I put a bony hand on his shoulder. "Man, you really let that leather guy *have it*, huh? Bam, bam, bam!! You're fast!"

We laughed.

Slinging my bow back onto my shoulder, I walked up to where the third Minecraftian, bunny ears guy, died. Only his wooden sword lay on the ground.

Reaching down, I picked it up.

I would have never thought a sword could be made from *wood*. But it was well-balanced, easy to handle, and might cut a bad guy, maybe?? True, the leather guy *stabbed* a burning zombie with his wooden sword, but there wasn't much of an edge to this one. It was more like a sharpened *club* that was *shaped* like a sword...

"You look like you're *familiar* with swords!" Zebulon said.

I shrugged.

Was I?

"Let's see what kind of stuff they dropped!" I said, and we ran over to where the leather guy fell. Gathering up the Minecraftian's leather armor and other random stuff in the grass, as well as another sword, we ran over to where the *orange man* died, but found nothing.

"That is odd," Zebulon said. "As I recall, *this one* dropped *many* things onto the grass when he was killed..."

"Yeah," I said. "He did. Weird."

After doing our best to usher the remainder of the roaming, burning zombies back into their houses, Zebulon and I went back to the library to look over the loot.

All in all, we ended up with two wooden swords, a full set of leather armor, several torches, another one of those *crafting tables*, some pieces of charred animal meat, three sections of ladder, and a Minecraftian tool made of stone and wood that looked close to breaking.

An axe, I thought.

How did I know that?

I handed Zebulon one of the swords. He looked up at me, black eyes bright, smiling.

"Take this sword," I said. "A *knight in training* should have a sword, don't you think?"

"Thank you, good Skeleton Steve!" he said. "Though *you* should take the rest! I feel that you are *destined* to become this village's hero! We would not have driven off those Minecraftians without your assistance!"

"Yeah, well," I said, "I couldn't have done it without you, either."

I looked over the leather armor. Aside from a few arrow holes and a scorch mark where the burning zombie struck the leather guy, the armor was in great shape. While it was pretty lightweight, I didn't much like the idea of *wearing* the bulky stuff. I preferred just my helmet, and keeping my bones free and clear to move around.

I had a feeling, however, that *someone* would like it...

Shoving the pile of armor across the table toward Zebulon, I said, "And take this armor, too. I already *have* a helmet. Think you can do something with this? Can you alter it to *fit* you?"

Zebulon gasped.

"*Truly*, Skeleton Steve!" He looked down and handled the leather shoulder piece, ran his small green fingers over the breastplate. "I believe I can make this work, my friend. One of the zombie villagers here used to be an *armor smith*, too. Thank you again!" The little mob carefully put the leather helmet onto his head, and looked at me, his small, black eyes dark and full of purpose in the shadows of the helmet's guard.

"Looks good," I said.

"Tis *destiny!*" he said. "Feels good! For *now*, I have become a *knight in training* … with armor and a sword!"

We laughed.

Looking over the other knick-knacks, I pretty much took the rest. The other torches, and everything else, went into my pack. That *crafting table* would be a good first piece of furniture in my *Zombietown* home, and I had an idea of putting the ladder pieces on the inner wall of the house, then *somehow* cutting a hole in the roof, so that I could have my *own* look-out area, accessible from inside only…

I put a few of the looted torches up inside Zebulon's library.

He was happy.

"Tis *so* much better for reading!" Zebulon exclaimed. "I can now read at *any* time of the night!"

S1E2
6 – Elias Returns

Zebulon and I spent the rest of the day hanging out in the library.

"Skeleton Steve," he said at one point. "Something *else* occurs to me—something that could truly help you recover your memories!"

"Oh, really?" I said. "What's that?"

"Many of the zombies here in town follow the same path as you, although, usually, *less* successfully. They *all* yearn to learn about their pasts and remember who they used to be, before … well … before they became the *walking dead!* So, when you and good sir Elias presented your case to me about your *wayward memories*, I did not think much of it!"

"Gee, thanks," I said.

"But—*bear with me now!*—I *just* remembered something else that could help. There is another zombie in town, Zenon, who found a way to *completely recover* his memories! If he has not *burned up* by now, you should be able to find him, and he could tell you more!"

"Zenon, huh?"

"Indeed! Twas something involving a *magical mountain shrine* or some such thing!"

"Hmm, okay," I said. "I'll check it out, thanks."

Well, it was *something*. At least a *little* lead that I could look into.

Between writing in this journal, taking the time to think, and experimenting with all of the Minecraftian stuff around me, I've been filling in a *few* blanks, at least.

Or have I?

I've been learning about things that I was already familiar with, but not truly *remembering* anything real from my past. Only reminding myself of old skills and previous knowledge.

No memories. No images.

Did *that* count?

Maybe this Zenon *could* help me! It was worth a shot...

I sure hope Elias gets back soon, I thought.

That evening, I was back in my new house, trying to figure out where to put my new crafting table, recently taken from leather guy. Ultimately, I set it up in the corner of the house closest to the front door. Heck, from there, I could experiment with the table and be able to see out of the front window at the same time!

I looked at the crafting table sitting in the corner, and realized that I was truly a mob with a house. Very cool...

As I was hanging a couple of torches, high up on the interior walls of my house, Elias the Enderman ninja returned!

Zip.

I heard the sound of my buddy teleporting just outside the front door. Plopping the torch onto the wall and bathing the darkening room with a warm, yellow light, I turned, and opened the door.

There was Elias. Standing outside. Tall, slender, black-skinned with glowing purple eyes. His blue ninja headband flowed gently with the light breeze. Little purple motes of light drifted down through the air onto the cobblestone street around him.

"Elias!" I exclaimed. "You're *back!!*"

My friend nodded, then teleported inside, into the center of the house.

Zip.

Purple light dust drifted down onto the wooden floor.

"*Hello, Skeleton Steve,*" he said. His mind voice seemed *subdued* somehow. Was this the feeling of Enderman … annoyance? "*How have things been here?*"

"I'm okay," I said. "Some *crazy stuff* happened with the Minecraftians this morning! *Three* of them attacked when the sun came up, trying to draw the zombies out into the daylight to kill a bunch of 'em. Zebulon and I killed *all three!* It was awesome!!"

Elias's face was blank, and his eyes narrowed a little as he looked off into space.

"*I am pleased that you are alright,*" he said.

"Yeah, I gave Zebulon a sword and some armor that we got from one of 'em, and now we have a crafting table and some other stuff!" I pointed to the table in the corner and the torch on the wall. "I was *just* hanging some torches." Pausing, I looked more closely at the ninja. Something was wrong. "What's the *matter??*"

"*It's...*" Elias paused. "*All is well. I am just processing a selfish emotion that has no place in the business of my Order. My master is wise. The council is wise.*"

"What happened?"

"*I reported on the energy and my discoveries in the ravine,*" he said. "*I cannot disclose to you the details of what my Order has decided to do, but I, myself, will not be involved with the ravine for now. I have been commanded to continue my Seed Stride, and leave the matter to some ninjas of ... a higher rank."*

"Sounds serious," I said.

"Indeed," Elias replied. *"The energy that is inside the ravine, attached to the artifact, attached to you in some unknown manner ... is a danger to this world—to this universe—your world and mine."*

"So what are you gonna do?"

"Do not confuse the voice of ego with that of intuition..."

"What?"

"I have already learned my lessons of letting my ego and pride blind me to listening to good wisdom and strategy. You were my teacher, back in your other form. I do not need a repeat lesson."

"So ... gonna let it go?

"Yes. I will continue my Seed Stride. With you."

"Well, that's good!" I said. "I'm sorry you're not going to be *on the front lines* in the battle with this big evil and all. But I'm definitely liking our time together!"

"*And I appreciate my time with you as well*," he said, seeming to clear his head. His purples eyes opened wider, and Elias seemed more … well, his face was impossible to read. But I could definitely *feel* some sort of emotion coming off of him before—anger, annoyance.

And it was gone now.

"Hey, I got a lead on recovering my memories!" I said. "Some zombie in town named *Zenon*. Zebulon said that this guy apparently found a way to completely get his memories back, something involving a magical mountain shrine maybe…"

"*That sounds promising*," Elias said. "*When were you planning to seek out this Zenon?*"

"Oh, it's getting dark, and all of the zombies are coming out. I was about to head out in a few.

Honestly, I was really hoping you'd be *back*, and could come *with me* for this."

"*I'm here now*," he said.

"And I'm glad," I said, smiling at my Enderman friend.

"*So are you ready to seek out Zenon and the magical mountain shrine?*"

"Yeah, in just a sec. Would you please help me put these other two torches up? You're waaaay taller than me!"

I approached my Enderman ninja buddy, and placed two Minecraftian torches into his hand...

Season 1, Episode 3:
The Mountain of Wisdom

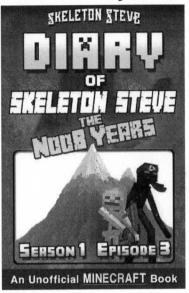

Skeleton Steve and the Mountain of Wisdom!!

Our amnesiac hero and his Enderman ninja friend are following their first real lead to recovering Skeleton Steve's memories--a local zombie who supposedly revived his mind at a magical mountain shrine! But ... they can't find the guy! When the duo delves into the dark undercity of Zombietown, will they finally find the answers?

And if they discover the way to the fabled Mountain of Wisdom, they'll still need to go on a dangerous journey to reach its peak! What challenges stand in the way of Skeleton Steve remembering who he is?

S1E3
1 – Searching for Zenon

I could see through the windows of our new house in Zombietown that the sun was going down, and I knew that the undead village would soon come alive!

"So who is this zombie we'll be looking for?" Elias said into my head, using his *mind voice.*

"His name is Zenon," I said. "According to Zebulon, Zenon found some sort of 'mystical mountain' where he came across a *magical mountain shrine* or something up at the top, and suddenly remembered who he was!"

"That sounds unlikely," Elias responded. *"How did he suddenly regain his memory?"*

I smirked.

"I dunno. That's all Zebulon said."

The little zombie knight-in-training was an interesting character for sure. In a town full of zombies with foggy minds, all living in the moment, maybe burning up in the sun on any given morning because of being so *scatter-brained* ... Zebulon himself was crystal clear.

Maybe it was all of the reading he did. Or maybe by focusing so much on his *knight's code*, he had something to stay *centered* on, and didn't lose his mind like all of the other zombies. But one thing was for sure—little Zebulon was a noble creature, indeed. He was like the caretaker for this town, enduring a humble life in the library and trying to keep his village out of the daylight.

Sure, he could have told me about Zenon and his 'magical mountain shrine' back when we first met, but, like the little guy said, Zebulon lived among plenty of zombies that were *always* longing for their minds and memories to go back to how they used to be.

I, *Skeleton Steve*, was no exception to that.

He must have thought that I was just another undead mob wandering Diamodia, trying to remember who he was...

So I couldn't hold it against him.

"*Very well,*" Elias said in my head. "*Once we find Zenon and learn of the location of this ... magical mountain ... then you're intending to travel there ... just to see what happens?*"

Standing tall in our Zombietown house, Elias looked down at me with his glowing purple eyes, the tails of his blue ninja headband draped over his shoulders. He crossed his long, thin arms over his pitch-black chest.

"Yeah, well, that's the plan..." I said.

The golden and pink light of sunset spread through the glass of our mostly-unbroken windows as the square sun outside dipped below the horizon.

"*It is a good plan,*" Elias said, nodding his head. "*Truly, this is the first real lead we've found on recovering your memories and learning about your origins, Skeleton Steve.*"

As the silver light of the moon bathed the village when sun was finally down, we stepped out into the streets to search for Zenon the enlightened zombie...

Darkness fell over the cobblestone roads, and dozens of undead emerged from the safety of their village homes, plodding through the streets with heavy footsteps and moaning as they walked.

I approached the first zombie near me.

"Hi there, excuse me!"

The green-skinned mob looked up, his dull eyes hazy until he focused on my face.

"Skeleton! Hello!" he said, his voice slow and thick.

"Do you happen to know a fellow named 'Zenon'?" I asked.

"I am not Zenon," the zombie replied, stopping and putting his arms down.

"You're *not?*" I said. "Okay, well, do you know where he is?"

"Where *who* is?"

"Zenon," I repeated.

"I am not Zenon," the zombie said.

"Heh ... right," I said. "I know. I'm just asking if you *know* who Zenon *is*, and where I can find him?"

The undead mob stared at me with dull eyes, his mouth hanging open in the moonlight. He reached up and scratched at his dark-green hair.

I waited.

The zombie scratched, looked at me, looked down at the cobblestone street, then looked up at me again.

"Oh!" he said, his voice dull but full of surprise. "Hello, Skeleton!"

"Uhhhh..." I said. "Hi."

I looked back at Elias, who stood behind me, looking down at the conversation with a passive, unreadable face. His arms were crossed, and the night wind made the tails of his blue headband flutter.

"What you want, Skeleton?" the zombie asked.

I looked back.

"Um ... well ... do you know a zombie named 'Zenon'?"

The zombie shook his head. "I am not Zenon."

"Okay, thanks," I said, clapping him on the shoulder with my bony hand. I looked back at my Enderman friend. "A little *help??*"

The Enderman ninja nodded to me, then turned back to the zombie. His blank, black-skinned face was unreadable, and his eyes flared purple in the dark night...

"No, I am not Zenon," the zombie said, looking up at Elias. "Are you talking *in my head?*"

I watched, as Elias and the zombie stared silently at each other, as the town full of undead mobs milled about around us. A handful of zombies down the street were talking about the Minecraftian attack I helped the village defend against this morning.

"Okay," the zombie said suddenly. "Bye!"

Giving a rubbery, green smile, the zombie turned, stuck his arms out in front of him, and plodded away.

I looked up at Elias.

"That zombie's mind was broken more than most of the others'," he said. *"He did not know of Zenon."*

"Let's go talk to *those* guys," I said, pointing at the group discussing the Minecraftian attack. "They at least remember *this morning.*"

Elias nodded, and followed me as I turned to approach the group of mobs.

"Hey there!" I said, causing the three of them to stop their conversation to look at me. Their eyes passed over me and my pack (*Zebulon had mentioned that it was odd that I wore this pack*), then they opened their mouths in awe as their eyes traveled over my shoulder, up and up, to Elias the Enderman.

One of them spoke.

"Hello, Skeleton Steve!" he said. "And an ... *Enderman companion??*"

I smiled. How about that? He remembered me!

"Yes," I said. "This is my friend, Elias." I jerked a bony thumb over my shoulder. "Maybe you can help us? We're looking for a zombie named *Zenon*. Do you know where he is?"

The zombie frowned. "I don't know a *Zenon*," he said. He looked over at his friends. "Do you guys know *Zenon?*"

Muttering and shaking their heads, the other zombies mumbled.

"No," one of them said, loud enough for me to hear.

"Yes," said the other.

"Yes??" I asked. "You know Zenon? Where is he?"

The zombie shrugged and shook his head. "I mean *no*," he said.

The mob's friend looked at him, and gave him a playful punch on the shoulder. "*You* know Zenon, Zander?" he said with a voice full of marbles. "Come on, where is he?"

Zander looked back at him. "No," he said. "I don't know Zenon."

"Then why'd you say *yes?*" I asked.

"I thought you asked if I wanted any *meat*," he said.

"What??" I asked, laughing.

His friend, the zombie I originally talked to in the group, shrugged.

That doesn't even make sense, I thought.

"Thanks, guys," I said, and Elias and I moved on.

We had several other conversations with zombies that night, but didn't get anywhere. It seemed that the whole town of undead didn't know Zenon or where he was. Or, at least, I should say that the *more clear-headed* zombies didn't know. Many of the zombies couldn't carry on a reasonable conversation at all, *or* even understand what I was asking most of the time.

At one point, I ran into good, old...

"Zed!" I exclaimed.

The zombie looked over at me, standing in the doorway of his house.

"Hi, Skeleton Steve!" he replied in a thick, slow voice. "Have you found a *helmet* for me yet?"

The mob smiled, his lips still crispy from when he caught on fire in the sun the other morning. His skin was greener than the last time I saw him, but was still a little baked and blistery here and there. Zed's clothing was black and charred, and, unless he found some new clothes, his outfit would always tell the world that he almost perished in the flames once upon a time...

"Not yet," I said. "Next time a Minecraftian attacks me, and he's wearing one, I'll save it for you, okay?"

The zombie smiled again in response.

"Hey, Zed," I said, watching several zombies emerge from the house behind his, "I'm looking for a guy named *Zenon*. Do you know him?"

"Sure!" Zed said. "I know Zenon. What do you want with him??"

I exchanged a quick look with Elias, who stood behind me, and breathed out a sigh of relief.

"Oh, awesome!" I exclaimed. "No one we've talked to yet knows him. I need to talk to him about how he got his memories back. Where can I find him?"

"Hmm," Zed responded. "I don't know where he is *right now*, but I haven't seen him tonight. He's probably at home."

"Where's he live?" I swept my skeletal hand across the air, indicating at the village. "Which house?"

"Oh!" Zed said, smiling broadly with his blistery face. "He's ... uh ... he's ... umm ..." Zed scratched at his face, twisting up his features in concentration. He stared at the street below him, then, looked up at me. "Wouldn't you know ... it's the *darndest* thing, but I just *can't remember* where he lives! Can you believe that?!"

I sighed, my attention once again going to the house behind Zed's little home. Several more zombies steamed out of the broken-down front door. That was what—*nine zombies* now that I noticed, leaving the house in the last few minutes? And that's only counting the ones I *consciously counted?*

"What the heck?!" I asked. "How many zombies can fit in a tiny house?"

"Oh!" Zed exclaimed, looking behind him at the zombies emerging from the next house down. "That's not just a *house*," he said. "That's the entrance to the *undercity*."

"Undercity?!" I asked, watching a couple more zombies wander out from there into the street.

Eleven.

Zed laughed, one of the burn blisters on his face popping as he did.

"There's a big *cave* under the village," he said. "You didn't think that *all of these zombies* spent the day in the houses, did you?" He laughed again. "Oh yeah—I remember now. *That's* where Zenon lives. In the undercity!"

Elias and I exchanged glances.

"Thanks, Zed," I said, and we walked toward the next house.

Three more zombies stepped out.

S1E3
2 – The Undercity

The entrance to the Undercity looked like just another small village house—square, short, made of cobblestone, with one window (broken), and a shattered wooden door in the front.

But there was something *different* about this tiny house—there were zombies continuously emerging from it, out into the night, like the modest home was a portal to another world...

In between two groups of zombies, I stuck my head into the doorway, then stepped inside. The Enderman ninja squeezed in through the small doorframe (small for *him*, at least) after me.

The difference between this house and the other tiny cobblestone shacks throughout Zombietown was that there was a huge, dark *hole* in the floor! It was as if a creeper had exploded inside the house at some point, long ago, even though the walls still stood, opening up the entrance to a cave down below.

Through the broken cobblestone floor, I could see that sand and other debris had collapsed into a make-shift staircase, and a tight, skinny tunnel wound off into darkness, deep into the ground...

Another two zombies stepped into sight, their gurgling growls echoing into the room from below, and they climbed the debris with ease, walking past Elias and I, into the night.

The tunnel was short.

Definitely *too short* for Elias.

I looked back at my friend.

"*I can sense your concern,*" Elias said into my head. "*The tunnel does not have enough clearance for an Ender like me.*"

"Yeah," I said. "What are we gonna do?"

"*You go,*" he said. "*After all, the undercity is nothing more than an extension of Zombietown. Find Zenon, then return. If a large cave system exists under this town, and you become lost, just follow the zombies back to the surface.*"

"Yeah, I was afraid you were gonna say that," I said.

"*Afraid?*" Elias replied.

"No, it's ... ah ... a figure of speech. Don't you know what a *figure of speech* is?"

"*How do you know yourself?*"

I stopped.

"Interesting point, Elias," I said. There were some things in my head that I just ... took for granted, but how did I remember some things and not remember others? "Okay, well, I guess I'll be back after I find Zenon," I said.

"*I will wait for you up here,*" Elias said. "*Depending on how long you take, I may be in the field outside of town seeking out Ender seeds...*"

"Alright, good buddy. Wish me luck," I said, turning to the dark hole and taking a step onto the sandy rubble leading down.

"*Good luck,*" Elias said.

I laughed, and looked back at him. "Thanks. *Another* figure of speech, I guess."

With that, I started down toward the Undercity...

I knew that this was just another part of town, and full of zombies that would be friendly toward me. Heck, some of these guys might even *like* me, because I helped defend the town from the attacking Minecraftians that morning!

So why did I feel so *nervous?*

Why did I feel like this deep, dark place was *not* a *friendly* place?

Natural caves and other places that hid from the sun and were dangerous for Minecraftian adventurers should be a *safe haven* for mobs like me, right? I was a mob, after all.

... *Wasn't I?*

I walked deeper and deeper into the tunnel, passing right under a large section of town, the path dropping a little lower every few steps.

Eventually, I passed by another couple of zombies that were heading to the surface.

"Hi, Skeleton," one said as they passed.

"Hey there," I replied, my voice echoing in the dark, rocky place. "Oh, hey!" I said, turning back to them.

The zombie turned.

"Do you know where Zenon lives down here?"

The zombie shrugged. "Nope. ," Then, he turned to finish hiking up to the surface.

"How long does this tunnel go??" I shouted toward their backs.

"Not far!" the zombie called back to me.

And he was right.

After I walked on for a short while, the tunnel took a turn to the right, and then opened up into a huge, open cavern!

All around me were the sounds of mobs making noises and chatting with each other. A few dozen zombies were scattered around the cavern floor, mostly clustered up into small conversing groups, growling and gurgling and talking with slow, syrupy voices. I heard the hiss of a spider, and saw a particularly large, fat, black one climbing the wall of the cavern, looking down at the zombies with bright red eyes.

Also across the cavern, I saw a pair of skeletons, standing together, talking, holding their bows. One looked over at me and waved with a bony hand. I waved back.

As I stepped into the cold, open space, I suddenly saw *movement* on my left, and must have jumped *two feet* into the air as I saw a creeper standing *right next to me!* The creature frowned at me, staring with his big, black eyes.

"Holy *creeper!*" I exclaimed.

The creeper frowned even deeper. "What'sss your problem, bonesss?!" it said with a raspy, crackling voice.

"Oh, I'm sorry—you just ... *surprised* me!"

"Ssss ... noob," it said, then turned and creeped away.

The cavern was large and long—a huge open space where mobs of all sorts hung out. Despite the diversity, however, this place was clearly dominated by the zombies. This was the undercity of Zombietown, after all!

I could see several other tunnels in the walls of the caverns, like this large open space was a hub for a very large cave system. Other zombies emerged from the small tunnels into the large area every once and a while, and sometimes, zombies in the large area made their way into one of the many dark tunnels...

Somewhere in this cave system, maybe in the main cavern, maybe in one of the offshoot tunnels ... was Zenon, the zombie who *remembered*...

Hopefully.

Talking to all of these zombies one at a time was going to take *forever*...

Taking a deep breath, I put my bony hands around my mouth in a way to make my voice louder...

"*Hey, zombies!!*" I shouted as loud as I could.

My yell echoed across the entire cavern, and all of the mob noises suddenly went quiet. A feeling of nervousness crept over my bones as I suddenly saw all eyes—dozens of dull zombie eyes, empty socket skeleton eyes, glowing red spider eyes, and dark and sad creeper eyes—on me...

"Hey ... um ... *everybody* ... uh thanks!" I stammered. "I ... um..."

One of the zombies coughed.

A spider hissed.

"Um ... my name is *Skeleton Steve*, for those of you who ... uh ... didn't see me *this morning*. Um ... I'm looking for a zombie named ... *Zenon?*"

Silence.

"Anyone know where ... uh ... know where he *is??*"

My voice echoed across the cavern.

One of the skeletons' bones *clunked*.

Suddenly, the entire crowd of mobs turned back to their conversations, and the cavern was bathed again in the sounds of them talking with each other and making their mob noises.

I sighed.

Great.

So much for the *easier* way...

But just as I stepped down into the cavern, ready to make contact with the first of many zombies in the *underground* search for Zenon, a large zombie fellow stepped out toward me from the crowd.

He was tall, broad-shouldered, and had a very stout face.

"Skeleton Steve," the big zombie said, his voice deep and slow.

"Yes, hello...?" I replied.

"You will find Zenon down that tunnel over there," the big zombie said, pointing at one of the tunnels burrowing into the cavern walls with a big, green hand.

"Over there?" I asked, pointing. "Thanks a lot!" I smiled. "What's your name, zombie?"

"Zarek," he said, then turned away to rejoin the group.

I didn't know it at the time, but, years later, I would meet Zarek again. I would remember *him*, but *he* would not remember *me*...

"Thanks, Zarek!" I said to his back, then, made my way to the tunnel.

Stepping into the opening, I delved deeper into the darkness of the underground world, and left the loud noise of the mob crowd behind me...

S1E3
3 – Zenon the Enlightened Zombie

The tunnel wound around and around, deeper and deeper into the belly of Diamodia...

I could see *just fine* in the dark, but for some reason, the darkness made me *nervous*, and I had a hard time ignoring the impulse to pull those Minecraftians' torches out of my pack to light the way...

Weird, I thought.

At one point, a couple of zombies passed me by, making their way up to the cavern.

I also saw a fellow skeleton deeper in, standing in the tunnel with no apparent purpose.

"Hi there!" I said with a smile.

The other skeleton's bones *clunked* as it looked over at me. He held a bow in his hand, and frowned, scoffing.

"What's with the *red eyes*, uh ... red ... eyes?" it asked.

"Huh?" I replied.

The skeleton scoffed again, and walked past me, up the tunnel toward the cavern.

I shrugged, and moved on.

Eventually, the tunnel brought me to a *square room* constructed of old cobblestone. The walls were coated with a fine layer of green moss and lichens. The room was dark, and the only light came from a weird, *fiery thing* sitting in the middle of the moss-covered cobblestone floor...

I looked at the strange, flaming contraption in the middle of the room. It was a small black iron 'cage' of some sort, with a blazing fire inside and a tiny, dancing *zombie*—smaller than Zebulon—flailing around inside!

Peering into the flames, I looked hard at the odd, little zombie in the fire. Was it some sort of ... doll? Or a toy? Was it even *alive??* The tiny zombie spun and spun in the flames, stuck inside the black-barred cage, its arms reaching around madly as it pivoted this way and that...

"Interesting, isn't it?" a dull voice said from a dark corner of the room.

I looked up.

Another zombie approached me, his appearance the same as any *other* zombie—dark blue pants, grey shoes, a disheveled, light-blue shirt, mottled skin green and rotting.

But his eyes ... those *dark eyes* were intent and crystal clear—not muddled by *stupid-brain* like most of the other zombies I'd been talking to.

"Zenon," I said.

"Yep, that's me," the zombie responded, walking up and putting a green hand on the fiery black cage.

"I've been looking for you," I said. "*Zebulon* sent me."

"Oh, really?" Zenon asked. "How's the little guy doing? Still playing *knight in shining armor?*"

"Uh … I don't know what *that* means," I said. "He's not exactly *playing*. He's a great guy, actually. He seems very *devoted* to Zombietown."

Zenon's eyes were deep, but gave me the sense of a *sadness* inside that I didn't understand. "Sure, whatever. Zebulon's a great little guy. *Zombietown??*"

"Um, yeah," I replied, shrugging with a smirk. "That's just what I *call* it, I guess."

Zenon looked down into the flame and watched the tiny zombie zip around.

"Zombietown," he repeated. "I like it. Has a nice *ring* to it."

"Yeah, I thought so," I said, looking down at the tiny zombie with him. "So the reason I'm here—"

"It's not *real*, you know," Zenon said, staring at the fiery cage. "The little zombie in there. It's a *construct*. Just a symbol. It tells you what's going to come out—"

A couple of puffs of smoke suddenly appeared in the air next to us.

"There," Zenon said. "Look now! Here comes *two more*..."

From the smoke, I suddenly saw *two zombies* appear!

The undead mobs materialized out of nowhere, standing still, dressed in their zombie blues. After a moment, they looked up, gurgled, raised their arms, and wandered off up to the cavern, their shoes clomping on the stone ground...

"What...?" I blurted. "What just *happened?*"

"New zombies for the world," Zenon said. "There they go! Off to wander around, make noises, and eat villagers and Minecraftians if they can. Maybe they'll burn up in the sun. Or maybe they'll be smart enough to figure out that they need to stay *out* of the sun. Maybe they'll become regular citizens of ... *Zombietown*."

"But," I said, "where'd they *come* from? Were they Minecraftians that died and became zombies? Or were they—"

"So what can I *do* for you, Skeleton Steve?" Zenon asked, looking up at me from the cage. "Why do you seek out old Zenon?"

"Uh ... well..." I replied. "My *past* is kind of a mystery, and I'm kind of a ... unique mob. My Enderman companion and I are on a quest to recover my memories. It's important—I guess my memories might hold the key to stopping this nasty *invasion thing* from taking over Diamodia...?"

"That's quite a story," Zenon said. "An Enderman companion, huh? Stopping an invasion? A *unique* mob? I can see that your *eyes* are glowing. That's certainly an *odd* thing for a skeleton."

"Yeah. So ... Zebulon said that you found a way to recover your memories up on some *mountain* somewhere, at some *magical mountain shrine?*"

"That's true, sort of," Zenon replied. "There's a huge mountain nearby, different than any other mountains you'll see on this world—as far as I know. I call it the *Mountain of Wisdom*."

"How did you get your memories back?" I asked.

"Well," Zenon replied, moving over to lean against a wall. He put a hand on a wooden chest that I hadn't noticed until now. "I climbed the mountain. It was very treacherous. Once I made it to the top, after exploring up there for a while and relaxing on the peak for the rest of the night, before seeking shelter from daylight, everything started ... coming *back* to me..."

"Just from you *being* up there?"

"Yep," he said. "Suddenly, the fog ... *lifted*, so to speak. I don't know if you're aware, but zombies aren't as stupid as they act! They're just victims of muddled minds—never able to focus, always forgetting things right away—like someone's always hitting the *reset button* in their heads."

"What's a *reset button?*"

"Anyway," Zenon said, "I could suddenly *think clearly*, and remember *everything*, all the way back to where I ... *came into being*."

"Did you remember who you were *before* you were undead?"

Two more puffs of smoke filled the room suddenly, and another couple of zombies appeared in the darkness, realizing their surroundings, then raised their arms and plodded away, up toward the cavern...

Zenon and I watched them go.

"Skeleton Steve," Zenon said. "I remember *everything* all the way back to my point of origin. And that point of origin ... was *here*."

"Here?" I asked.

"Yes," he replied. "This *spawner*."

Spawner? This *cage-thing?* Did this *spawner* create zombies out of thin air?

Surely there was more to it—more to zombie lives than just 'spawning' out of thin air from one of these weird cage things. Why, that would make their lives almost *worthless*, wouldn't it? Is that why Zenon seemed so depressed?

"You don't remember anything from before you ... spawned?"

"No," Zenon said. "Because there *was* nothing. I was *not.* And then, suddenly, I *was...*"

"I dunno," I replied. "Maybe you became a zombie after being a *Minecraftian* or something, and the *spawner*, as you call it, just transported you here from somewhere else!"

"It's an interesting point, Skeleton Steve," Zenon said, "but I don't believe it's true. There are scores of zombies here on Diamodia—*way* more than the number of Minecraftians, as far as I know—and we are here for some purpose that's still unknown to me. But we just *appear* from these little flaming boxes. We mobs have no souls, we're not *special*—there is no worth or uniqueness to the life of a zombie..."

"That's not true," I said.

"*You* came from a spawner too, you know..." he said.

Was that right? I thought, pausing. Was all of this—my quest, my growing sense of adventure and exploration, my friendship with Elias and the Enderman's *own* devotion to his order, Zebulon's *knight's code*—all just the worthless, fleeting dreams of empty, random—

I shook my head, rattling my bones.

"*No*, that's not true. I mean—it *might* be true, about the spawner and all, but it's not true that you and other zombies are worthless!"

"Explain," Zenon said.

"Well," I replied, trying to wrap my mind around it, "even *if* you didn't exist before you just *puffed* into the world from this *box*, you still developed your *own mind*—your own hopes and dreams, your own *personality* and everything else, all on your own! *You are Zenon*, and you're the *only* zombie like you. Even if you came from nothing special, you're special *now*. And so are all of those other zombies, as well. *Zebulon* is special. My friend, Zed, who almost burned to a crisp in the sun the other day—he's special in his own way, too."

Zenon stood quietly, staring into the flames of the zombie spawner for a time.

"That's an *interesting point*, Skeleton Steve. I'm not gonna lie—your words *do* make me feel better. I'll think about it some more." He walked over to the wooden chest and opened it with a *creak*. "I'm going to give you a small map I found a long time ago. That'll help you get to the mountain."

I followed him to the chest, walking around the fiery black cage.

Spawner, I thought. It's called a spawner.

"I don't need this anymore. I hope it can help you," Zenon said, pulling a rolled-up piece of paper out of the chest and unfurling it in front of me. "See, it's not a very *big* map, but I've lived here in what you call *Zombietown* for all my life, and it's sufficient to show the way to the Mountain of Wisdom..."

Holding the map out in front of me, I could quickly tell that it was, indeed, a lot *less* detailed than Elias's map—the one given to him by Balder the blacksmith—but I could easily make out the village and its surroundings. There was the big field and the river on one side that Elias and I followed

213

up to the ravine, and, north of town, *there* was a winding path through forests and rocky terrain that eventually led to a couple of large circles of stone, topped with white.

Snow, I thought.

Two mountains—a big one and a small one, side by side.

"I take it this big one is the *Mountain of Wisdom?*" I asked, pointing at the big circle of snow with my bony finger.

"That's right," Zenon said, handing me the map. "Be careful when you get close to the top. There's an area where the waterfalls can knock you off of the trail and send you falling *all the way* back down, and there's *another* area just before the summit where it's *really* steep, and you have to be very careful on the ledges."

"Zenon," I said, "how'd *you* find the Mountain of Wisdom?"

He stared off into space for a moment, recalling the memory. "One night," he said, "I saw a single Minecraftian. He was dressed like us zombies, in blue. But there was something *different* about *that* one. He wasn't like those Minecraftian *noobs* that hang around outside the edge of town and harass the village. He wasn't a tourist. He *belonged*. It's kind of hard to explain—suffice to say, he wasn't like the rest of them..."

I nodded. "Strange. So, what about him?"

"Well, this Minecraftian didn't mess with the village. Instead, he came, he saw us all, and he headed up into the forest. As a thick-headed zombie, like I was at the time, I *followed* him. I followed that guy for a long time, and was lucky enough to fall into a lake before daybreak.

"Now, at the time, I didn't know anything about anything, and if I climbed out of the water during the day, I would have burned up in the light! *No more Zenon*. But I was lucky, and couldn't pull myself up out of the water *all day*. By the time night rolled around, I finally found my way out of the lake, and saw the mountain standing before me...

"The Minecraftian was long gone by that point, but I was *curious*, so I climbed the mountain.

Like I said, it wasn't like any other mountain on Diamodia I've seen. You'll see it yourself—it's very smooth, and steep, and pointy at the peak. I ate whatever I could get my hands on, and wandered up and up until I reached the summit, then ... well you already know the rest."

"And you just *happened* to have a map on you when you were a muddle-minded zombie?"

"No," Zenon said. "I found the map later, and went *back* to map it out. At the time, I cared about helping my dumb zombie brothers to remember *themselves* as well." Zenon closed the chest, and leaned against it, smiling. "Your words really *did* make me feel better, Skeleton. I had never thought of everything from *that* perspective before..."

"Well, it's true," I said, smiling back at him. I put Zenon's map into my pack. "I take it you want this back?"

"Nah..." Zenon said. "Maybe you can get more use out of it than me, you being an *adventurer* and all, *questing around* with your Enderman friend. Keep it."

"Thanks."

"And Skeleton Steve?" Zenon said, as I turned to go.

"Yeah?"

"Good luck finding your memories."

"Thanks, Zenon."

S1E3
4 – The Journey

When I reached the surface again, Elias wasn't waiting for me in the street.

Immediately walking to the edge of town, I could hear him *zipping* around in the grass and trees a short distance away—at least I *assumed* it was my friend, and not just a random Enderman!

Seeing the faint trail of lazily falling motes of purple light—what Elias called his '*warp trail*'—I followed the drifting magic dust with my eyes until I saw his tall, black shape standing in the darkness of the nearby tree line.

He was holding a block of dirt. The fluttering tails of his blue headband told me that this was the right Enderman...

"Elias!" I called.

His purple eyes flared in the darkness of the forest, and I gave him a wave with my bony hand.

Zip.

The Enderman ninja closed the distance almost immediately, zipping across the field in between at an amazing speed, leaving a trail of purple motes in the air behind him.

"Hello, Skeleton Steve," he said into my mind. Elias looked down at the dirt block in his hands, like an afterthought, and tucked it away into his dimensional pocket. *"I found six Ender Seeds while you were away."*

"Awesome, buddy," I replied, and then I related to him the whole story of what I saw down below, as well as my conversation with Zenon. Showing Elias my little map, he pulled out his own large, detailed map, and we compared them. The mapped-out areas on the blacksmith's extensive map, much larger and more detailed than Zenon's, showed the terrain north of town for a while, but stopped *just short* of the two mountains, which would have been very distinctive and easy to notice.

"You can just barely see the beginning of the larger mountain's foothills on my map," Elias said, pointing at a sweeping curve of stone at the

edge of the drawn area north of Zombietown with a slender, black finger. *"We can use my map until we are at the bottom, then refer to yours."*

"Look at this," I said, pointing to a big blue blob at the base of the mountain. "This must be the lake Zenon fell into before he climbed the mountain." The blue lake shape was on *my* map, but not on Elias's.

"It looks like a day's travel, possibly more, to reach the top," the Enderman ninja said. *"Not accounting for moving slowly to climb the mountain itself..."*

I looked up at the moon. There would still be a few hours of night before the sun came up again.

"Maybe we should just leave now then."

"Good idea," Elias said. *"I am curious about what I will sense and feel meditating on the peak of this 'mountain of wisdom', myself..."*

We left Zombietown, heading north. By comparing our maps, we were able to determine which path Zenon had taken in the past. By looking at Zenon's exact path on my map, as well as examining the path's surroundings on Elias's map, the Enderman was able to figure out a route, off of the zombie's trail, that would take us to the mountain more quickly.

Less ... *wandering*.

If Zenon made this journey on the heels of a traveling Minecraftian, it looked like the Minecraftian was taking a very casual approach. According to the map, they had meandered into many random directions before reaching the peak.

By noon, we had reached the big, blue lake. Stepping out of the trees, my jawbone fell open at the sight of the massive mountains before us...

Most of the mountains I'd seen up until now on Diamodia were random and blocky, with various sheer cliffs and gradual, sloping changes. Either you could be walking through the woods, hiking up and up, and you'd suddenly *find yourself* on top of a mountain looking down, or, you could be passing through a grassy valley next to some extreme hills, and see large and sharp chunks of stone jutting out all around you suddenly, *towering* over you.

But *this*...

Up ahead, there were indeed *two mountains*, just like on the map. But they were almost perfect cones—a big one and a little one, connected to each other about halfway up the incline, which was gradual and change biomes the higher they went, from forest, to bare stone, to impressive peaks capped with snow.

Tall and majestic, the massive mountains seemed out of place in this world, taller and *neater* than other mountains and hills I've seen.

"Wow," I said.

"*Impressive,*" Elias replied, looking up at the tallest peak as his headband fluttered in the wind. "*These mountains are unlike any others I've seen on the Overworld up until now...*"

"I was just thinking the same thing, even though I haven't been around as long. How'd those mountains *get* that way?"

"Unknown," Elias responded. *"But they are indeed vast. We should begin our ascent right away."*

I nodded, and we walked on, passing the large, blue lake. I looked at the deep water with its sandy shores, and imagined Zenon, a long time ago, stuck down in the water during the daylight hours.

We hiked for *hours*, gradually making our way higher and higher up the mountain.

During the time that we hiked through the forest, the land was rather unremarkable—just another forest. The difference was, one direction led us *higher*, and the other direction went back down. I walked between all of the oak and birch trees, watching the sheep and other animals munching on grass in the shade. Once, I saw a couple of wolves run by, and felt the need to pull out my bow, just in case. I couldn't help but imagine how *attractive* I must have looked to those canines, a walking invitation of chew toys...

Elias pulled his compass out from time to time to check his bearing against his map, just to make sure we were still on course for the larger mountain's peak, but it was pretty obvious to me which direction we had to go.

Up...

Eventually, the air started getting cooler, and the oak and birch trees faded, giving way to the tall pine trees of a taiga forest. I kept my bow on hand, because I still heard the sounds of wolves howling here and there, just over the horizon. I was a little nervous about having to hit a moving target with an arrow; I did okay fighting the Minecraftians the other day, but I had a feeling that a charging *wolf* would be another matter entirely.

Once we reached the tree-line, stepping out onto a massive slope of slick gravel and naked stone, I was suddenly slammed with the realization of how high we already were...

Looking out at the land over the tops of the trees, now that we were exposed on open ground and had a great view of the world around us, I could see Diamodia go on for miles and miles. It was amazing that we couldn't see this *Mountain of Wisdom* from town! Then again, I couldn't quite see Zombietown either. We were far enough away. Maybe when we were on the way here, we might have been able to see the mountain from the treetops, but the entire journey was mostly through thick forests, so we never really looked *up*.

Elias and I stood above the tree-line looking down, and could see forever...

I could see the big, blue lake, now a small, blue spot far below.

And for as high as we were, looking up the mountain, I could see that we still had a *long way to go*...

Elias stood tall and thin like a shadow against the grey scrabble of the tundra, the intense wind whipping around the tails of his blue ninja headband. I wondered if he felt the *cold*. Endermen were, after all, *living* creatures, even if they weren't like Minecraftians or villagers or animals. I figured that it must be cold up here, higher than the trees could survive, but I didn't really feel it.

The undead don't suffer in the cold. Or, at least, *I* didn't...

"*We should continue,*" Elias said into my mind. "*We still have a few hours of travel before we reach the summit, by my calculations, and the sun will be going down soon.*"

"Yeah, sure," I replied. "It's just ... really amazing!"

"*Agreed,*" Elias said.

We made our way up the stone alpine tundra of the mountain, doing the best we could. I'm sure Elias could have just teleported his way to the top *very* quickly, but he stayed with me. He was doing this for me—it was my quest, to recover my memories, even though he's expressed his own responsible interest in it. He thought that my memories might hold some sort of answer about that 'red energy' he was so worried about...

Eventually, the mountain became so steep that we couldn't just keep climbing the incline anymore.

Elias *did* warp around a little at that point, scouting out whatever he could find in the way of a natural trail to the top.

Zip.

He appeared again in front of me, just as the sun started to dip into the horizon, throwing pink and gold colors all over the grey environment around us. Looking up, I saw the whole snowy peak *glistening* in the setting day.

"*I have found a path*," Elias said, then led me to it.

As we continued, climbing a natural cut in the side of the mountain, turning to follow switch-backs whenever our surroundings became too steep, I started to wonder if this was the same path that Zenon must have accidentally come across when he was here before.

I was answered when we heard the sound of rushing water up ahead.

We were following the path along a very steep incline, crossing the side of the mountain. In the distance, I could see the second, smaller mountain, starting its own peak across a great expanse of open space.

Up ahead, three *creeks* emerged from the melting snow above, and rushed down to cross the path ahead of us, creating three small waterfalls as they rushed over the edge of the trail. Looking over, I saw that the waterfalls plummeted over a hundred feet until they splashed and sprayed into a natural pool down below. The pool of frigid water run over as well, sending creeks of freezing water down the stony mountainside until disappearing into the trees far downhill...

We would have to *cross* those three streams.

Or, rather ... I would have to cross the three streams. Elias would be able to just *warp* past them...

And if I was swept up in that rushing water, I'd be—

"*Skeleton Steve*," Elias said suddenly into my head.

I looked up at him and his purple eyes.

"Yeah, I know," I said. "I've gotta cross the water."

"Unfortunately, I cannot help you with this," Elias said. *"Endermen cannot make contact with the water of the Overworld."*

"You can't?"

"The combination of hydrogen and oxygen in the precise molecular form of 'water' on this world is incompatible with my body."

"What the heck does *that* mean?!"

"It is," Elias said, thinking, *"like poison, you could say..."*

"Okaaay," I said. "What about snow and ice? We're going to have to walk on that *snow* eventually."

"That will not be a problem," Elias replied. *"Since I do not generate body heat like many living beings here, I do not have to worry about any snow in contact with my skin transforming into water."*

"Huh," I replied. "But you have to watch out for rain, eh?"

"Yes, I do have to watch out for rain."

I guess that also answered my previous wondering about if Elias suffered in the cold. If he didn't have to worry about body heat, he was probably just fine...

"Okay," I said. "Let's do it."

"*Skeleton Steve*," Elias said. "*Take care not to fall over the edge.*"

"Duh," I responded.

"*If you do fall, try to stay in the water to help protect your fall. But if you fall, and survive, it will take us several more hours to make up the difference.*"

"Gee, thanks," I said. "I guess if I *do* fall, and I *do* survive, then needing to waste a few hours catching up won't be a *big deal*, right?"

As I approached the water, Elias crossed with obstacle with ease.

Zip.

Suddenly, he stood on the other side of the three fast-moving creeks, his eyes glowing purple in the darkness up ahead.

I sighed, and cinched my bow and my pack down nice and tight.

Approaching the first creek, I watched the water speed past me, flowing from uphill, over and across my path, then dumping off of the cliff on the trail's edge, leading down to the pool *far below*...

One, I thought. *Two ... three!!*

Moving as quickly as I could, my bones *clunked* as I darted across the stream. Once my bony feet hit the water, I immediately felt the creek rushing against me, trying to sweep me up and throw me over the edge! A moment later, I was across and standing on stone again.

"One down!" I shouted to Elias.

The second stream was the same. I amped myself up again and did my best to run across the water, felt the current tugging against me, but made it to the other side.

"*You're almost across*," Elias said to me from up ahead. "*Take care on the last one. It is wider!*"

"Thanks, yeah, I can *see* that!" I said.

The Enderman was right. The third creek was *twice* the width of the other two.

On the first two torrents of water, my momentum was enough to carry me through to solid ground. Each time I crossed, I felt myself about to fall, but before my feet were swept out from under me, I was on stone again.

This time, I wasn't too sure...

Ready...

Set...

Go!!

I ran, bones clunking, and took my first step into the water. Took another—halfway across! Then, all of a sudden, my world spun around as my foot slipped, and I fell!

Splash!

When I hit the water, and saw nothing but blue for a moment, I realized that in another instant, I'd be thrown off of the path, and fall a hundred feet through the air down the mountain! In that moment, I felt Elias in my head, as if he was trying to exclaim some sort of words of—*Get up! OMG!*—*b*ut, it just came through as a vivid image of me *tumbling* off of the cliff and out into the open air...

I reached out to grab the stony ground under the water.

Nothing. Slippery. Just cold water.

Putting my bony fingers close together, I tried my best to swim against the current...

And I could suddenly *see and hear* again when my head broke out of the water!

Elias stood close to the edge of the stream, reaching for me with his long, black arms, but he couldn't reach far enough!

I pumped my bony arms, and scrambled with my legs for a foothold, and moved up the current a little more. Reaching out, I grabbed a chink of stone outside of the water, and pulled. The water pressed against me like a monster trying to hold me down...

Then, I felt Elias's strong fingers grabbing my ribs.

I heard a strange, otherworldly *cry*, and realized that it was the roar of an Enderman—the sound of pain from Elias's natural *non-telepathic* voice. He must have gotten some *water* on him...

"*Pull!*" Elias shouted into my mind.

I pulled, straining with my hand on the dry ground, trying to swim with the hand still underwater, trying to push myself up with *anything* I could feel under my flailing feet. Elias pulled against my ribcage...

And I landed in a heap on the trail on the other side of the stream!

Safe.

Elias and I sat on the trail for a while, the water of the third stream rushing past, as ice crystals froze on my bones and the Enderman nursed his injured arm.

S1E3
5 – Slinger the Spider

"Oh, come on!" I exclaimed, looking at the path ahead of us. "Really?!"

Elias stopped, walking ahead of me, and looked back, his glowing purple eyes showing no expression and his blank face without concern.

A ripping wind tore across us, and the blue tails of his ninja headband whipped around violently. It was a good thing I couldn't feel the cold. Good thing my Enderman friend couldn't either.

Once the waterfalls were behind us, we continued along the narrow path cut into the side of the mountain, always moving forward and up, up, up—across long and steep bowl-shaped fields devoid of all life, and occasionally turning around on a natural switchback.

I could *almost* see the top of the mountain now. Very soon we'd be in the snow.

But now, ahead of us, as the trail turned around a corner, it became a thin and treacherous ledge that appeared to be the *only* way across a vast and steep chasm!

The mountain was becoming so steep, that there would be no other way up, aside from crossing the ominously high and narrow ledge...

And it was *covered* in spider-webs.

"Spiders?!" I asked. "Here??"

Elias looked ahead, contemplating the webs, then turned to me again.

"*Yes, it appears that a spider, or multiple spiders, have covered the path ahead with their webs,*" he said into my head.

I scoffed.

"Yeah, I can *see* that, Elias," I said. "I was just ... being *indignant*, okay?!"

The Enderman turned to look at the obstacle again.

"*It does not look like the webs extend very far,*" he said. "*If you can get through them, then we can continue on our way.*"

Zip.

I saw the warp trail as Elias teleported to the other side of the webs, across the chasm on the ledge. Purple motes of light drifted down lazily, totally ignoring the crazy wind.

Magic dust, I thought.

Keeping close to the rocky wall, I slowly made my way along the ledge until I reached the beginning of the webbed area. Looking over the ledge, down into foggy darkness, my jawbone dropped open as I peered down the cliff. We must have been on the *back side* of the mountain—I didn't remember seeing this ridiculously steep area from the lake.

How *high* were we? And how far did that drop go?

In the crazy, windy weather up here, I could *barely* see the bottom of the cliff through the haze...

If I fell off of this cliff, I was done for...

For sure.

I'd be *bone dust.*

Reaching out to the thick spider webs ahead of me, I touched the nearest strand.

It was tight like a cable, and as thick as a rope, and worse yet—my bony fingertips stuck to it like it was made of tar.

I pulled, tugged, and worked hard to get my hand free without falling off of the ledge...

Sproing...

As I pulled my hand free, the sticky strand made a noise and vibrated the whole web!

Looking past the several webbed areas of the trail in front of me, I saw Elias in the distance scouting out the area up ahead.

Reaching into my pack, I pulled out the wooden sword I looted from the fight with the Minecraftians the other morning. Tightening my bow and my pack down against my bony body, I played with the heft of the sword before testing it out against the web, finally swinging down to make a solid hit against a sticky, rope-like strand.

Thwack!!

The strand was damaged a little under the blow, some sticky pieces of it splitting under the wooden blade's edge and snapping away.

I hit again and again. It seemed that as long as I was careful to hit *only with the edge* and not with the flat of the sword, I wouldn't have to worry about it getting...

Stuck.

My last swing *missed,* and the sword slipped and hit the web with the flat of the blade, getting stuck just as surely as my hand did!

"Dang!" I cried, then tried pulling on the sword, being careful not to fall off of the ledge...

Suddenly, I heard a loud *HISSSSSSSS*, and looked up to see a big, black spider body descending the cliff wall right toward me!

"Elias!!" I shouted, pulling on the sword to free its blade.

A large, fearsome spider landed on the path behind me, trapping me between the webs and its fangs...

It hissed again.

"Whoa there!" I cried, pulling at the sword and trying to smile. "Easy, spider!! No need to— *hey!!*"

The large spider twisted its abdomen around and, much to my surprise, launched a big, gooey ball of white, sticky web-stuff straight at me! The ball of web struck me square in the chest, plastering onto me like glue, and knocking me back into the very webs I had been trying to cut.

"Quiet, skeleton!" it said, glaring at me with bright red eyes. "I am very *hungry*, and you are in my *trap!*"

"Hungry?!" I cried. "Elias!!" I looked at the spider and tried to smile, shrug, still yanking at the stuck sword. My other arm was stuck to the mass of webs on the path. "You don't want to eat *me*, spider! I'm nothing but *bones!* How can you eat bones?!"

"I can *try*," it said, creeping toward me with its eight legs, its fangs playing up and down. "I can break your bones and see what's *inside*..."

Zip.

Elias suddenly appeared behind the spider on the path, now trapping *it* between him and myself. He quickly scanned the situation with narrowed purple eyes, motes of ender light showering down around him. I could feel his martial *energy*, tight and ready to explode...

But, when I expected the Enderman ninja to immediately *kick* the spider off of the ledge, like he did with the evil *red energy* spider down in the ravine, I was surprised when instead, the arachnid turned to him and gasped, its glowing eyes wide!

"It's *you!!*" the spider exclaimed. "You! The *hero Elias!!*"

I pulled at the sword again, and finally wrenched it free from the webs.

My Enderman friend relaxed his stance a little at those words. He spoke into both of our heads...

"*How do you know me, spider?*" Elias said. "*I do not recognize you.*"

"Oh, Elias!" the spider exclaimed, scuttling around before him. "I don't suppose you'd know just a young spider like me! But I've heard of *you!* You're the *ninja hero* that killed the Skeleton King and the dark undead army to the west of here!"

"*How do you know that?*" the Enderman responded, releasing his fists.

I used the wooden sword to try and free myself from the web behind me. One of the strands finally popped away from my arm with a *sproing!*

"Oh, I heard about it from my good friend, *Scott*. He met you once on a path south of the Minecraftian castle. Do you remember?"

As I struggled with the webs, I watched the conversation. Elias looked down for a moment in thought. Whatever was going on, however it ended

244

up, I knew that I *had* to get free! Would this spider *still* try to eat me? It was looking like it wouldn't, but still...

"*I do recall meeting a spider there*," Elias said. "*But I never got his name. Scott*." He nodded.

"Scott told me *all* about you, and that you were a member of the *Order of the Warping Fist* and all that," the spider said excitedly. Its legs drummed against the stone ground of the ledge. "I'm your *biggest fan*, Elias!" it exclaimed. "I'm training to be a ninja, too! You like my moves? My *trap?* I learned how to shoot my webs so that I can be *sneaky* like you!"

Elias folded his arms in front of his chest. "*Yes, that was very effective ... what is your name, spider?*"

"Slinger, sir!" the spider said. "I'm Slinger the spider ninja! Uh ... in *training* anyway. One day I'll be—"

"*Slinger*," Elias said. "*The skeleton in your web is my friend, Skeleton Steve. Do you think you could release him? We are on an important mission..."*

Slinger turned around and looked me over again with his four glowing red eyes. I couldn't read his arachnid face any better than I could read my Enderman friend's expressions. The creature's fangs twitched.

"Oh, sure!" he said with a hiss. "Well, uh, not *really*. I can't make the webs go away, but I won't *web* him any*more*, okay?" One of the four red eyes *winked* at me. "I won't *eat* you, okay?"

I felt a chill go up my spine, and as a skeleton, I'm not even sure how that was possible!

"Uh ... thanks," I said, finally freeing myself from the webs on the path. The massive sticky ball was still splattered all over my chest, plastering the strap of my pack to my bones, filling my ribs full of white spider gunk.

Gross...

"*Why are you setting your trap way up here?*" Elias asked.

"I'm waiting for Minecraftians," Slinger said. "I've been waiting for a *while*, too. I'm *so* freaking hungry!"

"But we're so high!" I said, pulling at the huge ball of yuck on my chest. I pried at it with the wooden sword. "You're not going to catch any food up here. No *Minecraftians*, anyway."

"Oh, sure I will!" Slinger said.

"What makes you say that?"

"Well, the top of the mountain is full of *torches*, for a start," the spider said, his fangs twitching.

"*Interesting*," Elias said. "*Have you seen any?*"

"Not yet," Slinger said. "But I just set up here a few days ago. Sure is a good spot for a *trap*, isn't it?"

"Boy, I'll say," I said. "You totally blocked the only way up to the top of the mountain. Heck, I hardly got through your webs at all! This is going to take *forever* to get through!"

The heavy ball of web-stuff finally pulled free from my chest, leaving sticky residue all over my bones. I tried to throw it off of the edge, but it was stuck to my hand!

I shook my hand. Shook it again. *Dang!*

"*And I have bad news, Skeleton Steve,*" Elias said. I looked up. "*The ledge up ahead becomes even steeper past the webs. Too steep for you. Unless, perhaps, I go down the mountain to gather enough dirt to make it ... passable for you—to build some sort of stairway. This will take some time, of course...*"

"Gah!" I cried, shaking my hand vigorously to be free of the web ball. "And we're *so* close!!"

Slinger looked back and forth between the two of us for a moment, Elias staring out into the sky, perhaps contemplating a quicker way to the top of the mountain, me swinging my bony hand again and again, trying to knock off the ball of his web...

"I have an idea," Slinger said.

We both looked at him.

"Let's hear it," I said.

"I'll make a *deal* with you two," the spider said. "I will help you get to the top of the mountain—it's easy for me—*if* ... you can tell me where I can find some Minecraftians to eat!"

I looked at Elias, and his purple eyes looked back at me.

"Well that's easy!" I said. "There's a group of Minecraftian *noobs* who live nearby, or, I *guess* they do, because they keep coming back to our village again and again!"

"And..." Slinger said quickly, "... you *take me with you!*" He turned to Elias. "Oh, *please* say yes, Elias! Teach me all about being a ninja like you! I won't let you down!"

I looked at the impossible path of webs in front of me, then looked up, craning my bony neck, trying to see the top of the cliff. Looking at Elias, I shrugged, and he nodded.

"*Very well, Slinger,*" Elias said. "*You may stay with us for the immediate future at least. And know that I will not be here for long. I am on my*"

Seed Stride, and will need to return to my world in time to continue with my ninja duties."

"Awesome!!" Slinger exclaimed with a hiss and a small hop. "This'll be *so easy*, you'll see!" He turned to me. "You ready??"

I pulled another chunk of web gunk from my ribs. "Ready for *what?*"

"*Hop on*, Skeleton Steve!" he said, waggling his fat abdomen and crouching down on his eight legs, low enough to make it easy for me to climb up onto his thorax...

"Hop on?"

"Sure!" Slinger said. "You can ride me to the top! I've never had a rider before, but I've known other spiders who have. You'll be my first!"

"Spider riders??"

I saw Elias watching with interest, his headband fluttering in the crazy wind.

"Yeah, sometimes skeletons ride spiders. Didn't you know?" Slinger said. "Let's go!!"

Looking up at my Enderman friend, I shrugged, then carefully climbed on, finding a place for my bony legs between the thick spider legs, and holding onto Slinger's front legs with my bony hands.

"Eh ... be careful now!" I said. "Don't *drop* me! That's a *long* way down!"

"Ah—don't worry!" Slinger exclaimed, then turned toward the wall. Just like that, he reached up with his lead legs, and we were suddenly climbing the wall as if it was nothing! His eight legs struck out in all directions, and I felt very oddly ... secure.

It felt good.

I never expected to ride a spider one day, and certainly never figured that it would feel this ... right.

"*I'll see you at the top*," Elias said into my head suddenly.

Zip.

I heard my friend disappear.

"Okay, Elias!" I called down to the path as Slinger carried me further and further up the wall. "See you there!"

S1E3
6 – The Top of the Mountain

Eight hairy spider legs drummed against the wall around me as the wind tore at Slinger and I, speeding to the top of the mountain along the sheer, stone cliff-side...

"Now *this* is a way to travel!" I cried out against the noise of the weather.

"Cool, huh?" Slinger said.

Pretty soon, we were in the snow and ice, and that spider was able to hold on to impossible surfaces just as easily. It was amazing!

Eventually, eight legs pounded into the frozen crust of the mountain's peak, the ground started to taper into an incline again, and we reached *the summit*...

Up ahead, through the snow and wind, I saw a large open area, as white as white could be, covered with the glowing yellow dots of dozens of Minecraftian torches.

Slinger wasn't kidding! There were *definitely* Minecraftians up here. Or, at least, there used to be...

The top of the Mountain of Wisdom wasn't just a sharp *tip* like I thought it would be. The summit leveled out and it was a pretty large area. Not as large as Zombietown or anything, but a sizeable area, big enough for a large house at least—if anyone was *crazy enough* to build up here. Most of it was a rounded flat top, with chunks of rocky outcropping here and there, all covered in a thick layer of snow.

The entire summit was lit up with torches, but I didn't see anything else. No *magical mountain shrine*—nothing but snow and torches.

And, more importantly, I didn't *feel* anything else.

I didn't suddenly remember who I was, or feel anything stirring in my head...

"Once I made it to the top," I remembered Zenon the zombie saying, *"after exploring up there for a while and relaxing on the peak for the rest of*

night before seeking shelter from daylight, everything started coming back to me..."

Would I have to *hang out* here for a while?

"I could suddenly think clearly, and remember everything, all the way back to where I ... came into being." The zombie's words echoed in my mind.

Zip.

I heard Elias warp somewhere, and saw his dark form appear in the storm on the other side of the summit. He was like a long, black shadow, stretched tall against the white world of the mountaintop.

Zip.

My Enderman friend appeared next to us, up to his calves in the snow. Purple motes of light settled down around him. I smiled at my pal.

"So here we are," Elias said into my head. I presumed he was talking to Slinger, too.

"Yeah, this is it," Slinger said, scuttling a little in the snow. He hissed. "There's not much up here. Lots of torches and snow!"

"What *time* is it?" I asked. "The snow is so thick, I can't tell!" The wind was *so* noisy...

"*Sunset*," Elias said. "*We reached the top sooner than I expected.*"

"Thanks to you," I said, reaching down and patting Slinger.

"When do we head back down?" the spider shouted against the wind. "I'm *so* freaking hungry!"

I climbed off of Slinger, and stepped down into the snow.

"Soon," I said.

"*Do you feel anything?*" Elias asked me.

I didn't.

"Not yet," I replied. "Zenon said that he was here all night, and his memories came back *gradually*. We should spend the night."

"*Very well*," Elias said. The Enderman looked around the summit with his hands on his hips for a moment, then sat down into the snow, crossing his legs. "*We'll see how things look in the morning.*"

Slinger hissed and scuttled around, peering over the edge of the summit in all directions. I didn't think the hiss was annoyance—from what I'd been noticing, spiders just hiss for no reason...

I walked over in the snow and sat down next to my Enderman friend.

Elias moved himself into his meditation position. He was settling in for the night.

Matching his position, I crossed my legs and put my hands on my bony knees. I guess I'd try to *meditate* too. Maybe it would help with the *remembering*...

S1E3
7 – The Mysterious Tower

Night passed, and I stayed in that meditation position, next to my friend.

The snow and wind blew all night long, and I never saw the moon. But when the morning approached, and the light of day started brightening the sky around me, the weather started to let up.

Before long, the sky was totally clear, blue, and I could see what seemed like *all of Diamodia* around me...

It was amazing!

As the sun rose, lightening the world with golden and pink hues, I could see for miles and miles all around. In the haze of the distant horizons, I could see *everything!* All around me was a mix of light greens and dark greens, grey and blue far away. Forests around the base of the mountain were huge, dark blobs of green color.

Standing, I looked around the edges of the summit, plodding through the thick snow.

Far below, I could see the big lake at the base of the mountain, now just a shimmering blue coin among shades of green.

I still couldn't see Zombietown, though—the village was either too far, or it was blocked from sight by forests or hills.

From here, I could easily see the top of the other mountain—the smaller and shorter counterpart to this one. The peak of the smaller mountain was not nearly as high in elevation. It was tall enough to pop up out of the tree line, but not high enough to be capped in snow—not very much, anyway. Not as *thick* as the permanent snow up here...

Yes, I thought. There was *some* snow. And ... also ... *what was that?!*

I focused my eyes, and stared at the smaller mountaintop. There seemed to be some sort of building on the top of the other peak. Some sort of ... stone tower. No farms, or animals or anything—

just a tall, strange-looking tower of stone, or *cobblestone*, sticking straight out of the top of the other smaller peak...

"*How do you feel?*" Elias's voice said in my head.

I turned and looked at my friend, who had stood up from his meditations while I was looking at the sights around us. Nearby, I heard a hiss, and saw Slinger hanging out on one edge of the mountaintop.

"I ... uh ... I don't really..."

Did I remember anything *new?*

Did this *Mountain of Wisdom* help at all??

As far as I could tell, I didn't *feel* any different—I didn't have any more memories than I did at the beginning of the night.

What the heck?!

Did I do something wrong?

Or was this Mountain of Wisdom just a fairytale? Did Zenon make it all up?!

I shook my skull.

"I don't remember anything new," I said, looking down at the snow. "At least, not as far as I can tell..."

"*So nothing happened,*" Elias said.

I smirked. "I don't think so," I said. "Back to the drawing board."

We all stood quiet for a moment.

Slinger ran up to us.

"I'm hungry!" he said. "Are we going to the Minecraftians now?"

"Not quite yet," I said.

There was that weird tower thing on the other peak. Was it possible that Zenon meant something *else?* Was there a mix-up somewhere, and he actually recovered his memories on the *other*, smaller peak? Could it be that the *tower* over there was actually the *magical mountain shrine* he had found?

"*What's your plan?*" Elias asked. "*I can sense that you are working on something...*"

"You're right!" I said. "Check this out!"

Leading the others to the edge of the summit closest to the other peak, I pointed across the expanse in between to the distant stone tower with a long, bony finger.

"What?" Slinger asked with a hiss.

"Over there, on the other mountain!" I said. "There's some sort of *tower*. Maybe *that's* Zenon's *magical mountain shrine!* Maybe his story or our directions were *mixed up* somehow, and *that's* the peak we need to be on! Maybe *that's* the magical shrine, and we'll find something in there that can help with my memories!"

"*Quite possible,*" Elias said. "*It's definitely worth checking out.*"

"Alright, alright," Slinger said, his fangs clicking. "So we're gonna head down this part of the mountain, and up *that* little mountain?"

"Yep," I said.

"And ... then?" the spider said. "*Then* we can find something to eat?"

We laughed, and I climbed onto Slinger's back.

I didn't know what secrets or magic the tower on the other mountaintop held, but we were going to find out...

Season 1, Episode 4:

The Mysterious Tower

Skeleton Steve and the Mysterious Tower...

Disappointed with what they found on the top of the Mountain of Wisdom, Skeleton Steve, Elias the Enderman ninja, and their new friend, Slinger the spider, travel across to the next peak over, where Skeleton Steve saw a mysterious stone tower, standing all alone on the top of the mountain.

But when the strange and abandoned fortress turns out to be something different than they expected, and the three of them end up lost and separated in a vast, old mineshaft underneath, will exploring the ancient Minecraftian place turn out to be more than the odd trio of adventurers can handle? And what's that strange, moaning sound, deep, deep underground??

S1E4
1 – Journey to the Tower

The sun was bright, and I took a long, thrilling look around at the miles and miles of Diamodia countryside all around us...

The *Mountain of Wisdom* was vast, and its peak was probably the highest I'd ever been before. I felt like I could see the *whole world!*

Heck—it was definitely the highest I'd ever been on *this* world. Especially since my memory only went as far back as when I met my friend Elias and his Minecraftian comrades back in that village, what—a couple of weeks ago, now?

I shook my head and my bones rattled. The time was all blending together.

The first thing I remembered was huddling down in the dirt, surrounded by cobblestone walls, with the Enderman ninja standing over me, ready to deliver a killing blow. A trio of Minecraftians stood nearby, two with diamond swords and one wielding a bow, and all around me were the broken bone bodies of the Skeleton King's army...

Was it already a couple of weeks ago now, since Elias and I headed east to Zombietown and started this chain of adventures to try and recover my lost memories?

A flurry of snow blew past, sweeping across my bones, reminding me that I was near the top of a *huge* mountain.

It was sunny, but also freezing up here! The cold didn't bother me, and apparently didn't bother my Enderman ninja friend, but I wondered about Slinger the spider. After all, spiders were living creatures! Wasn't he *freezing?*

The Slinger's legs pumped up and down around me as I rode comfortably on his thorax, holding my bow. We were making our way down the snowy peak, slowly and carefully since it was so steep.

Going *up* was one thing—I could just hold on to Slinger, and he could climb like a *crazy mob*, scuttling up the mountainside! But going down ... I had to hold on carefully, and he had to move slowly, so that I didn't fall off!

Zip.

I saw the warp trail of purple motes of light as Elias teleported past us. He would have had a hard time getting down too, if he wasn't an Enderman! As it was, he was trying to stay close to us, since we were a group, and just warping from solid block to solid block, bypassing the sheer drops and cliffs with ease.

Up ahead in the distance, I could see, quite clearly in the bright and clear day, that this taller peak continued to descend, *super steep* in some areas, but gradually started to level out into a more manageable incline. There, where the snow melted away, there was a huge expanse of shale and raw stone. Farther and farther down, the mountainside leveled out even more by the time the stone met with the tree line, and the mega-taiga and taiga forests led the rest of the way back down to the normal world of wooded hills and open plains...

But that's not where we were going.

Not yet.

Across the rocky area below the snowy tundra was a barren valley where the larger *Mountain of Wisdom* connected with a smaller, shorter peak! Across the rocky plain, the second, smaller mountain began to rise again, steeper and steeper, until it almost reached the elevation of the main peak's snowcap. The top of the second mountain had *some* snow, sure, but it wasn't the same as the permanent snow like this around me...

And on that second, smaller peak ... was the *Mysterious Tower!*

I could see it clearly in the distance, and watched the morning sun make shadows with the tall, cobblestone structure. It was a respectable size, and topped with strange battlements, with no windows, except for some slits in the wall near the top. From here, I couldn't see a door leading inside. The entrance must have been on another side of the structure.

Soon, we'd be off of this snowy peak, then crossing the stone valley, climbing the smaller mountain, and up *there*, searching for the way into the tower...

Zip.

While I was staring into the distance, I didn't notice when the ground leveled off, and Elias must have decided that it was safe to walk next to Slinger and me again.

I've gotta say—it sure is nice to have a *spider* to ride!

"Hey, Elias!" Slinger said, his head turning to look at my friend. "Is it okay—would it *be* okay if I asked you some questions about your ... *Order of the Warping Fist??*"

The Enderman ninja was tall and lean, and his long, black limbs and body were a stark contrast against the snow. He walked along in long, silent strides beside us.

Elias looked down, regarding Slinger with his glowing purple eyes, and nodded.

"*Very well, Slinger. I cannot divulge everything, but what would you like to know?*" he said into our heads. Or, at least, I *assumed* he said that into Slinger's head as well...

"Okay, sir," Slinger said, his fangs clicking. I supposed he was very excited. "What does your *headband* mean? How does that work? The symbol? Is it the *type* of ninja you are? Or your *rank* or something? I'm sorry—that was a *bunch* of questions..."

Elias reached up and touched the deep blue headband, its blue tails fluttering in the wind. He touched the white symbol in the center, as if making sure it was still in the right place on his smooth forehead.

"*This is the headband and the symbol of the 'Initiate' Ninja,*" he said into our minds. "*All lower ninja bear the 'white' symbol of the order, and the different levels of the lower rankings have different color bands.*"

"Different levels? And wait—you're an *initiate??*"

"*I am not an initiate anymore, spider,*" Elias replied. "*Well, technically I am, but I earned my*

272

acceptance into the lower ninja rank when I defeated the Skeleton King and revealed the danger facing this world to the council of elders. I just haven't been back to do my advancement trials and accept the official promotion yet..."

"Why not?"

"*I am on my Seed Stride.*"

"Seed Stride? What's a *Seed Stride?*" Slinger asked. We walked over a section of stone without snow, and his eight furry feet drummed on the ground as we passed.

"Off topic," I said suddenly. "You were going into the *ranks*. I'm interested in that myself!" I said.

"Okay, yeah, *sorry!*" Slinger said. "What about the ranks?"

Elias nodded, and went on. "*My headband and the symbol, together, indicate the rank of Initiate. It is the sign of an Enderman youngling reaching maturity and nearing the end of his training, but before attaining the first working rank of the Ninja. When I was a youngling in training, I wore a white headband with the same white symbol. Since I have now earned my rank as 'Lower' Ninja, once I return to complete my trials and ceremony, I will be trading this blue headband for a black one. I will still have the white symbol, until I am promoted again, later."*

"What's next?" Slinger asked.

"After Lower Ninja, if I am worthy, I will rise to the rank of 'Middle' Ninja, and wear a black headband with a red symbol. Above the Middle Ninja are the Masters, who have a purple symbol over a black band."

"Wow," Slinger said. "It sounds complicated! You must have ninja cities and all sorts of cool ninja stuff back on your world, huh?"

"The End is a pleasant place," Elias said. *"Although—maybe not for you creatures of the Overworld. You may find it difficult to get around without the ability to warp like we Ender, or to fly, perhaps."*

"What about climbing and jumping?" Slinger asked. "I'm *really good* at climbing and jumping!!"

I had *no idea* what sort of weird place that an Enderman would call home would look like. I could tell, from being around Elias all this time, that his homeworld must be *dark*, because he seemed annoyed by the sunlight, even though he toughed it out and moved around in the day anyway. And what sort of place would be hard to get around without the ability to teleport of fly? A place like *this mountain* or a ravine? Lots of cliffs and places to fall from, maybe?

By now, it had been a little while since we left the snowcap behind us, and we were having a rather pleasant trek across the flattening rocky area between the two peaks—still far above the tree-line, but the area around us was a nice, flat *bowl* of a valley. Up ahead, the slope of the smaller mountain rose gradually, then *suddenly*, leading to the shorter peak's summit and the tower...

"About the *Order...*" Slinger said. "Do you think it's possible for a spider like me to join it someday??"

"*I cannot say about joining, Slinger,*" Elias responded, looked down at us again with his purple eyes. "*Perhaps, one day, we may find a way for you to travel back to the End with me, and you can present your case to the masters.*"

"Really??" Slinger exclaimed, his fangs clicking. "You'd take me there?"

Elias went on. "*The Order of the Warping Fist is the guardian and guide of the Ender race.*" He looked down at me. "*At least on this world.*" Looking ahead again as we traveled, he continued. "*Our main goal is to maintain the neutrality of the Overworld, and to destroy abominations that upset the balance.*"

"Oh! Oh!" Slinger exclaimed. "*That's* why you were fighting the Skeleton King??"

"*Indeed,*" Elias replied. "*My mission brought me to the area to investigate the murders of many of my Ender people. That's where I discovered the Minecraftians, and eventually, the Skeleton King."*

"And you showed him who's boss, huh?" Slinger said. "That's *so intense!!* I mean—how did you manage to fight like a *hundred* skeleton archers, anyway? It must have been—"

If I had the ability to gulp, I suppose I would have. As it was, I adjusted the strap of my pack.

Slinger had *no idea* that I was the Skeleton King...

I *was*, anyway.

Used to be.

Was I still?

Elias seemed to think that I was like *this*, how I am now, *before* I became the Skeleton King, and I was warped and taken over by that evil bow!

But I had no idea...

That was part of why Elias was so intent on helping me recover my memories, I was certain. He was probably very intent on making sure I wouldn't turn into that monster again.

For all I knew, making sure I wasn't a *threat* might be his current *mission*...

What would Slinger do when he found out that I used to be the boogeyman he's so focused on in his fascination with the Enderman ninja?

I looked up, and realized that Elias was staring at me. His purple eyes glowed, boring into my skull, his smooth, black face passive and unreadable. Slinger was still blabbing on about fighting loads of skeletons...

"*Are you okay, Skeleton Steve?*" he asked into my head.

"Yeah," I replied. Was that out loud? Or in my head?

"*I sense much fear and confusion from you. Your thoughts drift to the ... other...*"

I smiled up at my friend. Slinger was still talking, unaware of our private conversation. "I'm alright," I said.

"—and they all had *arrows*, and I *know* that you can teleport, but *that many??* I mean—sorry, what was that, Skeleton Steve?" Slinger asked.

"Oh, nothing," I said.

"*It was indeed a challenge*," Elias said, returning to the conversation about the battle. "*And I was not entirely successful. At one point, I became too reckless, and nearly died.*"

"Holy smokes!" Slinger said, shifting his body under me as we started climbing the smaller peak. I settled in on his thorax and held a couple of his eight shoulders. Looks like we were going *up* again...

"*Ultimately, it was with a still mind and relaxed focus that I was able to defeat the army. And I defeated the Skeleton King with superior strategy and planning—not brute strength—along with the help of my friends.*"

"That's amazing! *You're* amazing, Elias! I hope one day I can become an *awesome ninja* like you..."

"Sounds like quite an adventure," I said.

"And where do *you* come into this, Skeleton Steve?" Slinger asked. "Where'd *you* meet up with Elias?"

I shifted in my seat on the spider.

"Oh, uh ... I met Elias ... *after*."

"Hmm, okay," Slinger replied. We walked along quietly for a moment, making our way up the ever-steepening slope toward the top of the smaller peak. "Well, Elias, how did you kill the Skeleton King??"

The two of them chatted about the battle for a while. I only half-listened. Everything leading up until my first solid memories was a ... *red haze*. But there were fleeting little pieces of the battle...

I touched the center of my ribcage with a boney finger. My sternum, the connection of my ribs in the middle, was solid. In that weird, *memory-flashback* Elias gave me back on the road to Zombietown about his fight with the Skeleton King, my ribs had *split open* here, making some sort of crazy, sideways *mouth* that chomped down onto the Enderman ninja! Elias had been too big to swallow, so I ... *he* ... had just crunched the ninja up and spat him out onto the ground...

Monstrous...

I shook my head to get the thoughts out...

Looking up, I saw the tower approaching, standing tall and exotic, much closer now.

We were suddenly climbing a sheer cliff, and I saw flurries of snow falling around me.

"There is is..." I said.

If there was supposed to be some sort of *magical mountain shrine* back on the Mountain of Wisdom, we must have missed it. That peak—the summit— was totally open, and *empty*, full of snow and torches.

I looked back, and saw the *larger* peak looming in the air above us. Its snowy cap looked pristine and peaceful in the daylight, but I knew better. It was bitter cold up there, and windy as heck...

As we stepped onto the solid, flat summit. Slinger springing up from the cliff-side and landing in the snow, I looked up at the large, cobblestone structure.

Was *this* the magical mountain shrine we were supposed to find on the *other* mountain? Was Zenon wrong about which peak we should have climbed? Why, it just looked like an old, Minecraftian tower! Was there some sort of magical area inside that would give me my memories back??

Was *this* the key to remembering who I was?

The snow definitely wasn't as deep on the peak of *this* smaller mountain. Still, compared to the other mountains I've seen on Diamodia (*and that didn't say much*), it was impressive! Tall and conical, majestic and not at all like the other mountains of the world.

But, next to the Mountain of Wisdom, it was a *small* peak. Nothing could stand next to that massive thing! The Mountain of Wisdom was definitely the most impressive natural wonder of Diamodia I've ever seen...

I stepped down from Slinger's back, my bones *clunking* as I moved my joints around again.

"Well," I said. "Let's check it out..."

S1E4
2 – Exploring the Tower

The *Mysterious Tower* sat in the middle of a small, level area at the top of the smaller mountain's peak. Being so far above the tree-line, there was very little grass. Most of the foliage up here was cold, brownish weeds and dense lichens, clinging to the stone. Not much plant life. Rocky outcroppings burst out of the summit here and there, but the large cobblestone structure was built solidly on the top of the mountain like a stout finger, pointing up at the sky...

Just like on the summit of the Mountain of Wisdom, there were many torches stuck into the ground and hammered into the stone, consistent but random, lighting up the entire area.

"Why are there *torches* all over both of these mountains?" I asked.

Elias shrugged.

"Who *uses* these torches, anyway?" Slinger said.

"*Minecraftians*," Elias replied. "*They require the light to see.*"

"Well it's *annoying*," Slinger said. "Makes it hard to see with so much *glare!* I kind of *don't want to be around* areas with so many torches like this!"

"Well, maybe that's part of it, too," I said.

"What do you mean?" Slinger replied with a hiss. "Keeping *me* away? Why would they want to keep me away?" he said, his fangs clicking and his red eyes glowing bright in the afternoon sun.

I laughed.

"Why, indeed..."

"*We must be wary*," Elias said into our minds, "*but I do not sense any signs of life inside the tower, not as far as I can tell.*"

The three of us eventually found the door to the tower on the *east* wall, facing where the sun would rise every morning.

"Interesting placement," I said, as Elias walked up behind me. "Other walls of the tower would have made more sense—there's more space outside those walls. More room to walk. This side's almost to the cliff!"

"*But it is facing the rising sun*," Elias said. "*If a Minecraftian built this, the front door facing the sun would make it safest to exit here in the case of any undead hanging around outside*."

"That's what I was thinking," I said.

Slinger came up next to us, his eight legs drumming on the stone ground.

"What's that *wood thing* in the wall?" he said, reaching up and climbing onto the cobblestone. "Well—I don't see any way in, so I guess I'll go *up there* and see if there's anything on the roof!"

I reached out to the latch, and opened the oaken door with a loud creak.

"What?!" Slinger exclaimed in shock, jumping back to the ground.

I smiled. "It's a *door*, Slinger."

"A *door...?*"

Pulling my bow and nocking an arrow, I stepped into the dark interior.

My eyes quickly adjusted to the dim, torched entryway of the tower. Stepping forward into the main level, I looked around, and Elias *zipped* through the short, open doorway to appear next to me. Slinger followed, pulling his way through the doorframe with his eight legs, giving me the *heebie-jeebies*. Even though he was kind of my *friend*, he still looked horrifying! I still thought of him as a *monster* at times. His many red eyes glowed. If I was a *Minecraftian*, I would be *terrified* to see a huge spider pulling its way through the door!

"Wow!" Slinger exclaimed, his fangs clicking. "*Look* at this place!!"

The main level was open and sparse. There were cobblestone stairs leading up to higher levels, and more stairs leading down into some sort of basement. Torches lined the walls, and several Minecraftian objects were clustered together in one area. I could recognize a lot of these things now—a crafting table, two furnaces, a chest, and several dark-colored chunks of metal that looked like a heavy, broken *tool* of some kind...

I walked up to the crafting area, my bones *clunking* and echoing through the room.

"What's this?" I asked, crouching to inspect the broken tool. It was a large, thick metal thing, big and heavy on top, with a stand at the bottom. What was left of it was covered with impact marks and gouges.

Elias walked up behind me.

"I'm not sure what that object is called," he said. *"But I believe I have seen an intact version of this tool at the village blacksmith's back where Balder gave me my map."*

An anvil, I thought. *It's called an anvil.*

"Umm ... I guess this is a broken *anvil*," I said.

Elias looked down at me. *"How do you know that?"* he asked.

I shrugged, my bones *clunking*. "I dunno. Wish I knew! I've been *noticing* that lately. Sometimes I just ... remember the *names* of stuff."

"*Perhaps the tower is bringing back your memory, as we expected would happen on the Mountain of Wisdom*."

"I wish I knew," I said. "Hope so..."

Even though Elias didn't sense any *signs of life* as he put it, I still couldn't shake the sense that there might be danger around a corner somewhere. Whatever Minecraftian built this place, or *group* of Minecraftians, they seemed to be serious. Who else would build a tall stone tower on the top of a cold mountain??

That said, there was also a very *homey* feeling to this place, even though it was clearly very *old*, and the cobblestone floors and furnaces and tools were coated with dust...

Heading to the stairs, we went up.

I led Elias and Slinger up to the next higher level. From what I could tell, comparing how high the main level's ceiling was to how tall the tower looked from the outside, I figured that the next level would have a *really* tall ceiling! Or, there would be a *third* level above that!

Making our way up the stairs, I emerged first into a large and open room. Old torches (*amazing that they were still lit!*) lined the walls, giving the room a flickering, yellow glow. There were no windows. Also lining all of the walls—except for the wall where the stairs were—were several large and dusty wooden *chests*.

"Jackpot!" I exclaimed, my voice echoing through the open stone room. My bones *clunked*.

"*Jackpot?*" Elias asked in my head, his own black head emerging from the stairwell into the room as he climbed with his long, black legs. "*What do you mean by that?*"

"Huh?" I asked, and looked back at him. His dark skin absorbed the yellow light of the torches. "Oh—*jackpot*. That's ... a figure of speech, I guess! I don't know or remember where it *came* from. More silly stuff locked away in my brain, I suppose. It means that we found a lot of *good stuff*. Look at the *chests!*"

Slinger hissed as he followed Elias up the stairs into the room. The drumming of his legs on the cobblestone floor echoed around us.

"I smell *meat!*" the spider exclaimed. "Delicious, desiccated *husks* of carcasses!" His fangs clicked together.

The staircase continued, leading up into a *third* floor above.

This level must have been some sort of *storage* room...

As I looked around, I noticed wooden slabs bolted onto the stone walls above each chest. On each wooden placard was there were words, scrawled by hand with black ink, probably indicating what was stored inside each chest.

My bones *clunked*, and I approached the nearest sign.

"Dirt," I said, reading the word on the wooden placard.

"*You can read that?*" Elias asked. "*Is it Minecraftian?*"

Interesting.

I could read it, indeed.

"Yeah, I can read it. I don't know if it's Minecraftian, but I understand these words!" I shrugged. "Weird..."

Walking up to the dusty chest under the sign that said 'dirt', I reached down with a boney hand, and popped the lid open.

The old *creak* rang through the room.

Dirt.

Of course. The chest was full of *dirt*. Not *full*, but maybe a *third-way* full of dirt...

"Yep," I said, closing the lid. "It's a lot of dirt, alright."

I looked at the other signs.

"Where's the *food??*" Slinger asked, a dangerous edge to his spider voice. "I'm *so* hungry!!"

"Well, let's see..." I said. "Cobblestone, gravel and sand," I read aloud from the signs, "wood, saplings, wood *stuff*, fuel—whatever *that* means, ah! Food!"

Approaching the chest with the 'food' sign with Slinger practically on my *heels*, I opened the lid with a sharp *creak*, and we looked inside. The container was mostly empty, but had several pieces of bread, and a few dozen dried-out chunks of charred animal flesh scattered among its wooden floor.

Slinger hissed loudly and immediately pushed me to the side with two of his powerful legs, pulling spider body halfway into the chest. I staggered off to the left.

"Jeez, Slinger!" I said.

"Hungry!" he exclaimed, and his arachnid head disappeared into the food chest, chittering and clicking as he rummaged around with his front legs and fangs. He emerged a few seconds later, sucking on a porkchop with both of his long fangs (*did I suddenly remember it was called a 'porkchop'?*). His red eyes were angry.

"*There are many Ender seeds in here*," Elias said into my mind, and I turned to see him sifting through the chest of dirt. He reverently pulled out one of the many dirt blocks, and slipped it into his dimensional pocket.

The spider cursed and threw the porkchop down onto the cobblestone floor.

"All dried out!" Slinger cried. "No juices! I'm so *hungry!* When are we going to find the Minecraftians?"

I walked over, and closed the food chest.

"*Soon*, Slinger," I said. "When we're done with the tower, we'll head back to town, and I'll show you where they were coming from."

"When we do that," Slinger said, "we should seek out where they live! I could build some traps!"

"Yeah, good idea."

I looked around the room some more. There were other chests, but, according to the signs, this storage room was mostly full of food and building supplies.

Nothing very interesting to *me*.

Although it *was* interesting how familiar all of this felt...

"Shall we continue up?" I asked. I looked over to the Enderman ninja, who was still rifling through the dirt chest, pulling out block after block. "Elias?"

My friend stood up straight, and closed the chest of dirt.

"*Skeleton Steve,*" he said, his purple eyes glowing. "*I just found nine Ender seeds, and there are more within.*" Was that *excitement* in his telepathic voice? "*Yes, let's continue, and I will return to this chest later.*"

"Great," I said. "I wonder what could be on the next level, if all of the Minecraftians' *stuff* was stored here, and the tools for making things were down below...?"

"*In my experience,*" Elias responded, "*the top level likely holds the beds.*"

We continued up the stairs.

Once I emerged into the next room, I was shocked and surprised by the stark beauty of it!

For one thing, the ceiling was much higher, and there were four narrow and tall windows, one on each wall, letting the light of the day outside flood the interior! The ceiling was also lit up by some sort of huge, flat window—a *sky* light of some kind—filled with glass blocks, just like what filled the *other* four windows, which let in the brightness of daytime while also keeping out the cold air of the mountaintop.

The other notable thing in this large, vaulted room was a *library*, set up in a corner and taking up most of the level. There was also a small, empty area of the room, built up on an elevated floor, covered in blood-red carpet with a single small chest on the platform's corner.

In the middle of the red carpet was an empty space, littered with fragments of wooden planks.

"Weird," I said, then turned to the bookshelves. My friends came up behind me.

As I approached the library, I looked over the strange arrangement of the shelves, shaped like a 'C' around an empty, central area...

Very odd, I thought.

The bookshelves back at Zebulon's library in Zombietown made sense. They hung from the walls in a way that if you wanted to find a book, all you had to do was walk up to the wall of shelves, look over the books, and find what you needed!

This strange shelving system was built around a central point, where if you wanted a book, you'd have to stand in the middle, and look all around you to find the book you desired.

It seemed that arranging the same shelves all along two of the walls would have made more sense up here. Such an arrangement would save space and keep the room more open! This 'C' of shelves didn't make much sense, unless they were built to stand around the central point *on purpose*...

Stepping into the ring of bookshelves, I felt a *crunch* under my boney foot.

I looked down.

On the cobblestone floor, amidst the dust that was all over everything, there where were chunks ... like *crumbs* ... of some sort of black rock. *Deep* black, like Enderman skin. And black dust.

"Huh..." I said to myself.

"*This is where the bed was*," Elias said. I looked over, and saw the ninja standing on the red carpet of the raised platform. "*I recognize these pieces of wood. I have broken beds before*."

"Is there anything in that little chest?" I asked.

Elias opened the chest with a *creak*, looked inside, then looked back at me.

"*Nothing*," he said. "*With the bed broken, I would surmise that this was the home of a single*

Minecraftian, and he left here, for whatever reason, a long time ago."

He closed the chest.

"There was also something *here*, too," I said, pointing to the open space in between the bookshelves. "There's something *broken*, or there *was* something broken, between all of these books..."

Zip.

Elias warped across the room to stand next to me, in between all of the books.

"Aw, *maaaan*," Slinger said, standing in the middle of the room and watching us. "The Minecraftians are *gone?* I was hoping we could ... you know ... find at least *one* of them!"

"Man, Slinger," I said. "Do you just think with your *stomach* all the time?"

"Well, I'm hungry!!" he exclaimed. "If you were as hungry as me, you'd be thinking with your stomach, too!"

"I'm undead," I said. "I don't *have* a stomach."

"*I also do not hunger,*" Elias said. "*At least not in the same way as you.*" He looked at the broken chunks of black rock. "*There is an interesting energy here,*" he said into my mind.

"Well la dee freaking da!" Slinger said. "I guess you guys won't be thinking about feeding *Slinger* anytime soon, eh?"

"Bad energy?" I asked. "Uh ... *red* energy??"

"*No,*" Elias said. "*Something similar to the power of the beacon. Nevermind—I'm sure you don't remember the beacon...*"

Something from the fight with the Skeleton King, I supposed...

"What's that black stuff?" I asked.

"*Obsidian,*" Elias replied. "*A very powerful mineral made from the remains of cooled lava.*"

"Why is there cooled lava up here in a tower with *books?*"

Elias touched his face with a long and slender hand, and narrowed his purple eyes.

"*I do not know*," he said.

My bones *clunked* as I shrugged, and I reached down to the nearest shelf and pulled out a random book.

"Well," Slinger said. "No more *up*. We should go down!"

I turned the book over in my boney hands and brushed the dust off of its cover.

The title was clear to me on the front in words that I could understand!

"Sir Gawain and the Green Knight," I said, reading aloud to myself. "... *Knight?*"

I thought of Zebulon.

Cracking the book open, I looked at a random page in the middle, then read quietly to myself.

"What you ask," said the knight, "you shall now know.

302

A most pressing matter prized me from that place:
I myself am summoned to seek out a site
and I have not the faintest idea where to find it.
But find it I must by the first of the year, and not fail
for all the acres in England, so help me Lord.
And in speaking of my quest, I respectfully request
that you tell me, in truth, if you have heard the tale
of a green chapel, or the grounds where a Green
Chapel stands,
or the guardian of those grounds who is colored
green.
For I am bound by a bond agreed by us both
to link up with him there, should I live that long.
As dawn on New Year's—

"What's that?" Slinger asked, climbing up onto the bookshelves.

I looked up suddenly.

"Oh," I said, closing the book. *Quests, truth, guardians, bonds*—this looked like something the little zombie knight-in-training would really appreciate! "It's just a *book*. And I know someone who would really *like* this book, I think..."

Slipping 'Sir Gawain and the Green Knight' into my pack, I looked up to see Elias watching me with his purple eyes.

"Are you feeling anything?" Elias asked. *"If this is the 'magical mountain shrine', as you say, is any of this stirring up memories?"*

Was I feeling anything? I stood and thought for a moment, trying to listen to my feelings.

"Um ... I don't *think* so," I said. "Not really. I mean—I'm *reading* stuff, and recognizing Minecraftian stuff here and there, but nothing *significant*. Not *yet*, anyway..."

The Enderman nodded. *"To the lower level?"* he asked.

"Sure," I said, leading them back to the staircase.

We descended the cobblestone stairs back into the storage room, then down to the main level. Crossing the room, we approached the stairwell that led into the lower level—or *levels*—and headed down. I could see the glow down below of torchlight...

The basement was another storage room, it seemed. There were no windows, of course, because this level was underground, cut into the mountain. Torches lined the walls just like they did in the *other* storage room, and this room was also full of chests, although not as many. Looking at the signs, I saw labels above each chest that said things like 'tools' and 'weapons' and 'armor', but when I looked inside, the containers were mostly empty. There were a few old, beat-up tools made of splintering wood and chipping stone—each just about *used up*.

"Junk," I said, throwing a piece of equipment back into the chest where it came from.

Pickaxe, I thought. That was a *pickaxe*.

"Hey, did anyone notice the *door?*" Slinger said suddenly, his fangs clicking.

Elias and I turned and looked at a single dark oak door built into the cobblestone wall in a darker corner of the large room.

"Oh yeah!" I said. "*That's* different!"

The three of us hurried over to the door.

"Do that thing you do!" Slinger said. "Do it again! I wanna *see!*"

"You mean...?"

"*Open the door*," Elias said. "*I sense nothing on the other side.*"

"Yeah!" Slinger exclaimed, his fangs clicking and his red eyes bright. "Open the door!"

I shrugged, and grasped the latch with a boney hand.

Opening the door, much to Slinger's excitement, I saw a dark tunnel on the other side— a long, descending stairway, delving down into the mountain deeper than even my undead eyes could see. The stairs went down, down, *down*, and with every several steps, a torch hung from the wall near the low ceiling.

"It goes ... *down*," I said, and we all peered into the darkness...

S1E4

3 – The Abandoned Mineshaft

I took the first step into the long, descending tunnel of stairs.

My bones *clunked*.

The walls were close, and the ceiling was low, and—

I looked and reached up to the blocky stone ceiling with a boney hand, and looked back to Elias.

"*It is okay, Skeleton Steve*," he said. "*I can fit.*"

Looking back down, I started the descent.

"What *is* this??" I asked.

Elias stepped onto the stairs behind me and followed. His head barely avoided hitting the cold, stone-hewn ceiling.

"*I have seen this before*," the Enderman said in my mind. "*It seems that Minecraftians have a preference for this kind of tunnel when seeking out stone and resources deep in the ground..."*

We continued down the stairs, down and down, passing a flickering torch every several steps. Even though I felt a sense of increasing depth and darkness, the passage was still lit up quite brightly—enough to hurt my eyes!

"Maybe there'll be a *Minecraftian* down there..." Slinger whispered, his fangs clicking.

"Honestly, I doubt it," I said. "Looks like whatever's happened here up on this mountain is *long* over. I wonder why whoever lived here before just *abandoned* this place like this...?"

"A fair distance away from here," Elias said, *"several days by your travel, the Minecraftians you met when you started your travels with me— LuckyMist in particular—built a tunnel just like this. And that was in a temporary home, in a cave. She created that tunnel very quickly."*

"Was it this deep?" I asked. We were still going down, and I had lost track of how many stairs were behind us. It's not like I was counting, but I was keeping a half-hearted count of the *torches* we passed at least, and I totally forgot what number I was on...

Up ahead, the tunnel continued, ever downward.

"*Yes,*" Elias said. "*It descended to what the Minecraftians called 'bedrock'.*"

"What for?" Slinger asked. "Why do Minecraftians cut through the world like this? It's *crazy!!*"

"*It is not crazy to their ways of life,*" Elias replied. My bones *clunked* as we continued down and down. "*The Minecraftians are strong in their ability to build ... and destroy ... and to create tools and technology to make them even stronger. They require ores and coal and other things to create their tools and armor and weapons, and those ores wait deep underground.*"

"If I could make stuff," Slinger said, his eight feet padding around on the stairs behind us, "I would make really awesome traps for capturing Minecraftians for *food!*"

"Figures," I said.

"What about *you*, Elias? What sort of cool *ninja* weapons and tools would you make??" Slinger asked.

Elias glanced back at the spider as we continued down the stairs. I could see that Slinger barely fit down the tunnel, and was happily struggling to keep up.

"*I cannot think of a single object, tool or weapon or armor or 'building block', that I require...*"

"What about *armor?*" Slinger asked.

"*My Chi Dodge is my armor,*" he said. "*My mind is my shield. Metal armor, or armor made from the skins of animals, would only get in my way and slow me down.*"

"How about weapons?" I asked.

"*My entire body is a weapon.*"

"I remember seeing those *shields*," I said. "I think one of the Minecraftian *noobs* had a shield?

Don't remember. But your Minecraftian friends back in the village *all* had shields!"

"What's a *shield?*" Slinger asked.

I looked back at him. My bones *clunked* as I stumbled on the stairs, then I looked forward again as we continued down. "It's a piece of armor made from wood and iron. The Minecraftians use them in battle to protect themselves from attacks. They hold it in one hand, like a weapon, but it's a piece of armor that they can move around."

"Hmm," the spider responded. His fangs ticked together, like he was contemplating my words. *Tick tick tick.* "If a Minecraftian used a *shield* to protect itself from *me*, I would just shoot a ball of *web* at it, and make the shield too heavy for it to lift up..."

"*That is a sound strategy, Slinger,*" Elias said.

The spider's hissing voice lit up. "You think so??" His fangs clicked. "*Thanks*, Elias!!"

I stopped, and the two of them quieted down and crowded up behind me.

313

Up ahead, the stairs ended, leveling out into a natural cavern—some sort of *cave*. The cobblestone walls transitioned into natural stone. I could see that past the last section of tunnel's ceiling, the top of the cavern opened up, revealing a larger room.

Listening, I only heard the sound of bats squeaking and fluttering around with their tiny wings in the dark.

"The end," I said.

"*It looks like the tunnel the Minecraftian was building intersected with a natural structure,*" Elias said in my head.

Why did I feel so *nervous??*

There would be nothing but other mobs down here—*friends* of mine!

My bones *clunked* as I continued down the stairs without a worry, and stepped into the stone opening. But when the cavern was visible to me— once I stepped down from the stairs—I was shocked to see that it wasn't a cave at all!

I stood in some sort of *structure*, cut and built into the stone underworld, not at all like the crisp and relatively clean cobblestone buildings of the Minecraftians, but something ... *older*.

Before me was the entrance to a *mine*. An ancient mine...

How did I even *know* that? What's *mining* to me? I'm a skeleton!

A flat-bottomed tunnel bore into the darkness ahead, barely tall enough for Elias to traverse, with old, wooden beams and posts built into the walls to shore up the sides. An ancient, rusting metal mine-cart track, bolted into the rough stone floor, led away into the unknown.

Loads and loads of cobwebs filled the mineshaft's ceilings and dark corners!

"What is this place??" I asked.

"*It does not look Minecraftian,*" Elias said. "*I see no cobblestone, and I have not seen mines supported by wooden structures like this. It is also dark, and full of the leavings of spiders, which I sense all around us. Small spiders...*"

"Wow!" Slinger exclaimed, scuttling into the tunnel. "What a *cool place!!* There are all *sorts* of great spots for an ambush!!"

"There's a *torch* way up there," I said, pointing with a boney finger to a spot of golden light up ahead. If we were to follow the metal track into the mine, we'd reach the torch.

"*I feel certain that whoever built this staircase stumbled onto this old place,*" Elias said.

I took a step onto the track, then began following the tunnel, dodging around the spider webs.

"Yeah, the *feel* of this place is *nothing* like the tower," I said.

As the three of us walked together down the tunnel, following the mine-cart track and weaving around the wooden beams and cobwebs, we watched and listened for any signs of the missing Minecraftian, or any mobs in general! When we reached the torch we saw from the stairs, I saw that a little *further* up ahead was some sort of ... *crossroads*.

"Hey, look!" I said, pointing and continuing to the junction.

My friends followed. Slinger was looking at the webs all around us as we walked, his many feet drumming on the stone floor.

"These webs are from *smaller* spiders," he said. "Smaller than *me*, anyway."

The crossroads was a four-way intersection of tunnels much like the one we were already in— shored up with wooden beams, dark, and full of spider webs. The metal track continued in the same direction it was going past the junction, and the *other* two directions had a bare, stone floor.

To the left, down a tunnel without the track, I saw the glow of another torch. The other two directions were dark. Looking back, I could see the base of the staircase fairly clearly, especially since there was a torch hanging from either side of the exit back to the surface.

"We have to be careful not to get lost," I said.

Elias nodded.

We continued to the left, toward the distance torchlight. I don't know what my *friends* were thinking, but I was curious to follow the path of the Minecraftian who had explored this place before us...

Several steps down the tunnel revealed another torch on the wall—the glow we saw from the junction.

Up ahead was another.

But when we reached the *next* torch, I saw something that was a little out of place in this old, abandoned mineshaft. The glow of the torch came from a *side room*, cut into the stone on the wall of the tunnel, hollowed out and built up from cobblestone.

"*Minecraftian*," Elias said.

The previous explorer had cut into the side of the tunnel several feet into the wall to carve out a room for himself, seemingly to store supplies, cook ore, and to build new items. Up against the back wall of the cobblestone room was a crafting table, two furnaces, and a large, wide wooden chest. In one corner of the room were splinters scattered on the floor, from something wooden being broken apart there.

"He must have had a *bed* here," I said, picking up a sliver of oak wood.

"*Correct*," Elias said. "*You remember the evidence of a bed from the tower...*"

I looked up at him and nodded, then made my way to the chest and furnaces.

"Any *food* in there??" Slinger asked, crowding up behind me.

I smirked, and opened the large chest with a *creak* that echoed down the tunnel behind us...

Stone. *Cobblestone*, to be exact, and lots of it!

There was also a pickaxe made of stone and wood, in good condition, and dozens of chips and shards of a red, crystalline substance I hadn't seen before. I passed a boney hand through it, and electricity crackled and flashed through the chips of red stuff as I did.

"What?!" I asked, scooping some of it up into my hand. "What's *this??*"

I held my hand up to Elias. His purple eyes glowed in his featureless black face, and he bent down to look at the stuff in my hand more closely. He didn't reach out to touch it.

"*I don't know,*" Elias said. "*A strange material—I have not seen it before. It appears to have its own inherent source of energy. Fascinating...*"

"Can I eat it?" Slinger asked, trying to see.

I pulled my hand back. "I don't think so," I said. "Something tells me that this would be *bad for your digestion.*" We laughed. Looking back in the chest, I saw that there was a pretty good-sized pile of the weird, red stuff. "I'm going to take some of it."

"*I will as well,*" Elias said. "*I will show it to my order and see if they know what it is.*"

The Enderman and I both took all of the red stuff. It crackled with energy as we moved it, *scoop by scoop*, into my pack and Elias's dimensional pocket.

I also took the stone pickaxe.

Looking into my pack, I saw that there was a lot of stuff in there! I was really starting to acquire quite a collection! There were apples, chunks of bread, three iron ingots, some baby trees (*saplings, I thought*), a ridiculous amount of arrows, courtesy of Elias and the Minecraftians, my wooden sword still covered with web-gunk, several torches, some sections of wooden ladder, a stone axe I captured from a Minecraftian noob, and now a pile of those strange, red shards and a stone pickaxe.

"I'm getting a lot of *stuff*," I said.

"*Me too*," Elias said. "*My Seed Stride is going very well. I have many Ender seeds...*"

My stomach, or where a stomach *would* be if I had one, suddenly felt cold.

I looked up at my friend.

"Does that mean you're ... *going* soon??"

Elias cocked his head, looking at me with his passive, unreadable face, his purple eyes glowing. He placed a long and slender black hand on my boney shoulder.

"*Not soon,*" he said. "*We still have much work to do, you and I.*"

"No food in there??" Slinger asked, poking the chest with a long spider leg. The lid fell shut, echoing a *boom* throughout the mineshaft.

"No," I said. I looked down the tunnel, the same direction we were headed before stopping off at this little Minecraftian hole-in-the-wall. "Shall we continue?"

Elias nodded, and I led the way down the dark tunnel, heading toward another glowing torch in the distance.

"*Help!*" a faint voice cried suddenly from far away.

We stopped.

"What was that?" I said.

322

"Someone said ... *help!*" Slinger replied, his fangs clicking.

"*Help!*"

There is was again, echoing through the mine.

It sounded like ... a *zombie*, maybe? The voice was thick and cottony, like the many undead voices I'd heard back at Zombietown. Was there a zombie in *trouble*, somewhere down in this mine?

"Help! Help me!" Its voice echoed through the tunnels.

Yep. Definitely a zombie.

"What is...?" I looked around at the faces of my friends, and then cried out loudly, "Where *are* you? We can help! Where are you??"

My voice echoed through the tunnels.

We listened.

"*The zombie is far away,*" Elias said. "*I cannot sense it, not yet...*"

A bat squeaked in the distance.

"Help!" the zombie cried.

We looked at each other again, then pressed on...

S1E4

4 – Lost

"Help!" the zombie cried from ... somewhere.

I stopped, and listened to the mob's voice echo through the tunnels, but still couldn't tell what direction the call was coming from.

We continued, following the Minecraftian's trail of torches, deeper and deeper into the mine.

Eventually, the tunnel we were in led to another junction, and the torches went off into two different directions. We turned onto a *new* path, still seeking out the glow of the torch trail, then, we came across *another* crossroads. Except this one also had a tunnel with stairs going down to another level of the mine...

We passed the stairs, and in time, crossed another mine-cart track, but continued following the torches instead.

Elias felt confident that we'd be able to find our way back, but I had lost track of direction a long time ago!

"Help!" the zombie shouted. His thick voice echoed through the tunnels around us.

"Where are you??" I called back. "We can't find you!!"

Slinger just followed along without a care in the world, admiring the many webs that lined the ceilings and wooden supports.

At one point, we even saw some of the smaller spiders! Following a track, heading to the torchlight we saw up ahead, we passed by a narrow passageway that led to a very dark open space with a wooden floor and wooden ceiling, and the cobwebs were as thick as the darkness, through and through.

That would have been a total *deathtrap* to any living creatures!

It was a good thing I was undead, and Elias was ... well ... *Elias*...

As we passed the opening into the web-infested lair, I saw a multitude of tiny, glowing green eyes staring back at me. Tiny fangs clicked together in the dark, and I heard chitinous shells brushing past each other.

Terrifying.

"Hi, there, little brothers!!" Slinger exclaimed as we passed, pausing to take a look.

A small spider that looked a lot like Slinger, only half his size, emerged from the darkness. Its green eyes were bright and fixed on us.

"I said *ahoy there*, my chitinous chum!" Slinger exclaimed.

The little spider turned and scuttled back into the safety of the webs. Many little green eyes blinked at us from the darkness. One small spider deep inside the nest let out a faint *hiss*.

Slinger shrugged his eight shoulders, and continued after us, his legs drumming on the stone floor.

"Weirdos," he said. "Those little guys don't get *out* much, I guess!"

"Help!" The zombie's cry echoed through the tunnels again.

"*I believe I can sense where he is*," Elias said.

"You can?" I asked.

"*Yes*," he replied. "*I will warp to him, and lead him back here. Continue on this path, and stay to the lit areas. I will find you again shortly*."

"Wait—what?!" I exclaimed. "We'll totally get lost!"

"*Stay to the torched path*," Elias repeated.

Zip.

In a puff of purple motes of Ender stuff, he was gone...

I looked down at Slinger, who stared back up at me with his glowing red eyes.

"Great," I said, and kept walking. Slinger followed.

After a while, the zombie called out again.

"Help!"

His dull voice echoed throughout the mine.

"Elias should have found him by *now*," I said.

"Maybe he got lost!" Slinger replied.

"Nah ... come on..."

Elias? Get lost? I supposed it *could* happen...

Of course, why would the Enderman ninja fear getting lost? He could just teleport back to the surface—couldn't he? But then, he'd have to come back down here and ... find *us*.

As we continued along the track, I saw another narrow opening in the tunnel coming up on the left again. More spiders?

Nope.

As we approached, I could see that this room was similar to the one infested with cave spiders, but *this* one was spider-free! As the narrow pathway opened up, I could see that the room was big and open, as dark as dark could be, and had a wooden plank floor and ceiling, just like the other strange room.

"What is this place?" I asked, stepping through the narrow hall toward the wooden room.

"*Hold it*, don't go in there!" Slinger said.

"Why not?"

"No torches! Elias said to stick to the *torched* path!"

I smirked, and stepped into the room.

My boney foot thumped on the wooden floor.

Oak.

I could see in the darkness just fine, but this room was very odd, and I was curious. The wooden floor and ceiling extended into other narrow

330

passageways leading away on the other three walls, all made of wood as well.

It was like a weird, wooden junction, but with extremely narrow tunnels leading away.

What in the world was this for? I thought, looking up to the dark ceiling and stepping into the center of the room.

It's as if it was the center of a great, big—

My foot landed in *air* where I expected a wooden floor, and my bones clattered as I wheeled my arms to catch my balance and *fell* through a small hole!!

"Ahh!!" I cried, tumbling through an opening in the wooden floor, down into darkness.

Crash!

In a heap of bones, I landed in a similar wooden room one level below.

Spider webs everywhere...

I could hear Slinger's feet drumming around on the wooden floor above me, scrambling to find me and wherever I disappeared to...

"Skeleton Steve!" the spider cried from above with a hiss.

Carefully, I struggled to my feet.

Okay, I thought. Not hurt too bad...

I picked up my bow.

"Skeleton Steve!" Slinger cried. "Where *are* you??"

"Help!" the zombie called out from somewhere in the mine, his voice echoing.

I looked up at the hole.

Wow, it was a good way *up* there!

"Slinger!" I called out. "I'm down here! I fell down a hole!"

I suddenly saw the spider's glowing red eyes appear in the hole in the wooden ceiling, previously the wooden *floor* I was standing on...

332

"Oh, holy smokes!" Slinger exclaimed through the hole. "Skeleton Steve! There you are! Are you okay??"

"Yeah," I said, looking around. Many of glowing green eyes looked back at me. "I'm on ... uh ... *another level*. Lots of cave spiders. I'm okay..."

"I'm gonna come and find you!" Slinger shouted.

"Can you send a web down through the hole or something? Lower yourself down?"

"Too small, I think," he said. "I'm gonna go back to the stairs we saw and come down to your level. Should be easy!"

"Wait!" I said. "I'll try to find my way up. You should wait up there for Elias!"

"No, it's okay!" Slinger said. "I'll find you—don't worry, Skeleton Steve! You can count on me!"

With that, his eight legs scrambled across the other side of the wooden ceiling, and he was gone.

I looked at the tiny, glowing green eyes around the room and laughed.

"Well," I said. "This isn't turning out very well, is it, little guys?"

The green eyes blinked back at me.

Brushing off my bones, I cinched up my pack, and walked out of the wooden room, toward where I figured I'd find another mining tunnel.

Everything was dark now.

Down here, there were no more torches. Either the Minecraftian never made it this deep into the mine, or he or she (or *they*) just passed through without leaving any light behind.

I had mixed feelings about the torches. Even though I didn't need the firelight to see in the dark, there was something comforting about having torches on the wall, something I couldn't quite put my boney finger on...

Then again, suddenly being in *total darkness* was very comfortable too, on a more *physical* level. The darkness didn't get in my way— I could see just fine. And without the light of the torches, my eyes felt a lot better, too. Being in the dark, like any other mob, was comforting in a *different* sort of way.

Man, I sure was one *mixed up* set of bones, wasn't I?

"Helloooo?" I called into the dark tunnel. My voice echoed forever, it seemed.

Bats squeaked.

"Elias?" I shouted. "Slinger?"

"Help!!" the zombie called back, his thick voice echoing, but ... was it *closer* now??

"Zombie!" I exclaimed. "Call out again!"

A pause.

"Help!"

Yes! I thought. *Definitely* closer!

Why, it sounded like he was right around the corner!

"Again!" I called, running down the tunnel, dodging around the wooden beams and webs. My bones *clunked*.

"Help!!" the zombie cried.

Louder. Closer. To the right.

At the next junction, I turned right, and saw the glow of torchlight in the distance.

"Elias!" I called. "Slinger!" My bones *clunked* as I ran. "I found him!! Come to me!!"

"Help!" the zombie shouted.

Up ahead and by the torches *for sure!*

As I approached the glowing light, I saw another room shoot off into the side of the tunnel, just like the Minecraftian's little, temporary 'bedroom' up above. *But no*, I thought, approaching the large cobblestone room carved into the stone. *Not the same*.

I found the source of the glow.

And it wasn't plain Minecraftian cobblestone! The room was made of cobblestone, *yes*, but it was *old* cobblestone, grown over with moss. In the center of it was something I'd seen before, back where I found Zenon the enlightened zombie in the undercity of Zombietown.

A *spawning* block.

Inside the little black cage in the center of the old cobblestone room was a blazing fire, and inside that fire was a tiny figurine of a zombie, flailing and dancing and twirling about on the whims of the flame...

Torches were placed all around the spawner, hammered into the cobblestone, lashed to the spawner itself—*eight* different torches placed hastily around the area.

"What the heck?!" I said, circling around the strange device.

"Help!" the zombie cried, and I could tell that his voice was on the other side of the cobblestone wall.

"Where are you?" I asked, walking up to the wall where I heard the voice.

"Help!! Help me!!" the zombie repeated, his voice muffled behind the cobblestone, but also echoing through the tunnel behind me.

Weird, I thought.

I felt along the cobblestone with a boney hand. It was solid.

What could I do?

"Are you stuck in the wall??" I asked.

"Help!" the zombie replied.

I sighed, looked into my pack, and pulled out the stone pickaxe.

Putting my bow on the floor and hefting the Minecraftian tool in my right hand, I shrugged, and pounded the pointy end into the wall.

Thunk!

Several cracks bloomed from my hit on the wall where I struck it.

"Huh," I said, looking over the pickaxe.

The tool was still fine. It didn't take any damage, as far as I could see.

"Uh ... stand back!" I said.

"Help!"

I smirked, then wound up my arm, and started pounding on the wall in the same place, hitting it again and again with the pickaxe! Cracks spread out from my target, then, cobbled pieces of rock in the wall started to fall off in chunks, and before long, the entire block crumbled away!

Picking up the piece of cobblestone I harvested, I looked it over and smiled, then threw it behind me.

Looking inside the hole in the wall, I saw the dark green skin and light blue shirt of a zombie. The undead mob's head turned, and he looked at me with full, dark eyes.

"*Hi!*" the zombie exclaimed. "I'm stuck!!"

"I see that," I said. "How'd you get there?"

The zombie shrugged and made an 'I don't know' sound. "You get me out??"

"Uh ... sure. Stand back," I said.

Using the pickaxe, I cut another hole in the wall, demolishing the block of mossy cobblestone that covered the zombie's legs. Once he was able, the undead mob sprang from his tomb in the wall, and began plodding around the spawner with a huge grin on his face.

"Thanks!" he said, his voice thick.

"How did your voice *echo* throughout the whole mine?" I asked.

The zombie shrugged. "I dunno," he said, and walked off, plodding down the mine tunnel.

"Uh ... *bye*, I guess..."

Approaching the hole in the wall, I stuck my head into the area where the zombie was trapped. How did he even *get* there? I remembered back to when I was talking to Zenon, how the zombies appeared quite suddenly from that 'spawner' in puffs of smoke. Did he just *spawn* into this cavity behind the wall?

It was just a *cavity*, alright—barely big enough for the zombie's body.

Then, I looked up, and my jawbone gaped open.

"Whoa..." I said, my voice echoing.

Above where the zombie's head was, I saw a tiny tunnel that led to a huge open space—some sort of massive cavern or underground *ravine*. It was a hole, not big enough for the zombie to fit through to escape, but *certainly* big enough to project his *voice* into the entire cave on the other side...

Using the pickaxe, I carved open the hole enough to let me climb up out of the mine and into the massive cavern. I could now see that the open space stretched *on and on*, up into darkness, and farther ahead than I could make out from this vantage point.

Here and there, throughout the darkness of the cavern, I could see glowing spots where torches lit up their immediate areas, and I could also see connecting sections of the *mine*, exposed to the open space!

S1E4
5 – The Portal

"Hellooo!" I called into the underground ravine, listening to the echo of my voice bounce around throughout the cavern and the mine complex...

Putting away the pickaxe, I smirked, cinched down my pack and bow, and climbed up into the huge cave.

I could hear the sound of trickling water from around a corner, and the squeaking of bats all around and far above echoed around me.

What a huge space! I thought.

Far ahead, across the cavern, a dozen feet or so above the ravine's floor, I saw the wooden beams of the mineshaft. There was a section of mine, wooden floors, mine-cart track, beams, cobwebs and a single, lit torch, just *passing through* a part of the huge cave's wall. Anyone walking along the tunnel there would suddenly find themselves looking out at *me*, with a great view of this big cavern!

As I looked around, I could see *another* section of tunnel of the mine-cart rack crossing the ravine even higher, its wooden floor acting like a bridge, supported by oak beams, all plastered with spider webs. The glow of a torch emerged from the tunnel boring into the rock wall on one side...

"Slinger!" I shouted. "Elias!!"

My voice echoed back and forth loudly. It probably passed through the tunnels of the mine just like the zombie's cries for help did.

What could I do from *here?*

I looked at the stone walls of the dark ravine. Could I maybe climb up onto one of those mine tunnels? Maybe if I could find a good enough place to climb, could I even get up to that *higher level?*

Walking out into the ravine, my bones *clunked* and echoed across the open, cold space...

The inside of the mountain, I thought. *Who knows* how deep underground I was...?

"Elias!!" I shouted again. "I'm in a *big cave!* Can you *hear* me??"

My voice echoed across the cavern.

Water dripped and dribbled nearby.

I heard a *hiss*, which echoed around me, and I looked up to the nearest tunnel.

There, emerging from the dark mine tunnel a dozen feet above the ravine floor, lit up by the golden light of the torch on a wooden post, was the head of a curious spider. Its many red eyes gleamed in the firelight, and its fangs clicked and rubbed back and forth on each other.

I felt a chill...

"Slinger?" I asked, my voice echoing. "Is that you?"

The spider perked up and stepped further out onto the exposed section of mine-track.

"Skeleton Steve!" the spider said. "There you are!! What are you doing in a *cave??*"

Yep. Slinger.

I relaxed as the large arachnid climbed over the edge of the wooden track floor, and descended the rock wall to the bottom of the ravine, the thumps of his spider feet reverberating across the cave.

"Hey!" I said with a smile, approaching. "I *found* the zombie!"

"You did?" Slinger asked, leveling out on the stone floor of the cavern. His spider head pivoted around, and he looked over the large, dark space. "What a *cool cave!* Where was he?"

"Back there," I said, jerking a boney thumb over my shoulder. "Stuck in a wall behind a spawner. Have you seen *Elias?*"

"Nope," Slinger said. "Those stairs led to a whole 'nother area. I've been looking for you for a *while!* Good thing you were out *here* when I passed by the cave!!"

I pointed at the lower section of mine he came from. "So that's the level under the stairs??"

"No," the spider replied. "Went up another staircase trying to circle around to where you fell."

"Jeez," I said. "This place is a *maze*..."

"You got *that* right." Slinger said, looking back over his shoulders at where the ravine led off into the dark. "Wanna see where *this* goes?"

"I guess, sure," I said. "I bet it connects with the mine again farther down."

Slinger looked up at the wooden bridge far overhead.

"*Or*," the spider said, "Maybe you should jump on my back and we head *up there!* That's closer to where we came in, I bet. Maybe *Elias* is up there!"

His voice echoed through the cavern as I thought about it.

"Yeah, that's a *better* idea," I said. "Let's go up there. Obviously the Minecraftian's already been there too. Maybe the torches keep going..."

Slinger sank down low to the stone floor and creeped over, close to me. When I climbed up onto his back and settled my boney legs in between his, the spider suddenly *vaulted* into action, scuttling across the cavern floor, then up the rocky wall!

I held on tightly as Slinger climbed higher and higher with his eight, sprawling legs. Tiny chunks of rock showered down to the cavern floor as he clawed his way up the wall.

"Holy cow!" I exclaimed.

"Wish you were a spider??" Slinger asked, his fangs ticking, as I watched the wooden bridge get closer and closer...

Eventually, my spider friend reached the edge of the bridge, and pulled himself over. We ended up standing on a mine-cart track that crossed the ravine, surrounded by wooden beams and spider webs. The tunnel extended on both sides of the cavern, and one side had a torch in the wall a little ways in from the ravine wall's edge.

"Wow," I said, looking down over Slinger's body at the ravine below. My voice echoed across the open space. Looking up, I could see the *top* now, which ended in a dark stone ceiling alive with fluttering bats!

"Elias!!" Slinger called, his hissing voice reverberating across the ravine and through the tunnels.

"Elias!!" I shouted, my voice echoing just the same.

I rode on Slinger down the tunnel, past the torch. We passed the lit-up area, and continued to the next glowing source of light farther ahead. After barely ducking out of the way of several cobwebs and a few wooden beams, I climbed off of the spider's back, and proceeded on foot.

The tunnel went on and on, like all of the others, and we continued following from one torch to the next.

"Maybe this *won't* lead back to the stairs," I said.

"It goes *somewhere*," Slinger said. "There are torches, right?"

"Yeah, I guess."

"*There you two are,*" Elias said into my mind suddenly.

I looked around quickly, but didn't see the Enderman.

"Elias!" we both said together, then laughed.

"*I have heard you calling out through the tunnels, but have not been in range to respond until now. It sounds like you found the zombie...*"

"Where *are* you??" I asked. "I don't see you!"

"*I am close by,*" the Enderman ninja replied, in my head. "*Continue down the tunnel until the next junction, then, turn left. That will take you to me...*"

"What are you doing? Come and join up with us!"

"*No*," Elias replied. "*Come to me. There is something interesting here that you should see...*"

"I hope it's food," Slinger said.

I smirked.

We continued along the tunnel. Eventually, I saw the junction up ahead, lit up brightly with several torches. As we approached, I could see that the tunnel perpendicular to ours was lit up with *a lot more light* than the other tracks we'd been following—there was a torch every few steps!

This must be an important tunnel!

"Shhh!" Slinger said suddenly, hissing as he shushed me. "Do you hear *that?*"

I listened.

"What?"

"*Shhh!!* Listen!"

At first I didn't hear anything. *Man*, I thought. Slinger sure must be a *cunning predator* with senses like that! It was a good thing I was an undead mob, and not something he considered *food*. Well, he *thought* about considering me food at first...

And then I heard it.

There was a low *hum*—a deep drone that warbled and vibrated in my bones a little. Very faint, but definitely not a normal sound of the mine. At least, not what we've been hearing up until now...

"What is *that?*" I asked. "I hear it!"

"Probably what Elias found, Slinger said. "Let's check it out!" The big spider sped off toward the junction, taking a left down the well-lit tunnel. "Whoa!" he exclaimed from around the corner.

I rushed to catch up. My bones *clunked*.

When I turned the corner, I saw a strange purple light emanating from a distance down the tunnel. At first, I thought it was Elias, but it wasn't. Shading my eyes against the glare of the many torches, I peered closer, and saw a *rectangle* of deep black...

352

"What??" I said softly to myself, then ran after Slinger toward the oddity.

Once I had left the junction a good ways behind, I approached the area with the strange object, and saw the long, tall shadow of Elias step in front of the eerie, purple field of moving light.

"*Skeleton Steve*," my Enderman friend said into my head. "*I found a Nether Portal.*"

Slinger cautiously approached the purple light in between the thick rectangular frame of deep, black blocks, but stopped himself *just shy* of touching the warping, wobbly sheet of magic portal-stuff.

"What *is* it?" I asked, stepping closer.

"*This is a portal to the third dimension of this universe,*" Elias responded. "*Do you remember when I told you about the three realms? There is this world—the Overworld. There is also The End, where I come from. There is also the third world—The Nether. This portal will take us there...*"

I watched the shimmering field of purple light for a moment. The portal emitted a constant and powerful low *hum* that vibrated my bones and warbled randomly.

What a spooky thing...

I looked up at Elias. "Um ... *will* take us there??"

Elias's purple eyes glowed, and I could swear that he was smiling inside, even though his face was blank.

"*Yes, Skeleton Steve,*" he said. "*This is a rare find, and it is a good opportunity to see if anything we see ... in the Nether ... will help to bring back your memories. We should take this opportunity to explore it—even just a little.*"

I felt a shiver go up my spine, and my bones *clunked*.

Reaching up to the bow on my shoulder, I felt along wooden limb of the weapon. It comforted me.

"Have you been there before?" I asked.

"*I have not,*" Elias said. "*But my people visit there regularly. I haven't bothered yet, until now.*"

"Okay," I said, looking at the portal. "What are those black stones?"

"*Obsidian*."

"Maybe that's where the Minecraftian went, and ... didn't come back?"

"*Perhaps*," the Enderman said. "*Although he obviously left the tower behind long ago*."

"Well, *what the heck*," I said. "I guess it's not every day we find a *Nether Portal*, right??"

I stared into the wobbly, warbling purple light. The low hum vibrated the tiny bones in my skull.

"I hope the *Minecraftian* is in there," Slinger said, his fangs clicking.

"Why?" I asked.

"Because I'm *starving!*"

Season 1, Episode 5:
Into the Nether

Into the Nether!

While exploring the abandoned Mineshaft under the Mysterious Tower in the last episode, Skeleton Steve and his friends found an imposing Nether Portal, left behind by the tower's previous owner! When Elias the Enderman ninja convinces our hero to visit the Nether to see if it will bring back memories, it seems like a good idea at the time, right?

But when the portal is snuffed out by a Wither's FIREBALL in the hellish dimension, how will the trio of adventurers manage to get home? A Magma Cube with a problem offers a solution, but will Skeleton Steve's Nether Adventure prove too much for him and his friends to handle?

S1E5
1 – Into the Nether

The ancient mineshaft was quiet around me except for the warbling, low moan of the *Nether Portal* vibrating my bones, and the faint crackling of torches...

"*Are you ready?*" Elias asked into my head. He must have included my spider friend, Slinger, in the conversation too, because the arachnid immediately answered.

"Yeah!" Slinger said. "Let's *go!* Maybe we'll find a Minecraftian to eat!"

My bones *clunked* as I considered the portal.

A huge rectangular frame of obsidian blocks stood at the end of this tunnel—a long and dusty stone corridor shored up with wooden beams and well-lit by dozens of Minecraftian torches. Whatever Minecraftian—or Minecraftian*s*—built the mysterious tower above us, long abandoned it seemed, must have built *this portal* here on purpose.

As deep underground as we were, there would be no way to hear this uncomfortable and constant *low drone* of the portal's magical purple field from up above in the tower.

Whoever built this place must have been very happy to discover the old, abandoned mineshaft that intersected the descending cobblestone staircase they were excavating down to the bedrock...

Bats squeaked nearby.

"Wait," I said.

My Enderman ninja companion looked down at me, his purple eyes glowing. Those eyes were the same color as the portal's warping magical field, stretching across the inside of the obsidian blocks.

Come to think of it, I thought, the portal was also throwing off the same purple motes of *Ender stuff* that Elias always left behind whenever he teleported!

Interesting.

Was the magic of the portal and the technology of the Ender people to warp around ... somehow related?

"*What's the matter?*" Elias asked in my mind. Slinger hissed next to me, his eight feet drumming on the stone floor in impatience.

"Umm..." I said. "What's going to be on the other side? What can we expect??"

"*Well,*" Elias said, peering into the twisting, shifting purple field of light. "*Like I said, I have not actually been there before.*" He looked back at me. "*But I have seen ... images ... from other Ender who have. The Nether dimension is hot, and red all over, and full of flames and lava. There are a variety of mobs that call the plane their home, all of them comfortable in the flames. From what I understand, the terrain is varied, and we should be okay if you watch your step. Since you cannot warp like me, you will have to be careful to avoid falling into ... dangerous situations—just like a Minecraftian would.*"

"What about the creatures that *live* there?" I asked. "Will they attack us?"

"*I do not see why they would,*" Elias replied. "*My people travel through the Nether frequently without any trouble. They are mobs just like you are. Although, I cannot recall any accounts of Overworld skeletons ever being seen there before. The skeletons there, in the Nether, are not like you...*"

I didn't know why I was so uncomfortable with the idea of going through the portal. Maybe because I didn't build the portal myself? Because I wasn't prepared or *intending* to go through before we found it?

But why? I thought. Why does that matter?

Why did the idea of visiting the Nether seem so ... dangerous??

They were mobs just like me, after all...

Just like my fear of caves, I thought.

Why was I so nervous about *other* mobs??

"Not like me?" I asked.

Slinger hissed, clicked his fangs, and drummed his legs again next to me.

"Come oooon!" the spider said. "I'm *hungry!* Let's get *moving!*"

"*They are different,*" Elias said. "*Taller. Stronger. They're also imbued with some sort of magic that I do not understand.*"

"I don't know why you think you're going to be *eating* anything there, Slinger!" I shouted. "Whatever Minecraftian went through here is *long gone!* He might be lost or dead on the other side, or he might have come back out and moved away and built a new tower somewhere else *years ago!*"

Slinger's fangs clenched together, and he looked up at me with his many red eyes wide. He blinked.

"*Sorry*, Skeleton Steve," the spider said. "I'm just ... you know ... I'm *hungry!*"

I put a boney hand on his back.

"Sorry for snapping at you," I said. "I'm just a little *nervous* I guess. Let's *do* this..."

I already had my bow in my hand, so I reached into my pack, and pulled out an arrow. Cinching my pack on tight and making sure my helmet was snug, I set the arrow on the string, and stepped up to the purple field of light.

The low moan made the tiny bones in my skull vibrate...

"*Just step inside*," Elias said. "*I'll be right behind you.*"

Looking up and around at the magical, warping field of energy, my bones *clunked* as I took a step forward. When my body splashed into the purple field, I didn't *feel* anything, but I could see the purple light taking over all of my vision, and hear the warbling moan more loudly than before, swallowing me up as if I was underwater!

"*Oh, one last thing,*" Elias said into my head, his *mind voice* wobbling as the world shifted around me. "*Do not attack the pigmen. No matter what...*"

"Oh, boy!" Slinger exclaimed, his voice faint and far away. "Let's go!" The sound of the spider and the crackling torches of the mineshaft faded away, and all I could hear was the weird drone of the portal as the world around me rippled and shifted into a purple haze...

And with an audible *pop*, all of the warping in my vision and my hearing was suddenly *gone*, and I was on solid ground again!

Emerging from the magical purple field that swam around my eyes, I stepped down onto a strange ground, and saw that the world around me was dark and red. I was suddenly aware of a *new* set of natural sounds—instead of the constant noises of bats and torches and wind that I never really noticed anymore, I now heard (*aside from the moan of the portal*) the sounds of crackling fire, bubbling and spitting lava, and...

A strange, whining cry rang through the air, filling me with an irrational sense of *fear*.

"What was *that??*" I said to myself, and my voice sounded strange in the other dimension's air.

I took another step, and realized that the ground was a little ... spongy. Looking down, it appeared that the entire terrain under my boney feet and around me was like ... flesh?

Meat?

Skin and meat?

Wild!

Some of it was on fire...

The portal's warbling groan became louder behind me suddenly, and I looked back to see Elias's tall and slender shadow forming in the purple magic-stuff.

Pop!

My Enderman friend appeared out of the purple field, his blue headband almost black in the weird ambient light of the Nether.

Pop!

Slinger emerged from the portal after him, and the obsidian gateway's drone died down to a low *hum*...

"Holy smokes!" the spider said, his hissing voice a little lost in the heavy, acrid air.

That scary, whining *cry* rang through the air again, like nails on a chalkboard in my skull. This time it seemed to call out to us in a high pitch...

"Aaaa .. Ooooooohhhh...?"

"What *is* that?!" I asked.

Elias stepped out onto the weird flesh-stuff and looked around. His purple eyes glowed brighter than normal in the dim, red light. He took a few long strides away from the portal.

I followed, looking all around.

The entire area was like a monstrous *cave*—much larger and more open than *any* of the huge, underground cavities I'd seen on the Overworld—and the strange, fleshy ground and twisting, convoluted terrain made it hard for me to understand how everything was laid out. I could see, looking up at the cavernous ceiling, that other rifts and gaping holes led to more large open areas above. Far ahead, I could see that we were on some sort of ... raised peninsula? Past that, tall and jagged cliffs extended all around us, all bathed in the orange glow of whatever ground was far down below...

Clusters of strange, glowing pods hung from the ceilings far above the ground, and patches of the meat-rock stuff were on fire here and there, the constant flames crackling and licking upwards, casting shadows and red glow everywhere in a confusing pattern...

"Where are we?" Slinger asked. "Some sort of ledge??" His arachnid feet drummed on the squishy ground, then he paused for a moment. "Gross!!" the spider exclaimed suddenly. "It *looks* like meat, but doesn't *smell* like meat, and doesn't *taste* like it either!"

I turned back to look at him.

"You *tasted* the ground??"

"Sure!" he exclaimed. "It could have been—
"

We were interrupted when a *huge* creature suddenly appeared from the edge of whatever platform we were on! It was *monstrous*—a pale creature, as big as a house in Zombietown, floating up from below! Large, black eyes as big as windows sat in stark contrast to its ghostly white face, eyes gunked up with some sort of *ichor* slime. The pale grey junk smothering its eyes ran down its face in streaks of slimy tears. As the creature climbed in the air just a dozen feet away from us, I could see that several flabby, white tentacles trailed along behind it, hovering and swinging in the air...

I gasped as its eyes burst open, flinging grey slime around its face, and it opened its mouth with a deafening *shriek*, spitting a chunky ball of flaming ichor straight at us!!

"Whoa!!" I cried, diving out of the way, stumbling down the slope of fleshy rock, desperate to dodge the fiery projectile zipping toward us! I saw Slinger scrambling to get out of the way just the same, and in that second, looking over to Elias, I saw *nothing*.

Where the Enderman ninja was standing just an instant before, all I saw were motes of purple Ender dust drifting down to the ground...

BOOM!!

The massive floating creature's fireball *exploded* next to the portal, sending chunks of the meat stuff flying. I fell to the ground, my bones clattering, and barely managed to avoid the blast. Pieces of ground-flesh showered down onto me.

The monster whined again, its strange cry loud and grating to my skull so close by...

"Stop!!" I cried out to it. "Don't shoot!!"

Raising my head, bow ready, arrow nocked, I looked around.

We were surrounded by fire. The ground was burning all around where the fireball had hit, choking the air with acrid smoke. The monster hung in the air above us.

It's ready to attack us again, I thought, and I raised my bow...

"*No!*" Elias said into my head suddenly. "*It's okay! Relax! It was just an accident. Don't shoot, Skeleton Steve!*"

"I'm okay!!" I head Slinger exclaim cheerfully from somewhere behind the portal.

The monster opened its mouth again, and I saw rows of small teeth as it spoke with a voice that was screeching and grating on my bones.

"I'm *sooooorry!*" it cried too loudly. "I thought you were one of the *oooothers!!*"

The creature closed its massive eyes again, and slimy, grey tears poured down its face!

I looked around for Elias, then saw his dark form standing on top of the portal frame. He was looking at the creature, probably engaged in some sort of telepathic conversation. When I heard the sudden sound of many feet plopping around on the foul, meaty ground next to me, I looked over, and saw Slinger rushing to my side.

"Skeleton Steve!" the spider exclaimed. "Are you alright? *Holy smokes*, that thing almost blew us up!!"

"Well I'm *soooooorry,* I said!" the monster cried out again in a loud whine. "I didn't *meeeean* it! *Jeeeeeez!!*"

The creature turned slowly, and started drifting away, sobbing loudly to itself. Grey, slime tears dripped down into the Nether air around it as the monster floated away.

Fires crackled around me—the blaze of the burning meat-ground was almost all I could hear. I eased up on the arrow in my bow.

Zip.

Elias appeared next to us suddenly, and stamped out the flames that had spread onto the ground right next to me. Little motes of purple light drifted down around him.

I stood.

The sound of another Ghast whining off in the distance somewhere made me jump. My bones *clunked.*

"Yeah," I said, looking down at Slinger. "*I'm* okay. What was that thing?!" I asked, turning to my Enderman friend.

"*That was a Ghast,*" he said. "*A very large mob—difficult to converse with. Lost souls, trapped in their own over-indulgent emotions...*"

"Wow," I said. "Well, it's a good thing we ended up *okay* from that. I guess the Ghast must have thought I was a *Minecraftian* or something...?"

"*Yes,*" Elias said. "*That is what I gathered from its mind. But now we have a bigger problem.*"

"What?"

The Enderman pointed back to the portal, and I realized that amidst the crackling of the flames, a particular sound we had been hearing up until now was suddenly *absent*...

Standing tall and dark on the meaty ground, the obsidian frame of the Nether Portal wasn't harmed *at all* by the explosion. But the magical field of purple light that was *inside* it—the way we would get back home when we were done here— was *gone!*

The portal's magic had been *snuffed out* by the Ghast's fireball.

I looked at Elias, then at Slinger, then back to the dead portal again, my jawbone gaping...

S1E5
2 – What Are We Gonna Do??

"The portal!!" I exclaimed.

"What's the matter—*ohhh*..." Slinger said. "The *purple stuff* is gone!"

"*Indeed*," Elias replied. "*The fireball killed the gateway. That presents us with a complication.*"

We were stuck here.

Trapped on this nasty, oily meat-world with terrible and dangerous mobs! I suddenly thought about the vivid green grasslands, the blue sky, the wind blowing through thick, rustling trees...

"Complication?!" I exclaimed. "You said everything would be fine!!"

"*We can solve this puzzle,*" Elias said. "*It is a minor setback—calm yourself, Skeleton Steve...*"

"Yeah, relax, buddy!" Slinger said. "Elias *knows* this place ... *right?*"

"What complication??" I asked. "Now we're *stuck* here, right? Is that what I'm to understand? No portal means *no way home*, right? Not for *us* anyway..."

"*That is true*," Elias said, folding his long arms together. "*But fear not, my friend. I will not leave you. We will find a way to activate the portal again.*"

"Come on, Skeleton Steve!" Slinger exclaimed. "I mean—how could Elias have known that a Ghast would have *freaked out* and blown up the portal? It's not *his* fault!"

I didn't know why, but for some reason, I *hated* this place! I couldn't stand the meaty floor, the fires and the smell of the oil and smoke. Staggering back away from the dead portal and my friends, I looked at the bow in my hands.

Something about *the Nether* felt very *wrong* to me...

"*Calm down, Skeleton Steve!*" Elias repeated. "*There is no need to fear! Trust in me! Stop backing up—you're going to—*"

"Stop!!" Slinger cried, and sprinted toward me, his eight legs pummeling the ground. *"Don't back up!* You're gonna—"

I stopped, turned around, and gasped, dropping the arrow I was holding.

Before me was the edge of the platform we were on. If I'd taken one or two more steps, I would have...

The arrow hit the fleshy ground, bounced, and fell off of the edge.

In front of me, over the rim of the platform, was a *massive ocean of lava*, glowing and burning and bubbling, a hundred feet or more below us, extending as far as I could see...

"Oh ... my ... *lava*..." I stammered.

Slinger appeared suddenly between my body and the edge, grasping at the meaty ground with his eight legs and pushing me back.

"Please be calm, Skeleton Steve," Elias said. *"We'll get through this. We will get you back home."*

"What is this—an island??" Slinger asked.

An island? my mind repeated.

What?!

"*Yes,*" the Enderman replied. "*We're on a floating island off of that peninsular there,*" he said, pointing off into a direction that didn't mean anything to me. "*That is where we will connect to the mainland. We may be able to find a way to reactivate the portal in the fortress.*"

I shook my skull, trying to snap myself out of the stupor of denial I was stuck in.

"Fortress??" I asked.

"*Yes,*" Elias said. "*Come and see. Do not worry, Skeleton Steve! I will see us through this.*"

As I walked back toward the middle of the island, Slinger followed behind me, giving me an initial *push* to make sure I didn't fall back toward the edge again.

How did I miss the fact that we were surrounded by an *ocean of lava* before??

Oh yeah, I thought. I *didn't*. Not really...

The way the light played through the air in the Nether was strange and disorienting. *Sound* also traveled differently—muffled and thick. But from the middle of the 'island' next to the portal, I could see a distinct orange *glow* coming up from below, as I noticed before, but I hadn't gone *close* to the edge until after we were attacked by the Ghast...

"Where?" I asked, following the Enderman across the fleshy ground.

We stopped, past the portal, near another edge of the island. I saw the ocean of lava appear below us as we neared the end of the platform. Vast, burning, and deadly...

Elias pointed into the distant darkness.

I peered into the shadows of the Nether, trying to see through the glare of the lava and the smoke...

There was some sort of *structure*, or the *silhouette* of it anyway, barely visible in the distance!

A castle? I could see multiple square towers, rising up out of the lava near the distant shore, a least a *couple hundred feet* above the burning magma, all supported by tall, thin pillars and ... a *bridge!* A long, black bridge reached from the fortress across an extreme distance of lava and rocky shores—presumably the same fleshy stuff as the ground under our feet—until it connected with the cliffs of the shores to its left.

From where Elias showed me the peninsula connecting to the mainland, it looked like we'd have to follow a ring of cliffs around the shores of the lava ocean, on and on, curving around to the right, until we could finally reach the bridge to the distant and complex Nether Fortress...

At least he had a plan...

"Alright," I said. "So if this is an *island*, how do we get across?"

We all walked over toward the point of the island Elias recognized as being closest to the peninsula that connected with the shore-cliffs.

As I stepped toward the edge, my bones *clunked*.

Down below, the lava ocean bubbled and burned, sending oily black smoke up toward us...

The nearest section of land was at least ... ten or so feet away?

Definitely a respectable gap.

We were truly on a *floating island* of meat rock, a big chunk of fleshy land hovering a *hundred feet or so* above a burning sea of magma...

"How is this even *possible??*" I said quietly to myself.

There was *no way* I could get across. Elias could just teleport, but *me??*

Zip.

As if hearing my thoughts, the Enderman warped across the gap, his trail of purple Ender dust drifting down toward the orange glow of the lava...

"No problem!!" Slinger exclaimed, looking up at me. His red eyes glinted, and his fangs clicked. "We can do it! Hop on!!"

I scoffed.

"Are you *kidding?!*"

Elias watched us silently from the other side.

"I've *got* this, Skeleton Steve!" the spider said. "I can make that jump *easy!*"

"Okay," I said, trying to laugh. What *else* could I do? "Don't miss!"

I climbed onto Slinger's thorax like I'd done several times already by now, cinching down my pack, and slinging my bow over my shoulder. With my boney hands, I gripped his largest shoulders as tightly as I could.

"Here we go!" Slinger exclaimed, breaking into a sprint, all eight legs pumping and clawing at the fleshy ground, and the spider gave a mighty *push*, and I felt the wind in my face as he leapt across the gap with me on his back...

382

For a moment, we were flying through the air a hundred feet over a brightly burning sea of lava...

And then, Slinger landed on the ground on the other side!

I realized that I was holding my breath, and let out a big sigh...

"See?" Slinger said, scuttling away from the edge toward Elias. "No problem!"

When he stopped, I climbed off, pulling my bow again.

"Good jump!" I said, looking back. I could now clearly see the island with the portal, floating in the acrid air with a fleshy, tapering tail hanging down below it.

The cliffs we were on followed the shores of the burning sea up ahead as far as we could perceive. I knew, from what we saw on the island, that *eventually* up ahead was the bridge to the fortress!

Fires on the spongy red ground around us played crazy shadows around me, and made seeing the surrounding land difficult. What a confusing, terrifying place!!

Elias watched me, his face blank, his purple eyes glowing, and I wondered what he was thinking...

The Enderman ninja's eyes suddenly darted to an area behind me. Elias turned to face whatever he was looking at with the same calm demeanor he always had.

I heard a crunchy *squishing* sound, and turned to look behind me as well...

Out of the fires and shadows, I saw something *glowing* heading our way. Whatever it was, it jumped up into the air, then fell back down again, closer, with another crunchy *squish!*

"Whoa!!" Slinger said, scuttling away to the side as if preparing for battle...

It was a large *block* of a creature. With its last jump, I could suddenly see it more clearly. The mob glowed orange and red like lava, and was surrounded by a black ... *crust*. Two bright and burning eyes blazed in the front of its face!

The creature jumped up again, stretching its entire body out with its leap...

Lava. Definitely lava. As the mob flew through the air, its crusty skin split open, and I could see the burning hot magma inside! It hit the ground again with a crunchy *splat* sound, and its whole body squished up like a *spring* before bouncing back into place.

Only its *eyes* remained unchanged, fixated on *me*.

It was some sort of amorphous creature—a *blob* made from burning lava!

I scrambled for an arrow, and backed away.

"Peace!" the cube-like blob cried out. Its voice was gravelly and harsh like it was made from ... well ... constantly changing *molten rock*. "No fight! I just want to *talk!*"

"*It is a Magma Cube, Skeleton Steve,*" Elias said into my mind, walking up behind me and putting a long, slender hand on my shoulder. "*I do not sense a coming attack*..."

The Magma Cube leapt again, closer, and landed with a *crunch*.

I could feel the *heat* pouring off of it...

Slinger approached to stand by my side again.

"Hi there," I said. "I'm Skeleton Steve. From ... the *Overworld*, I guess."

The lava mob stopped near us, its gelatinous body waving and bouncing, then settling down. It blinked with burning eyes.

"Greetings, Skeleton Steve," it said with its gravelly magma voice. "I am *Milo*."

"Good to meet you, Milo the Magma Cube," I said, nodding. I started to reach out to shake hands, but stopped myself. Not only did the cube not *have* any hands, but my own boney hand would probably *burst into flames* if I touched him!

"I saw what happened," Milo said. "With your *portal* going out..."

"*Are you aware of a way to reactivate the portal, Milo?*" Elias asked. "*We were about to walk to the fortress to seek help...*"

"Talking *in my head*, eh? Interesting!! To the *fortress*, eh?" Milo asked. "I *do* know of a way to reactivate the portal, yes. I've seen it happen with the Minecraftians before. I can help you—"

"You saw the *Minecraftians* come through?" Slinger asked. "Where'd they go??"

The Magma Cube's glowing eyes shifted to the spider. "The Minecraftian from the other side of the portal passed through a *long* time ago," Milo said, then looked back at me.

"How can we do it?" I asked. "How do we get back home??"

"I'll *tell* you if you help me," Milo replied. "Since you're going to the fortress *anyway*..."

"*How can we assist you, Milo?*" Elias asked. "*What does it have to do with the fortress?*"

"It's my *brother*," the Magma Cube responded. "I lost my brother in the fortress. Milo and I were separated there, and I need help to find him..."

"Milo?" I asked.

"Yes?" Milo said.

"No, I mean, you said your *brother*, Milo?"

"Yes, that's right," the Magma Cube said.

"You mean you ... *and* your brother ... are *both* named *Milo?*" I asked.

"Yes," the lava cube said. "*We* are Milo."

"Sure, we'll help you find your brother!" Slinger said. "How do we get home?"

Milo looked at the spider, then back at me. "I will go with you to the fortress. When you help me find my brother, I will tell you a way you can reactivate the portal. *Deal?*"

I looked at Elias. He was watching me, his eyes glowing purple, his blank face unreadable.

My decision.

Elias sure was letting me take the lead a lot lately. I wondered why...

I heard some grunting noises suddenly, and looked off to see several zombie-sized forms moving around in the distance. I saw the shadows of swords in their hands.

Looking back to the Magma Cube, I nodded. "Okay, Milo. Deal. Let's go find your brother..."

Pssssst!!
Liking the story? Don't forget to join my Mailing List! I'll send you *free books* and stuff! (www.SkeletonSteve.com)

S1E5
3 – The Shores of Fire

We followed along the outer rim of the lava ocean, sometimes together as a *group*, sometimes single-file, depending on how the terrain changed. As we made our way, Milo the Magma Cube hopped along behind us. The lava blob's *swooping* and *splatting* sounds of jumping and landing were very loud. *He must be very heavy*, I thought.

After a while, we started descending as the cliff became more of a slope, and I could see the island behind us and the peninsula leading to it stretching out into the darkness, high above the lava, over my shoulder.

What a crazy place!

My mind was certainly more *centered* now. When we first stepped into the Nether from the portal, and were almost immediately attacked by the Ghast, I was almost swept into a panic! Now, I was starting to see that while the terrain, cliffs, and outcroppings of weird flesh-stone; the caves, tunnels, and rifts were all *varied*, the Nether appeared to be very consistent.

Why had I been *so afraid??*

I didn't like the idea of melting in lava, of course, and that Ghast creature sure was ugly and terrifying, but this wasn't as bad as I initially thought it was. Not really...

The fleshy ground was ghoulish, and it was coated in a foul oil of some kind that was obviously flammable. I thought back to Slinger trying to eat it, and laughed. It probably *tasted* terrible! The acrid smoke that emitted from the areas of it on fire made me think that this environment must be very hard on living creatures like Minecraftians, but Slinger didn't seem to mind.

Maybe spiders were just unbelievably *tough*.

I didn't even want to *think* about what all of those nasty oils and stuff from the meaty ground was doing to the bottoms of my boney feet...

As we walked along, sometimes on jagged cliffs, sometimes on more open areas, I watched my step, because sometimes we passed pitfalls and sudden openings in the ground that led to caves and other levels below us.

And always, ever-present, were the *pigmen*...

"Zombie pigmen," Elias said at one point as we watched them. *"They are the most common mobs here. They live in family clans, are not very good ... conversationalists, and it's generally a good idea to stay away from them."*

"Why?" I asked.

"They have fierce tempers!" the Enderman said. *"If you offend them, especially if you try to hurt them, even by accident, from what I understand, they will try to kill you..."*

We passed through a group of them. I had my bow in hand, but kept it low, pointing at the meat-rock. Didn't want to give any of them the wrong idea...

As the pigmen milled around us, grunting like pigs from the Overworld and not really saying much, I observed that they were tall and stout, like large zombies from back home, and were *thickly muscled*. Their pink skin gleamed in the light, except for where their flesh was torn or rotted away, revealing chunky bones and ragged, green flesh underneath...

Every pigman carried a golden sword, most of them in disrepair, and they stared at us aggressively with dumb, dark eyes that reminded me a lot of the dull zombie eyes back home.

There was nothing slow about these creatures, though. Maybe their *minds* were slow, but their bodies were fast and ready. I felt a lot of *danger* coming from these mobs...

Once, as we moved through a group of them, one zombie pigman stepped directly into my path, making me stop suddenly to avoid bumping into it.

"Oh, excuse me, sorry," I said, looking into its dark, beady eyes.

The creature scowled and squinted at me, letting out an explosive *grunt*, and pushing its meaty chest into mine, forcing me back. My bones *clunked*.

Looking down at my feet, I stepped around the mob, and continued toward Elias, who was watching carefully.

Once we were past them, I looked back at the group, and at Slinger, who was following behind me.

He was clicking his fangs, rubbing them together, back and forth.

"They smell like *pigs*," he said.

"Don't even *think* about it!" I replied.

"I'm *so* hungry..."

"Slinger," I said, "They're not just *pigmen*. They're *zombie* pigmen. Do you eat zombies?"

"Well ... *no*," the spider said. "But I can tell from their smell, I think they'd taste like *pigs!*"

"*Do not attack the pigmen, Slinger,*" Elias said. "*That would be a terrible mistake...*"

The spider sighed with a hiss, and we continued.

Later, when we were taking a break to look around at the magnificent and terrible open space around us, I reached over to a meaty wall, and felt the red, organic rock that composed this world. It was mottled and knotted, like cords of muscles all bunched up and bound tightly together. Grabbing a piece of it with my boney fingers, I pulled, and was shocked at how easily I tore a chunk of *stone-flesh* from the block in front of me.

The red stuff disintegrated in my hand...

"What *is* this stuff, anyway? It's so weird and gross."

Milo sat near us, and I could feel the heat emanating from his body as if we were sitting next to a campfire. He watched us constantly with his fire eyes.

"Netherrack," the Magma Cube said with his grating voice. "The entire realm is made from Netherrack, except for the resources inside it."

"*Netherrack*," I said. "What about the fortress?"

The Magma Cube shifted its weight, bouncing a little as it settled. *Was that a shrug??* I thought.

"I *think* the fortress is made from Netherrack as well, but I am not sure..."

"Where'd it come from?"

"*Skeleton Steve*," Elias said. "*Where did the dirt and stone on your world come from?*"

I stared at the lava ocean for a moment, then shrugged.

"Okay," I said. "So it is what it is."

"Yes," Milo said, in his gravelly voice like grinding stone.

I looked over, and saw Slinger staring at a pair of pigmen in the distance. His red eyes were wide and bright, and his fangs were rubbing together.

"Slinger..." I said.

The spider snapped out of his longing and turned to the Magma Cube. "So, Milo!" he said. "How did you get separated from your brother?"

Milo looked off toward the distant bridge to the Nether Fortress.

"We were on that very bridge," the cube responded. "The day the Minecraftian came through, the trouble-maker ran along the bridge to the fortress, dashing the *wither skeletons* to pieces! I tried to stay out of its way, but it attacked us with its glowing, blue sword!"

"Glowing, blue sword?" I said.

"Yes," Milo replied, and went on. "When we were *separated* by the creature's blade, Milo stayed on the bridge, but I fell off of the edge into the ocean!"

"You didn't burn up in the lava, I take it?"

"No," Milo said. "Its essence and mine are the *same*."

"*Then* what happened?" Slinger asked.

"I tried to get back up to the bridge, to *these cliffs*, but it was a long journey from the bottom." His fiery eyes darted over the edge of the cliff. "By the time I reached the bridge, the Minecraftian was *long gone*, and the fortress had stationed guards at the bridge's entrance. They would *not* let me pass..."

"Milo," I said, "How do you know that ... um ... *Milo* ... is still *alive?*"

The Magma Cube stared off at the ocean, his eyes burning brightly.

"I *know...*"

"So, what are we supposed to do about the guards?" Slinger asked. "Are you expecting us to *kill 'em* or something??"

"*If the guards are still there,*" Elias said suddenly, "*we will be able to come up with something beneficial to all, I'm sure.*"

"Yes," Milo said. "Or *something...*"

S1E5
4 – Guardians of the Bridge

The ocean of lava was *vast*, and it was quite a long walk along the cliffs and high shores until we finally reached the bridge to the Nether Fortress...

"There they are," Milo said.

We all crouched around a large outcropping of Netherrack, peering at the entrance to the bridge through the smoky darkness. It was hard to see it clearly, but I could tell from this distance that the bridge wasn't made *just* from Netherrack. It was constructed out of stone-carved bricks, the same dark red color as the rest of this strange world.

The entrance of the bridge was protected by a brick portcullis, which was open, but guarded by two tall, dark figures. From here, I could only make out that they were almost as tall as Elias, were armed with swords, and wore helmets as well as chain-link armor on their chests...

If we had to *fight* these guys ... they looked pretty tough.

I was sure that Elias could handle them at least. I mean ... he handled *me*. As the *Skeleton King*.

Barely...

My mind drifted back to Elias's words about the wither skeletons before we stepped into the portal.

Something about *imbued with magic*...

"Just those two?" I asked.

"Yes," Milo replied. I could feel his intense heat as he sat only a few steps behind us.

In the red haze *beyond* the bridge, I saw the shadows of many pigmen doing wandering around, talking to each other in grunts and gestures. I heard their gruff noises in the distance.

Stepping out from behind the Netherrack, I slung my bow around my shoulder, and walked toward the bridge. My bones *clunked*.

"Skeleton Steve!" Slinger hissed from behind me. "What are you *doing?!*"

"Going to talk," I said.

I looked over my shoulder, and saw that Elias had disappeared.

Probably getting ready for battle, I thought. Being *sneaky*. Just in case...

"*Correct*," Elias said into my mind.

I laughed, and approached the wither guards.

As I closed the distance, I saw that they were much taller than me, and I was surprised to see that all of their bones were blackened and charred. I wondered if these dark skeletons were immune to fire like the Magma Cube was...?

"What's so funny, then??" one of them asked in a gruff voice. Their bones *clunked* as they moved to intercept me in the middle of the portcullis. The armor riding their ribcages shifted with metallic sounds...

"Look at this little guy 'ere!" the other said, sounding the same.

The two wither skeletons laughed raucously.

I approached and stood in front of them with a smile.

"What's with 'is eyes??"

"Oye, you!" the second one said, poking me in the ribs with his sword. The blade was made of chipped stone, just like the pickaxe and wood axe in my pack.

"Yes?" I asked.

"What's with your eyes?? Why they *glow* like that?"

Their own eyes were black pits—empty eye cavities like every other normal skeleton. These guys were tall and imposing, but they weren't unique—not like *me*, anyway...

"I don't know," I replied. "I've *always* been this way. It's some kind of *magic*."

"Magic??" the first one said. "What *kind* of magic??"

"The kind that ... makes me *know* things," I said. "Like I can tell that *you* guys ... you used to be *guards* in your previous life, didn't you?"

"Oye, check *this* guy out!!" the second one said, clapping his comrade on the back. "What do you mean *previous life*, then??"

"Well, you know, *don't you??*" I said. "*All* of us skeletons used to be living creatures. Don't you remember your old life like everyone else does? I do..."

The two wither skeletons shifted their weight on their large, bony feet, and exchanged uncomfortable glances with each other for a moment, then smiled again.

"Oh, *sure!*" the second one said. "I remember—of *course* I do!"

"Yeah," the first one said. "Just like *everyone else.* Me too! *Of course!*"

I smiled. My bones *clunked*. "So you *were* guards, right? Did I get it right? You look like very *skilled* guards..."

"You did!" the first one exclaimed. "How did you *know?*"

"The *magic*, of course," I said.

"Well what is it you're 'wantin, huh?" the second one asked.

"Well," I said, "My friends and I have business in the Fortress. Will you let us pass?"

"Fraid not!" the second one replied.

"No can do!" the first one said. "*No one* may pass, even a *smarty pants* like you!"

"Okay..." I said. "What if I could *do* something for you ... something with my *magic?*"

The second wither skeleton's bones *clunked* as he bent down to look me in the face.

"And what could *you* ... do fer *us*, little guy??"

"I can help you remember more from your old life..."

They laughed, hearty bellowing laughs that made their armor jump up and down on their bones.

"Okay, watch this..." I said.

Looking around, I made my way to the brick railing at the entrance of the portcullis, and found a block of bricks large enough to act as a table. Reaching into my pack, I began pulling out some of the Minecraftian food I'd saved, then set it out into two nice arrangements on the platform...

"What are you *doin??*" the first wither skeleton asked. Looking over, I saw them craning their boney necks to see what I was setting out.

"Sometimes it's good for us to remember being alive," I said. "If you let us pass, I'll help you remember *taste*. Can you remember *taste?*"

"What ... what 'av you got there??" the second one asked.

"I bet *you* remember taste, don't you?" I asked the second guard. "You remembered *being a guard*, after all! You've got to remember *taste*..."

"Hey!" the first one exclaimed. "I remember taste, *too*, I do!"

I heard their big bones *clunk* as they shuffled up behind me. Behind me, I saw the two big guards looking at each other, then smiling as they looked down at my place settings for them. Each setup had a cooked steak, an apple, and a chunk of bread waiting on the makeshift table.

"Oooh," the first one exclaimed. "That's ... I *remember* that's—"

"The steak?" I asked.

"*Oye*, yeah! The *steak!*" he said. "I remember the *taste* of the steak! It's so ... like *meat!*"

"And can you *smell* the steak?" I asked.

"I *do*, yeah! It smells like ... smells like a *steak!!*"

"And I do, *too!*" the second one exclaimed, giving his friend a shove. "I remember the taste, and the *smell*, of *that* there ... that ... *whatchacall* ... that there—"

"Apple," I replied.

"*Oh yeah!!*" he said. "I remember the *apple!*"

The second wither guard squatted next to the table, his bones *clunking*, shoving his friend aside, and he tore into the apple with his skeleton teeth, sending little bits of its white flesh and red skin cascading down his armor and onto the ground...

"What's the apple taste like?" I asked.

"Ooooh," the wither skeleton replied, chewing excitedly. "It tastes so much ... so much ... like an *apple*, it does!! I can *remember!!*"

"Hey!!" the first guard said, glaring at his comrade. "Don't hog it all, now! I want some steak and apple, too!!"

"And what about the *bread?*" I asked. "Do you guards remember bread??"

"*Sure*, I do!!" the first one said, suddenly *throwing* me aside and crouching at the table, dropping his sword onto the ground. "How could I forget the bread??" He fell upon one of the loafs, and seized a piece of meat.

"Me, too!" the second one said, grabbing a chunk of bread in his other blackened, boney hand.

I recovered my balance and got to my feet. My bones *clunked*.

"So we have a deal?" I asked. "You'll let us pass?"

The first wither skeleton was cramming steak into his mouth, dark and wicked teeth chomping up and down, tearing at the cooked meat. He pretended to swallow, but the pieces of steak just fell down the front of his armor and into his ribs.

"Oh, alright!!" he shouted. "Go ahead, then!" He turned to his buddy. "*So good!* Mmmmm! It's like ... it's like *meat*, it is!"

"I know!" the second one said. "I remember, too!" he gnashed on the apple. "This *apple*, I remember! It's like ... an apple! Oh *yeah!!*"

Brushing myself off, I cinched my pack around my ribs and walked to the open portcullis, waving for Milo and Slinger to follow.

As the spider and the Magma Cube came out from hiding, the two wither skeletons feasted on the Minecraftian food, arguing and trying to one-up each other with their made-up memories of times long gone...

The three of us started out onto the bridge. Once we were a good distance away from the portcullis, making our way along the Nether brick walkway, Elias joined us in a puff of purple Ender dust.

Zip.

"*Well done,*" Elias said into my head.

I smirked.

"Wow!" Slinger whispered in a hiss, looking back behind us to make sure we were far enough away. "I can't *believe* what I just saw! How did you think of that?"

"I dunno," I replied. "I was just kind of *winging it*."

"*Well, it worked*," the Enderman ninja said. "*We were able to make it past the guards without having to kill them. That is always a victory*."

"It was just something about their *attitudes*," I said. "I felt that I could, you know, *play* them off of each other? Especially since I already knew that they were *guards*, and then I just thought of all of that useless food I hung onto from before!"

"*Turned out to be not so useless*," Elias said.

"Yep, and I still have plenty left, too!"

Milo spoke up in his gravelly voice. "Thank you, Skeleton Steve. I have not been able to get past those guards on my own. I am sure we'll find my brother in *no time!*"

The bridge went on for a long while, held up over the ocean of lava by countless thin, Nether brick spires. We occasionally passed other wither skeletons as we made our way to the fortress, but they didn't give us any trouble. They must have thought that since the guards had let us through, we must have been okay...

At one point, an area of the bridge we approached was *broken*—probably by some past explosion—and only the side rail connected the section we were on to the section up ahead. Slinger and I carefully crossed the one-block-wide piece that held the structure together. I figured that I was more nervous about it than the *spider* was. Elias simply teleported across. I was worried that *Milo* would have a hard time crossing the thin rail connecting the gap, but that lava blob was very good at timing his jumps, and he *plopped* his way across with ease!

When we were most of the way there, approaching the complex network of fortress structures, when I paused and ducked to hide as I saw a new, *dangerous-looking* mob cross our path. I *literally* mean that it 'crossed our path', which is funny, since we were on a *bridge*, because the monster was able to fly through the air like a

Ghast! *Unlike* a Ghast, though, the creature was fast, and small. Or, at least, *my* size...

"What is it?" I whispered.

Elias, who stood next to me, unconcerned, replied. *"I believe that is a 'Blaze'. Nether creatures of fire. Elementals."*

"Is it dangerous??"

"Oh, yes," the Enderman replied. *"But not to us. Let's move on."*

The Blaze flew through the air from one section of distant fortress to another, surrounded by a nimbus of glowing and fiery rods—either made from lava or some other strange substance. Its body was surrounded by intense flames, and its head floated like a core within the bonfire, too far away to see clearly. The Blaze left a trail of smoke behind it as it passed, and I could hear the creature making odd, metallic scraping noises until it disappeared into a dark, square-shaped tower...

Eventually, we came across a junction in the bridge, and took a right to the nearest large structure. Connecting to a little 'guard house' or something small attached to the side of the bridge, we entered a large square building after going down some stairs, and stepped into the dark, mauve-colored halls of the Nether Fortress!

From outside, I could see at least *five* other large buildings like this, all connected by the bridge system, also sharing similar bridge-like connections at different levels.

This fortress was *immense*, and it was a maze...

We walked down long, empty halls, one after another, occasionally passing by a wither skeleton intent on its destination. The light was dim, but I could see just fine.

Deep inside the fortress, I felt a little more comfortable. These consistent brick halls reminded me a lot of dungeons and structures back home on the Overworld. But I *knew* that if I cut through one of the walls with my pickaxe, I would just see the consistent, smoky dark-red space of *the Nether*. And as if to constantly remind me that I was on another world, a distant Ghast wailed and whined every several seconds outside.

Once, after turning a random direction from an indoor four-way juncture, the hall we walked down made an odd, spiraling turn into a dead end. On the far wall, sitting all by itself, was a wooden chest.

"What's the *point* of this room?" I asked. "So much wasted space to turn into nothing!"

"*Perhaps the builders of these fortresses like to showcase their containers,*" Elias responded.

Slinger broke into a long laugh, his fangs clicking and his chuckles hissing as he gasped for breath. We all turned to him, and he cracked open his eyes, getting a hold of himself when he saw us staring.

The spider snorted.

"What?!" he said, regaining his composure. "That was *funny!* So what's in the *chest?*"

I turned back to the wooden container and pulled it open with my boney fingers. It *creaked* loudly.

"We must find my *brother*," Milo said. "He's *here*, somewhere! He is *close*..."

Looking into the chest, I saw two large and shiny bluish *gemstones*, and three blocks of gold, shaped like my iron ingots!

"What are *these?*" I asked, holding up a blue gemstone.

The light emitting from Milo's burning eyes and the lava cracks in between his splitting skin gleamed in the massive gem, casting rays of light throughout the room. It was...

"Beautiful!!" Slinger whispered.

"*I believe that is a diamond,*" Elias said in my mind. "*I saw my Minecraftian friends create weapons from the diamonds LuckyMist found deep in the ground...*"

"Cool!" I said. "I've never *seen* one before." I picked up the other diamond, as well as the three gold bars. "There are *two* of them, and three gold ingots!"

"What's the gold for?" Slinger asked.

"Don't know," I replied. "Makin *gold* stuff I guess..."

Since no one objected, I slipped the five treasures into my pack, and we moved on.

We walked down more dark Nether brick halls for a while, then, Slinger stopped.

"What is it?" I asked.

"This place is *huge!*" the spider said. "We're *never* going to find Milo ... eh ... *other* Milo ... if we're just *wandering around* like this!"

"*I do not sense another being with Milo's energy anywhere in the immediate vicinity*," Elias said.

"He is close," the Magma Cube said.

"Hang on," I said, looking around. Approaching another intersection, I looked down all of the other halls, and spotted a pair of withers down one of them, the two dark skeletons walking together, swords in hand. Running up to them, with my friends following, my bones *clunked*, and I waved them down. "Excuse me! Hey!"

The withers stopped, and waited for me to catch up.

"What do *you* want, short stuff?" one of them asked.

"Hey, uh, have you guys seen another *Magma cube* around here? Like *that* guy?" I asked, pointing to Milo.

"Nope," the 'short stuff' guy responded.

"I have," the other said. "There's this one weird Magma Cube in one of the gardens, *waiting for his brother* or something..."

"Really?" Milo asked, his grating voice bright and hopeful.

"Where?" I asked.

"Ah, it's the *next* building, I think," he replied, his bones *clunking* as he reached out with a long and dark boney arm to point. "Take this hall to the stairs, go *down*, and across the bridge."

"Thanks!" I said with a smile.

The wither skeleton sneered at me, then turned away.

"Come on!!" Milo exclaimed, hopping and plopping past us all.

We followed, sticking to the wither's directions. Just before I was out of earshot, I heard the dark skeleton scoff to his companion, and mutter, "Weirdos."

At the bottom of the stairs further down the hall, we followed the lower level corridor to the *left*, hoping to find the bridge. It was the right way, and we stepped out of the building onto the Nether brick walkway. Once again, we were surrounded by the vast open and dark space of the Nether and its smoke and gasses, peering to see through the shadows that mixed with the orange glare of the lava sea far below...

Across the short bridge (*much shorter than the bridge we came in on*), we approached another monstrous section of the complex. Stepping into the hall inside from outside and reaching the first intersection of corridors, we looked around in all four directions, and stopped.

"Sense anything, Elias?" I asked.

The Enderman stood still with his purple eyes closed and breathed deeply, listening closely to his *Chi.*

"*There is something faint,*" he said, "*that may be like Milo, below us and in that direction...*"

He pointed with a long, black finger before opening his eyes. We all followed his finger with our *own* eyes, and ended up looking at the corner in between two hallways.

"Well," Slinger said with a hissing sigh. "I guess that means we can take *this* hall, or *that* hall..."

I shrugged, and started walking down the corridor to the right. After several steps down the hall, I jolted to a stop when I suddenly heard the sound of weird, metallic *grating* from up ahead. Down the corridor in front of me, I saw the darkness of the turning corner *light up* with the yellow glow of ... *flames.*

"Oh *man...*" I said.

A Blaze appeared from around the corner, heading straight toward us.

The walls glowed and flickered around it as it hovered through the air, the elemental's strange, luminous golden metal bars, or *rods*, swirling around its core like a miniature firestorm. The brilliant inferno in the creature's center *flared* around it when it saw us, and I could see clearly now that its dark eyes were lustrous and deep, like obsidian gems set into its floating head...

It made that *noise* again, and continued toward us.

I flattened myself against the wall to let it pass.

"Excuse us, sorry," I said.

The Blaze looked at me, meeting my gaze for a moment as it approached, and I could feel that its face, its features, were just as alien and weird and unreadable as Elias's—more so, in fact. Elias at least had *eyes* with expression. This *Blaze* creature was a total alien to me...

The monster made a sound at me like grinding, screeching metal on metal, and I shuddered.

A creature like *this*, with dominion over fire, could just *annihilate* me, I was sure...

"Hey, you!" Slinger exclaimed. I gasped, and turned to see the big spider standing in the middle of the hall. "You! *Blaze!* You there! That's what you are, right? A *Blaze??*"

The fire creature paused, floating in the air. I could feel the heat from its flames pressing into me.

"*Yesss, ssspeak...*" it replied, staring at Slinger with its beady, gemstone eyes. The mob's voice was just like the sounds it made—like grinding metal on metal.

"Hey, *Mr. Blaze*, do you know where we can find another Magma Cube like this guy in this building?" Slinger pointed at Milo with one of his eight legs. "We heard it was around here *somewhere*..."

"*The flamesss sssenssse the burning one, yesss,*" it replied.

"Where can we find it?" Slinger asked.

Milo spoke up. "Yes, great *Blaze.* Where is my *brother?*"

"*Brothersss in flamesss, you wish to burrrrnn together, yesss? The flamesss hear you...*"

Fear ran down my spine like water...

"Yes!" Milo cried in his gravelly voice. I watched as the two Nether creatures spoke to each other, backing away from the Blaze as I felt my bones growing *dry*.

"*Very well, sssmall burning one,*" the Blaze responded. "*Find the other in the garden of sssoulsss down the ssstairsss. Now be gone, creaturesss of the world of tallow, before I ssset you all to burrrrnn...*"

"Thank you!" Milo said. "*Thank* you, Blaze!"

"Yes, sir!" Slinger said. "We'll get *out of your way*, sir!" He pivoted with his eight legs until he climbed up onto the wall, then rushed past the

Blaze. Elias followed us without a word as we left the elemental creature behind. Milo hopped along after us.

Once we turned around the corner, I let out a big sigh.

"Holy cow," I said.

"I know, right??" Slinger replied. "That guy was *intense!*"

"*There are the stairs, up ahead*," Elias said. "*I can sense the other Magma Cube down below.*"

"Milo!" the lava mob with us cried out with its stony, grating voice.

I heard the crunchy plop of *another* cube down below us...

"Let's go!" I exclaimed, and my bones *clunked* as I hustled to the stairs.

We went down, and emerged into a medium-sized room with another corridor heading out, away from the base of the stairs. Slinger scuttled down next to me.

"What?!" the spider exclaimed. "Where *is* he?? I can hear him!"

"Me too," I said, turning. The stairwell came down in the middle of the room, and there was *more* to the room on the *sides* of the stairs and *behind* it! "Weird layout!"

I saw a glow emanating from behind the stairs...

"*The garden of souls*," Elias said into my head, taking slow, easy strides down the Nether brick steps. Milo hopped his way down, taking care not to lose his grip and tumble.

"Yeah, what did he mean by *that*, do ya think?" I said, stepping into the area around the stairs.

My boney foot landed in something *soft* that sucked me in up to my ankle!

I looked down, and my foot was stuck in a disturbing plot of sand made of small, pathetic faces, moaning and wailing and *crying out* silently! The sand faces' eyes pleaded for help, turning

426

toward me, swallowing my foot and making their way up my boney leg...

"Gahh!!!" I cried, grabbing the staircase's rail and trying to pull my foot from the horrific sand. The miniature, tormented faces *pulled back*...

I heard the squelch of Milo landing behind me.

"Look out, Skeleton Steve!" the Magma Cube said. "That's *soul sand!* You'll get stuck!"

Pulling as hard as I could without risking pulling my leg out of socket, I grabbed the railing of the stairs, and eventually managed to *pop* my foot free from the sad, wailing faces stuck in the sand!

"Holy smokes!" Slinger said. "I've never seen anything like *that* before!"

The Magma Cube cried out past me into the soul sand. "Milo!" he exclaimed. "I'm *here!!*"

I saw the glow behind the stairs move, and slowly, *oh-so-slowly*, another lava mob that looked *exactly* like Milo appeared, half-buried in the sand!

"Milo!" it cried. "You're here!"

"Yes, Milo, I'm here!" our companion replied. "*Come* to me, brother! Get out of the sand! Join me again!"

"I will, brother!" it cried, and it jiggled, and writhed in the sand, cracking its crusty skin and sending spitting sizzles of magma out onto the writhing ground. The small crying faces wailed and swallowed the droplets of lava hungrily...

"Come on, brother!" Milo shouted from the stairs landing. "Get out of that sand! Come and join me again! You can do it!"

"Yeah!" Slinger exclaimed. "You can *do it*, other Milo! Come on!!"

The Magma Cube mired in the sand wriggled and waved, his ripping lava form rising inch by inch out of the quagmire, until finally *freed*, he leapt up above the sand, and made his way, slow hop by slow hop, toward us.

"I'm *coming*, Milo!" he cried, hopping and squishing into the soul sand again, struggling to get free, then hopping across a little more ground...

428

"Come on, brother!" our Milo shouted. "You can do it! Just a little further!"

Looking down, I saw something sitting on the Nether brick floor—something that I had jostled loose in the soul sand with my foot. I must have kicked it up out of the sand when I was trying to pull free...

"I'm *almost there*, brother!"

It was like ... the most *slow-motion* reunion ever...

I chuckled to myself.

Yes, it felt great to help this Nether mob reunite with his brother, but *good grief*, between the soul sand, and the natural slowness of the Magma Cubes ... this was the *slowest* and most dramatic family reunion ever!

Bending down, I picked up the strange object that was on the floor amidst clumps of sand that came out with my foot.

It was some sort of ... fleshy growth! Kind of *gross*. Like a mix between a mushroom and a ... *tumor*...

Tumor? I thought. How on Diamodia did I know what a *tumor* was??

"Oh, *Milo!*" our Magma Cube said. "At long last! Come to me, my brother!"

"I'm coming!"

Squish.

Squish.

I looked up at Elias, who was leaning on their stair railing, watching the slow reunion.

"What is *this??*" I asked.

The Enderman shrugged.

"*It looks a little like a mushroom?*" he said in my head. "*You should ask the Milos when they're ... finished.*"

Slinger watched the reunion with bated breath, seemingly all wound up from the suspense!

"Holy smokes, you guys!" he exclaimed.

The other Milo *finally* made it to the edge of the soul sand, and with one final, struggling hop, his big, magma body landed in front of his brother on our side, squishing solidly onto the Nether brick floor!

The two cubes stared at each other for a moment. I felt that if they had mouths, they'd be smiling. Then, they both jumped forward, and for a *moment*, I thought that they had crashed into each other!

Bloop!

But they didn't *crash*.

They *joined!*

The crusty black skin of cooling lava rippled and crumbled around each of them, and the cubes of molten rock inside bound up together in an instant! When they landed, the lava gave a little *splash*, then solidified, and now the two Milos were *one*...

One *big* Milo!

"Hoooly smokes!!" Slinger exclaimed with a hiss. "Awesome!!"

"What?!" I shouted. "Milo! You ... you..."

The giant Magma Cube was now bigger than I was, and as wide as Slinger, if not wider!

Its eyes settled in the middle of its massive face, two blazing coals, burning brightly in the dark room.

"*We* are Milo," it said in a booming, gravelly voice. "*I* am Milo..."

"Milo!" I exclaimed. "When I thought you wanted to *rejoin your brother*, I didn't know you meant ... *literally!*"

"This is *our way*," Milo said. "*Thank you*, Skeleton Steve, Slinger, and Elias for the assistance."

"*We are happy to have lent a hand, Milo*," Elias said in my head—our heads. "*You must feel a lot better being reunited with your other half after the Minecraftian separated you...*"

432

"Indeed, Enderman," Milo bellowed, like the rumbling of a volcano. "Thank you again!"

"What now?" Slinger asked. "You gonna help us get back to the island?"

"Yeah," I said. "How do we *reactivate* the portal??"

"Now that I am *complete* again," Milo said, "I wish to stay in the fortress. But you have *helped me*, and I will help you, as we agreed! A dead portal can only be opened again with fire. Open flames!"

"But we don't *have* any open flames!" I said.

"Yes, you do," Milo replied. "A *Ghast* is what put the portal out in the first place. All you have to do is ask a Ghast to send a fireball at the portal *again*. If it hits the portal with another fireball, the resulting fire will *reactivate* the magic!"

"Great," I said with a groan. The Ghast we dealt with before was a *terrible* creature—gross and irresponsible and annoying. Now I had to convince one to help us?

"Thank you again, Skeleton Steve and others," Milo said. "Good luck returning home. If you ever return, you will always have a friend here!"

"Thanks," I said, then jumped. "Oh, wait!" Holding up the weird, fleshy mushroom, I asked, "What's this??"

Milo's eyes were much bigger now, and burned brightly as he peered at the object in my boney hand.

"That is *Nether Wart*," he said. "It is grown in the soul sand. *Good bye*, adventurers..."

With that, Milo was off, leaping across the staircase landing and down the lower level hall with an agility that didn't look *possible* from a creature of his immense bulk. Every time the Magma Cube leapt, he stretched out his charred, crusty skin, revealing bright-hot lava underneath, and whenever he landed with a mighty, squishy *thump*, the light in the dark hallway went out until he jumped again...

Thump.

Thump.

Eventually, he was gone.

I looked around at my friends, and I could *feel them* smiling on the inside. Elias had no features on his face, and Slinger had, well ... a *spider* face, but I could *feel* the positive energy shared among us, and I *knew* that we did a good thing...

Looking down at the horrifying soul sand, I reached out and pulled up as many more Nether Wart plants as I could reach without falling into the wailing stuff that longed to suck me down.

After putting several of the weird plants into my pack, we started our walk back out to the main bridge—back toward the portal...

S1E5
5 – Piggy Problems

It took some time to find our way back to the main bridge, but when we did, I could barely see the floating island with the portal in the distance, almost lost in the red haze and orange glow coming from the lava sea below.

I couldn't *wait* to get back...

We traveled faster without having to wait for the slow Magma Cube plopping along behind us.

I wondered what Milo would do now, living in the fortress as a huge blob of lava. What was his life like before the Minecraftian came along and threw him into his little *adventure* of trying to rejoin with his brother? Er ... his ... *other self?*

Obviously a Magma Cube would be unable to write a journal like *this* one, since he didn't have any hands, and would probably *burn up the book* if he did. But maybe, once day, far in the future, it might be a good idea to come *back* to this fortress to find old Milo, and I could be his hands—to write *for* him—while he told me his tale...

The *diary of a Magma Cube*...

Once we finally reactivated that portal and got *out* of this nasty place, I'd have to make sure I could get back down to the portal *again* to return some day! Maybe I could put some signs in that abandoned mineshaft leading to the portal from the stairs, so I wouldn't get lost.

Heck, for that matter, if the mysterious tower was *truly* left behind by the Minecraftian who built it, maybe I should *move in!* I could fix the place up, get it all nice and clean and reorganize the chests! There was a library, all sorts of tools and things I might use, access to the mine...

I could be like a *regular Minecraftian*, and learn more about their technology until I could do everything *they* could do, all by myself!

My bones *clunked* as I walked along, my boney feet squishing on the caustic Netherrack as we followed the long path back around the cliff's rim above the ocean shores...

"*You are thinking happy thoughts,*" Elias said suddenly into my head. I looked up at my friend, who walked beside me, and smiled. He looked back down with his glowing purple eyes, and I could imagine that if he had a mouth, he would be smiling, too. Slinger's eight arachnid legs drummed along on the Netherrack behind us as he followed.

"I guess I *am*," I said. "I was thinking about the tower back on Overworld. I know we already claimed a house in Zombietown, but I was thinking of moving *into* the tower! That would be a really cool base for our adventures after this!"

"*Not a bad idea,*" Elias replied. "*It is within a day's travel of the village, and not too far from my Minecraftian friends, either. It would serve as a good home for your exploits in finding yourself, Skeleton Steve.*"

"And the library," I said. "I'm starting to get this *idea*—it's kind of funny ... *never mind.*"

"I *love* funny!" Slinger exclaimed from behind me. "What's so funny??"

"Not *that* kind of funny," I said. "Well, I'm still bouncing this idea around in my skull, but, I've been writing this *journal* ... and I know you, *Elias*, have been writing a journal, too..."

The Enderman nodded as he walked alongside me.

"I've been kind of developing this ... *concept* ... of collecting journals and stories of all kinds of *different mobs* across Diamodia." My bones *clunked* as we walked. "I *dunno*..."

"*Sounds interesting*," Elias said.

"Really?" I asked, looking up at him. "I just ... when we first *started* traveling, I felt weird about all of these mobs we've been coming across. But *then*, I started to see that they all have their own *stories*—their own different lives! I bet if I *really* get into it, I can probably help a lot of different mobs in their own personal adventures, *and*, build a really cool library of all of their *diaries* up in that tower..."

"Reading is boring," Slinger said.

I smirked.

"Yeah, maybe to *some*. I think these adventures—"

"Well *adventure* is cool," Slinger said. "I'm a spider of *action*, myself. I wouldn't want to sit down and write a bunch of gobbledygook. I want to hunt, and run, and jump, and *climb!!*"

I shrugged, and my bones *clunked*.

"Eh ... to each their own, I guess."

"I know one thing for sure," Slinger exclaimed. "I am *so* freaking hungry! I can't *wait* until we get back home and find this place where all of those *Minecraftians* live! I don't know if I'm going to make it! I'm wasting away here!!"

I listened to his many feet drumming and squishing along on the Netherrack behind me.

The snorts of several pigmen nearby took my attention for a moment. I watched their shadows move around in the dim, red light. Their golden swords reflected the many crackling fires, gleaming with danger...

"Like I was saying," I said, "I've really been loving these adventures! And the more we do together, the more I appreciate them. I feel like ... I dunno ... if I made it a *thing*—going on adventures with lots of new mobs and helping them with their struggles—that it would be really *fulfilling* somehow. Like connecting us all together, you know?"

"*I believe that is a noble idea, Skeleton Steve,*" Elias said. "*It feels to me like you've finally come to some cohesion in this idea*"

"It's definitely been bouncing around my skull a while..."

"*If it feels right to you, you should definitely pursue it.*"

"Thanks, Elias," I said.

"*It will also give you a good start to something to focus on after I am gone, as well.*"

"Yeah," I said, looking away at the lava ocean. "But that's not going to be for a while yet, right?"

The Enderman stopped. I stopped with him, and my bones *clunked*.

I expected him to face me, to put a hand on my shoulder, to try to comfort me, but he didn't. Elias's eyes narrowed to glowing, purple slits as he stared off into space, then his head snapped around to look at Slinger, who was walking along behind me.

"*We have a problem*," Elias said into my head.

I turned.

Slinger was *gone*...

"Uh oh," I said. "Where'd he go??"

I never noticed when the sound of his many feet drumming along on the ground had *stopped*...

We had been walking along a wide path of Netherrack up on the cliffs, high above the ocean's shore, and a good ways behind us, there was an open field of the fleshy, foul ground. That's where I saw the pigmen doing—

The Enderman snapped me out of my thoughts.

"*He's going to attack a pigman!*" Elias said. His eyes popped open, the purple glow flaring, and he pointed with a long and slender arm back into the recessed darkness of the Netherrack field!

"Slinger!!" I shouted. "Where are you??"

My bones *clunked* as I broke into a run toward the field!

Zip.

Elias disappeared in a shower of purple motes of light, and I could see the faint *warp trail*, telling me that he teleported far ahead into the field, among the group of pigmen, to find the spider...

As I ran into the field, into the group of zombie pig creatures, I weaved between the brutes, avoiding eye contact. The mobs stared at me with dumb, dark eyes, grunting and snorting as I surprised them and upset whatever they were doing.

"Sorry!" I exclaimed. "Excuse me!"

Once I was away from the cliff, away from the main group of pigmen, following Elias's trail, I finally saw the Enderman, standing tall in the red darkness, his purple eyes glowing as he stared into a dark corner of the cavernous area.

I barely heard Slinger's voice.

"But I'm *so hungry!*" the spider cried. "They can't *see* me! I did it like a good ninja!"

And then, there was a loud *squeal!*

With frightening speed, the entire group of pigmen behind me *startled*, then raised their swords and rushed the area where Slinger was hiding in the shadows, pushing past me and knocking me down to the gross Netherrack! My bones clattered as I fell.

At least a *dozen* of them converged on the area, charging in like a pink and gold wave of certain death, snorting and growling, as intent as a rushing river!

"Slinger!" I cried from the ground. "Get out! They're coming!!"

In the chaos of the pigmen charging into the area where Elias was dealing with Slinger, who was presumably trying to *eat* his victim, there was an explosion of movement as the furious mobs tried to fall upon the spider!

Elias stood by for a moment...

Those pigmen were intense and terrifying! The Enderman ninja must have been weighing how he could *help* Slinger without having the murderous group turn on him...

I jumped to my feet and pulled my bow.

Whatever happened, I couldn't let the pig people tear apart my new friend...

And then, I saw Slinger *leap* like a huge acrobat over the mob of pigmen, landing in the Netherrack between them and me! His red eyes were narrowed, and he sprinted toward me, all eight legs *ripping* at the Netherrack as he ran across the field!

He was *so* fast...

The pigmen were rapidly in *hot pursuit!*

"Kill!" one of the pigmen yelled in a grunting voice.

They could speak!

"Kill the spider!!" another cried between snorts.

"Hop on, Skeleton Steve!!" Slinger shouted as he sped up to me. My spider buddy paused next to me, flattening himself on the Netherrack with record speed...

I *did* hop on, swinging my boney leg over his back as fast as I could, and grabbing a shoulder with my free hand.

"Go!!" I exclaimed, patting his back.

Slinger *took off*, taking me with him, charging back to the cliff, then speeding along the path back toward the portal. Amidst the crazy, bumpy ride, I looked back for Elias...

The Enderman ninja had disappeared.

Probably getting up ahead, I thought.

I also saw the large group of pigmen chasing after us, much faster than I thought they'd be able to run, swords raised, rage in their squinted, dark eyes! They grunted and snorted and shouted for the spider's death.

"Kill it!" one said. "Kill the spider!!"

"Kill the *skeleton*, too!"

"Kill the spider and the skeleton!!"

Great, I thought.

"What the *heck*, Slinger?!" I shouted against the smoky wind in my face. "You couldn't wait just a *little* longer?!"

The spider shouted back at me between gasping breaths.

"I was so hungry! *I'm sorry!!* I thought I could get one of the weaker ones *all by itself*, and I did! I *webbed it* any everything! I did everything *right!*"

Up ahead, I saw the long, curving path that would eventually lead us to the peninsula, then back to the floating island. The smoke from the lava ocean glowed orange. Maybe if we could reach the island, and leap back across to it, the zombie pigmen wouldn't be able to follow...

Then, I saw in the fiery haze, the shadows of *several more* pigmen up ahead!

The distant zombie pig creatures turned, raised their swords, and were obviously running toward us...

We were cut off!!

"We're trapped!" I exclaimed, holding on with my knees and free hand for dear life as Slinger sped over the squishy landscape. "You've gotta *climb!* They're *everywhere!*"

Without a word, Slinger shifted toward the nearest Netherrack wall, made a quick jump, and was suddenly pulling himself up the sheer, meaty-rock surface just as fast as we had been moving on the ground!

I would have been very impressed, if I wasn't so terrified!

Looking down as I clenched onto the spider's body, I saw the dozen or more pigmen catching up to the wall where Slinger began to climb, swarming around the bottom like angry wasps! They snorted and grunted and called for our deaths...

"Cliff ahead!" Slinger shouted with a hiss.

I pulled an arrow out of my pack and set it on my bowstring. My skull jostled with the spider's rapid, bumping steps.

Slinger's feet pounded and tore at the Netherrack as he propelled us up the wall. I fought against a sudden attack of *dizziness* when the spider launched us over the edge of a higher cliff, abruptly running along the flat ground again!

We were in another dark red cavern, much higher that were before.

Two pigmen suddenly appeared in front of us, charging with their golden swords high, *murder* in their beady, dark eyes...

Slinger veered to the right and swung his thick abdomen around with amazing agility! I felt his body *squeeze* under me, and the spider launched a web ball at the nearest pigman! The sticky projectile flew through the air, and hit the mob *right in the face!!* The pigman dropped his sword onto the Netherrack with a *clatter*, and reached up with both hammy hands to pull the gunk off of him...

I aimed my bow at the other pigman and fired after a quick moment of focus. My arrow whistled through the air and pegged him on the side of the chest under his shoulder! The struck mob staggered back, grabbing at the arrow's shaft with his free hand, but kept coming!

Another two zombie pigmen appeared out of the darkness, rushing toward us.

"We can't keep this up!" I cried, scrambling in my pack for another arrow...

Zip.

The tall, black form of *Elias* appeared suddenly in front of us, immediately dropping low into a martial arts pose...

"Elias!" I beamed.

Three pigmen lunged in at the Enderman ninja. His dark blue headband tails settled onto his taught and muscular shoulder...

"*Find us a place to hide!*" Elias said quickly into my mind. "*Now!*"

Dodging the gold swords of the first two pigmen that attacked, Elias counterattacked against one of them with a flurry of palm strikes, then sent a roundhouse into the mob's chest that launched it back into the Netherrack wall behind it. The zombie pigman crashed into the fleshy stone with a *squeal*, its sword flying off into the darkness, and it crumpled up onto the ground, dead...

I jumped off of Slinger's back, pulling the stone pickaxe out of my pack.

If there was nowhere safe from the pigmen in *the Nether*, I would *make* a space!

My spider friend looked down at the pickaxe in my boney hand. "*Good idea*, Skeleton Steve!" Slinger exclaimed, and I ran to the nearest Netherrack wall.

Looking over my shoulder, I saw another jumble of movement between Elias and the other two pigmen. The one with the webbed face was still struggling to get the spider gunk out of his eyes.

Golden swords flashed. The Enderman's long, black body moved like *water* through them, and then I saw one of the pigmen thrown through the air, over the cliff! It squealed as it flew, disappearing over the edge...

Two or three *more* pigmen appeared in the distant red haze, charging with their swords to join the action.

I laid *hard* into the Netherrack with my pickaxe, intent to carve out a little cave as quickly as I could! When the stone pick sliced through the fleshy stuff with ease, I was relieved! My bones *clunked* as I worked, and I cut through the

Netherrack *quickly*, hollowing out the beginning of a tunnel, then the beginning of a *room*...

Behind me, I could hear the sounds of the Enderman ninja *decimating* his foes, and the grunting of the pigmen as they circled around him. Their swords clanged and clattered as their attacks missed, and the weapons were thrown onto the ground as they were separated from their wielders.

Zip.

I heard Elias teleport once, then the sounds of the battle resumed. Pigmen squealed and grunted.

"*Hurry!*" Elias said into my head.

"I'm hurrying!" I shouted, as I continued hollowing out a room in the nasty, meaty stuff!

Out of the corner of my eye, I saw Slinger, who stood guarding me, turn and launched more web balls into the growing crowd of attackers.

With a last quick look around, also making sure my little *meat-room* was tall enough for the Enderman, I stuck my head out and called for my friends, stashing the pickaxe, and pulling my bow and arrow once again.

"Slinger, come on!" I yelled. The spider abandoned his web attacks and crawled into the fleshy tunnel. "Elias!" I shouted. "Teleport in here! Plug up the hole with a dirt block!!"

The spider crowded into the hidey-hole with me, cramming himself into a corner and pulling his legs in close to his body. After an uncomfortably long wait, listening to the sounds of the Enderman ninja fighting the many pigmen outside, with a *zip*, Elias was suddenly in here too...

Without a moment's hesitation, the Enderman ninja produced a *dirt block* out of thin air, and used it to plug the hole, leaving only a small window through which we could see the Nether outside...

The pigmen cursed and grunted and snorted, stampeding around outside the hole!

I watched their stubby pink legs pump around outside the little window; watched the occasional flash of a golden sword.

One sword was smeared with black ichor, like ... *blood?*

"Elias!" I said. "Are you okay??"

The Enderman, wound up as tight as a spring, suddenly sat down on the rough, fleshy ground, and settled into his meditation post.

"*A little wounded,*" my friend said, "*but I'll be okay.*"

I sat down. My bones clattered. I let out a huge sigh of relief...

The pigmen churned and raged around outside, grunting and shouting, crying, "Kill the spider! Kill the skeleton! Kill the Enderman!"

Looking over at Slinger, the spider averted his many red eyes into a corner, and tried to make himself *smaller*.

"Elias," Slinger whispered, his voice a whimpering hiss. "Skeleton Steve, you guys—I'm *so, so* sorry!"

"Slinger!" I snapped. "Don't you remember Elias saying to *never* attack the pigmen, *no matter what?!*"

"*What's done is done*," Elias said into my mind. He sat meditating on the foul Netherrack floor. "*All we need to focus on now is getting past the pigmen to the portal, and getting back to Overworld.*"

I glared at Slinger.

"Do you realize Elias is staying here *for us??* He can go home anytime, but *we'd* be *stuck* here!"

Slinger shrank back into the corner even more...

"I'm *sorry*..."

I let out a long sigh, and tried to relax.

"Hey," I said, trying to smile. "We all make mistakes, right?"

Elias cracked his eyes open, and I could see the purple glow as he watched.

"I *said* I was sorry..." Slinger groaned.

"What's done is done," I said. "It's okay, Slinger. I'm sorry I was so *mean* about it..."

Looking out of the window, past the pink legs and golden blades of the many angry pigmen milling around, I peered out to the glowing, orange lava sea. Through the smoke, I saw the shadow of the peninsula, then the floating island. From here, I could barely make out the dark, hard-lined shape of the portal frame, sitting in the middle of the island...

"How are we going to get *out* of here?" Slinger asked.

"I don't know," I said. "We've got to get past all of *them. Then*, we've got to get a Ghast to help light the portal!"

"*I must meditate for a while to heal and recharge my Chi,*" Elias said. "*Let's see what happens after we wait a while.*"

Pulling the stone pickaxe out of my pack, I saw that the wooden shaft and stone head of the tool were pitted and ... *melting* a little? The tool gleamed with the sick sheen of the Netherrack's oily surface in the flickering light of a fire outside the hole.

That Netherrack sure was *nasty stuff*...

With this tool, I could cut through it easily enough, but this pickaxe wouldn't last much longer against that caustic material...

I stood, my bones *clunking*, and began to carve out a little more of the room.

If we had to *wait here* for a while, I could at least make the room a little larger—a little more comfortable...

After hollowing out our hideout a little more, and putting the damaged pickaxe back into my pack, I looked out the window at the island hovering above the fiery glow once again.

A Ghast moaned somewhere in the distance.

And I settled in to *wait*...

Season 1, Episode 6:
Invasion in the Rain
<u>Season Finale!</u>

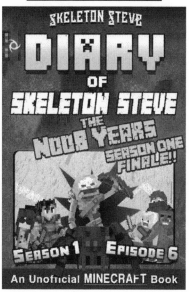

Invasion in the Rain!

The Season ONE Finale!!

Still stuck in the Nether, Skeleton Steve, Elias the Enderman Ninja, and Slinger the Spider struggle to reactivate the dead portal to get back home. But when they do, they're surprised to find Zombietown under full assault! The Minecraftian Noobs are trying to take over and wipe out all of the undead mobs!

And to make matters worse, when the trio of heroes joins the fight, it starts to rain, so the powerful Enderman Ninja is forced to stay out of the battle! Will Skeleton Steve and Slinger be able to save the village? And how will they stop a small army of Minecraftian Noobs that just keep coming??

S1E6
1 – Stuck in the Nether

Everything was dark and red...

Above the sound of the crackling flames outside, I heard the faint whine of a *Ghost* in the distance. A few seconds after, the foul creature followed up with a haunting and high-pitched "*Aaaa Ooooohhhh*..."

Peek-a-Boo, I thought. *I seeeee youuuu*....

What weird and eerie creatures, those Ghasts were...

To think that I'd have to convince one of them to help us when we finally left this foul Netherrack *cave*.

The pigmen outside the little window that remained—Elias had plugged up our desperate hidey-hole with *dirt*—stamped around on the meaty ground, snorting and grunting in annoyance.

Were they *calming down* somehow??

"Okay, so here's *another* one!" Slinger exclaimed, his fangs clicking. He relaxed in a corner of the room. The spider, Elias the Enderman ninja, and I, all sat facing each other in the dim red light, Elias sitting straight in his meditation posture, his glowing purple eyes mostly closed.

"To who?" I asked.

"Um ... *Elias!*" the spider said. The Enderman opened his eyes a little and nodded. Slinger spoke up. "What's the *longest distance* you've ever teleported?"

Elias closed his eyes again and replied into our heads with his *mind voice*.

"*Slinger,*" he said, "*I'm afraid you do not understand the complexity of that question.*"

"What do you mean??" the spider replied.

"*There are times when my warping can be measured in distance, like when I warp from where I stand to an area far away that I can see with my physical eyes. There are also times when I warp long, physical distances based on memory, like when I warped from Balder's village to LuckyMist's*" *cave, over a day's travel away by foot. None of these labels will mean anything to you, of course..."*

"Balder's village?" I asked. "The place where you ... ah ... *met me?*"

Elias turned to me and opened his purple eyes. *"Yes, Skeleton Steve. That village does not have a name, not like 'Zombietown', as far as I know."* He turned back to Slinger. *"However, Slinger, there are other times when my warps cannot be measured, at least not by any physical means I understand. Like when I warp back and forth between The End and the Overworld. Or, if I were to warp from here to another dimension. How do you measure such a jump?"*

"Well, that *sort of* answers my question," the spider said. "Now *you*, Elias!"

"Very well," the Enderman ninja replied. He was quiet for a moment, thinking to himself, then looked back at the spider. *"Slinger,"* he said into our minds. *"You have been very intent on eating Minecraftians, ever since we met you. My question is: have you ever actually caught and eaten a Minecraftian before?"*

Slinger laughed, clicking his fangs.

"Are you kidding?" he asked. "Of *course* I have! Why—did you think I was so excited about it because I haven't *done* it before? I've eaten *dozens!!*"

I smirked.

"Oh, really?" I said.

"*In my experience,*" Elias said, "*once a Minecraftian is killed, their body disappears. So how do you 'eat' them without them vanishing in a cloud of smoke?*"

"Oh, that's easy!" Slinger exclaimed, rubbing his fangs back and forth on each other. "First, I get them stuck in my webs. Once they're *helpless*, I poison them. Not enough to *kill* them—just enough to soften up their insides! Then, I suck 'em dry until they die!"

"Wow," I said, looking at the Netherrack floor.

Slinger's eyes were gleaming red in the faint firelight from outside the cave. Was he … smiling?

If a spider *could* smile, I could swear that he was smiling...

Elias shook his head. "*That is indeed gruesome*," the ninja said. "*Okay, Skeleton Steve— your turn.*"

I looked at my Enderman friend.

The tall, black-skinned ninja sat straight and returned my gaze, completely calm. I couldn't help but get the feeling that he was just ... *humoring* me. Our travels together so far were a mixture of us working together, learning and exploring, and lots of *fighting bad guys*. But there was always the undertone of him focusing on me a little *too* much...

Through everything we've been through together, Elias has always been very private about his own thoughts, but also very open about me and my search for my memories. Our focus together was always about me getting my memories back. Everything always circled back around to *that*...

But he's your friend, a part of me thought. *He's trying to help.*

But was he *really* my friend?

There have been many occasions now where he mentioned, basically, wanting to stick around until he was sure I would be okay. That I *wasn't a threat*. Was he really going to the lengths that a *friend* would, just 'helping' another friend? Or was it his *job?*

I shook my skull. My bones *clunked*.

Why did I think that?? Of *course* he was my friend!

"*What's the matter, Skeleton Steve?*" Elias asked in my head. "*I sense a struggle inside you. Are you thinking about ... the other ... again?*"

The Skeleton King...

Always thinking about the Skeleton King breaking out of me again...

"I'm okay," I said. "Just thinking of my *question*. Okay, Elias: how many *Ender seeds* does an Enderman need to gather to complete his *Seed Stride?*"

"It varies from Ender to Ender," Elias responded. *"Some Endermen walk their Seed Stride for a short while, feel satisfied, then return to The End to plant their seeds. Other Endermen stay on the Overworld much longer, seeking out more and more seeds until they feel like the phase is complete. Other Ender dedicate their entire lives to the Seed Stride, spending most of their existence searching the dirt, returning home to plant seeds from time to time, then warping back to the Overworld."*

"What about you?" I asked.

There was a moment of quiet in our little cave, and I heard the pigmen snorting and stamping around outside. Were they calming down? It definitely seemed like they were *less excited* than before...

"This is my first Seed Stride, Skeleton Steve," the Enderman ninja replied. *"I am not entirely sure how long it will last. I will follow my Chi, and I am confident that when the time comes that I feel ready to return, I will know. That said, I am also ... excited ... to partake in my ceremony and trials to*

increase my rank. However, once I officially become lower ninja, I will be bound to always focus on new missions for the Order, and will not have the freedom to adventure with you as I have now..."

I looked down. Did Elias resent me for keeping him from his promotion??

"Okay, my turn again!!" Slinger exclaimed, his fangs clicking. "Alright, *Skeleton Steve*: what did you do *before* you hooked up with Elias? What sort of adventures were you going on back then??"

Looking up, I saw Elias's purple eyes in the darkness, and realized that he had never taken his eyes off of me...

I looked over at Slinger, and sighed.

"Slinger," I said. "I'm gonna level with you there. If we're going to keep traveling together—and I *hope we do*, even though *you* got us *stuck in this cave*—you're going to find out sooner or later..."

The spider glanced quickly at both of us and shifted nervously at that. I didn't leave him time to awkwardly apologize again.

"The truth is, before I started traveling with Elias ... I was the *Skeleton King*..."

Elias's eyes widened. He was clearly surprised that I came out with it. Slinger gasped, widening his many red eyes.

Was that too blunt? I thought.

"What?!" the spider shouted. He laughed. "You're trying to *trick* me, aren't you?"

"I'm afraid not," I said, shrugging. My bones *clunked*.

"But ... how??"

"I don't know who I *was* before ... well, I don't *remember* my life before being the Skeleton King. I don't really remember even *being* the Skeleton King *either*, but Elias insists that I was, and I've seen some of his memories about it—also, I've got these *special red eyes*..."

"Is *that* what that is?" Slinger said. "I wasn't gonna *say* anything, but yeah—no other skeletons have glowing red eyes, you know..."

I smirked.

"Yeah. I know." I sighed and went on. "When Elias defeated me ... ah ... the *Skeleton King*, apparently, I turned into the ... *me* you know now. *Elias* and I have been trying to figure out more about my past ever since..."

"But," Slinger said, scuttling a little in his corner. "Is it ... safe?? I mean—I never laid eyes on the Skeleton King, but my friend *Scott* told me all about him, and the Skeleton King was a *huge monster!* And really *evil*, and created a big *army* of skeletons ... with ... glowing red eyes ... like ... *yours*..." His fangs clicked together. "What if you, like ... turn *back* into the monster again??"

I shrugged again.

"*Could* happen...? I don't know. I don't *think* so. Elias thinks that the transformation was tied to an evil artifact, and *that thing* is gone now." I turned to the Enderman. "Right?"

Elias nodded. "*There is a particular energy from another universe that is incompatible with our own. That energy was present in the Skeleton King's weapon. Once I disarmed him in battle, the Skeleton King shrunk down and turned back into*

Skeleton Steve. The weapon is no longer on the Overworld..."

"Holy smokes..." Slinger gasped. "I had no idea you guys were doing such *important stuff!!*" He looked straight at me with his many red eyes. "Skeleton Steve, you can count me *in* on this! Um ... as long as you give me some Minecraftians to eat when we get back. And some *other* times. Every once and a while, you know??"

We laughed.

"Sure, Slinger," I said. "As soon as we get *out* of here, back home, get out of the mine and the tower, and get back to Zombietown, I'll show you where we've been seeing some Minecraftians *right away!*"

"*My turn,*" Elias said. He looked at me again. "*Skeleton Steve, whenever my Seed Stride is indeed over, what do you plan to do?*"

Straight in for the kill. He's worried about me being a *threat*. So he *was* babysitting me after all...

I knew it!

"I don't rightly *know*, Elias," I said. "I'll probably hang around Zombietown, work on making the mysterious tower my *home*, and maybe start my whole 'mob journal' idea. Now it's *my* turn. Elias, good buddy, is it your *mission* to *stay* with me??"

Maybe it was just the energy in the cave, but it seemed like Slinger and Elias were both shocked by that.

I realized that I was holding my breath, and let it out.

Elias closed his eyes.

"*Skeleton Steve*," he said. "*Know that I was, indeed, given the mission from my master to resume my Seed Stride, and to keep you with me to make sure that you, and the energy that is attached to you, would not be a threat to Diamodia. I tell you this because—*"

"I knew it!" I shouted. "You were never *really* my friend, *were* you? All that focus on my memories? You just wanted to make sure that if I

474

ever remembered who I was, that I wouldn't freak out and destroy the world—is that it?!"

Slinger blinked, and shrunk into the corner.

"Skeleton Steve, I—"

"I was just a *mission*, huh? That's why you didn't want to give me a bow until you were forced to *leave* for a little while? That's why you commanded me to *stay* in Zombietown? You wanted to keep control over me, because it was your *job?*"

"That is not all there was to—"

"Forget it!" I said, cutting off the voice in my head. "Let's get the heck *out* of here. I don't have a choice either way, do I? You're gonna stay with me until you're done with your Seed Stride— whenever *that* is—because you're dedicated to your Order first, and you'll follow your master's command before anything else, right?"

The Enderman's purple eyes cracked open, and he looked at me. His blank, black face was as unreadable as always.

Elias didn't try to argue. He closed his eyes again after a moment, and resumed his meditation pose.

The three of us sat quietly in the Netherrack cave, listening to the fires, pigmen, and occasional Ghast noises outside. Slinger spun and played with a length of web between his longer front legs, idly making long and sticky shapes.

After a long while, Elias's purple eyes opened in the darkness again, and he spoke up.

"The pigmen," he said into our minds. *"I believe they may let us pass now. The group of them outside have calmed down considerably, and I do not detect any thoughts among them about us..."*

"Well let's hope you're right," I said. "Otherwise we'll eventually have to fight our way through."

"So how are we doing this?" Slinger asked.

"Let's start by removing the Seed block," Elias said, standing. His head almost hit the ceiling. *"I will venture outside, and see how the pigmen*

476

react. If everything is okay, you two should ride down the cliff, and we can make our way back to the portal."

"Okay, let's do it," I said, pulling my bow and an arrow. I looked at the spider. "No sneaky *attacking* any of them this time, *right?*"

Slinger shook his furry head. "No *way*, buddy! I learned my lesson, okay?"

When Elias pulled the dirt out of the opening, returning the precious seed to his dimensional pocket, he warped out through the small entrance with a *zip*, and stood out by the cliff, standing and assessing the situation.

Just several hours ago, he was fighting for his *life* out there, demolishing the pigmen attackers with his martial combat skills...

One zombie pigman stuck his pink and half-rotten face into the tunnel, snorting and looking at us with dumb, questioning eyes. The pigman squinted, blinked, then pulled his head out again, stomping away on his thick, muscular legs.

"Okaaaay...?" I said.

"Looks like all's good again, huh?" Slinger said. "Come on!"

We pushed our way out of the meaty-walled tunnel, and I was actually very *happy* to be in the open expanse of the *Nether* again! The massive cavern walls extended all around us, and the distant terrain, walls, and cave ceilings faded away into a dark red haze...

Much better than the foul, cramped cave of oily, fleshy *Netherrack*...

I still hated the Nether, but couldn't remember any rational reasons *why*.

Elias looked back at us from up ahead.

"*Looks like the coast is clear,*" the Enderman said into my mind. "*It appears that the pigmen have ... forgotten. Perhaps they share some mental traits with the zombies of your world.*"

I climbed onto Slinger's back, and we had a fairly uneventful ride back to the peninsula overhang that led to the floating island with the portal. It was rather harrowing, riding on the spider's back, clinging tightly to him with my free hand and my boney knees as he went *down* the cliff back to the main path we took before, and it was more harrowing still when he *leapt* across the gap between the peninsula and the island with me on his back! Once again, I held my breath and stared down at the brilliant lava sea—the orange glow of *certain death*—flying by under me, my life in the eight hands of this spider's *acrobatic* skill...

When we made our way back to the portal, I finally climbed off of Slinger's back. My bones *clunked*.

"*I will call a Ghast*," Elias said in my mind. "*Stand by.*"

The Enderman ninja stood tall and dark against the red expanse, his eyes closed. I leaned up against the obsidian blocks of the dead portal while waiting...

"I'm coooooommming!!" a loud, high-pitch voice whined, scraping against the bones of my inner ears. "Oookaaaay!! Hold *ooooonnn!!!*"

Looking up, I saw the large and pale bloated shape of a Ghast approaching, descending slowly toward the island from another cavern in the ceiling far above.

The monster was huge, much *bigger* than it appeared from afar, and *disgusting*. I was reminded again of our encounter with the *last* Ghast when I saw the slimy streaks of grey ooze streaming down its flabby cheeks and caking up around its puffy eyes.

"Gross," Slinger muttered with a hiss.

I guess *he* felt the same way.

Waiting until the monster descended close enough to have a reasonable conversation, I called out to it.

"Hello, Ghast!" I shouted, waving a boney hand. "My name is Skeleton St—"

The huge, pale creature suddenly *shrieked* in terror, a loud and ear-splitting sound that filled me with fear! Its big, black eyes popped open, spraying grey ichor all over its face, and it opened its mouth with a scream, spitting a big, flaming ball of gunk *straight at me!!*

My bones clattered as I scrambled to get out of the way! In the roar of the approaching fireball, I saw Elias teleport out of danger, and Slinger disappeared over a small ridge of Netherrack.

BOOM!!

The fireball exploded, showering dozens of chunks of the foul Netherrack material all around me.

"Again?!" I yelled.

There were fires all around...

I looked up at the portal.

It was still dead.

Darn!

"What is it with Ghasts *shooting first* and—?" I started.

"I'm soooorrrryyy!!!" the Ghast screamed. Its voice hurt my head. "Oh nooooo! I'm such a loooooooser!"

It sobbed, huge heaving sobs, spraying grey ooze all over. I scrambled back to avoid getting any of the nasty stuff on me, then stamped out a small fire next to my feet.

Slinger seemed to be okay, and he scuttled up to stand next to me.

"Be *nice*, Skeleton Steve!" the spider whispered with a hiss.

"Oh, *great Ghast*," I said, "It's okay! No harm, right?"

The creature howled. Its flabby tentacles swung around under it. "I'm sooooorryy!!" it repeated in an annoying, too-loud voice. "I didn't meeeeaaan it! You look like one of the ooooothers, with that heeellllmet? And that booow? And that ... how *taaaaall* you aaaaare??"

It sobbed some more.

I looked at Elias. He shrugged.

"It's quite alright, Ghast!" I shouted. "Listen, we called you here because—"

"Why do you waaaaaant meeeee? I'm such a loooooooser! What do you waaaaaaant??"

"Oh, gosh!" Slinger muttered.

"We need a *favor*, if you will, great Ghast! You're not a loser—you're *very good* at spitting those fireballs!"

"Reeeeallyyyy??" it said, its whining voice turning a little more positive. "You thiiiiink soooooo?"

"We do indeed! That's some *great* fireballing! I was wondering—could you please shoot *another* fireball, *right* at that portal there?" I pointed to the dead obsidian frame with a boney finger. "Just *right there* in the *middle* of that portal...?"

The Ghast stopped crying, focusing on me with its puffy black eyes. Under the grey ichor, they were sick and reddened around the edges.

"You want me to ... hit the pooooortaaaal? Whhyyyy?"

"Uh," I said. Would it make sense if I just totally told the *truth?* "We need some *fire* there to be able to get home! Would you, please?"

"I don't knoooooow," the Ghast whined. "I'm not suuuuuure I can dooooo that for others on puuuuurpose! I'm *shyyyyyyy!*"

"*Pretty* please?" I asked. "We would really, really appreciate it! Plus, it would look really cool! Like the last one! You're *really good* at shooting fireballs!"

The huge Ghast hiccupped back a sob, and a single slimy tear ran down its streaked face.

"Ooookaaaaaay," it said.

Taking a big breath, the pale creature screeched again and spit out a flaming hunk of ichor, which flew through the air as straight as an arrow, until it *exploded* next to the obsidian frame, sending pieces of Netherrack flying all over!

I turned my face away as the pieces of fleshy ground showered down around me.

Dang, those were big fireballs!

I heard a hissing *pop*, and I looked back at the portal...

The warbling purple field of magic was *back*, stretched over the obsidian frame from block to block! The low *drone* started up, and the hum of the gateway vibrated my bones.

This weird portal magic was terrifying to me before, but now I was ecstatic to hear the sound of it!

That drone was the sound of *home*...

The three of us stepped up to the obsidian frame and into the warping, purple light.

"Thanks!" I called back to the Ghast.

Elias was waiting to step in last...

And then, the purple haze and the warbling drone of the magic began to smother and surround me, and I lost myself in between...

S1E6
2 – Back to Zombietown

The weird, warbling magic that swallowed up my senses eventually faded away, and the next step forward with my boney foot landed on a cool, stone floor.

Yes!

When I could see again, my eyes were assaulted by the glare of the many Minecraftian torches lighting up the mining tunnel that held the portal, and I was no longer overwhelmed by the constant and foul sensations of the Nether.

Reaching out, I touched the stone wall on my left with a boney hand, and brushed away a cobweb.

"That's better," I said with a smile.

The wobbly sound of the portal became louder again behind me, there was a small *pop*, and I saw Slinger emerge from the purple haze.

"Hey!!" the spider exclaimed. "We're *back!!*"

A moment later, after Slinger scuttled out of the way, his eight arachnid legs drumming on the stone floor, the portal moaned again, *popped*, and out came Elias, his long limbs emerging from the magical field, purple motes of light drifting down around him.

"*Here we are,*" the Enderman said into my mind. "*Follow me. I know the way back to the stairs.*"

"I don't know about *you guys,*" Slinger said as we walked down the brightly-lit tunnel, "but I don't wanna go back there *any* time soon. Am I right??"

I nodded, and my bones *clunked* as I followed Elias to a junction and turned left. As we moved through the tunnels, I listened to the squeaking of the bats and the trickling of water far away...

The three of us walked quietly down another well-lit tunnel with a mine-cart track bolted onto the stony ground, then, went up some stairs made of cobblestone. It seemed that the Minecraftian who explored this abandoned Mineshaft before took it upon himself to create a staircase connecting this level with the one above. The clean (but dusty) cobblestone passage of stairs was *nothing* like the old, stone tunnels, shored up with creaky, wooden beams and plastered with old spider webs.

We soon found the *first* junction we came across when we originally started exploring this abandoned mineshaft.

"How did we miss the way to the portal *before?*" I asked.

"*We went a different direction when we were here last,*" Elias replied. "*Instead of the way to the portal, we followed the path that led to the Minecraftian's crafting room, remember?*"

"It'll be easy to get back to the portal next time," I said.

"*Next* time??" Slinger responded.

"Well, you know," I said. "Whenever ... *if* ever ... we want to come *back* again..."

Once we reached the stairs back to the surface, we climbed back up to the mysterious tower, step by step, that long, long way, until we finally reached the small fortress's basement.

"*Just to remind you,*" Elias said suddenly, "*I waited until we returned to gather more Ender seeds from the 'dirt chest' up above. I will do that now, and then we'll proceed back to the village.*"

"Um, *okay*, Elias," I said. That didn't sound very friendly.

I wondered if, since I called him out on his 'mission', if the Enderman would now drop the act, and not pretend to be my friend anymore...

"Please hurry!" Slinger exclaimed. "I'm *so* hungry!!"

As Elias dug through the dirt chest in the second level storage room, I made my way back up to the top of the tower—back to the bedroom and library.

There, I looked through the shelves again for any other interesting books. Some looked like they might be fun to read, but I was pretty sure that I already found the best gift available for the little zombie *knight in training* back in Zombietown...

I pulled "Sir Gawain and the Green Knight" out of my pack again, looking over the cover, and skimming over some of the words inside.

Yep, I thought. Zebulon would love it!

Walking over to one of the large, narrow windows, I looked out across the landscape that extended far below the tower. I scanned the horizon and watched the sun set over the forest *far, far away*. I looked across the distant stony valley between the two mountains, and watched the pink and golden light of the descending sun light up the massive snowcap of the *Mountain of Wisdom*.

I could definitely *live* here...

Once Elias was finished with the dirt chest, we stepped outside into the freezing cold of the smaller mountaintop, and started making our way back down to Zombietown in the dark of twilight. I decided to ride on Slinger's back for the journey, especially during the *descent*—he would be able to get down the cliffs and slippery areas much better than I could on my own!

When we reached the tree line, I started to see other mobs wandering the forest. Many of them eyed the three of us with wonder—I figured they might not see a skeleton riding a spider very often.

Eventually, once we reached the flats, we all started discussing the Minecraftian Noobs I had already seen.

"Okay," I said, riding the spider as he calmly made his way past the big, blue lake in the mountains' foothills. "So far I've seen *three* of them."

"What'd they look like?" Slinger asked.

"Well, *one* of them wasn't very distinctive at all. He wore the same blue clothes that the zombies wear, but was wearing leather armor, made of *animal skins*, all over his body! He had a skin helmet, chest piece, boots, and some sort of hard pants."

"Wow, that's vicious!" the spider exclaimed.

"What?"

"Killing animals and wearing their skins! Do you think he did it to make other animals *afraid* of him??"

Elias spoke up. "*Making armor and other things out of animal skins is a common practice with Minecraftians. He was just wearing it as some measure of protection, I'm sure.*"

"Sounds like a good way to inspire *fear* in your enemies!" Slinger replied. "Wear their *skins!* I should wear the skins of Minecraftians!"

"*Yeah...*" I said with a smirk. "So ... *anyway...*"

"What happened to him?" the spider asked.

"Um ... well, we *killed* him. Either Zebulon or myself, I don't remember."

"Wicked!!"

"That's where I got the wooden sword I was using to free myself from your web back on the mountain," I said. "The sword was *that guy's* weapon."

"Was," Slinger said, his fangs clicking.

"Yeah," I replied. "And I gave the armor to Zebulon, along with *another* wooden sword."

"Tell me about the *others!*"

"Okay," I said. "There was also this guy dressed in ... kind of a *ninja* outfit of orange and blue..."

"*The orange man,*" Elias said. "*Why do you say 'ninja' outfit? What is a ninja outfit?*"

Why would I associate the orange man with ninjas? Where did *that* come from?

More of those *weird memories* buried deep in my head, I guess.

"I don't know, exactly," I said. "I mean—it's not like I've *seen* lots of ninja outfits..." I laughed,

494

and my bones *clunked*. "You're a *real* ninja, Elias, and all you wear is your headband. But for *some* reason, when I saw *that* guy, I thought 'ninja outfit'. He also had weird, spikey black hair, and was trying to fight the zombies in *hand to hand combat!*"

"No weapons?" Slinger asked.

"No," I replied. "Don't know *why*. He was trying to *punch* the zombies! It didn't turn out well for him when I started shooting, but I dunno—those guys were *crazy*. The third guy had a sword, too."

"What did *he* look like?" the spider said.

"He was dressed *weird* for sure. That guy tried to sneak up on me with a wooden sword. He had a blue shirt, blue shorts, a bright green *backpack*, and was wearing a weird, white 'bunny hood' hat with little ears on top!"

Slinger scoffed below me. "Weirdos," he said. "You killed them all?"

"Me and Zebulon, yeah," I said. "But the zombies say that the Minecraftian *Noobs*—that's what they call them—come back every few days or so. They mostly harass the village, and never get very far before getting killed or running away, but they like to draw the zombies out into the sun to make them burn up and loot whatever they have!"

"That means that they must live somewhere nearby," Elias said. *"Minecraftians regenerate after death—they come back to life onto their beds. I have seen it..."*

"Well, if *that's* true," Slinger said, "then that's a good thing!"

"How's that?" I asked.

"Well if they die and keep coming *back*, then I'll have a constant source of food!!"

We laughed.

Psssst!!
Liking the story? Don't forget to join my Mailing List! I'll send you *free books* and stuff! (www.SkeletonSteve.com)

The trip back to Zombietown was uneventful. Quiet, even.

But by the time the undead village was in sight, we all *knew* that something was wrong...

"Are villages supposed to *smoke* like that?" Slinger asked.

"*The village is under attack again*," Elias said into my head, then teleported away with a *zip*. His faint warp trail shot like a comet toward the town, leaving purple motes of light in its wake.

"Let's go!!" I shouted, and pulled my bow off of my shoulder.

Slinger leapt into a run, his eight legs pounding at the forest floor, and I pulled and nocked an arrow from my pack.

Over the ridge, I heard a small voice boom out, "Elias! Thank goodness you've come!!"

It was Zebulon, the little zombie knight.

Knight in training, I thought. That's what he calls himself...

As we crested the ridge and the village came into sight, I gasped when I saw *a dozen or so* varied and colorful Minecraftians running around the field, fighting against a handful of zombies that were plodding around blindly in the sunlight, sheathed in flames! A crowd of zombies huddled in the shadows of the village, and Zebulon stood on top of the guard tower, watching the battle and trying to do ... whatever he could...

Two houses on the edge of the village were on fire! The wooden pillars and planks that filled the space in between the cobblestone foundation and load bearing walls were blazing with tall, orange flames, sending plumes of dark smoke into the air!

In the middle of a group of Minecraftian noobs (I recognized the *bunny hat guy* among them), Elias appeared out of his warp, crouched low into his martial arts pose as the invaders surrounded him...

Ka-BOOM!!

A clap of thunder split the air, and the sky opened up, suddenly darkening with a fierce storm!

Water poured down from the thick cloud-cover—*sheets* of it—and the sky was lanced by *heavy rain!*

As I felt the raindrops start hitting my bones and pinging on my metal helmet, I spurred Slinger on to the battle.

Then I heard Elias scream out in pain...

S1E6
3 – Invasion in the Rain

"It's raining!!" Slinger exclaimed, as he propelled us down the forest hill toward the battlefield.

"I noticed!" I replied, shouting against the torrent of water and wind.

Elias screamed—a hoarse and otherworldly sound, as alien as the sounds of the Blazes in the Nether! He screamed and screamed and screamed!

"Elias!!" I cried. "What's happening?!"

The strange and chilling sound of the Enderman ninja's howls of pain moved all around me, and I suddenly realized that Elias was teleporting randomly everywhere—*anywhere*—to get away from the rain!

The rain would *kill* him!

If he wasn't dead already...

The Enderman's screaming stopped.

Slinger and I arrived at the field, and several Minecraftian Noobs turned and looked at me in surprise.

Where was my friend??

If he was my friend...

Where was the Enderman??

"Elias!!" I shouted.

Was he dead?

I raised my bow and aimed at the first Minecraftian, a man dressed in a dark, long-sleeved shirt with a hood. He looked at me with bright, green, emotionless eyes, and held a metal sword— the first and biggest threat at the moment.

Hoodie, I thought. That's a hoodie.

Taking quick aim, I fired. My arrow flew straight through the rain, the sound of its whistling feathers muffled by the storm, and pegged him right in the head!

The Minecraftian dropped his sword, and fell to the ground.

"*Skeleton Steve...*" a voice called out into my head.

"Elias!" I cried. "Where *are* you?! Are you okay??"

A second Minecraftian charged at Slinger and me, holding a wooden sword in one hand, and a *shield* in the other! This one was dressed in white, had long, brown hair, and some sort of dark *glasses* over his eyes.

I fired again. My boney fingers had plucked another arrow from my pack and nocked it without me even realizing it! This bow was becoming *second nature* to me...

My arrow flew toward the charging Noob, and the Minecraftian stopped at the last instant and hid behind his shield.

Thunk.

"Dang!" I cried, reaching for another arrow.

Slinger swiveled in place, and I felt the spider's body squeeze under me. I looked back at my attacker just in time to see a ball of web stuff hurtling toward him through the air! The Minecraftian raised his shield again...

Splat!

Just like the spider said before...

Slinger hit the Minecraftian's shield with his heavy web-ball, and the Noob was perplexed, struggling against the weight of the gunk now stuck on his armor. When the shield dropped low, I fired again, and hit the Minecraftian in the chest.

"*The rain has wounded me,*" Elias said weakly into my head, "*but I have found safety for the moment. I am inside the watchtower. I am sorry, my friend, but I cannot help you with this...*"

I nocked another arrow.

The Noob with the glasses threw his gunked-up shield to the ground, and ran at us with his wooden sword. I could see the *bunny hat guy* charging at us now, too, armed with a sword of his own, crafted from *gold!*

"Elias! You're okay!" I yelled.

"What??" Slinger asked. "Oh, boy! Going backwards!!"

The two Minecraftians charged at us as Slinger scuttled backwards up the hill.

I fired at the guy with the glasses and long hair again.

My arrow flew through the rain and hit *glasses guy* in the chest again. The Minecraftian clutched at the arrow, dropped his sword, and fell down in a puff of smoke, immediately washed away by the intense falling water.

Bunny hat guy reached us, and hit Slinger on the leg with his golden sword! The spider hissed.

"No you don't!" I yelled, and pummeled him once on the head with my bow!

The Minecraftian looked up at me with his crazy face, stuck in a silent yell, his black-dot eyes unchanging under a yellow lock of hair that stuck out from under the white hat. He fell back with a grunt.

Slinger hissed like a monster, and *lunged* in, biting the Minecraftian with his long fangs!

"Yesss!!!" Slinger cried, sucking at the Noob who struggled on the ground, then, he reared back, and speared him with his fangs again!

The bunny hat man disappeared in a puff of smoke. His golden sword lay in the wet grass, gleaming in the heavy rain...

I looked around.

We were at the edge of the field. The last scuffle pushed us back up the hill to the trees again, but now there were *three less* Minecraftians. I couldn't tell how many were down there, but *three less* was good...

Nocking another arrow, I said, "Let's *go*, Slinger!"

"Yes siree!!" the spider exclaimed. I could feel a renewed since of strength in the lean arachnid body under me. Slinger pulled us into the fray with legs pumping, clawed feet pulling at the wet ground.

I aimed at the nearest Minecraftian and fired.

A Noob with a black scarf covering his face was chasing after a zombie in the rain, and took a head shot and went down, dropping his iron sword!

The fires had gone out, and now the burning buildings were just charred and smoking as the rain pounded all around us. The few remaining zombies in the field were now just drenched, blackened undead, plodding around, trying to catch the Minecraftians dancing past them.

Several more Minecraftians looked up as we charged in, and turned toward us.

"Gotta keep moving, Slinger!" I shouted. "Don't let them get around us!"

I nocked another arrow, and trained my aim on ... *the orange man!!*

There he was, running toward me, muscles gleaming in the rain, his orange and blue ninja outfit drenched. The Minecraftian's bare feet thudded against the grass, and his hands were clenched into fists. He yelled something to his comrades in a language I didn't understand.

In fact, come to think of it, they were *all* yelling stuff around the field. The Minecraftians shouted back and forth at each other in what sounded like gibberish to me. Elias told me once what their thoughts were saying, and even then, it didn't make much sense either. Something about them being ... *kids??*

I fired, hitting the orange man in the leg.

He staggered, but kept coming, his face unchanging from its ever-present angry, battle grimace...

Slinger scuttled suddenly to the side as a Minecraftian appeared out of nowhere, swinging at the spider with a metal axe!

"Whoa!" I cried, pulling another arrow and scrambling to aim at the attacker.

It was the *leather guy!!*

So far, I've seen each of the three Minecraftian Noobs I fought before, back and as alive as ever, but there were many more! In the crazy action, I couldn't even *count* them all. *A dozen*, maybe?

I fired, and the leather guy leaped out of the way. My arrow sank into the flooded grassy ground...

"Dang!"

Slinger's body squeezed twice under me as I reached for another arrow. I kept my eyes on the leather guy and didn't bother looking at whoever Slinger was shooting at, but I knew he was slinging web balls into the group.

Another Minecraftian ran up to my blind side, and I caught a glimpse of his sword gleaming in the rain, swinging down at my leg, before Slinger shifted and *pounced* onto the Noob with fearsome speed, knocking the sword out of his hand and piercing the attacker with his fangs!

The Noob under the spider made a sound of pain.

I aimed again at the leather guy. But just before firing, I aimed *up* a little, then released the arrow...

He fell for it.

Last time I fought this guy—at least I *think* it was this guy—he was very good at dodging my arrows by jumping! I anticipated that he'd jump when I fired, and I was right. This time, he jumped *right into* my arrow!

The projectile sank into his belly, and the leather guy staggered back.

"Skeleton Steve!!" I heard Zebulon's little voice bellow out from the watch tower, muffled by the intense rain. "Look out *behind you!!*"

Slinger heard it too, and spun toward two Minecraftians charging us from the rear.

"Get out!" I shouted. There was no time to say anything else.

My spider friend *leapt* out of the battle toward the field, making me grab onto him to keep from falling off as I was trying to fish another arrow out of my pack. Out of immediate danger, Slinger and I scuttled toward the center of the field and away from the group of Minecraftians that was closing in on us.

We couldn't do this alone...

And *Elias* was out...

"Zebulon!" I cried. "Help us!"

"I *will*, Skeleton Steve!" the zombie knight in training shouted back from the guard tower. "Do not let yourself be flanked! I will be down directly!"

I looked across the field to reassess the situation.

The orange man and the leather guy were both wounded. Another Minecraftian was laying in the wet grass, poisoned by Slinger's fangs, and suddenly disappeared as I watched, succumbing to the venom. There were at least six or seven others running *straight toward us* just about as quickly as Slinger could run himself...

Two wounded and burned zombies plodded through the field toward the group of attacking Noobs.

In the rain.

I gasped.

Not on fire...

"That's it!!" I yelled. "Zebulon!! Zombies!!"

Guiding Slinger with my knees, I turned toward the village.

Dozens of zombies hung back in the shadows of the little homes, inside or under the eaves of the cobblestone and wooden roofs...

Many, *many* dull, black eyes stared back at me through the pouring rain, set in green faces over gaping mouths.

Zebulon emerged from the watch tower's front door, dressed in his leather armor with his wooden sword in hand.

"The *rain!*" I shouted. Slinger scuttled to the side to get us further away from the charging

Minecraftians. "The rain will *protect you* from burning! *Attack!!* Attack! Everyone *attack the Minecraftians!!*"

I raised my bow and fired at the nearest charging Noob, hitting him in the belly and knocking him back a little as I immediately nocked another arrow.

At the edge of town, I saw Zebulon's face with a look of shock as he processed that for a moment—looking up at the raining sky, looking at me, at the remaining zombies in the field *not burning*. The zombies in town started to let out a collective moan as they thought about it, too.

Zebulon suddenly *dashed* out into the field, pointing his sword in the air and looking back at the huge group of undead citizens.

"Zombietown!" the little knight in training bellowed. "*To me!!!* Rally to me!! Attack!!"

Scores of zombies roared and moaned, plodding out into the field like a flood of green and blue!

I shot at the Minecraftian I wounded *again*, knocking him to the ground with a headshot, and he disappeared in a puff of smoke!

The two forces *clashed*...

Slinger and I darted around the field, me constantly reloading and shooting at any targets that looked good at the moment, the spider focusing on keeping us mobile and out of range of the Noobs' attacks. Sometimes, Slinger paused to launch a web-ball at a Minecraftian before rushing on.

Once, I saw a Minecraftian female with red hair and purple eyes get stuck by a flying web ball, and then she was immediately mobbed by several zombies, disappearing under the green arms and dirty, blue bodies. When the ravaging zombies let up, she was gone!

The Minecraftians were much faster than the zombies, but the undead were relentless, and any time the Noobs let themselves get cornered, they were *goners*...

Another time, I was *surprised* by the orange man. After taking a shot at a distant Minecraftian, the orange ninja Noob had *somehow* gotten around us. Then, the menace appeared out of nowhere, jumping onto me, grabbing my bones, and pummeling me again and again with his fists!

I pushed at him—stared right into his angry Minecraftian face! My arrow from before was still stuck in his orange leg, swishing around in the rain. Slinger scrambled in all directions, trying to knock the *orange man* from his back, but the Noob was strong, and held on tight, intent on breaking me to pieces! His fist crashed into my ribs again and again! *Crack! Crack!*

Suddenly, I managed to *head-butt him* in the face with my skull, and in that precious moment when he was stunned, I knocked the Minecraftian off of me with the end of my bow. The orange man fell to the ground on his back, scowling up at me in the rain.

Without hesitation, I nocked the arrow I had been holding, and fired straight into his chest.

The orange man let out a grunt of pain, then disappeared in a puff of smoke!

"Press the attack!" Zebulon cried across the field. "To *me*, brothers!!"

The fight was finally turning in our favor—I could see the wave of green and blue zombies pushing the Minecraftians back to the field, moving more or less as an organized unit, thanks to Zebulon. There were still little isolated fights between single Minecraftians fighting off handfuls of zombies here and there, but the Minecraftians' numbers were dwindling...

Or so I *thought*, until I saw the *bunny hat guy* again!

There he was, fighting with a wooden sword against the wall of zombies, his blue clothes and green backpack drenched in the rain, his white hat with little bunny ears standing out against the dreary colors of the storm...

I ducked suddenly as an arrow whistled through the air at me, over my head. Looking across the field, I stared back at the *leather guy*, aiming at me with a bow.

"What the heck?!" I asked. "Where'd *those guys* come from?"

"What is it??" Slinger asked.

Loading my bow, I took careful aim...

"Move *left* a little, Slinger," I said.

The spider scuttled slightly to the left just as another arrow sailed past.

Holding my breath and calculating for the distance, I let loose the arrow. It flew through the rain, and far away, I saw the leather guy fall back as I hit him in the chest!

Loading another arrow, I immediately fired off another to the same point of aim.

Across the loud storm, I didn't *hear* anything, but I saw the leather guy disappear in a puff of smoke.

Slinger surprised me suddenly when he pounced on a nearby Minecraftian, knocking him to the ground and draining the life out of him with his fangs!

It was the guy with long hair and glasses.

Were they coming *back to life* and running *back* to the battle?

"Elias!" I shouted. "What's going on?!"

We dodged out of the way as another Minecraftian charged in. This one was dressed in glowing blue lines over a black bodysuit—his head was hidden under a black cowl with a glowing blue visor. As Slinger stayed on the move, I put two arrows into him before he could reach us.

"Elias, can you *hear me??*"

Sure, the Enderman was *wounded*, but I was definitely *in range* of his *mind voice*, wasn't I? Wasn't he holed up in the guard tower? I looked back at the cobblestone building across the field.

Yeah, I've definitely talked to him across longer distances than *this*...

Did he pass out in there?

Or was Elias *watching*, unconcerned? After all, if it was his *job* make sure that I wasn't a threat to Diamodia, wouldn't it better to just ... let me die?? Then, I definitely wouldn't be a threat anymore! I scowled in the rain, and put an arrow into another Minecraftian.

Looking across the field, I saw the *orange man*, sprinting across the grass toward us again...

"*The beds*," Elias's voice responded weakly in my mind. "*Their beds are nearby. They die, and reappear there...*"

Of course!!

Just like I thought—the Minecraftians *lived* nearby. They were just jumping up out of their beds whenever they died, and immediately running back to rejoin the battle!

We had many zombies on our side, but if a dozen Minecraftians just kept coming back, again and again and *again*...

"Slinger!" I shouted in the downpour. "Find Zebulon!"

"Aye aye!" the spider replied, and launched into a sprint across the field, dodging through fights and zombied and *Noobs* alike...

We came across the bunny hat guy again as Slinger ran. The spider knocked him down to the ground, and I shot an arrow into him as Slinger kept running. I had no idea whether I killed him or not...

"Zebulon!" I shouted, and Slinger pushed through a mass of zombies. I saw the little zombie knight squaring off with a Minecraftian armed with an iron sword. Slinger spun around and shot a web ball at the Noob, who took it in the chest and fell to the ground, trapped by the sticky gunk.

The little guy looked up. "Skeleton Steve!" he shouted. "What a *fine day* for a battle, no??" The small zombie had a few gouges in his armor, and was completely drenched from the rain. He was grinning from ear to ear!

"Zebulon, they keep coming!"

"I *know*, my friend! What is the *meaning* of this??"

I saw that Zebulon wasn't making a move to *finish off* his Minecraftian foe, now stuck in the web. Maybe he wouldn't—perhaps it went against his *Knight's Code* to kill an enemy who was trapped.

No problem for me, I thought, releasing an arrow into the Noob's chest. The webbed Minecraftian disappeared in a puff of smoke.

"It's the *beds*, in the forest!" I shouted against the rain. "I've got to go and *destroy the beds*, or this will never end!"

"That is a *fine idea*, Skeleton Steve!" Zebulon bellowed with his little voice. "I will see to the defense *here!* If the rain stops, I will need to guide the village to *safety!*"

"Yeah, that makes sense. Be careful!"

"*You too*, my skeleton friend!!"

With that, Zebulon smiled, turned, and charged at another Minecraftian.

"Let's go!" I shouted to Slinger.

"Where to??" he asked.

"Into the woods! Let's go around, *outside* of the battle!"

With a mighty leap, Slinger jumped out of our position surrounded by zombies and Minecraftian Noobs, and we sprinted toward the tree line a good distance from where the invaders kept coming out of the forest.

"How do you want to do this?" Slinger shouted against the rain, his eight feet pounding at the wet, grassy ground.

"Real *quiet like!*" I said. "Let's get *as many beds as we can* before they figure out what's happening and turn on us!"

"How are you going to destroy the beds?"

"I'll think of something!" I said, looking into my pack.

S1E6
4 – The Hunt

"Shh," I said. "There's one!"

I pointed with a boney finger at a wooden bed, sitting in the grass in between two trees, covered with a dark red blanket. That blanket must be soaked from the rain...

"Why even put a bed out in the rain like this?" Slinger asked. "It doesn't make sense!"

"Weird, Minecraftian technology, right?" I asked.

"I guess so," Slinger said.

Pulling the old stone axe from my pack, I looked over the Minecraftian tool.

I had picked this up from my *first* battle with the Noobs, several days ago now. *Did it belong to the leather guy?* I thought, trying to remember. I shrugged, and my bones *clunked*. Rain pitter-pattered all over me, running through my ribs and shoulder blades, down around my helmet, making my pack slick and hard to open.

The axe was old and nearly broken. The connection between the wooden shaft and the stone head was stressed, and the stone head itself had a large crack running up the thickest section.

This tool would *break* soon, for sure...

But it would have to do.

I jumped down from Slinger's back, and my boney feet splashed into the muddy grass. Looking around for other Noobs, I approached the bed stealthily, and paused and ducked when I saw a Minecraftian darting through the woods toward the battle up ahead.

Slinger let out a low hiss. He saw him too...

Approaching the bed, I hefted the axe, and hacked at the wood and woolen object *again and again* until it was broken up into pieces!

The axe was holding together, and I was being careful with my hits to keep it from taking any more damage—as much as I could, anyway.

"That should do it," I said. "There's *one* down..."

From there, we quietly made our way through the forest to where I saw the Minecraftian *running from*, until we found *his* bed as well. The hard rain muffled the sounds of everything, so we had to take it slow to avoid being spotted. Twice along the way, I saw a couple of other Minecraftians running by!

At the second bed, I repeated the process, hacking up the bed until nothing but splinters remained.

"There's *another* one down," Slinger said with a hiss, trying to whisper in the rain.

"Are you okay?" I asked the spider. "I remember you taking a few hits back there..."

"I *did*, but I'm alright," Slinger responded. "Besides, I consumed a good bit of *Minecraftians* too, so *that* helped a little. Just a few bumps and bruises!"

I was so amped up in the battle *before*, that I never noticed the knocks I'd taken myself! But now—now that we were *slowing down* and sneaking around—I could feel every crack in my ribs from my fight with the orange man, as well as a few injuries on my hip and on one leg from other points in the battle.

It occurred to me that I didn't have any memories of even being wounded before!

Would these injuries heal? Would it take time, like with the zombies? I thought about Zed, my first friend in Zombietown, healing over a few days after almost burning to death in the sun. Would *time* take care of me? Or would I have to *eat* Minecraftians to heal, just like Slinger did? Did the zombies eat Minecraftians too?

Braaaaiiiiins, I thought, then laughed to myself.

"What?" Slinger asked.

"Nothing," I replied. "Let's find the next one!"

So we hunted through the woods for the beds, as quietly as we could, hacking them up where we found them. It was easiest to find the beds whenever we saw a Minecraftian running through the woods, because we *knew* that if we looked in whatever direction he was running *from*, we'd find that Minecraftian's bed!

Once, there were two beds almost right next to each other.

That was fortunate.

Until a Minecraftian suddenly spawned *right on top of* one of them!

With one final blow of my axe, I finished demolishing one of the beds as I saw a sudden puff of smoke appear on top of the *other*, and I was suddenly standing face to face with *bunny hat guy!*

"Holy smokes!" Slinger exclaimed as the Noob dressed in blue with the green backpack and white bunny hat leapt off of the bed at me, slamming his empty fists onto my chest, his face screaming at me without making any sound!

I swung the stone axe in reflex, connecting with the Minecraftian's body and knocking him back. The axe felt uncertain in my hands. Not wanting to break the tool, I threw it to the ground, and scrambled to draw my bow and arrow...

Slinger pivoted and shot a web ball at the bunny hat guy, but the Minecraftian was already sprinting at me again, and the spider missed! I heard the *splat* of Slinger's web hitting a tree.

The Noob clashed into me, swinging his fists, his face wild and black-dot eyes unchanging, as I tried to back away, drawing my arrow...

I fired, hitting the Minecraftian square in the forehead. I heard the sound of a *bell* ringing, and the Noob fell down dead in a puff of smoke!

"What the heck?!" I asked. "What was *that??*"

I must have rang his bell, I thought with a chuckle.

Just a moment after, there was another puff of smoke in the bed, and *bunny hat guy* was back!!

Slinger hissed.

"Web him!" I yelled, and the spider was already on it, spinning around to shoot a ball of web gunk from his abdomen.

As the Minecraftian was still getting his bearings, standing on the bed in the rain, he was hit by the web ball, and thrown back onto the ground, enveloped in sticky stuff!

"I've got him!" Slinger exclaimed, scuttling around the bed toward the downed Noob.

"Don't kill him!" I yelled, slinging my bow back onto my shoulder and picking up the axe. "Not until I break the bed!"

"Roger that!" Slinger said, and I heard the Minecraftian grunt in pain as the spider loomed over him...

I looked over just in time to see Slinger pulling his fangs out of the Noob's body.

"Slinger!" I snapped. "I said to *wait!*"

Hefting the axe, I went to work on the bunny hat guy's bed!

Thwack! Thwack! Thwack!

"Hey, relax, Skeleton Steve!" Slinger exclaimed. "I just poisoned him to make him *taste* better!"

I hacked up the bed until there was nothing left, then, Slinger finished off the Minecraftian, who disappeared in a puff of smoke!

The bunny hat guy didn't come back.

Where he was now? I thought. I couldn't remember if Elias had ever told me what happens if they die without a bed. Was bunny hat guy dead forever? Or would he have to wait until later?

As long as he didn't come back *here*, it didn't matter.

We continued hunting down the beds in the rain until the Minecraftians finally caught up to us...

Since we were breaking their source of regeneration, and their numbers were dwindling in the battle, I had to assume that Zebulon and the zombies were starting to really give them a beating. The rain was still pouring down like the oceans had moved into the sky, and it was still hard to hear anything over the roar of the pounding water around us, but whenever I saw the remaining Noobs running back to the battle, I saw them shouting at each other in the gibbering language. The Minecraftians hesitated more and more before going back, waiting until they were collected into a small group before charging into battle.

Eventually, they figured it out.

I was breaking another bed, surrounded by dark oak trees in the rain, when another Minecraftian suddenly spawned *on the bed* as I was breaking it!

It was the long hair and glasses guy, standing weaponless, suddenly drenched by the storm, quite shocked to see me! Instead of attacking me like the bunny hat guy did, he ran away, faster than we could react. And a few seconds later, the rest of the Minecraftians came running up with him!

The jig was up...

They were probably collecting all together in the same place by that point, so they were waiting for the glasses guy to join them before running back to the village again.

But now, the battle was *here*.

"Oh dang!" I cried, and the realization hit me that Slinger and I could fight them off, maybe, but they'd just reappear again *here* and keep going!

We were *boned*...

"Here we go!" Slinger exclaimed, and pounced onto the glasses guy at the front of the pack, sinking his fangs into the Minecraftian. As he drained the life out of the Noob, four others ran up and started pounding on the spider with their fists. Slinger hissed in pain.

The glasses guy disappeared from under my spider pal in a puff of smoke, then *reappeared* on his bed a moment later, unharmed!

"Dang!" I shouted, loading an arrow. "Slinger, that's not going to work!! Web them! Slow them down!"

With a might leap, Slinger sprang out of the group of Noobs, landing in the wet grass. They immediately turned on him again and pursued. My spider friend aimed his abdomen at the group and shot out a couple of web balls.

While the Minecraftians were distracted, I grabbed the axe and ran toward glasses guy's bed. My bones *clunked*. I almost slipped in the wet grass.

Looking over, I saw Slinger firing more web balls at the Minecraftians, scrambling to stay away from the angry group. The Noobs were all empty handed, and tried to surround and pummel the spider to death whenever they caught him. One Minecraftian was stuck to the ground with sticky webs, but was halfway to pulling himself free.

Nope, I thought. This wouldn't work for long!

Hefting the stone axe, I hacked at the bed. Hacked and hacked until nothing was left but splinters, and looked up just in time to see two Minecraftians running straight at me! Glasses guy was with them...

No time to fight, I thought, and I turned, running for the area where the other Minecraftians had had been gathering.

"*Hurry*, Skeleton Steve!" Slinger shouted from a little ways away. "Here they come!"

I looked back, and saw that Slinger, appearing quite beaten and bruised up, had pulled himself up into a tree. The spider pivoted, and fired web balls at the Minecraftians, who were now all charging after *me!*

My bones *clunked* as I ran into a clearing, and I saw *three beds!*

Three of them—all together!

"Get *back* here, Noobs!" Slinger was shouting from the tree. I heard his web balls *splatting* on the grass. "Come and get me! Leave him alone!!"

Was that the last of them?? Just these three? No—there was *one more*, right? Four guys and the glasses guy? Three beds left? No, that couldn't be...

Really, there was no way to tell...

The Minecraftians were right on my heels when I reached the first bed. The rain hammered against the red blanket and sprayed back up into my face.

Have to break the beds, have to break the beds, I thought.

Once my axe started chopping into the wooden frame, the Minecraftians caught up to me, and I immediately felt them punching my body. Their fists thudded into my bones, and I felt my ribs and shoulders cracking!

Almost there...

One of the Noobs *slammed* me in the legs, and my right knee buckled. I kept chopping as I fell, and the bed shattered into splinters as I dropped to the mud!

"Get *off* of me!!" I yelled, pushing back against the three noobs pounding on me with their fists. I swung at them with the axe, connecting with one of them, but my heart fell as I heard the *snap* of the axe breaking!

Broken!

We were *done* for...

And there were still at least two beds!

I heard a thud and a hiss as Slinger roughly jumped out of the tree, hurting himself to get to me...

But I didn't *see* it. I couldn't see my friend— I couldn't see anything at all! All I saw through the driving rain were the shadows of the three Minecraftians, beating me into the mud, my bones crunching and cracking, trying to keep them away from my head with my boney hands...

And then, all of a sudden, I heard the strange and grating otherworldly *scream* of an *Enderman* teleporting through the rain—the terrifying roar of pain as Elias warped into the glade, his body burning under the onslaught of the deadly downpour of water...

The Enderman roared a mighty battle cry, and I heard the sound of a bed smashing to pieces!

Zip.

He warped, screaming the whole way, the Enderman ninja roared fury *again*, smashing the *other* bed!!

I struggled to pull my broken bones back to my feet, and fell back to the mud again. The Minecraftians vanished from around me—probably running to attack Elias! Turning my skull on my creaking, cracking neck, I saw Elias, *barely standing* in the rain, his black body casting off dark vapors into the air, purple mots of light *pouring* off of him, facing off against three unarmed Minecraftians...

"Slinger!" I shouted. My bones *clunked* and clattered. "*Help* him!!"

In a flurry of action, the Enderman ninja *destroyed* the three Minecraftians with a series of palm strikes, kicks, and desperate attacks, using his strength and size advantage—anything he could to kill them *before he died*...

I tried to stand, felt something in my leg *snap*, and slipped into the grass again.

"Slinger!" I cried. "Slinger, save *my friend!!*"

As my skull crashed into the spraying water on the ground, I barely saw Elias vanish, heard the *zip*, and saw the motes of purple Ender stuff in the heavy rain as his warp trail *shot off* to somewhere in the trees...

He saved me...

Elias was wounded by the rain from before the battle, and came out here, through the rain that would *kill him*, to try and save me from the Minecraftian Noobs...

And now...

Was he *dead?*

Was Elias dead? My friend ... dead?

He was my friend.

He was my friend.

I knew that Elias was, indeed, my *friend*...

S1E6
5 – Just a Golden Apple

Do undead sleep?

Do they dream?

I only knew that I stayed in the dark, down in the muck, until I could *see* again.

How long was I out?

Was I even *out?* Or did I just ... *turn off* for a while?

When I opened my eyes, I saw the many red eyes of my spider friend looking back at me!

"Skeleton Steve!" Slinger exclaimed. "You're alive! Or ... *undead* alive? Or some sort of *state* ... in which you still ... exist and move around, right??"

I coughed, and my bones clattered.

"Elias," I said.

I was still in the wet grass where I had fallen down, but the rain had stopped, and the sun was shining. I could feel the sunlight on my bones, and felt a *little* better...

"*I live,*" Elias said into my mind.

The voice was quiet, but it was there.

Or had I *imagined* it?

"Where...?" I asked, struggling to sit up. My bones *clunked*. I felt many of them protest, cracking and creaking as I shifted in the grass.

"Hey! Don't move too fast!" Slinger said. "You're pretty messed up! Man, that was *crazy*, how you just kept *whacking at that bed* when they were trying to kill you?!"

"Where's Elias?" I asked. I looked around. The forest, brightly lit by the sunlight, swam around me. "Elias, where are you??"

"*I am here, Skeleton Steve,*" he said into my mind.

"It *is* you!" I exclaimed. "You're alive!"

"*I am.*"

"Where *are* you, Elias??"

"Hey, relax," Slinger said. "He's just healing up in the *trees* over there. *You* chill out for a while, Skeleton Steve! I bet you can't even *walk* yet!"

I looked up, and saw Slinger looking off over my shoulder. Craning my boney neck to look behind me, my bones *clunked*, and I could see a faint purple glow under the vast shadow of a dark oak tree. Looking back at Slinger, I saw that he wasn't hurt anymore. In fact, the big spider was practically *glowing* with vitality!

"What happened?" I asked.

Slinger hissed (*was that a sigh?*) and clicked his fangs together.

"Weelllllll," he said. "After you got your butt kicked, and Elias teleported in, breaking the beds and killing the rest of the Noobs while he freaking *melted in the rain*, you fell down and ... stayed there. You and Elias both were *really* messed up, and he crawled off under that tree over there to meditate. I came to check on you, thinking you were dead, but your *eyes* were still glowing, so I figured you just sort of ... *shut down* for a while..."

A sudden grunt caused Slinger to snap his head up and look into the distance for a moment. He hissed.

"What was that?" I asked.

He looked back down at me, his fangs clicking. "Oh, that was the *orange guy*."

"What?!" I exclaimed, trying to sit up. My bones cracked, and I fell back down again.

"Oh, don't worry about *him*," Slinger said with a laugh, rubbing his fangs together. "I took care of *him* alright!"

"What do you mean? Did we get his bed?"

"No," Slinger said. "Not *really*. As far as I can tell, his bed is the *only one left*, since no other Minecraftians have attacked me lately! But, after you guys were out, this guy came by to—I dunno— finish you off? Well, he didn't know that I was hiding like a spider *ninja*, and I webbed him good! Then, I ... you know ... *ate him* a little. But *just* a

542

little! When I found his bed past *those trees over there*," he said, motioning with his fangs, "I set up a *huge* web trap around it. Then, I didn't have to worry about killing him and him *reappearing* there!" Slinger smiled—or at least it *seemed* like he was smiling—and rubbed his fangs back and forth on each other. "I've eaten him ... *oh ... three times now!*"

"Gosh," I said.

"In fact, you should just relax here for a bit. I'm gonna go ... *check* on that guy..."

Slinger turned and sauntered away, his eight feet drumming lightly on the ground.

After a while, I could feel my bones holding together a little stronger. I sat up, and looked down at my broken leg.

It wasn't broken anymore...

One of those bones broke in the fight, I thought, running my fingers along the different sections of my leg. But they were intact now.

I guess *that's* how I heal. Just like the zombies. Some sort of *slow regeneration*...

When I could, I started half-crawling, half-walking toward where Elias was hiding from the sun under a tree. My bones *clunked* and clattered as I stumbled across the clearing, but once I made it to the shadows, I plopped down next to my friend.

My bones *clunked*.

"*Skeleton Steve*..." Elias said into my mind. His mind voice was quiet and weak...

The Enderman ninja sat in his meditation pose like he usually did, but appeared thin and emaciated—like he was starving. His deep black skin stretched over whatever Endermen had for bones, his blank face sick and skinny. The ninja's blue headband rested on his forehead, its dark blue tails draping over his sunken shoulders. Black vapor poured off of his body like smoke—like a strange, black flame—drifting up and away every time the wind blew through the trees.

"Oh my gosh ... *Elias*," I said.

This was all my fault.

I should have never been such a *jerk* to him. Ever since we were in the Nether, I've been treating him like dirt! Maybe his master did assign him to watch over me, but that didn't mean he wasn't my friend. Just as *he* had become *my* friend.

It's a good thing he showed up when he did, or you wouldn't be reading this book!

But still, I felt *terrible*. There was a thick knot of coldness where my heart would be, if I was alive, and I was struggling to say something—*anything*—to make my friend feel better...

"*You're wrong*," he said. "*It is not your fault.*"

"Aww, man—really?" I said. "Can you really just ... *read my thoughts* like that?"

"*Not like you would think*," Elias responded. "*I perceive the images. Feelings. Emotions. And I accept your feelings, Skeleton Steve. You are my friend. I am sorry our circumstances caused you to question that, but make no mistake. I am your friend.*"

If I could have cried, I would have.

"I'm sorry, Elias," I said. "I'm sorry I was a jerk to you. Thank you for saving my life."

"*There is no need to apologize, Skeleton Steve,*" Elias said, cracking his eyes open. He looked at me, his purple eyes a little dimmer than normal. "*I can understand and appreciate your position. Know that my wounded state is not your fault. The battle could have gone no differently, whether our friendship was in question or not.*"

We sat in silence for a moment.

"I guess you're right," I said. "That was just a *tough spot*, wasn't it?"

"*Indeed,*" Elias said.

"When did you think of me as more of a *friend* than ... you know ... your *mission?*"

Elias looked at me with his weak, purple eyes. Black vapor drifted up from his face.

"*When I returned to keep you with me for my Seed Stride, it became immediately apparent that you are of good heart, Skeleton Steve,*" he

546

said. *"As we progressed deeper into the problems of the red energy and the search for your memories, I came to know that our destinies were to be intertwined. There will be a time when I leave you, my friend, but I will always be your friend, and I expect we will always see each other from time to time after my Seed Stride, and my mission, is complete."*

I sighed.

"Are you going to be okay?" I asked. "You look *terrible...*"

Elias closed his eyes again and moved his head back into his meditation posture.

"I will be," he said. *"Truthfully, I have never been this injured. Except for, perhaps, after my first fight with the Skeleton King. The hydrogen and oxygen of the rain, in the configuration you know as water,would have completely disintegrated my body on a cellular level. I am rebuilding the outer-most molecular structure of my form. It may appear very ... disturbing, but I will be okay in time..."*

So we sat, a pile of broken bones and a half-melted Enderman, under that tree for a long time.

Slinger came back and forth, checking on us occasionally, and snacking on the orange man.

What a terrible fate for *that* guy...

Eventually, the spider came back perplexed, but fat and happy.

"I don't get it!" Slinger said. "Every time I killed the guy, he reappeared on his bed, and would try to escape, but get stuck in my webs. So then, I'd just feed on him until he died again, then, we'd do the *same thing* over and over again!"

"So what's the problem?" I asked.

"Well, the last time he died, he reappeared on his bed, but just stood there staring at a tree for a few seconds, then ... *vanished!*"

"Vanished?"

"Yeah, just *pop!* Gone, into thin air!" Slinger looked up at the sky, and clicked his fangs together.

"Weird," I said.

"*Indeed*," Elias said.

Long after the sun went down, and we all sat together in the darkness, Elias and I healing oh-so-slowly, with Slinger just hanging out making shapes out of his webs on his front feet, we heard a commotion of moans coming from the village!

"*Do not worry*," Elias said. "*It is only the zombies from the village come looking for us*."

"You know," I said, "It's really nice having someone like you around that can *tell* these things before they happen."

And Elias was right.

It was just the zombies from town. Or rather, a *search party*, led by Zebulon. The little zombie knight-in-training led the pack of Zombietown citizens through the woods, calling our names.

"Skeleton Steve!" Zebulon bellowed out to the forest. "Good Elias! Where *are* you??"

Over a dozen zombies followed, moaning out at the darkness, occasionally groaning one of our names.

My bones *clunked* when I waved my arm from the darkness.

Yep. I still had to *heal* some more...

"Zebulon!" I called. "We're over here!"

I watched the little zombie peer through the dark night in our direction, then he broke into a run when he saw my waving, boney arm.

"Oh, goodness me!" Zebulon bellowed as he led the group of undead mobs toward us. "Skeleton Steve! Elias! And ... your good *spider* friend, *well met!!* We have been *searching* for you—we feared that you had *perished* in the battle!"

"Yeah, we *almost* perished," I said.

"Good gracious!" the little zombie exclaimed, approaching closer to Elias. "My good Elias! Enderman, sir! You look to be on *death's door!* Is there anything I can do??"

Elias shook his head weakly.

"*No, Zebulon. I will be fine after I regenerate. Thank you for your concern.*"

"You three have *surely* rescued the village for complete destruction! What *bravery* in the face of extreme danger!! That was *brilliant thinking*, good Skeleton Steve, seeking out the brutes' *beds* like that! And, Elias, never before have I seen an Enderman *intentionally* teleport *into* the rain! Such heart! Such *gallantry!*"

"Thanks," I said. "It's just *what we do*, I guess."

"Heroes!" Zebulon said, looking up at the moon. "So you have scattered the *Minecraftian Noob* threat from these woods?"

"Sure did!" Slinger said. "Except for one back there, but don't you worry about *him!*"

Zebulon cocked a little green eyebrow, but smiled and nodded.

"*Outstanding!* It is good to find you and know that you are well. Is there anything we can do to *help* you all? Any way we can help get you back to town, perhaps?"

"*I will wait here for a while*," Elias said. "*We will likely return tomorrow some time.*"

"Actually, there *is* something," I said.

Zebulon nodded to Elias, then looked at me.

"Anything, good Skeleton Steve," he said. "What do you need?"

"Do you know where *Zenon the Enlightened* is? We're going to need to talk to him when we get back."

Zebulon opened his mouth to respond, but another voice called out from the crowd behind him.

"I am *here*, Skeleton Steve."

It was Zenon himself, the hermit of the undercity. The zombie who discovered the Mountain of Wisdom stepped forward from the group, and approached. Just like last time, he looked exactly like every other zombie, but his eyes were crystal clear, and gleamed with intelligence.

552

"Zenon!" I said with a smile. "What are *you* doing out here with the others?"

"I saw the *battle*," he said. "I asked to be a part of the search party to make sure you were okay. What do you ask of me?"

"Well," I said. "I was just wondering about the *Mountain of Wisdom*..."

Zenon rubbed his green chin with zombie fingers and looked off in the direction of the mountain. I knew he wouldn't be able to see it from here, but I guess he had a pretty good idea of which way to go to get there. According to our previous conversation, he had been there what— *two times?*

"What about it? Did you find it?"

"I did," I said.

"And did you find your memories?"

"No," I replied. "Not really. And we spent the whole night up there, just like you did. We even went over to the *next* mountain over to explore the old cobblestone tower there, thinking *that* might be your magical mountain shrine instead!"

"Oh, *that?*" Zenon said. "Nah, that's just an old *Steve* tower."

"*Steve* tower??"

"How strange," Zenon said. "And you spent *all that time* relaxing and contemplating?"

"Yeah. There was nothing up there but a bunch of *torches*."

"Hmm," Zenon said. "Well, *that's* not right. There wasn't a *spawner?*"

"A *spawner?*" I asked. "Like the one where I found you in the undercity?"

"Yeah, a *zombie* spawner, more specifically," the undead mob responded.

"No, I didn't find one, and we looked *everywhere*. Where was it?"

"Well, it's not like it matters, but it was right at the top, kind of covered up in snow, depending on what time of the year you go up there..." He trailed off, looking up at the sky. "Well, I *guess* it might be covered up in snow about now..."

Seriously? I thought.

"*What's a Steve tower?*" Elias asked.

"Oh, hello there, Enderman!" Zenon said, nodding his head. "My, don't *you* look like death warmed over? The *Steve* is the Minecraftian guardian of *this* universe."

"I hear weird stuff," Slinger said suddenly, scuttling closer. "What's all this?"

"*Guardian of this universe?*" Elias asked, opening his purple eyes. "*Please explain yourself.*"

"No, that's enough," Zenon replied. "I've probably said *too much* already. At any rate, I guess the spawner must have been *covered up with snow* when you went up there. Didn't see any *zombies* up there, did you?" He looked back at me.

"Uh ... no," I said. "No zombies."

"So it was still *well-lit*, but just covered up."

"Wait—why didn't you *tell us* about the spawner? Wasn't that relevant?? We searched *all over* for that magical mountain shrine!"

"First of all," Zenon said, "I never said anything about a *magical mountain shrine*. That's just *hearsay*. Second, I didn't think the spawner was relevant. It was just a cobblestone room with a zombie spawner that *the Steve* disabled, with a chest."

"The Steve??" Slinger asked.

"What was in the chest?" I asked.

Zenon rubbed his green chin. "Oh, not much. Just a saddle, a golden apple, some bread—that kind of ... oh ... *wait*..." He frowned.

"What's a golden apple?" I said. My bones *clunked* as I sat a little straighter.

The enlightened zombie laughed, looking up at the sky. He covered his brow with one zombie hand, smiling, then looked back at me. "You know, I'm *sorry*, Skeleton Steve. All this time I never connected the dots together! I just went up there as a *muddled zombie*, then something wonderful happened, and I must have thought I figured it out back when I was still ... *muddled!*"

"What do you mean?"

Zenon smiled, as if enjoying his own private joke. "You see, I climbed that dreadful mountain, poked around the spawner room, ate the golden apple, took the bread with me, left the saddle, then *sat* up on the mountain until my memories came back to me and I could *think* clearly! I guess I always thought my memories came back because of some sort of mysterious *magical quality* to the mountaintop! It *is* a very odd, unique mountain, after all—*you've* seen it!"

"That it is. So what...? The *golden apple?*"

"Yes," Zenon said. "Maybe. Probably. Golden apples do have an effect on zombie memories. *Of course!*" He *thwacked* himself on the forehead and laughed. "How did I never *consider* it?? I'm *sorry*, kiddo!"

I exchanged glances with Elias.

"Could it *really* be just a golden apple?" I asked him.

"*Possible*," Elias said. "*I've only seen golden apples on one occasion before. And they are rather special.*"

"And they can be found as *rare treasure* at times!" Zenon interjected, raising a green finger.

I looked back at the enlightened zombie and smirked.

"Who *are* you??" I asked.

"You *know* who I am," Zenon said. "I'm Zenon! They call me the enlightened zombie."

"*How do you know so much about the universe?*" Elias asked.

"*That's* a tale for another day," the zombie replied, then looked at me. "But I hope it wasn't a waste of time. It sounds like you explored the *tower*, didn't you?"

I nodded, and my bones *clunked*. "I did. We did. Have *you* been inside?"

Zenon rubbed his chin and narrowed his eyes. "So it sounds like your *next step* should be finding yourself a *golden apple*, eh, Skeleton Steve?"

"Yeah, I guess so," I said. "Were there any *more of them* up in that chest on the mountain?"

"Nope," Zenon replied. "I ate the only one. But if you find more dungeons—more *spawners*— you should find one eventually! Maybe you can find one in the desert temples far to the *east...*"

"*Thank you for the information, Zenon,*" Elias said.

"My pleasure, Enderman," he replied with a slight bow. The zombie looked back at me. "Skeleton Steve, I want to thank you for pulling me a little out of that pit of *nihilism* I was in when we met before. I'm sure you have *many more questions* about many more things, but you have more traveling to do before we address any new topics. So, is that all, my *skeletal friend?*"

I looked down and thought for a moment.

Zenon seemed to know a lot more about this world than he let on before, even when I was surprised by how much he knew! This zombie seemed out of place and unconcerned. Amused. Whatever he learned from his experience on the mountain rocked his world.

I never got the same message *he* did.

What left him so unconcerned with life as a zombie? He acted like a man who thought that ... reality ... *wasn't real?*

I shook my head. Where was I going with this?

"Zenon, does any of it matter?" I asked.

Where did *that* come from?

"What a *peculiar question*, Skeleton Steve," Zenon replied. "You've got *quite a brain* in in that skull, kid. To answer your question: no. It doesn't. But *you* had the right idea! You may as well have *fun* along the way!"

I nodded.

"Bye, Zenon."

The enlightened zombie turned back to the group and faded in to the throng of zombies that looked just like him.

"Brave heroes," Zebulon said. "Are you going to be *okay* here? Would you like us to stay with you until morning?"

"I think we'll be okay, Zebulon," I said. "You guys can head back. We'll be there in the—*Oh! Wait!*"

I groaned in pain as I reached around for my pack, and pulled out the book—*Sir Gawain and the Green Knight*—from the library in mysterious tower. I brushed the droplets of rain off of its cover.

"For me??" Zebulon said when I held the book out to him.

"Yeah!" I said. "It's a book about *knights*, I think. Or, at least, a *couple* of knights. I found it in the tower up on the mountain. I thought you might like it, you know—to add it to your *collection!*"

Zebulon took the old book in his little, green hands, and peered at the cover with bright eyes.

"Sir Gawain and the Green ... *Knight??*" he read aloud, grinning ear to ear.

"Yep," I said. "It had mentions about being *bound*, and *promises* and *vows* and such things in there. I thought it'd be right up your alley!"

The little zombie smiled as if he could hardly contain himself, and looked at me with dark eyes full of adoration. When I thought he was about to *burst*, he finally reached out and clapped me on the shoulder. My bones *clunked*.

"Truly a *great gift*, Skeleton Steve! Thank you! I will honor this book *forever*, my good friend!"

Eventually, the rescue party of zombies made their way back to the village, leaving the three of us alone to sit quietly and heal in the darkness of the forest.

Slinger sat in the dirt under the huge tree, making shapes with long, sticky strands of web with his front feet.

"So what now?" I asked. "Look for a *golden apple?*"

"I've got to admit," Elias said. *"That does seem like a logical next step."*

"Where are we gonna *find* one of those things?" Slinger asked. "Back up the mountain?"

"No," I said. "Zenon said that he ate the only one there."

I thought about the zombie spawner I found at the bottom of the abandoned mineshaft, but I didn't remember seeing a chest there. In fact, there were torches planted all around the spawner itself. Maybe if the Minecraftian—*the Steve*—disabled that spawner, he took the chest and whatever was in it with him.

"How about we go to that desert and look for *temples* or whatever?" Slinger asked.

"I believe I have a more practical idea," Elias said. *"My Minecraftian friends back west had large amounts of various treasures back at their castle. I saw such things even back when I was there, looking through their chests, when their home was occupied by the Skeleton King. We should go there.*

They are likely to have one or more of these 'golden apples'..."

"Yeah, that *is* a good idea," I said.

"Minecraftians?" Slinger asked, rubbing his fangs together. I expected more of the same, but when I looked over at my spider friend, I saw that his many glowing red eyes were troubled.

"What's the problem?" I asked.

"Well," Slinger replied. "I've got to assume that since they're your *friends*, I can't *eat* them."

"*Oh course you can't eat them*," Elias replied. "*They are also powerful, so you would likely fail if you tried.*"

"Yeah," I said. "They fought me and my army back when I was the *Skeleton King*..."

Elias shot me a look with a cocked brow.

"*...Apparently*," I amended. "Not as if I *remember* or anything..."

Slinger sighed with a great *hiss*, and sprawled his legs out in the grass.

"It's just gonna be *hard*," he said.

We laughed.

I sat with my friends, wounded and healing, under a great dark oak tree.

In a little while, we would be able to see the sun rise.

And soon, we'd be following the setting sun back toward the Minecraftian castle north of Balder's village.

I looked over at Elias, and observed the wounded ninja, sitting in his pristine meditation posture, black vapor drifting off of him, purple motes of light popping out of his skin from time to time and lazily falling to the ground. The Enderman sat with his eyes closed, his blank face perfectly *at peace*...

What a warrior he was...

Then I looked over at Slinger, who was sprawled out in the dirt, a monstrous spider, focusing on entertaining himself throughout the bored night by playing with his web strands in the tiny claws on the ends of his front legs. His red eyes all blinked, then he looked at me, and made a motion with his spider mouth that I was coming to understand resembled a *smile*.

I didn't know how long these two would be traveling with me, but I welcomed it. And I didn't know what would happen when I finally bit into a golden apple—if anything would happen at all. Maybe I'd *never* get my memories back.

But I'd make lots of new ones, with my good friends...

I sighed, and my bones *clunked*.

Looking up at the square moon, passing slowly through the sky to the west, I smiled.

And I thought about what tomorrow would bring.

I didn't realize until much later that there were also several sets of glowing red eyes watching the same moon that night, just on the *other side* of the clearing. Watching me. Watching *Elias*, especially. And *they* were planning *their* next moves, too...

Wanna know what happens next??
Go to the NEXT BOOK in Season 2!!

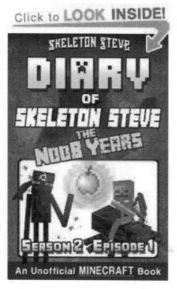

Love MINECRAFT? **Over 20,000 words of kid-friendly fun!**

This high-quality fan fiction fantasy diary book is for kids, teens, and nerdy grown-ups who love to read epic stories about their favorite game!

Hunting the Golden Apple

Skeleton Steve, Elias the Enderman Ninja, and Slinger the Spider are back for more, heading west from Zombietown in search of a golden apple, hoping that it will revive our hero's memory like it did for the mysterious enlightened zombie, Zenon. But as they travel to the castle of Elias's Minecraftian friends, stopping to see new sights on the way, they have no idea that they aren't alone...

And to make matters worse, when they reach the castle, no one's home! A dark and intense attack late in the night by the evil and terrifying Doomstreak Clan reminds Skeleton Steve and his friends that something dreadful is creeping in Diamodia, and Skeleton Steve is directly involved! Will our heroes be able to survive the evil Endermen ninja clan? Will Skeleton Steve get his bony hands on that golden apple?

CHECK OUT
SKELETONSTEVE.COM
... to find the NEXT BOOK!

Sign up for my Free Newsletter to get an *email* when the next book comes out!

Go to: **www.SkeletonSteve.com/sub**

Want More Noob Years?

1. Please go to where you bought this book and *leave a review!* It just takes a minute and it really helps!

2. Join my free *Skeleton Steve Club* and get an email when the next book comes out!

3. Look for your name under my *"Amazing Readers List"* at the end of the book, where I list my *all-star reviewers*. Heck—maybe I'll even use your name in a story if you want me to! (*Let me know in the review!*)

About the Author - Skeleton Steve

I am *Skeleton Steve*, author of *epic* unofficial Minecraft books. *Thanks for reading this book!*

My stories aren't your typical Minecraft junkfood for the brain. I work hard to design great plots and complex characters to take you for a roller coaster ride in their shoes! Er ... claws. Monster feet, maybe?

All of my stories written by (just) me are designed for all ages—kind of like the Harry Potter series—and they're twisting journeys of epic adventure! For something more light-hearted, check out my "Fan Series" books, which are collaborations between myself and my fans.

Smart kids will love these books! Teenagers and nerdy grown-ups will have a great time relating with the characters and the stories, getting swept up in the struggles of, say, a novice Enderman ninja (Elias), or the young and naïve creeper king

(Cth'ka), and even a chicken who refuses to be a zombie knight's battle steed!

I've been *all over* the Minecraft world of Diamodia (and others). As an adventurer and a writer at heart, I *always* chronicle my journeys, and I ask all of the friends I meet along the way to do the same.

Make sure to keep up with my books whenever I publish something new! If you want to know when new books come out, sign up for my mailing list and the *Skeleton Steve Club*. **It's free!**

Here's my website:

www.SkeletonSteve.com

You can also 'like' me on **Facebook**: Facebook.com/SkeletonSteveMinecraft

And 'follow' me on **Twitter**: Twitter.com/SkeletonSteveCo

And watch me on **Youtube**: (Check my website.)

"Subscribe" to my Mailing List and Get Free Updates!

I *love* bringing my Minecraft stories to readers like you, and I hope to one day put out over 100 stories! If you have a cool idea for a Minecraft story, please send me an email at *Steve@SkeletonSteve.com*, and I might make your idea into a real book. I promise I'll write back. :)

Other Books by Skeleton Steve

The "Noob Mob" Books

Books about individual mobs and their adventures becoming heroes of Diamodia.

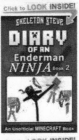

Diary of a Creeper King
Book 1
Book 2
Book 3
Book 4

Diary of a Skeleton Steve - The Noob Years
FULL SEASON ONE

Skeleton Steve – The Noob Years
Season 1, Episode 1 – ***FREE!!***
Season 1, Episode 2
Season 1, Episode 3
Season 1, Episode 4
Season 1, Episode 5
Season 1, Episode 6
Season 2, Episode 1
Season 2, Episode 2
Season 2, Episode 3
Season 2, Episode 4
Season 2, Episode 5
Season 2, Episode 6
Season 2, Episode 6
Season 3, Episode 1
Season 3, Episode 2
Season 3, Episode 3
Season 3, Episode 4
Season 3, Episode 5
Season 3, Episode 6

Diary of a Teenage Zombie Villager
Book 1 – ***FREE!!***
Book 2
Book 3
Book 4

Diary of a Chicken Battle Steed
Book 1
Book 2
Book 3
Book 4

Diary of a Lone Wolf
Book 1
Book 2
Book 3
Book 4

Diary of an Enderman Ninja
Book 1 – *FREE!!*
Book 2
Book 3

Diary of a Separated Slime – Book 1

Diary of an Iron Golem Guardian – Book 1

The "Skull Kids" Books

A Continuing Diary about the Skull Kids, a group of world-hopping players

Diary of the Skull Kids
Book 1 – *FREE!!*
Book 2
Book 3

The "Fan Series" Books

Continuing Diary Series written by Skeleton Steve *and his fans!* Which one is your favorite?

Diary of Steve and the Wimpy Creeper
Book 1
Book 2
Book 3

Diary of Zombie Steve and Wimpy the Wolf
Book 1 *COMING SOON*

The "Tips and Tricks" Books

Handbooks for Serious Minecraft Players, revealing Secrets and Advice

Skeleton Steve's Secret Tricks and Tips

Skeleton Steve's Top 10 List of Rare Tips

Skeleton Steve's Guide to the
First 12 Things I Do in a New Game

Get these books as for FREE!

(**Visit www.SkeletonSteve.com to *learn more***)

Series Collections and Box Sets

Bundles of Skeleton Steve books from the Minecraft Universe. Entire Series in ONE BOOK.

Great Values! Usually 3-4 Books (sometimes more) for almost the price of one!

Skeleton Steve – The Noob Years – Season 1
Skeleton Steve – The Noob Years – Season 2

Diary of a Creeper King – Box Set 1

Diary of a Lone Wolf – Box Set 1

Diary of an Enderman NINJA – Box Set 1

Diary of the Skull Kids – Box Set 1

Steve and the Wimpy Creeper – Box Set 1

Diary of a Teenage Zombie Villager – Box Set 1

Diary of a Chicken Battle Steed — Box Set 1

Sample Pack Bundles

Bundles of Skeleton Steve books from multiple series! New to Skeleton Steve? Check this out!

Great Values! Usually 3-4 Books (sometimes more) for almost the price of one!

Skeleton Steve and the Noob Mobs Sampler Bundle
Book 1 Collection
Book 2 Collection
Book 3 Collection
Book 4 Collection

-

Check out the website
www.SkeletonSteve.com
for more!

Enjoy this Excerpt from...

"Diary of an **Enderman Ninja**" Book 1

<u>About the book</u>:

Love MINECRAFT? ****Over 16,000 words of kid-friendly fun!****

This high-quality fan fiction fantasy diary book is for **kids, teens, and nerdy grown-ups** who love to read *epic stories* about their favorite game!

Elias was a young Enderman. And he was a NINJA.

As an initiate of the Order of the Warping Fist, Elias is sent on a mission by his master to investigate the deaths of several Endermen at Nexus 426. Elias is excited to prove himself as a novice martial artist, but is a little nervous--he still hasn't figured out how to dodge arrows!

And now, when the young Enderman ninja discovers that the source of the problem is a trio of tough, experienced Minecraftian players, will he be in over his head? And what's this talk about a 'Skeleton King' and an army of undead?

Love Minecraft adventure??

Read on for an Excerpt for the book!

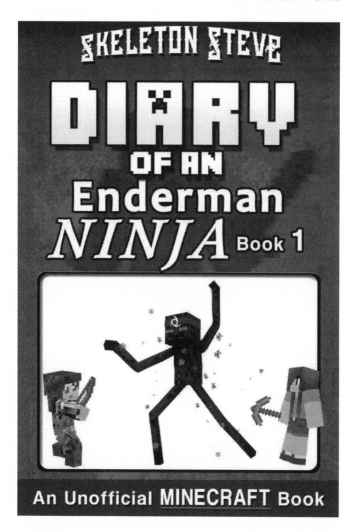

Day 1 - Overworld

When I teleported to the Overworld, I never thought that I would be starting a *diary*.

It is always interesting, the adventures that life puts in my path. So here I am, an Enderman, sitting on a rock and penning words into this empty book I found in a chest.

The day is clear today. Warm. Very pleasant.

It feels strange, trying to think of things to say with my fingers instead of with my mind, to use this archaic quill and ink to put words on paper.

The grass, and the leaves in the trees, are swaying and whispering in the wind, as I scratch these words onto paper in this leather-bound book resting on my lap.

Such is the way.

I am reminded frequently by the flow of the world around me to ignore my expectations, because once I expect something to go *one* way, the universe opens like a flower and teases me into another direction.

But I am ninja, so I flow like water.

Or, at least, I *try* to.

So I embrace this journal. This diary.

I will write of my adventures on my *Seed Stride*, and it will become part of my way. A painting of this path on my journey of life.

My name is Elias, and I am Ender.

I am also an initiate in the Order of the Warping Fist—a unique group of Endermen *ninja*. By now, I would have normally been granted the title of 'lower ninja', but the end of my initiate training was interrupted by the Seed Stride.

It occurs to me that writing this diary gives life to my story, and my story may travel on away from me once it has life. One day, my story and I may go separate ways—my body and my words separate, but together.

So I must explain.

The 'Seed Stride' is a rite of passage for young Endermen. Just before we reach adulthood and become full members of the Ender race, we are compelled to go on a Seed Stride. This is the first of many Seed Strides I will take over the course of my life, to help contribute to the well-being and expansion of my people.

We Ender, as a race, rely on the Pearls, our *Chi*, to produce more Ender, and to attune ourselves to the rhythm of the universe. Our Chi is also the source of our power to teleport, to warp between worlds, and also enhances our ability to communicate by the voice of the mind.

Such things we Ender take for granted. But it is possible that *you*, whoever picks up this book, as my story decides to *travel* later, may not understand the simple concepts that I've known since my birth.

So, now that you understand, *know* that my first Seed Stride was the reason my initiate ninja training was interrupted before completion.

Mature Endermen all understand, either through training or experience, how to dodge arrows and other missile weapons through the awareness they achieve by being in tune with their *Chi* and the world around them.

I'm still working on it.

When it was time to begin my Seed Stride, I was a little concerned that I hadn't yet mastered the Chi dodge, but as a ninja, I am comfortable enough in my combat ability to make up for my lack of skill in Chi.

Once my Seed Stride is complete, I will return to my master to complete my training. Then, I will increase in rank to lower ninja and start participating in real missions.

I understand that I am supposed to control my emotions. But the idea of finally being a real ninja and going on missions for the Order excites me! I'm sure that such excitement clouds my mind with impatience...

But I've got that impatience under control—really, I do!

So, I mentioned that the Ender people rely on the pearls. The pearls are the source of our enhanced power; the technology of our race.

I received my Ender pearl when I was very small. After going through the trials like all Ender younglings, I was chosen for the order. Some Endermen are more naturally in tune with their Chi than others. My connection and potential showed that I would be one of the few chosen to protect and further the race.

And now, I was almost fully-grown.

Though I recognize the value of humility, I was confident in my strengths.

I'm strong. And fast. And my martial arts skill is among the highest in my class.

I was sure that my connection with my Chi would catch up.

But I was out of time.

The time of my Seed Stride had come, so my training was paused, and now I am sitting on a rock in the sun, being one with the wind and the grass, and writing in this book...

Earlier today, I found a jungle.

The tall, green trees and lush ground was a most interesting biome! There were pools of water here and there, and I realized that a place so green had to experience frequent rain.

Warping through the environment, searching for pearl seeds in the dirt under thick vegetation, I knew that I needed to stay sharp—I wouldn't want to get caught in the rain!

But it didn't rain.

And I found *four* pearl seeds in dirt blocks during the time I traveled and warped through the interesting and lush environment. Trying to sense the Ender energy within, I picked up and discarded block after block of dirt until I could feel the pull of the Chi inside.

Whenever I found a dirt block containing a pearl seed, I opened my dimensional pocket, and stored the block with the other seed blocks for my return home.

The dirt blocks I collected would stay inside the dimensional pocket until I returned to the End at the completion of my Seed Stride.

There was no requirement or limit on the amount of blocks an Enderman was expected to collect on a Seed Stride. Finding the pearl seeds for our people was something engrained in us from an early age—something we were expected to do as a service to our race.

I figured that I would know when I had collected enough seeds. My heart was open, and I would listen to my instinct. Once I finished this Seed Stride, and was satisfied with my service to the Ender people, I would return to the End to plant my seeds and continue my ninja training.

Some Endermen collected more seeds than others. And some dedicated their *entire lives* to the Seed Stride, walking the Overworld forever in search of the dirt blocks that held the promise of a growing pearl.

I would work hard, and collect many seeds. My life as a member of the Order was sworn to a duty to the people, after all. But my real goals lay in the path to becoming a better ninja.

I loved being a ninja. And once I rose to the rank of a lower ninja, I would at least have the respect of my peers.

Yes, maybe I suffered from a *little* bit of pride. I was aware.

But I knew what I wanted.

I wanted to be the best.

The strongest and fastest ninja. I wanted to be a shadow. In time, I hoped that I could even become a master, and be able to channel my Chi into fireballs, and do all of the other cool ninja stuff that Master Ee-Char could do.

So far, I had twenty-seven seeds. Pausing to peer into my dimensional pocket, I counted them again. Twenty-seven blocks of dirt, all holding the promise of growing an Ender pearl to be joined with twenty-seven Ender younglings in the future. Perhaps one of them would also become a ninja, like me.

When I was in the jungle, earlier today, I found an old structure. Old for *Minecraftians*, I guess.

The small building was made of chiseled stone blocks, now overrun with vines and green moss.

As I explored the inside of the old Minecraftian structure, I noted that it was some sort of *temple*. My ninja awareness easily detected a couple of rotting, crude traps, and I avoided the trip lines and pressure plates without effort.

Inside a wooden chest, among a bunch of Minecraftian junk and zombie meat, I found *this book*.

Out of curiosity, I experimented with the levers by the stairs, until I revealed a hidden room with another wooden chest. Just more junk. Pieces of metal and bones.

Those Minecraftians and their junk...

At least, I *figured* it was Minecraftian junk. I had never personally *met* one of the creatures before. From what I'd heard in my training and tales from other Endermen, the Minecraftians were small and weak, but were intelligent, and were able to transform the Overworld into tools, armor, and other technology that made them stronger.

The older Endermen told me stories about the famous *Steve*, as well as other Minecraftians that came and went frequently on the Overworld. We even saw a Minecraftian or two appear every once and a while on the dragon's island, stuck on our world because of dabbling with portal technology they didn't understand. I've never seen them myself, but I've heard about the incidents from Endermen who were there at the time.

Usually, the visiting Minecraftians had it out for the dragon.

It never lasted long.

Apparently, they were usually surprised when they appeared on the obsidian receiver, and realized that there was no way to get home! I've heard that when they inevitably decide to attack the dragon, the great, ancient beast just *plucks them up* and throws them out into the void.

Well, now I had a piece of their junk. This book was constructed from leather and paper, which was likely constructed from something else. This ink was created by Minecraftians as well—all components derived from plants, animals, and minerals of the Overworld, to be sure.

What a beautiful day!

This Overworld is very bright during the day—uncomfortably so. But it's very peaceful and lovely.

I think I'll meditate for a while and write more tomorrow...

Day 2 - Overworld

After meditating, filling my Chi, and exploring the Overworld during the night, I decided to stay out in the open again during the next day.

I ran into another couple of Endermen during the night, a time when exploring is a lot easier on our eyes. But now, during the day, now that the sunlight is flooding the world around me, I'm all alone again.

During my training, I was never told to only go out at night, but it seems to be an unspoken rule of my people on the Seed Stride here. And I can understand why. The sun was so bright and hot on my eyes! But I didn't care. Let the others go into hiding or warp back to the End during the day. I had *seeds* to collect and an infinite world to explore!

Today, I observed the animals and the Overworld's native mobs.

There were several different kinds of beasts that I found, as I teleported from valley to valley, hillside to hillside, as the sky lightened with the rising sun. White, clucking birds, fluffy sheep, spotted cows, pink pigs. I was able to understand them by using my Chi to perceive their thoughts, but their language was very basic and they mostly communicated with each other through grunts and noises.

"*What is your name?*" I asked a particular chicken with my *mind voice*.

"*I am a chicken,*" it thought back. "Bawk!" it said aloud.

"*What is your purpose?*"

"*I am eating.*"

The bird scratched at the ground with its goofy yellow feet, pulling plant seeds out of the tall grass.

As the morning went on, I noticed that some of the larger, more complicated creatures, the *mobs*, as I was taught they were called, *burst* into flames as the sun settled higher into the sky!

Skeletons and zombies raced around, frantic and on fire, until they burned up and left behind nothing but piles of ash, bones, and charred meat.

What an interesting world.

As I teleported into the shadows of a tall, dark forest, I found a lone zombie hiding from the sun under a pine tree. He held a metal shovel in his hand—a Minecraftian tool.

"*Excuse me*," I said into his mind.

"Who...? Who's there?" the zombie asked in a dull, slow voice. The creature looked around with black eyes.

I stepped out from the shadows to where it couldn't help but notice me. It's not like I was *trying* to hide before—I don't know how it didn't see me.

The zombie's face stretched in surprise. "Oh!" it cried. "You surprised me! So sneaky!" It settled down, paused, and stood vacant for a moment before speaking again. "What you want?"

"*I was wondering … why does the sun sets zombies on fire?*" I said into its mind.

The zombie was shocked. "The sun sets zombies on *fire?!*" It was suddenly very aware of the sunlight just outside of the shadow of the tree, and the poor undead creature clutched at the pine's trunk to keep away from the light.

"*Elias,*" I suddenly heard in my mind. The voice of another Enderman. "*Behind you.*"

Turning, I saw, across a sunny valley, was an area of deep shadow under a cliff—probably a cave. Another Enderman stood inside. From here, I could see his eyes glowing purple in the dark, and I could barely make out the white symbol of the *Order of the Warping Fist* on his black headband.

Another ninja.

I left the zombie, teleporting across the valley to stand before the other Enderman.

"*What is it, sir?*" I asked. It was Erion, a lower ninja from the rank just above me. He had finished his initial training, and would now be expected to perform minor missions while still taking training from his master. His headband was black instead of blue (like mine), but still bore the white symbol of a novice.

Soon I would have a black headband like his.

"Elias, you have been summoned by Master Ee'char. He has ordered that you return to the Temple immediately."

"But ... my Seed Stride...?"

"Master Ee'char is aware that you are on Seed Stride. He has sent me to find you and ask you to return to him, still." Erion broke eye contact for a moment, and glared around at the sunny valley. *"What are you doing exploring during the day?"*

"Thank you, Erion. I'll return directly," I said into his mind.

The other Enderman ninja nodded, then disappeared with a *zip* and a brief shower of tiny, purple motes of light.

I turned, and noticed that the zombie I was talking to was gone. In front of the tree, outside of the shadow and in the sunlight, was a pile of charred meat … and a shovel.

Huh.

What a strange world.

Teleporting around on a single world was easy. It was a lot like making a long jump—didn't require much energy, much of my *Chi*. I could overdo it, of course. If I warped around too much in too short a period of time, I would … get tired, in a way. If my energy became too low, I would have to wait, or meditate for a while, until I had enough Chi to teleport again.

While exploring during my Seed Stride, the more I practiced harnessing my Chi for warping, the more I could do it without resting. I suppose there would come a time when teleporting on one world like I did here—hill to hill, place to place— would become as easy as blinking my eyes. In time.

But not yet. I still had to try. Still had to focus. And I could still get tired.

Teleporting was easier today than it was yesterday, though. With practice, I'd be able to warp more without resting and recharging my Chi—I was sure of it!

Jumping to another world was a different matter, however.

Going back and forth between the Overworld and the End was difficult, and required me to focus and have very strong Chi. The act needed *all* of my energy. And I'd probably need to recharge quite a bit before I could do it again.

So I sat on the cool stone in the shadow of the cave mouth, my legs crossed, my hands open and resting on my knees, receptive to the Overworld's Ender energy.

I meditated for a while, and let my thoughts dissipate. Focused only on my breathing, I willed my body to be a *receiver* for the energy of the world—the combined energy of all of the pearl seeds hidden in the blocks around me ... the energy of the world's core. It all funneled into me, moving up my arms, my legs, spiraling to my center ... to my *Chi*.

My Ender pearl was warm inside of me.

And I warped home.

CURRENTLY FREE!!

Enjoy this Excerpt from...

"Diary of a **Creeper King**" Book 1

<u>About the book</u>:

Ever heard of the **Creeper King**, mighty Cth'ka?

Read the adventure diary of a young creeper who was looking for a way to protect himself without *blowing up*!

When Cth'ka the Creeper and Skeleton Steve leave the forest to ask the local witch for help, they are soon on a long and dangerous journey to find a **secret artifact** that will allow Cth'ka the power to move blocks *with his mind*! But will the difficulty of traveling across the Minecraft world, a village under attack, hiding from a fully-armored killer hero, and finding the way to a hidden stronghold be too much for a creeper and his skeleton companion to handle?

Love Minecraft adventure??

Read on for an Excerpt for the book!

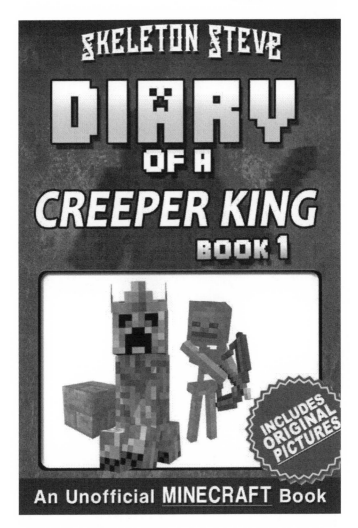

Day 1

Let's see ... is this '*Night* 1' or '*Day* 1'? I figure I'll write these entries in terms of *days*, since I never sleep. I will try to ignore the fact that, since I don't have hands that I can write with, I'm sitting under a tree right now *dictating*, saying my story out loud, to my good friend, Skeleton Steve.

He says that I should just tell the story like I'm writing it. I'll give this a try.

My name is Cth'ka. I'm a creeper. I don't know if that's the *real* name of my race, but that's what everyone calls us, so it works.

Other creepers would probably say that I'm a weird guy. An oddball.

But other creepers don't say much.

That's what's different about me. I don't know very much about where we came from. Heck, I don't even remember much about a year or so ago.

How did I get here? As far as I know, I've always lived in this forest. Skeleton Steve calls it "Darkwood Forest". He says that there are hundreds—*thousands* of other forests, so he likes to give names to places.

I do love this place.

The hills rise and fall, and the trees are thick, tall, and dark. *Dark oak*, Steve says. It's a very large forest too. I've never felt much of an urge to leave.

On one side of the forest, where the hills slope down, there's a thick jungle where the trees are different. On another side, the hills rise higher and higher until the trees stop, and snowy peaks reach into the sky.

I never go there, to the cold mountains. Hardly ever, really. I prefer to be in warmer places.

The jungle is nice and warm, but it's also full of water and rivers, and I don't care for water—not at all.

On the other sides of Darkwood forest, the hills continue for quite a ways with tall, dark oak trees, until they wind down into some grassy plains full of flowers and horses.

I love this forest, but I'm getting side-tracked.

Creepers are very solitary. I've seen many creatures in this world, living in and passing through my forest. Some creatures have moms and dads. Most of them are babies and then grow up. The zombies and skeletons don't. I don't know where *they* come from. Where Skeleton Steve came from. I think he was something else before he became who he is today.

I don't know much about my past. Or where my race came from.

I don't remember having a mom or dad. And I don't remember being smaller, or growing up in any way. I hope to find out about these things in time.

Creepers don't exactly have a library of their race's past. There's nothing to study. Nothing we can learn from our elders. I can't even tell the difference between a young creeper and an old creeper! I assume that I'm young, but maybe we just don't have very good memories. Who knows?

And the creepers I see while I walk around my forest don't have much to say either.

Earlier today, I was in my favorite part of Darkwood. My *clearing*. Near the very middle of this forest is a large clearing, a place where the trees break, and a wide valley of grass stretches out a long way. Red and yellow flowers pepper the open expanse. I love to go there during the day and watch the flowers sway in the breeze, feel the sun on my skin, and watch the clouds roll by.

At the time, Skeleton Steve was back in the forest. He doesn't sleep either, but he can't explore with me during the day. If Skeleton Steve steps into the sunlight ... *foom*! He'd catch on fire. I've only seen it happen once before—he's pretty careful. But I guess that's just part of being undead.

So Skeleton Steve was back in the thickest part of the forest, waiting out the day in the shadow of a large dark oak tree, and I was watching another creeper walk across the clearing.

Whenever I see another creeper, I always try to make conversation, to learn about them. It's always my hope to learn more about my people, and to make friends who are like me.

"Hi there," I said.

The other creeper noticed me, said nothing, then turned to continue moving away. I followed.

"My name is Cth'ka. What's yoursss?"

The other creeper stopped, and turned to face me. "What you wantsss?"

"I don't sssee othersss like me very often. Where did you come from? Where are you going?"

"What doesss it matter to you?" he said in a gravelly voice. He turned, and continued walking through the valley.

"I jussst want to be friendsss," I said to his back. "Pleassse tell me about yoursssself!"

I stopped.

The other creeper kept moving, without speaking again, and I stood in the sun and watched until he disappeared into the shadows of the dark oak trees.

Later that day, when the sun went down, I walked back to where I knew Skeleton Steve was waiting for me. In the shadows of the darkening forest, I could see the glowing red dots of his eyes, hovering in the middle of his empty black eye sockets, watching me approach.

"Why do you always try to talk to the other creepers?" Skeleton Steve asked after I told him about my day. "They always act the same way."

We were walking along a ridge, watching the moon rise into the sky. Skeleton Steve's face was silver in the fading light. I could see in the darkness just fine, but when the light faded away, the colors of the world disappeared too. I did love the daylight, when everything was bold and colorful. It was too bad that Skeleton Steve always had to hide in the dark.

"I've got to try," I said. "There have to be more creepersss out there like me. I want to know more about why we're here. How we creepersss *get* here."

"So many creepers are just ... grumpy, it seems," Skeleton Steve said.

We walked in silence for a while.

"I wonder if we're ssstuck like thisss, or if there will ever be sssomeone to bring usss together. If there are other creepersss, sssmart like me, I'm sure we can do *great* thingsss."

"Why are you so interested in other creepers?" Skeleton Steve said.

"I think … it would be a good thing for usss to come together," I said. I wasn't quite sure what I was getting at, but I knew that I wanted creepers, as a *people*, to find strength together somehow. To have a real race, a real history. Something unique that we could pass down to whatever it meant to be the next generation. I didn't even know if creepers had children, or how more creepers came to be. "We could maybe be—I don't know—a *real race*. Develop ourssselvesss instead of jussst being like animalsss wandering around all alone."

"You mean like creeper cities? A creeper nation?" Skeleton Steve said, smirking.

"I don't know," I said. "I jussst feel like, we could be … more."

Day 2

I stayed with Skeleton Steve in the dark during the day. We were close to the jungle, and I thought it might be fun to walk along the border when the sun went down. We might even see some areas of the jungle that were dry enough to let us walk down into it for a while without having to cross any *water*.

It would be nice to feel the warmth of the tropical forest. I hadn't visited the jungle in a long time.

Another creeper passed by, and I was at least able to get his name. Car'nuk. But we didn't talk about much else. I tried to find out how old Car'nuk was, and where he lived, but, like all of the others, he scowled at me, and went on his way.

It was a little sad, how difficult it was to communicate with my people. It's like we creepers were designed to never have anything to do with each other. And that was a pity. Creepers are natural-born explorers. We walk, all day and all night, and I'm sure there would be *plenty* to talk about if the others like me weren't so grumpy about having conversations.

When the sun went down, Skeleton Steve and I walked to the next ridge over, where we could look down into the jungle. Even in the fading light, I was surprised at how *green* the area was.

Some of the trees were squat and so thick that it made it hard to see the ground beneath them, and they were covered with vines that descended like green, ropy sheets from the treetops. Other trees were massive and tall, popping out of the canopy with large clumps of leaves extending in multiple directions.

I bet it rained a lot here.

It was hard to see through the trees, but I could see water here and there, down below. There must be rivers and pools *all over*.

I could never live in the jungle. I don't like the water. Never have. I've always had a hard time with the idea of floating in the water, even though I've seen other creepers swim before—I don't know how to ssswim, and didn't know if I'd ever be able to figure it out.

With my little legs, the idea of not being able to keep my head out of water, the idea of sssplashing and ssstruggling to get back to sssolid ground .... my lungsss filling up with water .... Sssssssssss ... sssssssssplashing, ssssssstruggling ...

No thanksss. Just the *thought* of being stuck in water gets me all ... excited. I've always thought it would be better to avoid water altogether.

As Skeleton Steve and I walked along the ridge, we looked out over the expanse of trees into the dense jungle below. The ridge descended gently into an area of jungle that wasn't as thick.

I hesitated.

"It's okay," Skeleton Steve said. "I don't see anything bad in there. It's just *part* jungle. Do you want to see what it looks like inside?"

I walked with him down into the tree-line. Darkwood Forest was behind us now, just on the other side of the ridge. There were no rivers or pools in the immediate area. No water.

We stood, peering into the depths of the jungle, and I was thinking about heading back to the forest when I saw movement! Green.

Another *creeper*!

I saw the distinct shape, its head turn, a face like mine looking back at us from the darkness for just a moment before it turned again.

"Hey!" I shouted. "Hello there!"

The creeper stood still, then turned to look at us again.

"Let'sss go in!" I said.

Skeleton Steve shrugged, and followed me deeper into the jungle.

We approached the creeper, and I called out to him again from a distance. "Hi there, fellow creeper! I'm Cth'ka! Do you live here in the jungle?"

As we continued making our way to my new friend through the heavy underbrush, I saw the creeper suddenly snap his attention to one side, then stagger back a few steps. I could hear him

630

hiss, unsure at first, then again—intensely! The creeper fell back again, and I saw something on its chest—a *blur* of a creature, dim without color, but ... *spots*?

The creeper was under attack?!

I was suddenly afraid, and faintly heard Skeleton Steve, at my side, pull out his bow and nock an arrow. The creeper hissed again, a continual, rising, sputtering sound! It was definitely an animal of some kind, a spotted creature, small, clawing and biting at my intended friend.

"Ocelot!" Skeleton Steve said.

Expanding and shaking, hissing even louder, the creeper suddenly *exploded* with a thunderous *boom!*

What?! *How*?

How did that ...?

Shocked, I stood, staring at the spot where the creeper and the ocelot were fighting, now a crater of raw dirt and shredded plants, and I felt fear wash over me again when I saw two white and yellow forms darting through the bushes … straight at *me*.

Two more ocelots! Little greens eyes, focused on me.

"Run!" Skeleton Steve yelled, and I stumbled backwards as an arrow suddenly struck one of the cats. It turned and sprinted off to Steve.

As I focused on the ocelot about to attack me, trying to force my body turn and run away back up the hill, my *hearing* seemed to tighten around my heartbeat, my vision darkened around the edges, and Skeleton Steve's shouted warnings suddenly seemed very far away…

The ocelot leapt through the air at me, and I felt its claws and teeth sink into my body. I tried to turn and run, but it was hanging onto me. My hearing, now weird and hollow like I was in a deep cave, was focusing more and more on a … hissing sound … I ssscrambled, tried to essscape, tried to call for Ssskeleton Sssteve … Sssssssssss …

"Sssteve!   Ssssssssssssssssssssssssssssssave
me!"

An arrow appeared out of nowhere sssticking out of the ocelot'sss ssside, and the cat fell. I turned and sssaw Ssskeleton Sssteve nocking another arrow, aiming past me.

I ran up the hill. Turned. Sssaw Ssskeleton Sssteve kill the ocelot. He ran to catch up to me, his bonesss rattling.

We ran back up the hill out of the jungle together, back up to the ridge.

"Are you okay?" Skeleton Steve said.

I could suddenly hear again, see again, like normal!

"Yesss," I said. "What … sssssssssss …. What happened?"

Skeleton Steve sat on the ridge, looking out over the jungle, his bow still in his hand.

"Those were ocelots," he said. "Mostly harmless animals. Strange that they attacked. Usually they mind their own business. I know they don't like creepers, but I've never seen them *attack* one before."

"What happened to the creeper?" I asked. "It *blew up!*"

Skeleton Steve looked at me. "You don't know?" he asked.

I shook my head.

Skeleton Steve's glowing red dots of eyes looked me over. "That—blowing up—that's what creepers *do*. They explode. In self-defense, and also when they're attacking a *Steve*."

"When they're attacking *you?*"

"No," Skeleton Steve said. "A *Steve*." He looked off at the moon. "My name is Steve, yes, but there is another creature on this world named 'Steve' as well. He's different than us."

"But why *explode?*" I said.

"That's all that the creeper *could* do," Skeleton Steve said. "When the ocelot attacked him, he exploded in self-defense, and killed it."

I was so confused. Why would he defend himself ... by killing himself?

"It doesn't make sssensssse," I said.

Skeleton Steve looked at me. "No one knows why creepers explode, Cth'ka. There's no other way for them to defend themselves, really. And I've never seen a creeper really *care*. I've seen creepers launch themselves at Steve and happily blow up in his face!" He regarded me for a moment. "*You* were about to explode too, you know. When that ocelot attacked you? I'm surprised you didn't, actually."

I looked down at my body, at the wounds where the cat had ripped at me.

So *that's* what that was—when I was losing concentration, when my vision and my hearing changed. Was I preparing to blow myself up?

"Why didn't I explode?" I asked.

"I don't know," Skeleton Steve said. "Maybe you're a little different? Maybe with how *smart* you are, compared to other creepers I've seen, you're able to control yourself better? We'll have to look into that some more—so you can survive longer. I'd hate to lose you as my friend, if you ever get attacked again and blow up, or if we run into the *Steve*."

What a twist to my pleasant little life, roaming around in my forest! I had never seen a creeper explode before. I didn't even know it was possible. And now, there was a way that, if I was freaked out enough, I could lose control of my mind and blow myself up, too?

No way! That's crazy. I had a life to live. I wanted to bring 'creeperkind' together and learn more about our race. To learn more about our past and our culture ... if there was one. Surely there was more to the creeper race than random solitary creatures that avoid having friends and then eventually blow themselves up?

What could I do?

I was defenseless. If Skeleton Steve wasn't with me, I would have been helpless, and killed by those ocelots. Or turned myself into a living bomb and ended up *dead* just the same.

"How can I defend mysssself?" I muttered.

We sat quietly for a few moments. The tall grass swayed in the night breeze.

"I have an idea," Skeleton Steve said. He was watching me as I sat, thinking. "*You* are special, Cth'ka. I'd like to see you learn to control your 'defense mechanism' and be able to defend yourself properly, but you can't use weapons like me, and you can't run very fast. We should go and talk to the witch! Maybe she'll have an idea."

"Witch?" I asked.

"Yes," Steve said. "There's a witch not too far from here, named Worla. I've dealt with her in the past, and she's very clever. She might be able to figure out why you're different. Maybe she'll have an idea about how to make it *easier* for you to survive without blowing yourself up one day."

For the rest of the night, Skeleton Steve and I traveled to the edge of the forest that was closest to the swamp. Before the sun came up, we found a small cave, and decided to wait out the day in there.

Day 3

When the sun went down, and undead could walk around outside safely again, we departed for the witch.

Standing at the edge of the forest, I could feel Darkwood behind me like a warm, safe hug, and the plains stretching out ahead of us, the empty rolling hills in the distance were … unknown.

We struck out, down from the shadows of the dark oak trees, into green and yellow fields. A group of horses of different colors stood quietly in the grass far off to the left, staying still in the night. A couple of zombies roamed aimlessly in the valley nearby.

"So, over those hills ahead," Skeleton Steve said, "is a swamp where Worla lives."

"A ssswamp?" I said. "Like, full of … water?"

Skeleton Steve laughed.

"Yes," he said. "Swamps are full of water. But that's where *witches* live."

"Can't we just have her come to usss?"

Skeleton Steve looked back at me while we walked. "Cth'ka, sometimes, to get good things, you have to take *risks*."

We walked across the great, open valley, then up into some sparse hills, as the wind whistled across the plain and the moon slowly moved across the sky. The hills were mostly devoid of trees at first, then started sprouting white trees here and there. Skeleton Steve called them 'Birch' trees. The hills rolled on, with more and more trees, until we seemed to be heading downhill all the time, and the trees turned darker.

Eventually, vines started growing from the trees, then further on, thick *sheets* of vines cascaded down their sides, a lot like the trees we saw in the jungle. The ground flattened out, and we were suddenly standing at the edge of a huge swamp, with random dirt and mud and water alternating as far as I could see, full of weeping trees. The air was hot and wet, and large lily pads spotted the surface of the water.

"That'sss a *lot* of water," I said.

"It's okay," Skeleton Steve said. "We'll stay on land where we can, and you can use the lily pads when you need to."

Lily pads? A sssaucer of *plant stuff* being the only thing keeping me from drowning in the murky water of this dreadful place?

"Where'sss the witch?" I said.

"Worla's hut is a little ways past that outcropping of rock over there," Skeleton Steve said, pointing to a spire of rock sticking out of a small hill, deep in the swamp.

Over the next few hours, we traveled across the bog. There was a *lot* of water, but Skeleton Steve was right! He was careful in planning where to walk, and planning ahead, and we stayed on dry ground most of the time. There were a few places where I had to cross water, but we were able to avoid swimming by finding areas where the land was close together, and joined with lily pads.

Once we reached the spire landmark, Skeleton Steve pointed deeper into the swamp, and I saw, in the fog, a small, dark dwelling standing on wooden stilts. The light of a fire inside made the hut stand out in the darkness.

"I've never ssseen a witch before," I said.

"Just be respectful, and certainly stay calm!" Skeleton Steve said with a smile.

When we approached the little building, I was relieved to see that it was mostly on land. I was afraid that I would have to cross more lily pads or even try to cross open water to get there. A rickety wooden ladder was lashed to one of the stilts, and it led to the deck on the front of the little house, and standing on the deck...

"Who goes there?" a woman's twisted and sharp-edged voice rang out in the quiet, dark night.

I saw a strange creature standing on the deck, just outside the doorway, her body wrapped in a dark purple robe, her hands hidden inside, and a black cowl hid most of her face. Her features were angry, and a hook-like nose curled down in front of a scowling mouth.

"Reveal your intentions," she said, "or I'll set you on *fire*!"

"Worla!" my bony friend said, "It is I, Skeleton Steve, and my companion, Cth'ka, come to consult your wisdom!"

She seemed to think for a moment.

"Skeleton Steve," she said, her voice suddenly much more friendly. "*You* are welcome, but I cannot risk your creeper companion destroying my home! I'll be down directly. Have a seat." She disappeared back into her doorway.

Skeleton Steve smirked at me. He looked around the clearing where we stood, and walked over to a circle of fallen logs. He sat on a log.

I followed.

A few minutes later, the witch descended her ladder with ease, and approached us. She sat on a log opposite Skeleton Steve so that we could all speak. A torch stuck out of the ground in the middle of our circle, which I didn't notice before, and it *flared* to life, casting fiery reflections and dancing shadows all around us.

"I am Worla," she said to me, "the witch of Lurkmire Swamp."

"I am Cth'ka," I said, "creeper ... of Darkwood Foressst?"

Skeleton Steve laughed. Worla laughed. I relaxed.

"What can *my wisdom* do for you tonight, Skeleton Steve?" she said.

"We've come because of my creeper friend here, Cth'ka," he said. "He is on a quest to learn more about his race, and to bring his people together, but is in need of a way to *defend* himself without blowing himself up."

Worla cackled. "A creeper trying to *avoid* blowing himself up?"

"Why isss that ssso funny?" I asked, my tone a little harsher than I intended. Skeleton Steve flinched a little.

"Because," the witch said, "creepers are quite *happy* to blow themselves up. It's their *destiny*. It's how they make *more* creepers."

What?

"Sssss … *More* creepersss?" I said. That was absurd!

"Look into my eyes, young creeper. Let me look into your *destiny*." She leaned forward toward me.

I looked at Skeleton Steve. He shrugged. Looking back at Worla the witch, I took a deep breath, steadied my fear, and held still, looking right into her beady, black eyes. In the flickering flames of the torchlight, I saw my frowning, green face reflected back at me in her eyes. Worla's face was still and passive, then it transformed in surprise!

"Oh my," she said, her black eyes unmoving but her face animating around them. "My, my. What an *interesting* path you have, mighty Cth'ka…"

Mighty?

She continued. "I can see what lies ahead for you, most interesting creeper. Interesting, indeed!"

"What isss?" I asked.

"Yeah," Skeleton Steve said. "What's so interesting?"

Worla laughed, breaking her eyes out of the dark and stony stare that held my own eyes in a tight grip. My attention to the swamp around me suddenly snapped back into focus.

"Cth'ka the creeper," she said. "I *will* help you, yes. I will tell you the location of an ... *artifact* of sorts, something that will allow you the ability to act with *hands unseen*, strong hands that will let you *smash* your enemies and defend yourself without using your ... last resort. Is this idea to your liking?"

I had no idea what she meant by all of that. Hands unseen? Some kind of weird magic?

"What do you mean?" I said. "Handsss unssseen?"

"Yes," she replied. "A magical item that will let you manipulate the world around you with your *mind*. The only possible defense for someone of your kind, assuming you don't want to destroy yourself."

She waved her hand, and the torch snuffed out like magic. A snap of her long, spindly fingers, and it flared to life again.

"I will give you items to assist in your journey as well. I only ask a small price in return..."

"What price?" I said.

"I am ... building my interest here in Lurkmire still, and will require your assistance in the future. I ask for three favors upon your return with the artifact, and in exchange, I will give you the knowledge and ability to attain the power to fulfill your destiny and *lead your people*."

Everything I wanted.

But at what price?

What could the witch possible ask of me that I wouldn't be able to give her, especially once I had the power to manipulate the world with my mind and bring my people together in a nation of creeperkind?

I looked to Skeleton Steve. He returned my gaze without emotion.

He wasn't going to help me with *this* decision.

Wasn't this kind of idea what we traveled here for in the first place? Could I trust Worla the witch? If I asked Steve for his opinion, I would basically be asking him whether or not he thought I could trust the witch. I might offend her, and she might change her mind about the whole thing!

"Okay, I'll do it!" I said. "I'll get the artifact, then help you with your three favors."

She instantly pulled her hands out of her robe, her fingers like white spider legs in the darkness, tipped with thin claws. "Say it again," she commanded. "Repeat—I, Cth'ka the creeper, in exchange for assistance in finding the *Crown of Ender*, will perform three favors for Worla the Witch when she requires in the future."

I repeated her words, and she traced patterns in the darkness with her fingertips as I did. When I completed the sentence, she lashed out with her index finger, and touched my forehead. I flinched in surprise, caught control of my hissssssss, and felt a warm sensation bloom between my eyes then disappear.

Some sort of magic?

"You are unique, creeper," she said. "You will learn to control your *last resort* with your willpower. I can sense that already you can calm yourself back down. In time, you will be able to fight your enemies while keeping your mind calm, and not have to worry about exploding at all!"

Her hands disappeared back into her robes, then she produced three greenish-blue and yellow spheres. When she held out her palm to show us, the three spheres floated above her hand, throwing off purple motes of light. In the center of each sphere was a black slit of a pupil. They were *eyes*. Weird, magical eyeballs.

"These are eyes of Ender." She looked to Skeleton Steve. "Use them wisely. They will show you the way to the underground stronghold where you will find the Crown of Ender. Use one at a time, and *only* when you need to find the way. They will burn out in time. Follow the eyes to the location of the stronghold."

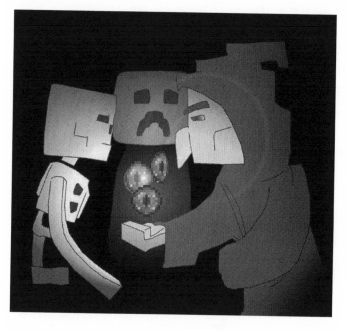

"Thank you," he said. Skeleton Steve took the eyes and put them into his pack.

"Remember," she said. "Only use them when you need to. Don't squander them!" She stood, pulling her robes about her. "And take care crossing the desert, my skeleton friend!" Worla laughed, and pulled the black cowl over her face again. The torch went out. "Good luck, mighty Cth'ka. Return to me once you have obtained the *crown*." She looked at the sky. "The night will soon be over..."

With that, Worla turned, and moved back to her hut with a speed and dangerous grace that I wouldn't have imagined.

I looked at Skeleton Steve. "I guesss we're ssstaying out of Darkwood Foressst for a while?"

He nodded, and we traveled back the way we came, stopping to spend the day under a large tree at the edge of the swamp.

The Amazing Reader List

Thank you SO MUCH to these Readers and Reviewers! Your help in leaving reviews and spreading the word about my books is SO appreciated!

Awesome Reviewers:

MantisFang887 EpicDrago887

ScorpCraft SnailMMS WolfDFang

LegoWarrior70

Liam Burroughs

Ryan / Sean Gallagher

Habblie

Nirupam Bhagawati

Ethan MJC

Jacky6410 and Oscar

MasterMaker / Kale Aker

Cole

Kelly Nguyen

Ellesea & Ogmoe

K Mc / AlfieMcM

JenaLuv & Boogie

Han-Seon Choi

Danielle M

Oomab

So Cal Family

Daniel Geary Roberts

Jjtaup

Addidks / Creeperking987

D Guz / UltimateSword5

TJ

Xavier Edwards

DrTNT04

UltimateSword5

Mavslam

Ian / CKPA / BlazePlayz

Dana Hartley

Shaojing Li

Mitchell Adam Keith

Emmanuel Bellon

Melissa and Jacob Cross

Wyatt D and daughter

Jung Joo Lee

Dwduck and daughter

Yonael Yonas, the Creeper Tamer (Jesse)

Sarah Levy / shadowslayer1818

Pan

Phillip Wang / Jonathan55123

Ddudeboss

Hartley

Mitchell Adam Keith

L Stoltzman and sons

D4imond minc4rt

Bookworm_29

Tracie / Johnathan

Jeremyee49

Endra07 / Samuel Clemens

And, of course ... Herobrine

(More are added all the time! Since this is a print version of this book, check the eBook version of the latest books—or the website—to see if your name is in there!)

Made in the USA
Monee, IL
16 October 2021